CITY OF ICE

JOHN FARROW

CITY
OF
ICE

For Ann Marie
An icy look at Montreal.

HarperCollins*Publishers*Ltd

[signature]
Montreal 2000.

CITY OF ICE
Copyright © 1999 by John Farrow.
All rights reserved. No part of this book may be used or reproduced
in any manner whatsoever without prior written permission
except in the case of brief quotations embodied in reviews.
For information address HarperCollins Publishers Ltd,
55 Avenue Road, Suite 2900,
Toronto, Ontario, Canada M5R 3L2.

http://www.harpercanada.com

HarperCollins books may be purchased for educational, business,
or sales promotional use. For information please write:
Special Markets Department, HarperCollins Canada,
55 Avenue Road, Suite 2900,
Toronto, Ontario, Canada
M5R 3L2.

First edition

Canadian Cataloguing in Publication Data

Farrow, John, 1947-
City of ice

ISBN 0-00-225517-0

I. Title.

PS8561.A785C57 1999   C813'.54   C98-932570-9
PR9199.3.F47C57 1999

99 00 01 02 03 04 HC 6 5 4 3 2 1

Printed and bound in The United States

in memoriam
Daniel Desrochers
1984-1995
a child of Montreal
killed by a biker's bomb
at age eleven

CONTENTS

PROLOGUE

ANGELS AND WOLVERINES

Friday, September 17

They called themselves *Wolverines.*

In the freight elevator, Sergeant-Detective Émile Cinq-Mars
ascended to the fourth floor of an office tower in Montreal's north
end. He got off and walked left down a brightly lit corridor, then right
at the first junction. As instructed, he rapped three times upon a door
marked CLOSET. It opened a crack. The detective displayed his gold
shield next to his face. The door closed as the chain lock was disen-
gaged, then opened fully, and a guard wearing a bulletproof vest and
toting an automatic rifle let him in.

The man's finger was on the trigger, the barrel aimed at the floor.
Émile Cinq-Mars stepped inside.

His eyes required a moment to adjust to the dimmer light of the
palatial suite. Plainclothes officers, their backs to him, were lined up
at the windows like pigeons on a rooftop turned to face the wind. In
shadow, the cops stayed three steps away from the glass to preserve
their secrecy from the outside world. Two snapped pictures with tele-
photo lenses. Three others observed the scene through high-powered
binoculars. Another wore earphones. The cop who had opened the
door remained at his back, standing guard. Four more were occupied
by traditional police work—they were sitting around waiting.

These men were the cream, the privileged few. Wolverines.

Across the busy intersection below them, they monitored activity at
a bar where the Hell's Angels Motorcycle Club was throwing a party.

"Ah, Cinq-Mars!" a man with a crew cut who sat slumped in a

1

comfortable armchair announced. "Come in! Take a load off. Glad to meet you." He rose and the two men shook hands. The host officer did not identify himself. The prevalent odor in the room was stale smoke, not body sweat—remarkable given the number of cops present and the oppressive heat. "Welcome to our stakeout. I'd introduce the surveillance team, Sergeant-Detective, but, as you can guess, I'm not free to do that yet."

"Not a problem," Cinq-Mars said in a cool tone. His manner indicated that, had it been left up to him, he'd choose proper introductions over the secrecy. A tall man, six-two, in his fifties, the detective was conservative in his dress, reserved in his demeanor. His outstanding feature was a magisterial nose, a proud, immense beak, ideal for lining up his famous hawkeyed gaze. His auburn hair was thin but wavy and, save for the receding line along his tall brow, he still enjoyed full coverage. Cinq-Mars was already perspiring as he accepted an offer to be seated. The man who had greeted him was younger, not as tall, and substantially thinner, yet he occupied more space. He spread his knees as he sat down while his elbows flared outward. The man smoked, and waved the cigarette as he talked, as if inscribing words on air.

"Lemonade? Coffee?"

"No thanks." Cinq-Mars shook his head, confirming to himself that only an officer of the Royal Canadian Mounted Police would offer lemonade. He was curious about the man's identity. Who else but a Mountie would turn off the air-conditioning to give his long-range listening devices an extra measure of quiet? And only a very earnest Mountie would cut his hair that short. He wasn't wearing his suit jacket and had slackened his tie. The temperature was unseasonably hot for September, still in the high eighties as evening settled. The man wore his service revolver on the back of his belt, which Cinq-Mars knew was more typical of city detectives than Mounties, or SQ, the Quebec provincial police, for those guys tended to be more hidebound when it came to regulations.

Not having been introduced, Cinq-Mars had his back up.

"Sergeant-Detective," the crew cut said, lowering his voice to signal an intimate aside, "you know we wanted you with us from the beginning."

Three police departments had committed elite officers and resources to form a new tactical squad, a strike force, and a crack investigative team. Put together as a desperate measure to combat increasingly powerful biker gangs, they had as targets two warring enemies, the Hell's Angels and the Rock Machine.

"I wasn't interested then," Cinq-Mars reminded him. "I've never been interested. I'm not interested now."

Wanting a menacing name for their squad, the cops had called themselves the Wolverines. "You're the best cop in the city. Your record is exemplary—without parallel, I'd say. You have contacts no one can begin to emulate. You've set the ethical standard for policemen in this town. Stop me if I'm embarrassing you."

Cinq-Mars smiled briefly. "I appreciate the flattery. That doesn't mean I'm influenced by it. Do you think I could call you by your rank, at least?"

The crew cut waved his cigarette around, mulling it over. "It's Lieutenant," he conceded. "Cinq-Mars, we could use a man like you."

The city detective shook his head. "Gangs don't interest me much. I prefer to investigate petty crime. Your work is out of my league, Lieutenant. In my opinion, if we arrest crooks we'll win. Conspiracies, international plots, organized crime—that kind of talk addles my brain." He did his best to laugh him off.

Cinq-Mars recognized the smile on the face of the younger officer, a man in his early forties. Little more than a polite scoff, really, it was the smile of a man who didn't believe him.

"Company's coming," a voice at the window called out.

The lieutenant signaled with his chin for Cinq-Mars to move across to the windows with him. "What've we got?" They gazed down upon the intersection and the bar under surveillance. Beyond the immediate scene, through the dust of late summer and the heat haze, above the drone of traffic, low apartment buildings and duplexes were chockablock for miles, their flat, tar-and-gravel roofs forming a vast, desolate moor.

"Toyota 4Runner, just went up the block and parked."

"Ah," the crew cut lieutenant murmured, looking through binoculars.

"Significant?" Cinq-Mars inquired.

3

"George Turner, the bikers' banker. Take a look, Detective."

Cinq-Mars checked out the bar through the glasses, an instrument so powerful that he had a better view than if he was down there himself. Motorcycles were crammed across the side patio, tables and chairs stacked out of the way. A neon light flickered dimly. *Bar Salon.*

"Doesn't it rot your socks?" the lieutenant whispered. "The Hell's Angels have decided to put themselves on display. A show. They ride their bikes around the neighborhood. Cause a sensation. Now they settle into one of their own bars to have a good time. Why? So they can bait the press. They'll say, 'See? We're out in the open. We're not a secret organization. All that stuff you read about us is bullshit. We're not killers. All we want to do is ride our bikes and be left alone.' They show their colors, their leather jackets and leather pants, the tattoos on their arms, their rat's nest hair, their beards, their wild women, all to demonstrate that they're public, not a covert criminal organization. People lap it up."

"Coming down," a voice at the window warned.

"Tell me about this guy," Cinq-Mars requested.

Of medium height and build, bald across the scalp, the man from the Toyota 4Runner wore a smart, understated gray suit with a pinstriped white shirt and dark blue tie. Through the binoculars Cinq-Mars could see every detail. He caught the red glint of the setting sun off the man's diamond ring. Caught the shine off his shoes. He had the clean pores of the rich. He was carrying a leather satchel with brass fittings and Cinq-Mars could make out his initials stamped in gold lettering. He'd read about satellites that could track the flight of a golf ball, but he'd settle for a pair of these if he wanted to watch the world at close range. He figured they'd cost a month's salary. The Wolverines, it seemed, owned a few nice toys.

"George Turner lives on the mountain in upper Westmount. Attractive wife. Two kids. Well connected. Often seen in the company of politicians. An accountant by trade who carries only one client. The Hell's Angels. He's rarely seen with them in public, so this is significant. This is a move."

"Who else is inside?" Cinq-Mars asked, doing his best to mask his interest.

"Wee Willie, wearing biker colors for a change. The gang's Number One. We hardly ever get to see him out of his sports shirts and dress slacks. The boys are putting on a show for some reason." The detective sucked a drag off his smoke as if inhaling bad news. "Tonight he's bare-chested, showing off his tattoos. He got his name, by the way, from his tiny eyes, not his bulk. The fact that he's three hundred and fifty pounds is incidental. Another guy in biker colors is Plug. A runt, no bigger than a hydrant. We've never seen him out of a suit and tie until this afternoon. He's the gang's computer nerd, a whiz kid. The other top Angel we identified is Jean-Guy. He's in a suit—dapper white threads, wouldn't you say, gentlemen? Black tie, yellow shirt. Greaseball haircut. Jean-Guy is the gang's munitions expert. Nobody knows dynamite like Jean-Guy."

Outside the biker bar, the man called George Turner had paused for a smoke before going in. He looked out of place leaning on the saddle of a Softail Harley. A passerby might easily mistake him for an innocent, be tempted to warn him away. At the side entrance, a burly biker stood guard.

"Giuseppe Pagano is inside, too," the Wolverine lieutenant continued. "Old-guard Mafia. Got turned away when the local Italians split up, so he threw in with the Angels. Also present is Max Gitteridge, their lawyer. That means they've called their lawyer, their banker, their allies, their bomber, their computer expert, and their Number One to this meet, and some dude we don't know. Something's going down."

"Who's the guy you don't know?" Cinq-Mars inquired.

"We call him the Czar. We've heard about him, but we haven't identified him yet and we've never seen him. Couldn't get a picture today either. Not so far. He's wearing a Panama hat and a cape, if you can imagine that. In this heat."

Down below, Turner finally ditched his smoke and entered the bar.

"So the one person you don't know is the one person you haven't been able to photograph," Cinq-Mars pointed out.

The officer shrugged. "Maybe when he comes out. This meeting is in public view, so we figure he's the reason for the show. From wiretaps we know there's a Russian on the scene, looking to do business. He might be the guy. If he is, he heads a coalition of Russian gangs.

Either the Angels want to prove to him how tough they are or they want to demonstrate that they're free to spit in our face any time they choose. That's why the meeting's public. We're guessing it's the Czar they want to impress."

"They must know you're here. They know you're taking pictures."

"Sure they do. Check out the guard, Cinq-Mars, through the glasses."

Cinq-Mars looked him over. He was a scary individual, muscled and huge. Ponytailed. The detective mused that tough guys now wore earrings. That was something he'd never seen in his early days as a cop.

"Read his biceps."

The glasses were that strong. The tattoo read, *The Filthy Few*.

"Know what that means?" the lieutenant pressed him.

"He's a killer." The designation had been widely reported.

"It means he's killed on behalf of the Angels," the lieutenant specified. "Do you see our problem here? They openly brandish the fact that they're murderers, they know we're taking pictures and they don't give a damn. You're too good a cop to let this happen in your city, Sergeant-Detective, on your turf."

They went back to the dim lounge area of the office. The room was probably used for business luncheons in normal times, and as a space to entertain clients. A portable wet bar was set up in one corner, which the cops weren't using except to mix lemonade, and the sofas and coffee tables were on casters so that the room could be rearranged to suit any occasion.

Seated again, Cinq-Mars waited for the detective to make his pitch. The man he presumed was a Mountie butted out one smoke and lit another off his lighter, waved it around, and looked Cinq-Mars in the eye as he took a deep drag. Then he scrunched up his brow and declared, "Sergeant-Detective, we need you onboard. We're putting together a crackerjack unit. The Wolverines are going to inflict some damage, mark my words."

"I wish you well."

"Don't give me that. This is where you want to be. With us. A Wolverine."

"It's not my style."

6

"From what I hear, you practically run an independent version of us already. You have contacts inside the Mounties, contacts inside the SQ. Near as anybody can tell, you run your own intelligence unit. I respect that. What we can provide is better resources, Cinq-Mars, top-notch people, ace equipment. State-of-the-art from top to bottom. No screwups, no foul-ups, no bureaucratic glitches."

"You can promise that?"

"No sweat."

"Truth is, Lieutenant, I'm not much of a team player."

"We're flexible."

Cinq-Mars realized that there was no point to being polite with this man. He wasn't getting it. "Lieutenant, I don't want to be involved with your organization. I wish you well, but I work on my own, within the limited restrictions of my department. You're putting good people together, you should be able to do good work. But life on a special squad is not for me and I don't think it answers the real problem. You watch the bikers, but they're able to monitor your movements, too. They know you're here. They're toying with you. Why play their game?"

"Police work sometimes means playing ball with the bad guys."

"Not my police work."

"Really? Listen, Detective, don't take this the wrong way, but the call has gone out, you understand? If you don't join us, you know how it goes. I don't see many promotions being tossed your way."

Abruptly, Cinq-Mars stood up. "Now you're threatening me?"

The officer stood also, holding up a palm as a signal to stop. "Don't get excited. I'm not threatening. I'm just saying. The call's gone out. If you say no, a smudge is bound to appear on your record."

"Sorry," Cinq-Mars confirmed tersely, turning to leave, his lips pressed hard together. "Not interested."

"Won't you at least think about it? This will be the real thing, Detective. On the edge. It's important for the security of our citizens. These bastards have already killed forty-seven people—"

"They bump off other bikers."

"With bombs!" He thrust out both his palms. "The innocent are bound to die in one of those blasts. When they do—"

7

Cinq-Mars wanted him to complete that thought, and waited.

"—when they do we'll be blessed with a budget so huge we'll have trouble spending it. You'll want to be with us then, Émile. The work that we can do!" The man made two fists. The muscles in his neck flexed and the skin reddened. "Think of it!"

"Coming out!" came the call from the window.

Cinq-Mars and the lieutenant moved over to that side of the room with quick long strides. The accountant, George Turner, was walking up the street back to his 4Runner. Other gang members were milling around outside the bar now, climbing onto their bikes and starting their engines. Still others were heading off to their cars and vans. Cameras inside the surveillance room clicked repeatedly. Outside, the bikers had the setting sun in their eyes, the street and rooftops cast in a red tint.

"The man's going home to Westmount, Sergeant-Detective, to high society. He'll chat with his political cronies and his big-business neighbors. We need to bring people like him down."

A proficient police force, state-of-the-art equipment, a decent budget that might balloon, a chance to assail a brutal criminal organization, this was not a trifling opportunity. "I'd work alone if the department didn't force a partner on me," Cinq-Mars mentioned, testing the waters, seeing what might be offered.

"You can adapt."

Independence, then, was not on the table. Cinq-Mars watched as George Turner climbed into his 4Runner. He hated the impunity with which the man lived his life. Hated his social connections, his contented lifestyle earned through nefarious work. He was thinking these things over when the Toyota lifted off the ground and blew. *Whooooommmm!* Brilliant white light flashed. The concussion of the blast came next, the change in pressure, then the roar, rattling the windows and causing the high-rise to shake. The air continued to rumble. Men in the surveillance room had ducked, a reflex action. The guy with the earphones gave a howl and threw them off. Suddenly they were all convulsed, each man shouting at once. Orders were jabbered out, officers scrambled to the corridor.

"Get down there!" the crew cut lieutenant hollered, pulling on his

8

sports coat. "Keep those cameras clicking! Get a shot of the Czar! We might get a look in the confusion!" He was running from the room when he remembered the man he'd been trying to recruit.

Cinq-Mars was calmly observing the smoking wreck of the car through binoculars, the roof blown clean off. The rest of the vehicle was rubble. The body had at first lifted clear with the roof, then fallen back onto the car seat, upside down, the legs missing. Tissue would have to be scraped from the walls of apartment buildings on both sides of the avenue. Cinq-Mars saw chunks of limb tumble down through the trees, and he believed that he spotted the sparkle of a ring on a severed finger. He put the glasses against his chest to look only with his eyes, to spare himself the grotesque images. On the street, traffic was in turmoil. Collisions were rampant as stunned drivers forgot to brake, or braked prematurely, or pressed gas pedals to the floor in a panic to flee.

"Do you get it now, Cinq-Mars?" the lieutenant baited him. "This is where it happens. We're at the center of things. This is where you want to be. *Come on!*"

Cinq-Mars put the glasses down and followed him out to the corridor, where confusion reigned.

"What's going on?" the lieutenant bellowed. He couldn't believe that his men were still there.

"The elevators are stuck, sir."

"Take the stairs!"

"They've been barricaded."

"Oh, *Christ!* Call downstairs! Get people up here!" The lieutenant took note of Cinq-Mars then. "All right, Sergeant-Detective, so this isn't our finest hour." Furiously, he punched the elevator button as if that would do some good.

"Let's hope there isn't a second bomb, this one under our feet." Émile Cinq-Mars spoke in a flat voice, conveying both calm and dread.

The lieutenant raised an eyebrow. He was trying not to look down at the floor. "You win some, you lose a few."

"You said no glitches. No screwups. How could you promise that? The Angels knew you were here. So did the Rock Machine. The Machine just committed murder under your nose and they've stalled your access to the scene. They're mocking you. That stranger you're after? The Czar? He's long gone. I saw him jump into a van, his cape held high. You never got a photo."

"What do you want from me, Sergeant-Detective?" The crew cut Wolverine was digging for his smokes again. "Tell me what it takes to get you onboard. There's got to be something we can do."

"No, nothing. But thanks for the offer. I appreciate the flattery, but I've thought it over, Lieutenant. I've decided not to join your band of Wolverines. Call it a hunch. I feel I'm better off on my own."

Policemen had arrived on the other side of the stairwell door, busily removing the steel bar wedged between the door and a concrete pillar, blocking the exit. Sergeant-Detective Émile Cinq-Mars couldn't help himself. He was shaking his head, and he sighed heavily, unable to conceal his disapproval, his disdain for failure. He detested bungled operations, and he really hated it when the bad guys had things go their own way.

ONE

STEEPLECHASE ARCH

1

Christmas Eve

The St. Lawrence River flows from west to east, out of the Great Lakes to the Atlantic Ocean, connecting the industrial heartland cities of Chicago and Detroit, Cleveland, Buffalo, and Toronto, to the sea. The river is often a border between two countries, separating Canada from the United States—the province of Ontario from the state of New York—and serves the commerce of both nations. As it flows east it increasingly turns north, into the province of Quebec. Where the river bends up and begins to widen toward the Atlantic, it is joined by the waters of the Ottawa, and there divides around a city established upon an ancient volcanic island. At one time the volcano soared above the clouds. Over aeons it was worn away, rubbed down by nature's relentless chafe. Glacial debris backfilled the crater, then ice, miles high, compressed it. Time eroded the lava crust, the river carried the dust away, and all that remained of the immense volcano was the hardened, tenacious core, the crater's plug.

A faint replica of its former glory, the plug is called a mountain now. In English, Mount Royal. The city shares its name with this sweeping, imposing promontory that has steep escarpments on its south side. *Mont-réal.* Montreal. The mountain dominates the downtown skyline. Most of its surface is either park or cemetery. Lovers are drawn to the winding, wooded trails and the vistas, and the lonely wander there also, to be soothed and consoled. Families play on the slopes. In summer, barbecues sizzle. Tourists ride horse-drawn buggies to lookouts, for it's rare to gaze upon a city from a natural

13

precipice, to be above skyscrapers and traffic and pedestrians and noise while standing amid trees, rock, and birdsong. They come to the top to feel the thrum of a city from a height that confers a meditative moment, a sense of wisdom, perhaps, a lofty perspective.

Below them is a French city, primarily, and English, too, home to countless nationalities, mingling on the one hand, blending languages on the streets, but also carefully guarding their separateness, one culture from the other. They enjoy a city graced by the mountain's beauty, made fortunate also by the river, the calm, powerful St. Lawrence, connecting the island to the world.

Rivers forge corridors through the surrounding territory, northeast to the ocean, west and southwest. An eastern tributary connects south to Lake Champlain, the great waterway of Vermont and New York State. A French trading post before the *Mayflower* landed, the first settlement had links to both the Canadian West and the lands that would become known as the American Colonies. So the city is steeped in the history of commerce. And yet, after the first post was abandoned by the French, written off as a business failure, the island became instead a center for saints and visionaries. The city was founded on the spiritual notion that, from here, all savages would be converted.

From the Prohibition era, when great whiskey fortunes were created by distilling and smuggling booze into New York for distribution throughout the States, through decades of traffic in heroin and cocaine, Montreal crime syndicates have positioned the city as a side door into New York. The border has always been an easy crossing. Nothing that guns and bribes and secret back roads can't open. The city offered a retreat from pressure imposed by the FBI. Italian gangs were connected and related to the New York Mafia syndicates a mere six-hour drive south, where they did good business, especially in narcotics. From time to time they'd call for help to battle rival French gangs at home. The tactic was learned by both sides in these wars— always work internationally, maintain brotherhood with those across borders. The associations would prove profitable, and you never knew when you might need allies to wage a war at home.

Crime became entrenched, the proceeds lucrative, the turf wars never-ending, the combatants increasingly brutal. When the Mafia began losing its power in both Montreal and New York, new gangs arose, notably the Hell's Angels. When they retreated to the Quebec countryside to rebuild after a tenacious police crackdown, another biker gang, the Rock Machine, secretly formed in their absence. That gang was cobbled together, in part, from Mafia remnants. When the Angels, reorganized and strong again, wanted back into Montreal, war ensued. Alliances were formed and tested. Russian gangs—thanks to liberal immigration laws more were operating out of Montreal than in New York and Miami combined—were asked to choose sides.

Bombs and chain saws became the weapons of choice.

Dynamite rocked peaceful neighborhoods.

On Sunday mornings, church bells pealed in every sector of the city, the bright, triumphant ringing of old, but all the savages had yet to be converted, and even among the penitents were citizens who aided and abetted, and in some cases worshiped, the criminals.

On the lower slope of the mountain in the *quartier* known as the student ghetto, three and a half months after the George Turner bump, Sergeant-Detective Émile Cinq-Mars was seated behind the wheel of his unmarked car along Aylmer Street, next to a hydrant. Only a few people were outside in the cold, walking briskly toward shelter. The severe temperature had shunted everyone else indoors. Apartments here were of different sizes and styles, thwacked together in an architectural mishmash. Older, elegant three-story homes rubbed up against the new and garish. Tall, skinny buildings loomed over the squat and stunted. Private residences elbowed for a little breathing space between raucous rooming houses for students. In his car, Émile Cinq-Mars shivered, and fluttered his lips with impatience. His new partner had loped off for coffee ten minutes earlier and was now overdue.

"The English," he muttered under his breath in English. *"Pfffft!"*

He swore aloud the moment he spotted the new man tilted into the wind carrying a cardboard tray. The young detective trudged along the sidewalk kicking up snow like a draft horse. He lumbered on, then bundled himself into the front seat and passed Cinq-Mars a styrofoam coffee cup.

"Idiot." His pronunciation fell somewhere between English and French.

"What'd I do now?" Detective Bill Mathers wanted to know.

"Put a flashing light on your head. Pop a siren in your mouth."

"Excuse me?"

"They told me you were a good detective."

"Who told you that? I know I'm all right, but who told you?"

"Wear a sandwich board," Cinq-Mars taunted him. "Write on it— *Undercover cop on duty! Please do not disturb!* Trust me, if the bad guys made themselves as obvious as the police we would not have crime."

"You don't want me bringing you coffee?"

"Bring me coffee. Don't bring me coffee in a cardboard tray with steam rising out of it like a chimney. Who sits in a car all night with the engine off when it's thirty below?" Cinq-Mars quizzed him. "Who else but us dumb cops, and guess what, Bill? The bad guys know that."

Mathers warmed his hands on the cup before he removed the lid and blew across the surface. "Know what?"

"What?"

"If only cops freeze their tails off because the motor's not running, let's turn ours on. That would be less suspicious."

"You're an imbecile."

"Wouldn't that be less suspicious?"

"What're we supposed to be doing in here, kissing?"

"Also less suspicious," Mathers deadpanned.

The point was well taken. "You forget," Cinq-Mars recovered. "We're not here. We're invisible. No motor. No heat. Just steam rising from our coffee cups."

"I know what you're after. You want to crack my nuts off."

"You're a better detective than I thought to figure that out so fast."

Mathers chafed. "Suit yourself. This isn't my first initiation. Odds are it won't be my last."

"Knock on wood," Cinq-Mars advised him, which gave his junior officer pause. "It could be your last. Who's to know?"

Having no wood handy, Mathers knocked three times upon his own cranium.

"Sounds hollow to me," Cinq-Mars commented.

Under the city that night, within the mountain, where track for the commuter train ran a tunnel through rock, a jury of homeless men was gathering for shelter from the wretchedness of winter. Although the tunnel was not a warm place, men found refuge there from the bitter winds and made fires from old newsprint they had gathered and soaked with snow to prolong the burning time. The tunnel had become their safe haven. The men entered after the last of the rush-hour trains had passed, the intermittent evening trains still to follow, and they would stay the night, to be awakened from their lair by the violent alarm of the morning's initial locomotion.

On this Christmas Eve they were joined by Okinder Boyle, a junior columnist out to make a name for himself. His editor had wearied of his sage pieces on the homeless, so he needed to devise new ways to tell a familiar tale. *You want to write about the homeless? You're so fascinated? Give me the underbelly, Boyle. Back off the sop. God, I'm sick to death of your sop. Makes me want to puke. Your sop quotient got used up aeons ago.*

Boyle had a talent for creating interesting sets, and he was certain as he entered the tunnel on Christmas Eve that he had found the ideal location for the holiday week. While the remains of turkeys were being picked over, he would give his readers an image of their city they hadn't imagined. He knew nothing of the people there, precious little of their lives, but he had discovered a tunnel—*a tunnel!*—where the disinherited huddled against the cold and dodged morning trains on their retreat back to sunlight.

You want underbelly? he rehearsed his conversation with the grouch of a city editor who'd love to squash him like a sow bug. *I'll give you friggin' underbelly. These people live*—and he would delay his next word—*under*—and he would repeat it—*under the mountain. They live inside rock.*

For Christmas Eve Okinder Boyle joined the ranks of the homeless beneath the city, where trains ran riot and marauding winter winds took up a ghostly howl and paper fires choked the foul air with pungent warming smoke.

"I might as well tell you," Bill Mathers said to his new senior partner, "I asked for this dance. I put in a request to ride with you."

Sergeant-Detective Émile Cinq-Mars embellished upon his usual grunting response. "I'm impressed, I suppose. How impressed am I, Bill?"

"Don't give me such a hard time, Émile. You've done a lot. I'm letting you know I respect that. I asked to be your partner. Maybe I can learn from you."

"Miracles have been known to happen," Cinq-Mars concurred.

"What'd I ever do to you?" The young man possessed a round, cheerful, boyish face distinguished by large, brown, bovine eyes. He wore his hair with an exacting part along one side—as if he was a Mountie, Cinq-Mars considered with disdain. His new partner seemed as earnest as that crew cut lieutenant Mountie he'd met in the Wolverines at the time of the Turner bump. The junior detective was in his early thirties—looked younger— but Cinq-Mars guessed that he'd been behaving as a forty-year-old for the past decade, as if he had repudiated, and thereby forfeited, his youth. "Why are you giving me such a hard time, Émile?"

Cinq-Mars gazed down the street through the light fall of snow that had just commenced. He checked his side mirror again, more from nervous habit than concentration. The street remained remarkably quiet.

"My last partner spied on me," the detective revealed. "You should go talk to him. This time I worked things with the brass so they wouldn't dare stick me with another spy, but they're not going to do me any favors either. They wanted me hooked up with deadwood, take me down a peg. So I looked over the deadwood, and guess what, Bill? I found you. I heard you're a good cop. Steady. Unremarkable overall. Brass decided I deserved a squarehead. They figure you'll be no earthly good to me. Considering the choices, I was happy enough to take you. Now get out," Cinq-Mars instructed him, "prove them wrong. Clean off the rear window, or do you think I can see through snow?"

Mathers did what he was told without complaint, using the sleeve of his topcoat to clear a patch on the window. Falling in this temperature, the snow was so dry and weightless that he could just as easily have blown it away. Cinq-Mars had summed up his career as unremarkable overall, and he was pondering that assessment with gloominess. He had been chosen from among the deadwood. With that sort of praise he had no further need for criticism in his life. He knew that his advancement in the force was considered tokenism, a bone tossed to the English. English officers believed the best among them were held back in favor of those less capable, assuring that no English cop would shine. That was the theory. To suit the theory English cops had a tendency to act dumb around brass. He wondered if he had ever done that, unconsciously or inadvertently. He knew he was an ambitious cop. That's why he was so excited to have been paired with the eminent and legendary Cinq-Mars.

Before climbing back in the car Mathers trained his own practiced eye up and down the block. He opened the door and clambered in.

"Start her up," Mathers said. "Get around the corner. I've been made."

Cinq-Mars turned the ignition over immediately. "Tell me."

"Santa Claus. Straight behind."

A man in a Santa Claus outfit carrying a sack of toys slung over one shoulder scaled a snowbank and came down the other side. He crossed the street and hurried to safely avoid an oncoming car. A line of traffic gently fishtailing on the slippery surface went by him and traveled past the detectives. Cinq-Mars asked, "Can you see him?"

"Sometimes." Mathers added, "He's going in."

"Wait now."

"He's in."

"Wait," Cinq-Mars whispered. "You got the door?"

"Got it."

"No mistake?"

"I got it, I said."

"Let's go," Cinq-Mars ordered. "Lock your door. Don't slam it. I'll leave the motor running. The extra key's in my right coat pocket. Let's take it nice and easy."

"You're forgetting something," Mathers mentioned.

"What?"

"I might be your new partner but I'm no rookie."

"Then don't be so touchy. Let's go."

They opened and closed the car doors gently. Mathers followed as Cinq-Mars headed across the street at an angle away from their quarry and charged into an apartment building that was not the one entered by the pursued. Inside, Mathers asked, "What're we doing here?"

"East of Aldgate," Cinq-Mars told him and unclasped his side holster and removed the revolver.

"What does that mean?"

"Put your gun in your pocket. Carry it with the safety on but ready to fire. Now listen, Bill. Don't shoot yourself in the foot, but most of all, don't shoot me."

"You're expecting trouble."

"Always do. Don't you?"

"Call for backup?"

"Is there some benefit to chaos I don't know about? The more cops the better chance for a screwup."

"You're not following procedures, Émile," Mathers criticized, but he was smiling.

Cinq-Mars blew air through his lips to signal that he dismissed the rules. "Let's go."

They vacated the foyer of that apartment building and strolled up the street to the rooming house where their prey had vanished.

"In first," Cinq-Mars commanded. He was the one smiling now.

"What're you grinning at?"

"Now you know why I took a squarehead to be my partner."

"Do I?" Mathers asked.

"If somebody's going to take a bullet for me, he might as well be English."

Mathers beamed back at him. "I figured it had to be something like that," he answered in French.

They entered, each officer clutching a pistol concealed in his coat pocket, in pursuit of Santa Claus.

Okinder Boyle's nightmare began as a low murmured howl, indecipherable from the wind's roar at the tunnel's entrance. Occasional colored lights made grimy by diesel fumes and generations of mountain dirt lit his way. Scant help. He walked on and pounded his feet against the ties to keep himself a trifle warmer.

This time the complaint was sustained and Boyle stopped and listened and waited and soon knew what was wrong. Bearing down upon him from the opposite direction now—a train. He had to quell an immediate panic. He sucked a breath and drew it in deeply. The freezing air stung his lungs. Ahead glowed the wee aperture of a dim red light, and he jogged toward it. At the light he looked around. No evidence of shelter was apparent. He shouted once, "God!" Then spun, not knowing which way to go. And spun again. He cried out, a noise. Boyle whispered aloud, "Okay. Calm down." The train was still far off. One train, parallel tracks. No need to panic. To be sure he was okay he checked behind him again and this time spotted the light of another oncoming locomotive.

Now—panic.

Boyle carried no memory of an alcove or bay in the rock behind him. Best to forge ahead. He jogged along the wall toward the next light. Beyond it shone a bright white lamp. He dragged one hand along the wall to detect any opening, any break in the concrete perimeter, and kept his eyes high in hopes of discerning a shelf. Nothing. He ran on, the train ruckus louder now, ferocious. Again at the next red light protected by a wire cage no safe cubbyhole presented itself, no ledge. A safe zone had to exist somewhere. He scrambled toward the lamp. The train bellowed now. The track curved slightly. He was dazed by the bright lights of the nearer locomotive, and paralysis set in. Plastering himself against the side wall probably would save him, but he deplored the risk, the very notion of odds. He could stand on one track and hope to hell the first train passed before the second bore down, jump from one track to the other, but he didn't want to rely on dumb luck.

Controlling his panic, he jogged on in desperation into the lead engine's gaining light, but it was the light from the locomotive behind him that revealed a safe ledge. He might not make it, he might not reach that destination, and if he fell—*what if I fall! God!* He saw stairs in the train's blazing light—three iron steps that led to a narrow gangway. He jumped to the first step and ascended to the gangway and in his relief lay down and pressed himself against the wall. The first train was not yet upon him. He had overestimated its speed, its nearness.

He'd had more time than he'd guessed. Boyle groped the wall, his face against the stone. He lay straight and held his hands and toes, knees, hips, chest and face squeezed against the cold wall while the trains came on. The huge sound and then the crush of wind eclipsed his breath and staggered his heart. He gasped and exhaled with fear as both trains exploded past him and the very wall against which he had sought refuge shook and groaned. He believed the trains would never end, that the night had come undone, that he could not endure their violent passage. *War's like this,* he thought as the locomotive on the near track charged by him, and the lights of the passenger cars flashed upon him. The trains escaped into the darkness as quickly as they had emerged and Boyle was abandoned on his iron trellis, his body conjoined to rock.

Pushing himself to his knees, he listened keenly to the trains. They had thundered a moment ago and now were gone from view. Soon they'd be silent. That frightened him, made him wary. How quickly they came up, then vanished. He would have to move more rapidly through the tunnel and stay alert.

Boyle crossed along the catwalk to where the white light shone brightly enough that he could read his train schedule and double-check his watch. The outbound had been the ten-forty, the last in either direction for the night. A mercy. He stepped down a ladder to the tracks and walked deeper into the mountain. The men at the mouth of the cave had directed him into its core. He'd find his best story there, they promised. That's where the hermit lived, the man known to them as the Banker. Boyle did not go far before spotting a flickering fire, which had to be his destination. He approached warily, mindful of his inner coldness, as though his fright had claimed the remnants of a residual warmth. Close, he called out, "Hello, there! Hello, the Banker!"

Shadow moved. Out of the campfire a flaming piece of lumber was lifted and upraised as a sword, and a phantom man wielded the weapon and lurched to his feet. Flames swung through the air in haphazard design, then the torch was aimed at the interloper, the flames dancing wildly.

"Are you the one they call the Banker?" the journalist called out.

"Who goes there?" a voice shouted back. "Friend or foe?" The torch swished.

Boyle had to restrain his laughter. He half-expected to discover that he had slipped through a whorl in time, that he was engaged now in a medieval joust. "Friend," he answered.

"Fat chance!" the fire-wielding dungeon dweller yelled back.

"Listen, I write for the papers. My name is Okinder Boyle. Some of the boys at the entrance to the tunnel said I should come down here and talk to you. Do you have a story to tell? Or were they just shooting the breeze, playing a trick on me?"

Unsure of his answer, so it seemed to Boyle, the man chose to wave his stick of lumber around. "What do you mean, a story?" he asked in a moment.

"You know, how you came to be living here."

"I don't live here. Only a damn fool would live here. I only sleep here and pass the time, you nut."

"That's what I mean. I can use that sort of detail. I'd like to know your story. Starting with, if I might ask, why they call you the Banker."

"Long story."

"That's why I'm here. To listen. Can I come up there?"

"Well," the Banker stated, then he fell silent.

"What do you say?" Okinder Boyle pressed him.

"Maybe you should come up here," the Banker suggested, as though the idea had originated with him.

"I'm climbing up there," Boyle informed him. He placed his gloved hands upon a cement ledge, heaved himself up, and scrambled onto the catwalk to join the older man by the fire. The Banker had squatted down again, both palms faced toward the flames as he warmed his hands through his mitts. He had returned his torch to the fire. Boyle hunkered down across from him on a board, the small smoky campfire between them.

"So who're you?" the Banker asked him.

Boyle studied his hermit. A full round face, he wasn't underfed by all appearances. A scruffy two- or three-day beard. Impressive eyebrows and smallish eyes. Under one a scar glowed in the firelight, odd-shaped in that it was almost square, as though a patch of skin had surgically been removed from his cheek. He wore a heavy black wool cap.

"My name's Okinder Boyle," the young man answered. "I'm a journalist."

"Yeah," the Banker reminded him, "I heard all that. But who are you?"

Boyle was momentarily disadvantaged. "That's not important," he said finally.

"Maybe yes, maybe no," the Banker mused, his voice level now, he was sounding sane, "but that's the part I want to hear. Humor me. You do the talking, son. I'll listen in."

The two detectives moved with stealth, attuned to the sound of their ascent. On each floor the hallways were dimly lit, the stairways between them worn and narrow. Student rooms emitted the muffled beat of the music channel, or the laugh tracks of sitcoms, a quieter night than was common with many residents gone home for the holidays. The men moved upstairs in search of Santa Claus, to the second floor, then the third, Mathers in the lead, Cinq-Mars a stride behind. They were looking for Room 37, found it easily, and listened at the door. No sounds came from within.

Cinq-Mars stood to one side and rapped gently, a friendly knock.

No answer.

He waited.

No sound.

He knocked harder. Then gestured with his chin.

"What?" Mathers whispered back.

"Try the knob."

It turned.

Cinq-Mars arched an eyebrow.

Mathers opened the door and peered through the crack. Then he gave the door an easy shove and let it swing open, both men concealed behind the casework on either side, weapons drawn. Mathers gave the room a quick glance, pulling his head back in a wink both to entice fire, if it was forthcoming, and to avoid it. Cinq-Mars did the same, to get a mental snapshot of the room. He put a finger to his lips to indicate they'd move in without first shouting a warning, then flashed his thumb for his junior partner to go first.

Mathers swung low, his pistol held in both hands in front of him as he stood in the doorway. Not much to see. The room was empty of people, pretty much empty altogether. A tall, pine wardrobe, a table with Santa's bag of toys on it, and that was all. Mathers crept forward, his eyes taking in the room, and headed for the kitchen. That long, narrow space proved barren as well, save for the remnant of a cardboard box. He turned, and Cinq-Mars gestured to maintain silence.

A small alcove was built into one end of the main room on the right, and a door led off it. Cinq-Mars listened first, then proceeded. Bent at the knees, he flung open the door, his pistol upraised. Straightening, he reached inside and flicked on the light switch. The john was empty. Even the curtain on the shower stall was missing.

"Back way out?" Cinq-Mars asked.

"Kitchen door," Mathers told him.

They entered the kitchen together. They had a choice between two doors. The one ajar led into a small pantry. Empty. The other was locked. Mathers flicked the light switch beside it and peered through the keyhole. "Stairwell, looks like," he commented.

"Santa's chimney," Cinq-Mars muttered.

"Break it down?"

"Why bother? If Santa wanted to lose us, he's lost us."

"So this was a wild gooser?"

"With all the trimmings. Why, though? What's up?"

Mathers holstered his pistol. He walked back into the main room, and his steps echoed off the hardwood floors and bare walls. "Somebody cleared this place out."

"Not quite," Cinq-Mars noted. He leaned against the kitchen jamb. Motioned with his chin. Mathers simultaneously opened both doors to the wardrobe. Then just stood there, gaping.

"Bill?"

"Jesus!"

Cinq-Mars came around. Inside the hutch, Santa Claus hung from a rod. His head was tilted askew, as though the neck had snapped,

25

and his bloated, pale face was largely concealed by the phony Santa's beard and by the extravagant white tufts of Santa Claus hair. His slack mouth was open in an oval. Around his neck, across his red Santa's uniform, a cardboard message had been slung on a string, a few words of greeting, which Sergeant-Detective Émile Cinq-Mars recognized as being addressed to him.

The victim's eyes indicated that Santa Claus would not be riding his sleigh tonight. The eyes and the limp body confirmed that he had no pulse. Cinq-Mars checked anyway. The body was cold to his touch.

On top of the mountain that night, on a floodlit frozen pond away from the city's noise, a young woman was skating to the drone of Christmas Muzak. Aware of a man's careful scrutiny, she knew that she was being recruited. Roughly twice her age, the man shivered by the edge of the oval and regarded her as he stomped his boots on the hard-packed snow to keep his blood circulating. Equally cold, the skater turned her head from the breeze and hunched her shoulders to keep her collar high. Her name was Julia Murdick. She glided one more time around the ice before returning to his side.

"Now I understand your walk," he said, his breath a bright cloud in the snapping cold and under the lights.

"My walk?" She sound offended. Flattered by his attentions, curious about the nature of his enterprise, Julia believed that she could resist his advances. She was willing to let him try. She wanted to experience mental combat with a pillaging male and, having tested herself, triumph over the intricacies of seduction. Julia recognized her weakness here, the vulnerable points that he exploited, but most of all she was keen to know what he wanted her to do, and why she'd been chosen.

The man kicked one stinging foot against the other. Over his suit he wore a mauve scarf and a taupe woolen topcoat. A jaunty sable cap decked his head. "That was the second thing I noticed about you, Jul, your springy step, the way you push off with your back foot. You walk as you skate, young lady, and you skate beautifully."

"My walk's dorky. That's what you're really trying to tell me. Don't sweat it, Selwyn. It's nothing I haven't heard before."

The man's name was Norris—Selwyn Emerson Norris—and the

young woman had not known him long. He had lovely eyes in her estimation and a decent manner and an intriguing air about him. Always impeccably groomed, he was so damned handsome. He had old-fashioned manners, always seemed interested in what she had to say, and loved conversation. She had little more to go on than that and no sound reason to be keeping his company.

"There's a name for it, you know," she said.

"For what?"

"My walk."

"Really?"

"But I'm not telling! It's way too demeaning. Wild horses! My walk is physiological so don't try changing it. It's not in your domain. *Yikes*, I'm stiff. I'm so *cold*." She bobbed at the knees to keep herself in motion.

Norris placed her boots on the ice as she stooped to untie the laces on her high-top skates. Unable to manage while wearing mittens, Julia pulled them off between her teeth and attacked the knots with fingers numb from the cold. Supporting her weight against him, one hand in his, mitts in her mouth, she kicked a skate loose and tucked her foot into the frigid boot.

"Sel!" Her shout was muffled. Extracting the mittens from between her teeth, Julia put them on again. "Why's it so freezing out? This has got to be the coldest Christmastime ever ever *ever*."

"How does a bowl of hot soup sound to you?"

"Like the sound of one hand clapping, I guess." She pried the second skate off and pulled on her boot.

"Snoop—"

"You don't mean here. You can't mean *here*." Julia abhorred the public chalet where children retreated for *poutine* and warmth and the familiar comfort of their own racket.

"I think not."

Which had to be considered also—the drive in the Infiniti, the food of fine restaurants—although she did not dwell on such ancillary offerings for long.

"Let's run," she said.

"You go. I'll catch up."

Hugging herself, Julia Murdick ran, disappearing along the path through the woods. Selwyn Norris next saw her in the parking lot jumping in place by his car. He walked across the hardened snow, and the crunch of his boots was clear and sharp in the night air. He unlocked the doors of the Q45 from a distance. Julia heard the gay electronic *blip!* of the locks releasing, opened her door, and bounced in. She watched Norris carry her skates around to the trunk and deposit them there, then come back and slide in behind the wheel.

"Start her up, Selwyn. It's so cold!"

She got a kick out of saying his name. The oddity of it spoke of a class distinction, of a cultural epoch not her own, of a boundary she was being invited to cross. Each time she spoke his name she wondered if it was for real, or fabricated, and if his true identity would ever be disclosed.

"You're the one who wanted to skate, Snoop."

"So press charges."

He fastened the seat belt.

Charmed by the self-mockery of her youthful conceit, he smiled. The quality endeared her to him always and Norris mulled over how the attribute could be used to advantage and under what circumstances the virtue might prove a liability. He started the car, and the engine purred confidently in the cold.

"What was the first thing you noticed about me?" she asked.

"Good work, Jul! Well done. Nicely underplayed. Always delay the question. Allow time, enough for the person with the answer to choose to want to talk. Diminish the tenor of your interest. Make it sound as though you're engaged in idle conversation, nothing more. You carried that off exceptionally well."

"Bugger off, Selwyn."

"You're right. We'll discuss this another time. A cup of hot soup," he said. "Coming up."

The Infiniti tagged on to the end of a short line of cars traversing the mountain. The road turned and cut through a blasted trench of rock, and soon the vast eastern expanse of the city was revealed on their right. Norris turned into the overlook alongside lovers in their cars. Before them lay the great glacial plateau of the city, lights twinkling, chimneys smoking.

"Consider," he said, as though he was offering her all that she surveyed, "the world."

"Okay," she consented, "let's."

"The former Soviet Union has been ground to dust. Republics mutate and subdivide quicker than anyone can redraw the map."

"The place is a shambles, Selwyn," Julia agreed, and shivered even as she was warming up. "What's your point?"

"A superpower has re-created itself as a crime state. Dweeb bureaucrats make tens of millions of dollars. Bankers are billionaires, and fifty a year die gruesome deaths. It's astonishing. For so many criminals to flourish, extraordinary organization has been necessary, with a plan that includes intimate and ever-expanding contacts with the West. The roots and tentacles of crime are growing together to span the globe."

Julia listened, skeptically, as she surveyed the city from the precipice. "Come on, Sel," she argued, "we've always had crime." She was irritated by his condescending, smug air, as if he had all the answers while she still struggled to ask the right questions.

"Out there," he said, and nodded to the city lights, "the Hell's Angels and the Rock Machine are in a fight to the finish. Bombings. Murders. They use chain saws as weapons. Now imagine this, Snoop. These bikers are fighting to side with foreign gangs operated by displaced members of the KGB. It boggles the mind. The illicit enterprises still flourish, but now the opportunity has emerged to broker the world's merchandise. Never mind drugs, although drugs remain big. But CDs. Jeans. Condoms. Cars. High fashion. Gasoline. There's a market opening up more huge than the USA. Russia wants it all and needs it all at bargain basement prices. It's made crime the true growth industry of the next century and, for what it's worth, crime fighting the most beleaguered profession."

"But this is where you come in, right, Selwyn? You'll keep us safe from harm? Put on your Superman cape and fly around the room, do something?"

"Actually," he whispered, "I was hoping that this might be where you come in."

"Me?"

"You, Snoop."

"Don't think so, Selwyn. I have no inclination whatsoever to hang out with fat sweaty bikers."

"Fat and sweaty is only for show these days. The upper echelon is groomed, scented, jauntily attired. They work out at sports clubs."

"Still not interested."

Together, they stared across the broad plateau of the city where rival gangs vied for a chunk of floating ice. In the dark of winter, the peace of the season was disrupted by the periodic detonation of dynamite in unsuspecting neighborhoods.

Norris backed out and changed gear and drove slowly through the parking lot. "Suit yourself," he advised. "It's your world, Jul, spread out before you. Your generation. You'll have to live with the consequences."

He scared her sometimes. Selwyn Norris gave off the air that he knew more than he was willing to say, that he knew how things were meant to be and how they would evolve. She hadn't yet determined if this had to do with an acuity in him or a deficiency on her part. She hadn't learned how to think around him. Julia knew that she was slipping, but she remained determined not to fall.

The investigating detectives rummaged through the contents of Santa's sack, which lay on the wooden table dominating the unfurnished room. The bag contained a collection of empty shoe boxes adorned in Christmas wrapping, a light load for any erstwhile Claus. Nothing would be found, Sergeant-Detective Émile Cinq-Mars believed. The bag had been part of the uniform, part of the ruse. He leaned against the wall by the window, at times gazing idly upon the street three stories below, at other times staring off into space. The snow had stopped now, the soft powder that had cleansed the city in time for Christmas sparkling in light cast by streetlamps.

From the room, from the kitchen, from the corridor beyond the apartment the familiar sounds of investigation wandered through to him, the muted voices, the hushed commands and desultory responses. Sounds echoed in the abject emptiness of the room, off the hardwood floors and vacant walls. A sensation impressed him. He was weary of being at the scene of a crime. Ever closer, retirement loomed as an antidote to the barbarism that had occurred within these walls.

Strange that only two pieces of furniture occupied the apartment—the table, on which lay the spoils of Santa's largesse, and the wardrobe, in which Father Christmas hung like a rack of beef. A meat hook, they'd determined, administered with high velocity and strength, had entered through the back and pierced the heart. The instrument remained embedded in the dead young man, and the round handgrip hung him from the rod across the wardrobe. Blood had run down the youth's back to the floor of the cabinet.

Detective Bill Mathers wandered in from outside carrying two cups of coffee. He came straight through to Cinq-Mars and handed him one. "Drink up. It'll help bring you around."

The older man scarcely acknowledged him but received the coffee and pried open the plastic lid with expert fingers. He sipped, and gazed back into the room. "Where the"—and he swore, rare for him—"is forensics?"

"It's Christmas Eve. We had to get them from home. Not that they'll have much to tell us."

"You're the expert?"

"Get off my case, Émile. The man was killed with a meat hook."

"When?"

"When?"

"Is there an echo in here?" Cinq-Mars chided.

"We know when he was killed, Émile. We watched Santa enter the building. We were inside within a minute and a half, two minutes. That's when he got whacked."

"Think so?"

"I know so," Mathers claimed. He was frowning. The old man was treating him like a child, it seemed to him. He was sensitive about it because he often had that problem with tough city cops. The baby-face thing again. His looks caused cops, and the bad guys, too, to underestimate him.

"Good for you. I'm not so sure. I guess senility comes with old age."

"You're making no sense, Émile. Do dead men walk?"

"Do the dead go cold in two minutes?" Cinq-Mars asked him in return.

"Listen, after coming in here and opening that door and looking at that mess, I'm in no mood for your riddles." Flustered, Mathers angled his back to his superior.

"Do the dead go cold in two minutes? Answer the question."

"I was outside just now. Feel my hand. It's still cold."

"That's not the same thing."

Forensics arrived at that instant, a studious young intern leading a senior colleague to the deceased. For the first time since they had opened the cabinet, Cinq-Mars emerged from his funk, moving across to watch the men work. He stood to one side of the closet to spare himself further visual discomfort.

"Time of death?" he asked.

Below a shock of untamed white hair the pathologist's thin, angular face appeared quaintly academic. He acknowledged the policeman's query with a nod and continued his ministrations, staying at the work for ten minutes without speaking. He examined under the Santa suit for other injuries after his junior had stepped back with nothing more to do.

"Can I see what he looks like again?"

The pathologist slipped off the fake beard and pushed back the Santa hair. Removing his gloves, the senior pathologist commanded, "Bag him. If he's riding back to the North Pole tonight, it's in a hearse."

The detective raised a hand, and two uniformed officers entered from the hall with a gurney and body bag. The officers struggled with the dead man's weight to get him down, unsure what to do about the meat hook.

"Take it out of him if you've a mind to," the pathologist suggested. "Spare me the trouble." The officers looked from one to the other, hoping the doctor was kidding. The physician let them stew before he added, "Otherwise bag him as is." The uniforms chose the latter option.

"Can you take that sign off him?" Cinq-Mars requested. "It's sacrilegious." In an English scrawl, the sign, written on cardboard torn from the side of the box in the kitchen, declared, *Merry Xmas, M5.*

The intern held open a plastic bag, and the senior physician tossed his latex gloves inside. He looked up at Cinq-Mars. "Personal, is it?"

"Doesn't fit the season."

"That may be true, Émile, but the sign stays on him."

The detective conceded to the doctor's jurisdiction.

"You got here quickly."

"Not quick enough," Mathers offered.

"Marc, how long has he been dead?" Cinq-Mars wanted to know.

"Since when do you do homicide, Émile? Who's the IO?"

"LaPierre. He's in the crapper. Flu, he says. His partner's in the building somewhere—what's his name, Bill?"

"Alain Déguire."

"That's it. He's talking to the other tenants. How long, Doc?"

"Three hours, three and a half, four," the pathologist told him.

"Hey," Mathers objected. "That's not possible. That means he died two or three hours before we got here."

"You have a problem with that?" the physician inquired.

"Could be. You're telling me that this man died two, maybe three hours before I saw him walk down the street and enter the building."

"Now that's a feat," the doctor marveled.

"I'd say so."

"Thanks, Marc." Cinq-Mars took the physician's elbow in his hand and turned him toward the door. "You didn't have to come out tonight. We appreciate the exception. One more favor—will you copy me the full report?"

Mathers leaned into the physician as he went by. "Here's a tip. Death by meat hook. Natural causes won't wash in this case."

The doctor freed his arm from the detective's grip to take up the younger man's challenge. "I didn't catch your name."

"Mathers, sir."

"I'm Dr. Wynett. I make it a point to give my students one tip a day, Detective Mathers. Here's yours."

"I'm not one of your students, sir."

"Maybe you should be. Listen to what you hear, Mathers. Not to what you want or expect to hear. This man was not killed by a meat hook but by having his neck broken three to four hours ago. The neck break preceded the meat hook."

"I saw him—"

"You saw a Santa Claus," Cinq-Mars interrupted quietly before his partner embarrassed himself further. "Not this one."

"Émile," Wynett said, "I'll copy you my report to LaPierre, but there's something you might want to tell him right off."

"What's that?"

"The boy's genitals were hot-wired. High voltage. He got burned up bad before they killed him."

"*Merde.*"

"I also have good news. Before somebody snapped his neck, he was choked. The throat's bruised. There's tissue and blood under the boy's fingernails—most likely the perp's. He scratched him."

The zipper on the body bag was done up and the corpse swung carefully onto the gurney, avoiding further damage by the hook. The officers took their time strapping him in, making certain that the body would not slip free when they descended the steep stairs.

Chastened, Mathers followed Cinq-Mars back to the window. "It makes no sense," he whispered. "This has to be the same Santa. If not, where's the other one now? Why were we tipped off about a deal with Santa if there was no deal? You're the one with the contacts, Émile. You should know."

"We were tipped off because some people wanted to deliver a Christmas present to me. There it is," he said, nodding toward the gurney. "Now, do you want to take this up with my contact? Do you have a beef with him?" Cinq-Mars asked, suddenly turning angry.

"This is off the subject. Don't get nasty, Émile."

"Do you want to meet an errand boy who can take you to my source? He has good information. The prime stuff. My source has even better stuff. Would you like to meet him? Introduce yourself then." Cinq-Mars turned back to face the room.

"What are you going on about?" Mathers asked.

"Just unzip the bag and say, 'How do you do, pal? I've been look-ing for somebody like you most of my life. You've done wonders for the career of Detective Cinq-Mars, what can you do for me?' Go ahead. There he is. He can help you along with promotions, at least lead you to someone who can. Say hello, Bill. Go ahead. Unzip the bag and say hello."

His mouth open, Bill Mathers looked at the bag as though he might actually be tempted. He appeared to regret not having done a more careful study of the tenant. "That's him? That's your stoolie?"

"He was never a stoolie, Bill. Respect the dead in their presence. Don't let me hear you call him that again. He was a conduit. An intermediary. A go-between. Everybody knows I have one great secret source. This kid's not him. But he was on the pipeline, he was connected to him."

"Santa Claus?" Mathers's eyes were as wide now as his mouth. As the new partner to Émile Cinq-Mars, he had hoped to gain his trust and someday make the acquaintance of his contacts. Cops knew that he had to have extraordinary contacts to have accomplished all that he had. Mathers just never expected that an introduction would occur during his first few hours with the man. Nor had he expected the contact to be dead, which did spoil the moment.

"In the flesh," Cinq-Mars confirmed. "So to speak. At Christmas people give one another presents. I was just delivered mine by Santa himself. Why am I so lucky, do you think?" Cinq-Mars abruptly raised his hand and called to the policeman he had spotted in the outer corridor. "Detective!"

A detective the same age as Mathers came into the room looking from side to side as though expecting someone, his partner perhaps, to jump out at him.

"Déguire, isn't it?" Cinq-Mars asked.

"Yes, sir. Hi, Bill," he said to Mathers, who nodded.

"Anything from the tenants?"

The detective checked through his notebook as though his memory was faulty. "Not much," he concluded in the end. His black hair was thick, curly, and cut short. He kept it trimmed around his ears. A deep, permanent horizontal crease in the man's brow suggested perpetual concentration, but the way his forehead protruded over his wide-set eyes gave the impression that all the concentration in the world had never helped him to arrive at a conclusion about anything, that he was constantly perturbed. "It's a rooming house for students mostly. Half went home for the holidays. Some were out shopping during the day, visiting friends at night. One guy's stoned. Says he saw a moving van. Stuff being hauled out of a room on this floor, could've been this one. Must've been. Another guy went to mass if you can believe that. Nobody heard a thing. Like one kid said, everybody plays their music so loud in here nobody can hear nothing. That's a quote. That's what he said." He seemed nervous about addressing Cinq-Mars.

"What name on the moving van?"

"Once he got started he was on a roll. He offered around seven choices. I suggested a few more, and he agreed it could've been one of those, too."

"Great. Who lived here?"

"Our victim. Everybody I spoke to gave me a positive ID off the Polaroid. Nobody knows anything about the Santa Claus routine. His name's Hagop Artinian."

"Hagop? That's a name?"

"Yes, sir."

"It's Armenian," Mathers put in.

"All right. Déguire, get in touch with the building owner in the morning. He might have plans to double his income this week. I want the apartment sealed until New Year's."

"I'm off tomorrow, sir," Déguire declared. He stuffed his notebook in his pocket and faced Cinq-Mars, challenging him to repudiate his statement.

"You're what?"

"Off," Déguire testified. His chin was a pronounced nub, which aggressively extended forward. "It's Christmas."

"You won't do this one little thing?"

His nervousness was apparent, but whether he was being defiant of Cinq-Mars's authority or was merely intimidated by his reputation was difficult to discern. Perhaps his upset had everything to do with the disruption to his Christmas, as he had stated, and he was mad that once again a superior officer had messed up his plans. "Yes, sir. I'll take care of that."

"Good man," Cinq-Mars told him, although he did not sound impressed.

Déguire lurched out of the apartment as if spooked by ghosts. Émile Cinq-Mars watched him go, trailed by the dead man, who was finally being wheeled out. Then he left also, with Bill Mathers shuffling along after him.

Behind a wall in that stark room a toilet flushed in the wake of their departure. Moments later, wiping his nose and mouth and sneezing, once, violently, the investigating officer, Sergeant-Detective André LaPierre, emerged from the bathroom. He looked around. He checked the empty closet. Then he yelled for a uniform to get the hell back in there and tell him what had happened to the body. "Where's my corpse?" he hollered. "Who took my corpse?"

2

One A.M., Christmas Morning

Detective Émile Cinq-Mars drove west from the mountain and the Christmas lights of downtown Montreal across the broad, flat, and largely English suburbs that would yield to countryside, where he lived, where his American wife slept peaceably, where his problems followed him around as if they were doting pets at his heels, yappy and insistent, affectionate and needy. He drove his own car, a blue Taurus wagon, and set the cruise control fifteen clicks above the legal limit, his usual allowance in winter. Friends thought him foolish to undertake this drive daily. For Cinq-Mars the trip was enjoyable, the quiet time restorative, and crossing the bridge to leave the urban island behind inevitably provided a jolt of relief. He was headed for horse country, an area of woods and open fields and white fences, a leisure community of large homes surrounded by vast yards and farms where, on a crisp, clear winter night like this, the sky was filled with stars.

Christmas morning now, Santa would be aloft, traversing the heavens in his chariot, swinging low to rooftops to scurry down chimneys into the dreams of children. *Good*, Cinq-Mars thought. Good, he meant, that the world periodically returned to its fictions and fairy tales, good that those whose job it was to separate a department store Santa from a savaging meat hook were shunted aside for a while, their stubborn reality dismissed for a day. Beyond the city, across the bridge, off the island, under the stars, Émile Cinq-Mars drove, and as he drove he brooded. As any man on the downward curve toward

38

retirement might do, he reflected upon those matters in his life that had carried him so gently to this juncture.

No one might have guessed, least of all Émile Cinq-Mars, that he would rise to become the top cop of his time and place. He had prided himself on being particular, a fusspot for detail, pragmatic and diligent by nature, artful by design. "Unremarkable overall" was how he had described the career of his newly attached partner, Bill Mathers. His own career path had made a similar impression through his early years as a police officer. He was known to be thorough, someone who got the job done, a plodder, a man of caution and integrity, unflappable, unexciting, a bore when he wasn't drinking, an oddity and a practicing Roman Catholic. He was promoted through the ranks on the basis of his reliability and service, all in due course, nothing rushed. That's how the job was for him, until it suddenly changed.

During his early years on the force Émile Cinq-Mars had specialized in petty crimes. Armed robbery, murders, rapes, headline-grabbing drug deals, and white-collar larceny were not the areas where he had first demonstrated talent. Car thieves, on the other hand, purse snatchers, B & E artists working a neighborhood, pickpockets and muggers—the pests, he called them—were criminals for whom he had a nose, a sense. Their activities suited his methods of investigation. Cinq-Mars did well because of his natural inclination to stick to it. He held an innate belief that the quick-strike petty criminal did not merely fade away into the welter of humanity, never to be identified, but that he distinguished himself, even shone forth, that he radiated the nature of his being and the manner of his crimes and all that any cop had to do was to keep on looking until the perpetrator showed up to declare himself. Often Cinq-Mars solved crimes he was not investigating. He never let a crime go, never forgot the circumstances, the pattern. Meddling in the affairs of the criminal world invariably unearthed both clues and suspects, and it was more a question, he had found, of matching suspects to a crime than the other way around. Where others might investigate a bank robbery and get nowhere, Émile Cinq-Mars would study the habits of an unsavory individual he had stumbled across and discover the bank robber his colleagues pursued. He liked to say that he didn't solve crimes. Rather, he figured out what criminals had been up to lately.

Cinq-Mars publicly maintained that shoddy police work was the chief reason petty crime flourished. "Crooks," he had declared while imbibing at an officers' party, "are like horses. They look smart going over the jumps, but they're still dumb animals." That remark had won the approval of his colleagues and a satisfying round of laughter. Cinq-Mars, however, had had quite a few whiskeys that night, and he continued on with a final aphorism, "The main thing dumb-ass crooks got going for them is dumber-assed cops," an opinion that failed to garner a laugh, or even a smile.

Still, the career of Émile Cinq-Mars had been predictable enough, and while he was respected and over the fullness of time would earn appropriate honor, the principal credits that had made him worthy of promotion were duty and years of service. He was not on an accelerated path, nor did he do anything of a dramatic nature to help himself. Cinq-Mars had nothing to contribute to the operations and teamwork put into play against the New York-Montreal Mafia connection or the Toronto-Montreal alliances or the Hell's Angels. His prey were the miscreants, the street toughs, the rough boys out to hot-wire a buck. Some he pursued because they were salvageable, others because they weren't. Most he tracked down because that happened to be his job. He was considered too genteel, too small-town, too hick country, to be a real street cop, but that's what he had become, in his own way, a street cop with a degree in animal husbandry, and his counterpoint, his reason for being, like the cow to the farmer, was the street punk.

But that would change. Everything would change. By the age of fifty-two, when most men were taking a sobering look at the limits of their careers, at the finite and shrinking choices of their lives, at the victory of boredom over ambition, of regret over aspiration, at a time when most men were choosing to settle for less and those who labored within large bureaucracies were settling for less than they had deemed imaginable, Émile Cinq-Mars would see his world turn, his wheels slip, his life and circumstances take a harrowing swerve. His career bounced once, twice on the tarmac, and then took off.

Cinq-Mars drove on.

Provided that those who were judging his appearance had an eye for extremes, character, and a blurred racial mix, the detective was a handsome man. His prominent forehead and amazingly large, aquiline nose, with the dominant crown and the steep ski slope down to a hefty nub, spoke of both his French-Norman roots and the Iroquois bloodlines a few generations past. A further French mix—paradoxically, Huguenot—irked him. At times he felt that that Protestant ingredient, in a grandmother, impinged upon his Roman Catholic soul, deformed him internally. Fifty-six now, he looked his years. Not younger, not older. His severe, erect bearing moved him through the world with an attitude of eminence. He could readily be mistaken for a judge or a bishop rather than be identified as a policeman, and politics might be guessed as his hobby before horse trading. Yet a measure of his authoritative stance was his inclination to be recalcitrant, to disavow power, to choose his own judgment over the rules, his own path above the accepted method. In the way that he pursed his lips, how he bobbed his head from side to side in a kind of ritual incantation, in the manner that he arched his rather extravagant and eccentric eyebrows, Émile Cinq-Mars displayed a thorny, rebellious temperament that caused those who knew him personally to fear him as much as those who knew him by reputation alone.

In answering a call on a wintry night such as this, he had agreed to visit a familiar motel on rue St. Jacques, in the city's west end before the onslaught of the suburbs, a predominately English-speaking neighborhood. Told nothing of what he might find there, in Room 23, he was, in effect, being dared to go and to go alone. Cinq-Mars did not call for backup, although he recognized the motel as the night headquarters for an Irish gang that controlled the nearby turf, a place where members monitored police radio frequencies and doled out small jobs to underlings and wanna-bes. He went alone as instructed and knocked at Room 23. A woman's voice spoke from the opposite side of the door. Cinq-Mars identified himself as a police officer. He stated that he had received a complaint. Opening the door, the woman threw herself into his arms.

She had been beaten by her husband and stowed away in the motel room while her wounds healed. She was the wife of a diplomat, Cinq-Mars learned, always an impossible arrest. He was curious, however, about the choice of motel, a possible link between the diplomat and the local tough guys, who were usually referred to as the West Enders. The coincidence could be brushed off, but he was not inclined to do so. He drove the woman away and established her in another motel along the same strip, calling paramedics to her side. Then the detective returned to Room 23 and awaited the diplomat's return.

He had nothing to go on and no hope of arrest. And yet, he waited.

The diplomat, when he showed, was a small man, British, refined in the customs of protocol, self-assured to the brink of inflated importance. Cinq-Mars endured the man's rebuff and his snooty tone, and worked the man's manner to his own advantage. If the gentleman was determined to treat him as loutish, he would assume the role and play it through. He assured the diplomat that his wife had been photographed, that the photos would be sold to tabloids back in London, that he'd do the selling himself, that he would pocket the change to put toward his retirement. Seizing the obvious opening, the diplomat offered a higher bid.

"Now that you have confirmed your guilt——" Cinq-Mars began.

"It won't stand up in a court of law," the diplomat rebutted, chiding the detective for his ignorance. His name was Murray. *Jonathan James Murray, Esq.*, his embossed card had read.

"Who mentioned court?" Cinq-Mars countered. "We're not going to court over this, Murray."

"Don't be so bloody familiar, sir. You may call me Mr. Murray."

"Mr. Murray, sir," Cinq-Mars repeated dryly, "I'm not interested in your money and we're not going to court. What I want is information. It's the only currency I accept."

The diplomat duly smirked. Cinq-Mars reiterated a description of his wife's appearance, both eyes blackened, the nose pulpy, the mouth bloody. He conjured possible headlines, each vying to more rudely smear the man's reputation. "What do you call that London rag? *The News of the World?*"

With bluster and harangue, the small man protested. He raised the specter of diplomatic immunity, he shouted harassment, he accused the policeman of kidnapping his wife and swore he'd have him arrested. He insisted that his contacts could strip him of his badge and Cinq-

Mars disputed nothing of what he had to say, nevertheless the photos would be sold or the diplomat would soon tell him something that he did not already know.

The debate carried on through the night. By dawn the Englishman tendered a plea for clemency. Immunity from prosecution he already possessed, but he had come to crave freedom from scandal. Cinq-Mars revealed that he merely wanted to toss a spanner into the works of the boys downstairs. Whipped, defeated, the diplomat pulled out an unanticipated confession. Within days Émile Cinq-Mars single-handedly cracked a white-trade ring operating on behalf of minor London sheiks, foiling the sale to a brothel in Europe of ten Quebec girls who had recently arrived in the city from the countryside. In the Montreal tabloid *Allô Police!* the policeman was enshrined as a local hero.

He never gave the tip that had initiated the entire process a second thought. A maid, a child, a chauffeur, a friend, an employee at the British Trade Commission, one of many could have instigated the leak, others may have passed it on. And yet, within a fortnight, he had heard again from the same telephone voice, and Cinq-Mars used the new information to disrupt a band of young fur thieves stealing from restaurant cloakrooms and art galleries. A mere three weeks later he exposed a stolen car ring that had been supplying western Canada with mid-market automobiles. Repeatedly, Émile Cinq-Mars racked up impressive arrests leading to convictions. He was a continuous source for front-page and television news material. Any time he mentioned that his main method to break a case was to wait patiently by the phone, nobody believed him, and he was referred to as a modest man. After a few such experiences, he kept that explanation to himself. Local tabloids turned him into the stuff of legend. At *Allô Police!* he had grown godlike.

He survived it all, even the envy of fellow officers. The frequency of the tips would diminish after the initial flurry, but several times a year Cinq-Mars made stunning arrests. Jewel thieves who had eluded the work of a task force were apprehended, tried, and convicted after Cinq-Mars had given them a week's attention. An automobile-tapedeck company passing along its daily list of new clients to thieves was unmasked. A gang that had robbed banking machines by battering the walls that contained them and carrying off the machines with a truck and a forklift was nabbed in the act. A postal theft ring had their warehouse raided. His information, its breadth, its accuracy, its pace, baffled friends and confounded enemies. Cinq-Mars himself grew curious about the origins of his knowledge. He heard from only one voice, although no single informant could gather such a gamut of intelligence on his own. Of interest, and particularly astonishing in his experience, he was never asked to pay back the information with either cash or favors.

As his professional life ascended to new heights, his personal life had also come under review. He and his new wife had found living together more difficult than had been their long-distance courtship when she'd been in the States. Cinq-Mars consented to her desire to move to the country and raise horses. They had originally met and courted around horses, and the move was meant to rekindle the initial spark. Cinq-Mars viewed it as an attempt to keep her occupied whenever he was not home, himself occupied whenever he was. To that end, the move had been a good one. Life in horse country had done less to heal the divisions in their marriage than to entrench them, but tensions had eased.

Cinq-Mars drove on that winter's night, down the country road. At an entrance to a horse farm he pulled over, shut the motor, and stepped out. Ill-advised in such a climate. A car that would not start again would leave him in life-threatening cold, with no one passing at that hour. He was willing to risk it, although he knew that people were as likely to freeze to death close to home as anywhere. Cinq-Mars needed to get at a nagging thought, and he preferred to do it here.

The thought was an aggravating and grievous one. Had he, or had he not, sold his soul to the devil? He had accepted information and profited from the steady flow. And yet, when had he agreed to the purchase price? This youth tonight, this twenty-something, student-looking Santa Claus, was part of a network that had fed him. The boy was one of the few he had met previously, briefly. Now the boy was dead, his neck snapped for the betrayal of nefarious friends, his body savaged and deployed as a cryptic warning to Cinq-Mars. Who was this kid? He didn't know him. He had benefited from his information and from the risks the young man had taken. Why had he done the work and who had put him up to it? Cinq-Mars had no clue. All he knew was that the youth had sacrificed his life and he had reaped the benefit. Standing in the blizzard of cold air, Cinq-Mars endeavored to convince himself that he shouldn't hold himself responsible.

Think fast. The night was too cold not to demand an immediate conclusion, however rash. Cinq-Mars determined that fundamentally he was not to blame. But if he was not responsible, then who was? Not the dead Santa, nor any of the others. The breadth of information indicated a small coterie. Someone had recruited them. Someone had trained them and set them to work. That had been obvious to Cinq-Mars for a long while, but he had let it go, impressed by the results. Therein did his guilt reside.

Émile Cinq-Mars climbed back into his car. He held his breath and started the ignition. It kicked over. He eased out onto the country road and headed home to his wife and horses. "That's who," he said aloud, and he did not bother chastising himself for the unwelcome habit of being vocal whenever he was alone in his car at night. "Okay, somebody killed that boy. But the one who put him into that company, that's who sealed his fate, that's who should be held accountable for his death."

Cinq-Mars thought silently, as though the notion impressing itself upon him now was too grave, too bedeviled by consequence, to be spoken aloud—*As of this moment, that's the one I'm after.*

The official investigation would pursue the actual killers, and probably to no avail. Cinq-Mars figured that one way or another, and it would be tricky in the world of department politics, he was going after the one who seemed to believe that he—or she, or they—controlled him. He was going after the one who had recruited and possessed the soul of the dead boy, and probably other young people, and he would track the culprit down as a personal crusade.

Cinq-Mars had to admit that he did not know where to begin, how to proceed. He was even uncertain that he could successfully define the crime. All he understood was that he did not want another dead boy on his conscience. His job now was to thwart the powers behind his own success. If he hurt himself and his career in the process, so be it. In the clear, cold air of Christmas Eve night, his new resolve gave him sufficient peace of mind that he could, at least, go home.

3

Christmas Day

On Christmas morning Émile Cinq-Mars and his wife, Sandra Lowndes, awoke before dawn to tend to their horses. They worked diligently in the cold damp of the stables, feeding and watering, and when they were done emerged to a beautiful sunrise sparkling across the white fields of snow. They changed out of their work gear and had a special breakfast of pancakes and sausage before opening presents. From her husband, Sandra received a saddle she had first spotted at a country fair in August and coveted but decided was too expensive. Unbeknownst to her, her husband had sneaked away under the guise of finding a Johnny-on-the-Spot and made the purchase. After that triumph, Cinq-Mars opened gifts of underwear and socks, shirts and a new pair of boots from L. L. Bean before he received his ultimate gift, a recent translation into French of Stephen Hawking's book on the universe. Both recipients felt like happy kids.

After they had cleaned up, Cinq-Mars made a suggestion. Never before had he seen fit to bring his wife along on an investigation, but he asked if she'd accompany him into town. He had promised that he'd be around for Christmas Day, he didn't want to disappoint her. Sandra agreed. She might even have been pleased. On the drive in, Cinq-Mars let it slip that they'd be stopping by a crime scene.

"Émile," she sighed, "you take the cake."

He was not familiar with the English expression. "What cake?"

Sandra smiled, suspecting that his invitation had been extended as a gesture of affection. "What crime?"

46

"Murder."

Her laugh was a full-bodied burst that ended in a giggle.

"What's so funny?"

"Santa's murder? On Christmas Day you're taking me to the place where Santa Claus was killed? Merry Christmas to you, too, Émile. What will we do there, exchange presents? I know! We should take each other's presents *back*. That would be symbolically appropriate."

"Sorry. I know it's not the ideal Christmas. But I need to have access when no one's around."

"Don't I get to go in?" She had initially been attracted to him, in part, by the nature of his work. Seeing him in action would be a treat.

"Of course," Cinq-Mars conceded. "I just meant, I want to be there with no cops around, or witnesses jabbering in my ear, or a coroner telling me what he thinks. I can't function at a crime scene when it's busy and hectic and everyone's on edge. I prefer the quiet, when I can hear myself think."

Sandra put her head back and playfully tossed her hair. "Or, could it be that since you're not in Homicide, you have no business being there yourself?" A mock smile fended off his look, and she laughed again. "Émile, I promise. I'll be the mute, dutiful wife."

Upon reaching the city and coming off the expressway, Sandra asked if he'd like some coffee. "Great idea," he said.

"Good! Because I could use a bathroom."

That confused him. "Why didn't you just say so?"

"Because now we're stopping for your sake, not mine. I'm not holding you up. The investigation of Santa's murder will not be retarded by my presence." She was smiling, her little finger poking into a corner of her mouth. When Émile shook his head, smiling back, she stuck out her tongue.

Cinq-Mars stopped in the heart of downtown along Peel Street, where the normally congested traffic was sparse on the holiday, and parked. The two of them popped into a McDonald's, but the place was too gloomy to stay on a festive day, the customers homeless or merely loveless, and at Sandra's urging they took their coffees into the park across the street. In the frigid air and gusty winds, they had the place pretty much to themselves. As they strolled along the plowed

47

serpentine paths, shivering and sipping, Cinq-Mars described the square's significance to his wife, who still had much to learn about the city.

Dominion Square provides a respite in the center of downtown. Covering two half blocks on either side of a wide boulevard, the park offers a broad view of the sky amid the tyranny of buildings, places to sit and be restful amid the hubbub. The War Memorial is here, and an array of old cannons challenges pedestrians. Shade trees, well spaced, provide an intermittent canopy in the summer, although in bleak midwinter the bare branches contribute to the city's pervading sense of chill, of dark, of endurance. Monuments to the poet Robert Burns, to Queen Victoria, to Canadian veterans of a war in South Africa, to French and English politicians, speak to the city's diversified history and influences. On opposite sides of the boulevard stand the old Sun Life Assurance Building and Mary Queen of the World Basilica.

The Sun Life is entered on broad stairs between massive Doric columns that are repeated to a lesser scale twenty floors up. The concrete building rises in narrowing blocks, a solid look, as though no quake, no maelstrom can dent its structure. Mary Queen of the World is also concrete, a low rectangle protected along its roofline by a walk of apostles standing beneath a copper dome. Once the power in the province of Quebec, the Roman Catholic Church doled out land to parishioners. A Frenchman wanting to farm requested a plot from the Church and promised to be faithful. If an Englishman desired land, the priest placed a fraternal hand upon his shoulder and suggested that he look first to Ontario, or slip across the border into the United States.

The process was accepted until history intervened. Famine besieged the Lake District in England, prompting massive emigration to Montreal. Under pressure to provide for the arriving and starving English, the Church offered land in Quebec it didn't want, or where it had not as yet created a parish. Granting the English farmland created a problem for the Church, for it had no means of distributing property among *les autres*—the others, the Protestants, the English. So the bishops contracted with the Sun Life Assurance Company to do the job. English farmers, then, had to approach Sun Life on bended knee to beg land, just as the French bowed at mass on Sundays.

"For the early homesteaders," Cinq-Mars explained to Sandra, "Sun Life became the equivalent of the Catholic Church. The French put their faith in redemption after a life of devotion, the English in redeeming policies after a life of premiums. It's one of the ways the French and the English remained culturally separated, even though our history in this place is merely different sides of the same coin."

Both the Church and Sun Life would be left behind by the times. Politics became the new religion of the province, politicians its new saints and bishops. Parish churches emptied, the power of the priests was stripped away. The new political might of the French proved too much for the scions of Sun Life, who chose to flee, packing their head office into trucks in the middle of the night and scurrying three hundred and fifty miles down the highway to Toronto.

"It leaves you out of the loop," Sandra suggested to her husband.

"How do you mean?"

"You're a religious man, but your church is becoming a shell. You love your city, but it's not as prosperous as it used to be. Politically, Montreal's ripping apart at the seams. How do you feel about all that?"

Cinq-Mars swallowed the last of his coffee and mashed his styrofoam cup in his hand. "Like everyone else, I wait, watch, and worry," he said gravely. "I study the situation. Change is always difficult. Political uncertainty chases away industry. So many people out of work, so much lost opportunity. Which makes my business more hectic than it should be." Getting cold, Cinq-Mars turned his face away from the wind and exhaled a giant billow of air. "Trouble is, change becomes a religion to some. Was it really necessary to categorically ban English on signs? Shops, okay, that's only natural, but tourists die on the highways because they can't comprehend our signs. The people who believe in that should clean up the blood and guts. They should be the ones to tell the victims' families." Cinq-Mars sighed and banged his boots together to chase off a chill.

"But for me, there's something else." He glanced at a homeless woman lugging her bag of belongings across the park like a weary Santa Claus with his sack of toys. Where was she going in such a determined fashion? Out of the cold, perhaps, or to a free Christmas meal? The image of her reminded Cinq-Mars that Santa Claus had been murdered, and that he was pursuing his killers. "What scares me most around here, what worries me about political upheaval, is those seams you were mentioning, the ones that are being ripped apart. When the political, the economic, *and* the social structures of a city crack, criminals take up residence along the fault lines. They entrench. They dig their way into the dirt, they become part of the new foundation. That's an aspect of political instability nobody talks about. We can't contain the biker gangs now. Imagine if our resources were depleted or distracted by secession, and suddenly you have thousands of people leaving, and others arguing to divide Quebec land among the English and the French. If more business leaves and people go hungry, if the currency fails, if we have riots— scary in itself, but nobody, nobody is thinking about what that will do for organized crime. Except, maybe, the bikers."

They were waiting for a taxi to pass so they could cross the street back to their car. "Do you really think that bikers talk politics, Émile?"

Cinq-Mars regarded her in a thoughtful manner. When they'd first met they had enjoyed discussing American politics. The situation in Quebec was another subject, so embedded was it for Cinq-Mars with fret. Perhaps, though, now that she was living here, discussion of the local situation ought to become part of their daily lives, as it was with most families. "I know they do," he told her.

He spoke in a particularly gentle voice. Sandra nodded. She understood. Like the buildings at her back, the Sun Life and Mary Queen of the World, the import of his words lay beyond their apparent architecture.

Julia Murdick went home for Christmas.

As she had explained to Selwyn Norris, she was not going *home* home but to the farm her family used as a retreat. They were gathering for the holidays—her mother, her father, her father's new wife, and her mother's latest boyfriend—and she was expecting the usual wretched quagmire.

Buses took her beyond Ottawa, a two-and-a-half-hour trip, where she disembarked on a barren highway surrounded by open fields. Frigid winds stung her cheeks and, going right through her wool coat, made her shiver. She waited for her dad, getting madder by the second. If her father ever showed up she'd brain him. Just then, Julia spotted his car descending a hill on the secondary road and waved as he passed to access the highway ramp. Given that the bus had arrived early, he was not terribly late. Never mind. She would impress upon him that unless he planned to buy her a very expensive, much warmer coat he'd better never be late for a wintertime pickup again. He ought to show up at least an hour ahead of schedule. *If* he loved her, *he* should have been waiting for *her*. And yet, when his car sidled up to her and he smiled broadly, Julia was simply glad to see him. She'd been away from home for so long and away from her father for longer still.

Inside they kissed cheeks and she slammed the door shut. "Good thing I'm a student," she barked.

Her father ceded to the trap. "Why's that?" His name was Ron Murdick, and he owned several restaurants in the Ottawa area. A good-looking man of forty-five, rotund, with a carefree disposition, he'd gained a shock of white hair when he'd been in his twenties. Ron Murdick was always a sucker for her gibes.

"I'm financially dependent on my parents. Otherwise"—she made a twisting motion with one hand—"a shiv through the heart."

"I'm not late."

"You're not early."

"You're hard to please," he lamented.

"I'm frozen stiff! Another minute, I'd be a goner."

"I came as soon as I could get away."

Julia laughed. "Like I'm going to believe that!"

Enjoying being ribbed by her again, her father laughed lightly also. "It's the truth," he said. "You don't have to believe me."

"I know better."

They drove into the broad and rolling countryside, past snowbound fields and copses, through small villages that served the agricultural communities around them, the old stone homes of the early settlers still prominent, and they carried on toward what they referred

51

to as the family farm, although no plow had tilled the soil in twenty years and title had never wholly resided in family hands.

Through most of her childhood and adolescence, Julia had journeyed to the farm from Toronto for her summer and winter holidays. Along with eight others, including her father, her mother had bought the property in the early seventies, before Julia was born. The group had scraped cash together and made the purchase for a pittance, inspired by talk of forming a commune to live off the land.

"Now that's a scary thought," Julia had scoffed one time. "You guys living off the land. Yeah, right. Like maybe for a weekend."

She had reason to be cynical. Rather than being a retreat for an alternative lifestyle, the hippie commune had become a mark of affluence. Swank summer cottages replaced the pottery and weaving studios, and the original barn had been bulldozed to make room for a four-season house. Fields had gone to seed. Beehives envisioned next to a wildflower meadow had given way to a three-car garage. Space for the stables had been appropriated for a pool.

The henhouse, the pig sty, the milking barn, the lambs' pens and rabbit warrens had slowly collapsed over time, never knowing a welcomed tenant. The vegetable garden—worked for a few years—had been paved for parking, and the original farmhouse where Julia and her family stayed now offered, after three additions, ten bedrooms and four bathrooms to accommodate the expanding and multiplying families.

Where four couples had originally been involved, now there were nine, divorce having been the catalyst for growth.

"Look what the cat dragged in," Margaret commented as Julia entered the house through the kitchen door. "Nice of you to drop by for a visit."

Julia beamed at her stepmother. Luckily, she could give as well as receive. "Is Mummy here?" she asked, promptly putting her father's wife in her place.

Margaret Murdick smiled back. "There's another one who thinks Christmas is just another inconvenient smudge in her appointment book. No, Julia, your mother is not here yet. Who knows if she'll make it? She might be throwing a Christmas brunch for diplomats.

Maybe she's doing her nails. Perhaps she was on her way but met a new man in some roadside diner."

"She's busy," Julia reminded her. "Doing well, I hear."

Her stepmother—annoyingly thin to Julia's mind, but at least she had mousy hair that never set properly—hung tough. "Being an indentured slave to the government, dear, is not working. Think of it as an extended vacation with pay."

"What about you?" Julia shot back. "Found a job yet? Or are you still looking?"

Her stepmom grinned so brightly that Julia worried she might be defeated in her foray, but the smile proved to be another ruse. "There's a good job out there with my name on it, sweetheart. My spirits are high, my disposition sunny. I'm thinking positively. Someone will snap me up."

"I hope it's an orgasmic experience for you," Julia muttered as she moved through to the large living room before Margaret could respond. She slipped her backpack off her shoulders.

"I heard that, young lady!" The piercing voice from the kitchen trailed after her. "That's not the sort of language we tolerate in this house. Carting yourself off to a university does not give you the right to be vulgar."

"Orgasmic is a word, Margaret. It's look-up-able."

"A word like that you can find in places other than a dictionary— and I know what sorts of places!"

"Oh, lay off." She ascended the stairs. "It's Christmas Day. I don't want to kill you on Christmas Day. Somebody already butchered that poor sod Santa Claus last night, did you hear? That's enough violence for a while."

Margaret stood at the foot of the stairs, gazing upward, where Julia had vanished. "I told you this would happen," she said to no one in particular.

Julia lay down for a few minutes in the quiet of her room. *This is going to be nuts. Wait'll the gang's all here. This'll be hell.* She had deliberately delayed arriving until the last possible moment, and she didn't intend to stay long. She felt weary and utterly alone, less resilient, less formidable than expected. Funnily, she was missing Selwyn Norris, missing his attentions, she even missed battling his intellect. *This'll be the worst visit ever.* Somehow she had to suppress her anger, make it through until her real mother arrived. After that, with any luck, she might scrape by.

Julia had to hope that her mother showed up soon. Hope as well that she wasn't in one of her crankier moods.

Merry Christmas, she told herself. *Welcome home, Julia kitten.*

Sandra Lowndes hung back as she and her husband entered the small apartment where Santa Claus had swung from a coatrack. Émile Cinq-Mars moved about the rooms in stages, observing, concentrating. She wondered if he detected the cries of the victim, or picked up an echo of the killer's words. Could he identify criminals through intuitive revelation? Émile was eighteen years her senior, and at times she felt his age, the gap apparent in his weariness at the end of the day when an evening's whiskey caused him to slur his words. Often he fell asleep in his armchair after dinner. They had met around horses, where his concentration in the midst of a negotiation was fearsome. He could detail an animal's attributes and shortcomings in rapid-fire succession and take command of any deal by virtue of his superior knowledge. She had been impressed. Here, in the room where the frightful crime had occurred, she saw again the knitted brow, the eyes moving over the objects of their interest while the head remained perfectly still, the occasional gentle tapping of a middle finger upon the hard bone behind his ear to indicate that notions were alight, in the air.

She watched him crouch before a blank wall, stand on tiptoe and peer at the dust on top of the refrigerator. He seemed scarcely to be breathing. He spent considerable time in the common living and sleeping room, less time in the kitchen, no time at all in the bathroom. He seemed more interested in blank spaces than in the cabinet where the boy had hung, or in the plain dark pine table centered in the apartment. He did stand upon the table once, observing both the top of the cabinet and the room's central light fixture.

"All right," he said finally. "Let's go."

"Émile?" She leaned a shoulder against the wall next to the entry door, where she had remained throughout. "Tell me what you see," she requested quietly. "Please." Her husband was a reserved, reticent man. In the heady days of romance spontaneity had never been a problem, but marriage had proven the less successful sojourn. Daily she felt him becoming more removed from her, his secretive nature taking up residence between them as a third and somewhat hostile entity.

Cinq-Mars gazed back into the room. He considered his thoughts, as though uttering them aloud might diminish their import, or tarnish his ideas in such a way that they'd lose their impetus.

"The furniture was removed from this room," he pointed out, "and only the fridge and stove are left in the kitchen. You can see by the shadows where light faded the floor in some places and not others. The bed was here. Over there, a dresser. The way this small rectangular shape turns toward the large one suggests a television aimed at a sofa. No cable. Here, these small shapes? Bricks, placed in a row to support bookshelves. Someone removed every stick of furniture, except the closet and the table, which they probably needed to remain behind."

"For the murder?" Sandra asked.

"They hung him in the closet. But he wasn't murdered here. The meat hook might have been driven into him here, but the boy was already dead. I think they left the table because it's so plain, so simple, they know it holds no secrets."

She was especially intrigued now, folding her arms together. "What do you mean, secrets?"

"Here, look." He invited her over to a wall and crouched. She placed a hand on his shoulder and leaned down. "The wall socket. What do you make of it?"

His wife did a quick study. "It's a wall socket all right."

"Look closer," gently, he commanded.

She did so, crouching herself. She examined the device carefully, smiling, warmed by being in her husband's company for a change, and enchanted by the possibility that something was to be seen here that she could not see. Her husband often spotted attributes or blemishes in horses that she had missed on first inspection. She liked to tease him that he had a pathology for detail, while she preferred the overview, the big picture. He'd get defensive then, saying that he noticed details because he understood them in the context of the big picture. She didn't doubt it, but kidded him anyway. In this environment Sandra viewed neither. What she was looking at carried no significance for her. "I see a wall socket, Émile."

"Ah, but look." He ran a finger along its edge. "The room was painted some time ago, but it's fairly fresh, within the year I'd say. The socket was painted at the same time with the same color. Now look. The paint's been chipped around the plate and scratched off the screwhead. Which means the plate was removed recently." He straightened a little stiffly to an upright position again. "We know that a moving van was here yesterday, so it's reasonable to assume that all the furniture was moved out then. Notice how well the apartment's been cleaned. Swept and vacuumed. But look, check along the quarter-round, a few flecks of paint remain, trapped under the molding. They fell from around the socket. If I had to guess—and I do—I'd say the sockets were opened up and inspected yesterday, after the furniture was removed, before the cleanup began."

"Why would anyone want to look in the socket?" Sandra asked.

"Here, the light switch? Same thing."

This time she knew what she was looking for. "The paint's been cracked."

"Not excessively. Whoever took the wall plates off and put them back on again took care. The perpetrator didn't want us to notice." Cinq-Mars took out his key chain, which doubled as a pocketknife. He inserted the end into the screw on the light switch. "I won't find anything. This has already been investigated, by the killer presumably. But there's no harm looking." He pulled the plate off and found the cavity to be as he anticipated.

Sandra slipped an arm through the crook of her husband's elbow. "What do you make of it, Émile?"

Cinq-Mars grimaced to indicate that he hated being limited to mere speculation. "Someone went through this apartment with a fine-tooth comb. The furniture was probably removed so it could be inspected, torn apart, analyzed thoroughly. That's my best guess. Student's furniture, where bricks are used for shelves, isn't worth stealing, certainly not worth killing for. I think someone opened up the sockets and the switches to see if anything was hidden in there. Or to remove what he knew to be hidden there, that he might have hidden himself. A listening device. A key. A code. Something."

Noting that her husband was speaking slowly, with an unusual quietness, she squeezed him against herself. He breathed deeply, sighed.

"What this tells me is that the perpetrator is extraordinarily meticulous. He's thorough, he's organized. He had help with the furniture and the cleaning. We already know he's ruthless, because of how he butchered the boy. Moving the body here and hanging a sign on him tells me he's cold-blooded. I hate to say it, but whoever is behind this crime is also professional. Very professional," Cinq-Mars told her gravely, a further idea dawning upon him. "Almost as though whoever did this was trained."

She leaned into him, hugging his arm and burying her head in his shoulder. He moved his arm, pulling it gently from her grasp, then drawing her small frame into his side. He led her to the door, where he turned and stared back one more time.

"Curious," he said, "that someone would be so meticulous in cleaning up a crime scene, yet leave DNA under the fingernails of the victim." Émile Cinq-Mars turned off the light.

In the corridor, Sandra Lowndes kissed him lightly on the cheek. "Merry Christmas, Émile."

"Thanks for allowing this," he said.

She managed a smile. "I guess it's part of being a cop's wife."

They had been married a few years now, not so long. She was still learning of such matters.

In Julia's eyes her mother possessed a unique and prodigious talent for devastation. She was a mood wrecker. Solemnity had to be dispatched with spontaneous raillery, calm deposed by riot. A party animal, her mom could rarely tolerate the notion of solitude and believed that people standing around by themselves were either rude or demented. Conversation had to include everyone in the room, and she had no time for contemplation or pause. She liked to talk, she was also happy to listen, and she expected the same from others. To Julia, her mom was like a child, full of questions and observations, often delirious with news. She preferred quick repartee to the carefully considered reply, and while she was intelligent and could discuss most matters under the sun, she preferred to talk about very little at all, she just loved the babble. Julia was fond of her mom but the woman exhausted her. Even as a child she had wished that her mother would grow up before she did, get serious, give herself and others a little space.

"Knock knock," her mother said, sticking her head through the doorway.

"Get lost."

"Oh, honey bunny, I haven't seen you in months!"

"That's why, dumb-dumb. I can't take this. I need my peace and quiet."

Dinner had been consumed and wine swilled in abundance and presents opened and wrappings strewn everywhere. Constant chatter, yet every meaningful observation was engulfed by trivia. Julia could not cope with the bedlam. "Fiddlesticks," her mother said. Her name was Grace Olfield.

"Fiddlesticks nothing," Julia protested. Grace was already in the room, closing the door behind her. "Mummy, I just want time alone, 'kay?"

"Forget it. We're chatting." She was a heavy woman, a half foot shorter than her daughter. Grace Olfield had always carried weight, and had had to assure Julia from time to time that their body types were not similar. "When I was a little girl I was plump," she'd tell her, truthfully, "when I was your age I was fat, now I'm a mature full-figured gal! You may need to watch your weight, sweetheart, but your thighs will never match mine. Yours are matchsticks by comparison." The mattress sagged as she sat down beside her daughter.

Julia jumped up. "All right, come in since you're already in, but you're on the clock!"

"I just want to catch up."

"Great." Julia tidied the books she had unpacked into one safe corner. She stowed the ginch she had just received as a gift in the dresser out of harm's way. She bounced back down on the bed beside her mom. "What's up?"

"With you, dear."

"Come again?" Her mom's eyes were bright, excited. She'd missed seeing them every day.

"With you. What's up with you?"

"Nothing. Why?"

"That's why!" She shook her head with her mouth open for a few seconds. "There's nothing. You go away to university for four months, you live on your own for the first time in your life, you're in a new city, and so far you have told me nothing, nada, diddly-squat."

Julia collapsed on the bed and hugged a pillow. "Oohhh, Mummy."

"So tell. Gossip. The blues. Who your friends are. Your best parties. I want to feel like I'm there myself."

"Hey. It's my youth. You're not invited."

"Vicarious living. It's my style. Shoot."

"Mummy!"

"Talk, child, you're not mute. Talk or I'll tickle."

"All right, all right. Take it easy."

"Good. Now take your time. We've got all night."

"*All night?* I'm tired!"

"Go. Begin."

"Well," Julia started off, flopping down beside her mom and enjoying having her temple caressed, "to cut to the chase, there's no boyfriend yet."

"That's okay. You've got one back home."

"I'm quitting him."

"Really? Have you told Brian this?"

"Yes."

"I saw him yesterday. He didn't mention it."

"The mail is slow at Christmas," Julia said quietly.

"Oh, honey," her mother said, snuggling down with her. "You should tell him yourself. Over the phone, at least."

"Can't. Won't. Too chicken. I've never dumped anybody before. I have absolutely no experience at the job."

"Brian's a nice boy."

"He's a geek, Mom."

"I know, honey, but he's such a nice geek."

They laughed, mother and daughter, and Julia was happy to be held, to be cuddled. Their conversation would span the globe, cover politics, fashion, books, dance, theater, men. Grace Olfield roused herself to leave only when it was clear that her daughter was all but asleep.

Julia stretched, catlike, as her mother opened the door to leave.

"Julia? Have you had yourself checked out yet?"

"Not yet—"

"Honey—"

"I have an appointment."

A phone was ringing down the hall.

"That's good. An appointment is good. It's progress."

"It's not as though I've had to use it."

"Use it or lose it," her mother said.

"What kind of a mother are you anyway? Use or lose it—*my ass!* That's disgusting!"

"Good night, sweetie."

"Sweetie schmeetie. Use or lose it. You can't say that to me. I'm your daughter. It's indecent. *Be an adult!*"

A shout arose from downstairs that the phone was for Julia. She scrambled up and took it in the hall. Her mother waited by her side, retreating only when Julia gave her a stern get-away-from-me look.

"Okay. I'm history," Grace Olfield conceded, scrunching up her nose. "Good night."

"Good night, Mummy."

She picked up the receiver. "Hello."

"Hi," the voice said.

Strange, Julia was thinking even while it was happening, that they both seemed to be waiting for the same signal. She did not speak until the click of the other phone indicated that whomever had answered downstairs had hung up. Strange how she instinctively knew to do that when talking to Selwyn Norris.

"Hi," Julia replied.

"It's good to hear your voice," he said.

"Even if it is monosyllabic."

"Listen, Julia. I need to speak to you."

60

"Okay."

"I want you to call me back. Call collect."

"When?"

"After everyone there has gone to bed. Do you have a phone you can use that's private?"

"Sure. At least, it'll be private when everyone's in bed. That might not be for hours, Selwyn. My father and stepdad-in-training are into the Calvados. Who knows when they'll retire."

"Doesn't matter when, Snoop. As long as you call. Okay?"

"Okay."

"Bye now."

"Bye."

Now what's this about? Julia wondered as she returned to her bedroom. Lying down, she crushed her pillow against her chest and questioned why she hadn't mentioned him to her mother. She had revealed just about everything else. Of course her mother would disapprove, but that was no big deal. The tingling excitement, the *anticipation* that she felt, this was what she could not convey, could scarcely acknowledge to herself. She did not know if she was in love—she assumed that she was not. But what, then? Attraction, yes. And the man was a mystery. He intrigued her. He beguiled her. He set her on edge. But what was it? What kept her coming back for more, wanting to know more, to comprehend the spheres of his knowledge, the limits of his influence on her? What was it about Selwyn Norris? And why was she dating an older man? Could she really call it *dating*? Could she? What would *he* call it? He hadn't so much as tried to kiss her. What would he have to say when she called him back? Why did he have that urgency, that irritation in his voice? What was wrong? *Oh, damn him!* He made the most routine matter seem fraught with interest, mystery, deviation, terror. *What's up with this guy?*

Julia hoped that she would sleep, that she would wake up when it was time to call. She was bone-weary. But after brushing her teeth and crawling into bed, she could not close her eyes for long. She lay there, awake, waiting for the hour when she could telephone her mystery man.

61

Julia dozed off and awakened startled, disoriented. For a moment she wondered where she could be. The darkness of the country night frightened her, she had no notion of time. Too sleepy to locate the bedside lamp, she wrapped her short kimono around herself and felt in the dark for the doorknob, switching on the light only after she opened the door.

That dim glow led her down to the second-floor landing as she moved sleepily toward the bathroom. There the overhead blinded her and, after getting her bearings, she turned it off and peed and soaked water into her eyes in the dark. Her eyes had adjusted when she emerged and she was awake now. The light from her bedroom guided her across the landing toward the stairs. With both hands on the walls, Julia worked her way down.

In the living room she stepped over the Christmas debris and empty wine bottles to the sofa, where she sat with the telephone in her lap. She turned on the floor lamp to dial. She was thinking of hanging up the phone on its fifth ring when Norris responded.

"Hi," he said.

"It's me."

"You sound sleepy."

"Well, *duh*. What time is it?"

"Quarter of." She had noticed that he always used the American way of defining time. Did that mean he was American? Had to be.

"Quarter *to* what?"

"Two."

"Guess I fell asleep. Did I wake you?"

"No."

"Liar. So what's the urgency? What's the big news?"

"I've got to know, Snoop. I have to find out where you stand."

"Oh—you—you're so infuriating! What d'you mean, where I stand? I don't stand anywhere."

"Keep your voice down," he cautioned her.

"Don't be shushing me, Mister Buddy. You've got some hare-brained scheme I know nothing about and you're asking me where I stand? What do you think I am, some neophyte groupie who'll do anything you please no matter what the miserable fuck it is?"

"Ssshhhh."

"Shush yourself. It's two in the morning. I'm so tired. What's the matter with you? Are you nuts? I'd like to know." She didn't like her feet. Her toes, anyway. Julia wrapped a finger around her big toe and squeezed it while she talked. *My toes are too long.*

"Things have changed," he said.

"What's changed?"

"Circumstances."

"Selwyn, nothing has changed for me. I'm spending Christmas in the same old country home with the same old nutty relations fighting the same old boring fights. I would *love* a change of circumstances. But no such luck for me."

"I don't need an answer now."

"Too bad, I'll give you one now." *My arches are too flat.*

"Think about this first. Matters have accelerated. We've had some good fortune and some bad luck. There has been an escalation in the terms of engagement."

"Selwyn—"

"I have a spot for you, Jul. It's safe. It's exciting. It's in the thick of things. You won't believe your adventures. Engage the world. That's what I'm asking of you. Look around your country home while you're up there. Take a good look at your elders. Decent enough folk, I'm sure, despite your quibbles."

"Quibbles!"

"Look at them, Julia. Each man, each woman, has one life to live. How is he or she living it? Are they bored with their own lives? With their spouses? Are they tired and burned out? Do they repeat the same old discussions they've had a thousand times before, and is that really passion you hear in their words? Become one of them if you want, Julia. Or choose to live by your wits where you'll never feel bored or useless. You'll never feel disconnected from the world. You'll never experience what it's like to believe that life has passed you by."

"What have you been snorting? You're on a roll."

"Look around you, Jul. That's all I'm asking for tonight. While you're up there, think about the life that's ahead. Think about what's waiting."

"You're crazy, you're an absolute loony bird. Why do I bother talking to you?" *I have lame duck feet. Duck feet and emu kneecaps.*

"You talk to me because I'm offering what you can't get elsewhere. A chance, Jul, to live a real life. Engaged. Valuable. Vital. I'm offering you the chance *not* to seep slowly into your dotage, to live on the edge. Maybe you can walk away from that, maybe you can't. That's what I need to find out. The only difference between today and yesterday is that now I need to know soon."

"Why? What's changed? What happened that's so important, Sel?" *Give me something, anything.*

"I can't tell you that, Julia."

"You're so insufferable! If you can't tell me, then I can't help you out."

"I can't tell you if you're on the outside looking in."

"Give me a hint then."

"A hint?"

"You're a smart man. I'm sure you can do it without compromising your precious secrecy."

"All right, I'll give you a hint. It has to do with Santa Claus."

Julia listened to the distant buzz across the telephone line.

"Jul?"

"Somebody stuck a hook in his back. That's what they said on the radio."

This time she could hear Norris breathing at the other end. She waited. "I didn't think the news would have made it up there," he responded eventually. "As I said, matters have escalated. I know— you don't have much to go on, Snoop. But you're smart and savvy and you can think for yourself. That's why you're important to me. I don't have time for groupies. I'm nobody's guru. I need people who can think on their feet and I need people who are committed. I can't give you the details. All I can say is this, you can step away any time you choose. Just take one giant step back. But first, take a baby step forward. Take that step. Then decide. Think about it, Jul. Will you promise me that, at least?"

She wished that she held his throat in her hands at that moment rather than the telephone so she could choke him. "Think about what,

Selwyn? Think about some vague concept of which I know nothing? Think about being a valiant hunter chasing down the villains of the world? *Exsqueeze* me, but saying I don't have much to go on is a ridiculous understatement. Give me something to think about, Sel."

"Santa Claus was murdered. A young man your age. Ask yourself about whether or not you want his killers to go free."

"Hello! Hello! Earth to Space Cadet, Selwyn Norris! This has absolutely nothing to do with me!"

"It has everything to do with you."

"How so? Just explain that part and maybe we can get somewhere."

"If you work with me on this, Snoop, the boy's killers will be apprehended. If you don't, they'll get off scot-free. It's as simple as that. Justice in this case is in your hands."

"Oo, you're so aggravating! You have no idea!"

"The truth is rarely convenient, Snoop."

"Oh, screw you! You can't engage in philosophical debate when only you know what we're discussing."

Norris was chuckling to himself.

"What's so funny?"

"You are. You're a riot."

"I'm glad you're so amused."

"Think about it, Jul."

"Yeah yeah."

"Think about it."

"Good night, Sel."

"Good night, Snoop. If you're looking for a New Year's resolution—"

"Good night, Selwyn."

Julia sat on the sofa in the aching silence of that country house. She switched off the lamp. She was fully awake now, although inert, unable to move much. She wanted to belt him. Julia let her body slide down the sofa until she was on the floor, and she sat there in the ambient dark, listening and wondering what there was to think about. What she hated most was that she had no arguments to refute him. Common sense warned her to run from the guy. Yet she had no reason to do so.

Everything he said was enticing. She didn't have to look around, for years it had been obvious that parents and stepparents and older folk were playing out their run without enthusiasm, with little aspiration, devoid of any zest for the ideals they had once coveted. The farm was supposed to have been a colony for an alternative lifestyle, instead it was a paean to the great sellout, the relinquishing of expectations and values. She knew about the slide. She had seen it with her own eyes, she feared it, she had always feared it, and Selwyn Norris, she knew, played to the heart of her fears.

What she hated, and what she dreaded, was that she could imagine herself consenting. She wanted to. She wanted the unknown over the known. The adventure over the banal. Risk over prudence. *Damn him!* He knew how to work her.

4

Tuesday, December 28

A child, his name was Daniel, was walking to his local rink for a game of pickup hockey during his Christmas vacation. Skates were slung over one shoulder. He carried his stick while kicking a puck. The eleven-year-old loved soccer most of all, but in the winter he only got to kick pucks along the sidewalk. Sometimes the puck became embedded in a snowbank, and then he used the stick to dig it out. He figured that was all the stick was good for. Hockey was not his game and Daniel usually embarrassed himself on the ice, but the other kids knew he was a hotshot soccer player so they never teased him about it very much.

The street in the east end along which Daniel walked was rundown, overcrowded, with mostly crummy two-story walk-ups occupied by large families. At eight o'clock in the morning those off to work were starting their cars in the cold. One such man was short and exceptionally well dressed for the neighborhood. He had been visiting a new girlfriend overnight. Daniel did not know, nor would he have cared, that the man who kicked his puck back at him was a physician who did private consults for the Hell's Angels. In a time of war the man had been kept busy. Daniel welcomed the challenge, did a little feint with his feet, and kicked a goal between the man's legs. The doctor laughed, fished his keys out of his coat, and climbed into a Camry.

The puck had careened into a snowbank and Daniel was digging for it. He wasn't sure where it had gone after darting past the man.

67

He thought he saw it and thrust his stick deeper, but the bank contained ice and he was unable to dislodge it easily. The boy hacked away at the ice to reach the black object there, then worked the blade of his stick under it and heaved with all his might. The ice broke free, the puck floated aloft and bounced off the hood of the car.

The physician was not amused. He opened his car door, put one foot down on the pavement, and stepped halfway out. He warned the boy to watch it. Daniel said that he was sorry. He scaled the snowbank and came down the other side and saw his puck lying on the road. The man was telling him that he could've put a dent in his car, that it was a lucky thing for him he hadn't. Daniel gripped his stick and began to stickhandle the puck past the man and the automobile.

The doctor never put his key in the ignition. He never closed his door a second time. The car erupted just as Daniel was stepping past him, and they were both annihilated that instant.

The Wolverines stated that the bomb had been detonated by remote control, that the Rock Machine had taken out a Hell's Angel sympathizer, that the killer could have waited for the boy to leave the area, or for the car to move on, but hadn't bothered.

The same day, thanks to the immediate and intense public outcry, the Wolverines were granted the budget they'd been requesting. In the history of Canadian law enforcement, no agency had ever operated with such generous fiscal resources. Along with the check they were handed a simple mandate—break the backs of the biker gangs.

At last, the Wolverines said to one another, the bad guys had lost their shine, public opinion would finally turn against them. The people would demand justice, wouldn't they?

An unofficial spokesman for the Hell's Angels stated that his gang would never have done such a thing, none of their members would kill an innocent child. They weren't animals. The Rock Machine, he said, was too stupid to be believed, too stupid, he stipulated, to be allowed to live.

To the astonishment of the Wolverines, out on the streets, as the days went by, citizens, in their rage and sorrow, were looking not to them but to the Hell's Angels to exact revenge.

5

They drove into the poor neighborhoods that spread southwest from downtown. Made narrow by winter, the streets were lined by snow-bound parked cars in igloos. Red-brick row houses were crammed together, never a gap between them, two- and three-story flats with crooked exterior staircases made of wrought-iron railings and worn wood steps, hard against the sidewalks. Some entranceways had been tramped smooth by boots, others had been shoveled out. Balconies, holding mounds of snow, were pitched in different directions, shifting with time and rot, and windows were sealed by plastic wrap and old newsprint to bar drafts. At the rooflines, snow drooped like wisps of white hair on aging gentlemen. Trees, leafless, rose from the snow-banks as knurly sentinels, their upper branches run through with electrical wire. In the front windows of a few homes, Christmas lights, off now, had been strung in the shapes of squares or circles or stars, a cheery defense against long winter nights. People waiting for a bus or tramping through the snow looked cold, scrunching their shoulders up and tucking their heads down into their collars as though they had no necks, their faces concealed by scarves, like bandits.

"Give me his name again." Cinq-Mars let Bill Mathers drive. He equated driving with thinking, except when the roads were this perilous.

"You're not good at names," Mathers observed.

"French ones I am."

"Hagop Artinian. It's not that difficult." Mathers turned up an unplowed side street. "That the garage?"

69

"Should be," Cinq-Mars guessed.

Above a broad garage door flush to the sidewalk a faded sign declared the premises to be Garage Sampson, bodywork and foreign cars the specialty.

"Watch first or go in?"

"Park. Give it a minute."

What interested Émile Cinq-Mars was the innocuous style. By appearances the business was legitimate, although it had done little to advertise itself. No specials on fenders or tires, no night lights for the sign. He gave a moment's thought to the little boy who had been killed the day before. At Headquarters, everyone was feeling both angry and saddened by the event. Not that rage or sorrow was going to win the war.

Mathers glanced across at the senior detective a few times.

"What's on your mind, Bill?"

"Nothing. Forget it."

"Come on. Spit it out."

"I was wondering what we're doing here."

Cinq-Mars could see that he was nervous. He didn't bite his fingernails, but he kept bringing them up to his lips as though he was tempted to do so. "You mean this isn't our case?"

"Something like that."

"You haven't taken an interest?"

"Like you said, it's not our case."

Cinq-Mars didn't seem inclined to explain himself. No sign of life was visible from the garage. A minute passed before he spoke again, and when he did his voice was grave and Mathers listened intently.

"I received a call one night, directing me to a tavern in the east end. I was to go inside, sit down, order a draft, then look for a young guy sitting under the clock. I did what I was told. The guy would get up to take a leak, then leave. On his way out he'd stop to put on his hat and gloves. The moment he did that, the boys on his immediate right were the ones I wanted for a series of violent muggings. Bad boys, Bill. They didn't just rob their victims. They pistol-whipped them, threatened them with knives, and always they were old people, men and women both. My contact inside would leave the tavern and

I was to let him go. Which I did. I made my arrests. The young man who'd been sitting under the clock was Hagop Artinian, not that I knew his name back then. The night he died, Bill? The sign he wore around his neck? *Merry Xmas, M-Five.* That's me. March the Fifth. To show contempt, the bad guys—especially the French—they say my name in English. So I've taken an interest in this case, Bill."

Mathers nodded. "You told the IO all this?"

"I told LaPierre squat and I'll thank you to do the same. We're on this case, Bill. It's not official, but we're on this case." Cinq-Mars stared at him to gauge his reaction.

"I'm square, as long as you can skate us around the department."

"You let me worry about the department."

"What about Sergeant LaPierre? I don't know much about the guy, but he catches us messing with his case—" He'd not had to deal with these issues working in the suburbs. They had internal political problems there, too, but nothing that skirted so far around the rules. Bill Mathers was a man who stayed within the lines, but he was not so much inclined that way as fearful of doing otherwise. He was coming up against his own trepidation, rather than a moral dilemma.

"Relax. He's doing his duty. Today's the boy's funeral. LaPierre's attending."

Mathers offered a little smirk. "You think of everything."

"Let's go."

They clambered out of the car and walked up to Garage Sampson. The door to the side office was locked. Lights were on inside, and they could hear a radio.

Mathers rang the bell.

The radio was switched off.

Mathers rang again, and this time they detected a motion down a lengthy corridor. A figure advanced toward them. When he was near he shouted in English for them to hang on a second. Momentarily they identified the figure as a young man approaching with a ring of keys. He had to open several locks.

"Is this Fort Knox?" Mathers inquired in French when the door swung open.

"What?" the young man asked in English. He was dressed in a

mechanic's greasy coveralls. Steel-toed boots protected him from mishaps.

"Never mind." Mathers pushed his coat back and showed his hip badge. "Police. We'd like to come in, ask you a few questions."

The youth promptly stepped aside. Cinq-Mars gave him a nod as he followed Mathers through the door and did a broad scan of the premises.

"You alone here?" Mathers asked the mechanic. He offered a wide smile, to suggest that he was the one person he'd want to trust in all the world.

"Yeah."

"What's your name?" He was good-looking, dark-haired, thin, and Mathers guessed that Cinq-Mars would describe him as not having a criminal appearance. He looked the part of a grease monkey. He wore what girls were calling hockey hair, long at the back and on top, shorn on the sides.

"Jim Coates. This about Hagop?"

"You know Hagop Artinian?"

"Yeah, he works here. Or— I mean. You know. He did. I can't believe he was killed, man. Whew. He's a good guy. Nobody deserves something like that. What was he doing in that Santa suit anyway?"

"Were you friends?"

"Sort of. Not really, but, you know, we worked together."

"Here?"

"In the garage, yeah."

"What did he do?"

"Mechanic. I do bodywork, he did engines."

Cinq-Mars listened to the boy as Mathers questioned him, catching his tone. An underlying excitement was apparent, as though the investigation was enough of a novelty, despite the grim circumstances, to give him something to talk about later. He seemed nervous but not frightened. Without bothering to ask permission, Cinq-Mars wandered into the garage bays to do a general snoop.

"How long did you know him, Jim?" Mathers asked. His pen and notepad were poised to record the answer, and the boy leaned slightly forward on the balls of his feet to make sure that he did so.

"I been here about three months maybe. Something like that. I knew Hagop since then. We didn't hang out or nothing, but we talked to each other at lunch and stuff."

"You didn't work together?"

"I'm body, he's mechanics. When I'm working it's not so easy to carry on a conversation."

"Where's everybody? Why are you here alone?"

"Christmas holidays."

"Cars crack up around Christmas, don't they?"

"The boss gave us the week off."

"Except you."

"Tough luck. I got the least seniority. I got a couple of cars to do, but mostly he wants somebody down here telling customers to come back next week."

"Isn't it a strange time of year to be closed down, Jim? With this weather, don't you have a lot of fender benders?"

"I guess so. Yeah. Maybe."

Mathers moved around the office, in between desks, casting his eyes on the paperwork waiting in abeyance, order sheets, invoices, much of it left as if the staff had suddenly been spirited away. He wanted to see if the young man would try to stop him, but he didn't seem concerned.

"Christmas holidays, is this something that goes on every year? Did you know about it in advance? Or did the boss just spring it on you?"

"We had the day off before Christmas, and Christmas and Boxing Day. Then on Boxing Day, after we heard about Hagop and that, we got called and told to take the week off. Me, I was told to come in. The boss came down here and we took care of a few customers and the rest we told to come back."

"So it came as a surprise. A last-minute sort of thing."

"I guess so. Not much of a surprise for me. But it's been a quiet week for me too."

Cinq-Mars returned to the office area. "I see only one car out there," he said.

"Yeah. We're closed."

"Did Hagop have friends here?" Mathers asked.

"He kept to himself a lot. The boss liked him. He hung out with the boss a bit. That made the rest of us, you know, a little careful around him."

Cinq-Mars had wandered through to the executive office and plucked a business card from a tray. "This your boss's name—Kaplonski?"

"Yes, sir," the youth said. He was showing more nerves now. The line of questioning had not been what he might have expected. He had hoped to get details he could share with others.

"What's that," Cinq-Mars called through, "Armenian?"

"Polish," Mathers answered.

Cinq-Mars joined them again. "They left you in charge," he said to Coates.

"Yes, sir."

"You must be a big shot to be left in charge."

"I'm at the bottom of the heap. Everybody else gets a holiday."

"Maybe everybody else deserves one. Did you think of that?"

"Yes, sir. I mean, no, sir." The boy was flustered now.

Cinq-Mars loomed a head taller than the young man, and he stepped closer to him and stared down the ski slope of his nose. "Where do you work in this place usually? When you're not listening to the radio and reading *Penthouse* in the back like you were when we rang the bell, where would you be working?"

"In the back."

"In the body shop? Where that Buick is?"

"Yes, sir."

"What kinds of cars do you work on back there?"

The young man shrugged. "All kinds. Damaged cars."

"What makes?"

"All makes."

"Mostly new or mostly old?"

"I don't know. Mostly old, I guess. New ones, too."

"Up front, where you don't work, what kinds of cars get worked on up there?"

The boy shrugged again. "Different cars."

"Mostly what kind would you say?"

He seemed to not like where this was headed. "Mostly German, I guess. I don't know."

"Mercedes-Benz?"

"Yes, sir."

"BMW?"

"Yes, sir."

"What about Japanese cars? Lexus?"

"I seen some of those, yeah."

"Those were mostly new cars, I suppose."

"I guess so."

"Do me a favor," Cinq-Mars demanded. "Don't guess."

"It's just an expression."

"Don't express yourself, son. Just answer the questions."

Coates remained quiet. He was beginning to rebel, Mathers noticed, against this inquiry. He kept looking over to Mathers as though the younger officer might help him out.

"What kinds of problems do they work on up front here?"

"Mechanical. I don't know. It's not my department. Tune-ups, I guess."

"Tune-ups," Cinq-Mars spat out. "Son, if you owned a new Mercedes-Benz would you bring it down to this shit-box garage in this rat-box neighborhood for a tune-up? Would you?"

The mechanic looked from Cinq-Mars to Mathers and back again. Then he looked down. "Probably not," he said.

"Son, you've got stolen cars coming in and out of this place every day, don't you?"

The boy kept his head bent down.

"Well? Don't you?"

"I don't know," he said. "I work on older cars. I talk to the customers. I know those cars aren't stolen."

"We're not talking about the body shop. We already know that's a front. We're talking about the cars at this end of the garage. The ones that get priority treatment. Those cars. Does it come as a surprise to you to hear they're stolen?"

The boy shrugged in his compulsive manner. "I don't know," he said.

"What *do* you know?"

He squared his shoulders this time. "I don't know nothing about stolen cars. Honest. I just do bodywork in the back."

"A boy can get into serious trouble working for a stolen car ring."

This time the young man raised his hands in his own defense. His glance was shifting around, but he wouldn't look at anyone's eyes. "I got nothing to do with that. I was out of work a long time, then I got this job. I mind my own business, that's all."

"Hold your hand out," Cinq-Mars ordered.

"What?"

"Are you deaf? Hold your hand out!"

The boy did so, his left. He held it out as though expecting to be strapped by the school principal.

Cinq-Mars removed his own hand from the pocket of his topcoat and dropped small rectangular pieces of metal into the boy's palm.

"Your hands are dirty now, son. Tell me what you're holding there."

The boy examined the contents of his hand. "Oh shit," he said.

"Tell me what you got there."

"You know what they are."

"I want to hear it from you."

"VI numbers."

"The VINs of hot cars, to be precise. Am I right?"

"Look, when I got here, the boss, he said, 'Can you work?' I said yes. He asked me if I knew how to mind my own business. I said sure. That's it. That's all I know."

"Go on. Touch them. Rub your fingers on them. I want a good set of prints on those tags. Go on. Do what you're told."

"I don't want to," the boy said meekly.

"You do what a crook tells you to do you can damn well do what a cop tells you to do! Now put your fingerprints on those tags." The boy did what he was told. Cinq-Mars lifted the flap and pulled his coat pocket open. "Now I want you to slip that evidence into my pocket here." The boy did so. "Good. I guess your goose is cooked now. But I'm only guessing and that's only an expression."

The mechanic stood grimly silent.

"What're you going to do?" he asked in a whisper.

"That's not the question," Mathers interjected, and he stepped toward the boy as Cinq-Mars backed off. "The question is, what are you going to do? Do you think you know too much, Jim?"

"I told you, I don't know nothing about what's going on."

"Do you think Hagop Artinian knew too much?"

The mechanic thought about that. "Maybe," he allowed.

"Look what happened to him. They dressed him up in a Santa Claus suit and broke his neck and stuck him through the back with a meat hook. I'm the one who opened the cupboard where they had him stashed. Not a pretty sight. You know something now, don't you, Jim? You know you're working as part of a stolen car ring. You know how dangerous that can be. If I were you I'd start looking for another job. One with improved benefits. Someplace where they don't kill you for what you know. Get that job, Jim. Then give Mr. Kaplonski two weeks' notice. That's what I would do if I were you."

"Here," Cinq-Mars butted in, "I took Kaplonski's card, so you take mine. If you ever get the feeling there's a meat hook in your future, give me a call. In the meantime I want you to go back to your *Penthouse* magazine and turn on your radio. We're going to have a look around. You'll forget about the whole thing, right?"

"Yeah," the mechanic agreed.

"Good," Cinq-Mars confirmed. "Get his address and phone number," he told Mathers.

"Start looking for that new job," Mathers warned him as he wrote down the particulars. "Work is hard to find but you have an incentive now. You should have an easier time than before. Working here you've added some experience to your résumé."

The two policemen opened drawers and scanned papers. Cinq-Mars moved slowly through files labeled with the letters *P* and *C*. He examined telephones and lamps, and Mathers checked under desks and the bottoms of drawers until he found a bug.

Cinq-Mars put a finger to his lips. They'd discuss this elsewhere.

Satisfied, the two men shouted a good-bye to Jim Coates and departed.

Outside, Mathers asked, "One of ours?"

"What are the choices?"

"One, it's ours. Two, it's theirs, and they keep surveillance on their own people. Three—unlikely—it's some other gang."

"Four," Cinq-Mars cut in, "it belonged to Hagop Artinian. Or whoever he was working for. My contact. The person who calls me with good information. Hagop was on the premises. So that's a point for that theory. It could be us. It's primitive, so whoever planted it was on a budget. Which could be us, which could be anybody, I suppose. Outside gang? Like you said, not likely. We found it in the outer office, right? Who'd want to know what the secretaries talk about? The boss, maybe. My contact, I'm sure, would plant a bug in the boss's office, if he had a choice. So would we. That's a point for the boss spying on his staff, and less likely it was my contact or cops."

Mathers opened the driver's side door and got in. He reached across and flipped the latch for Cinq-Mars, then started up. He spun the tires on the hard snow pulling out, and they headed off down the street. They saw Jim Coates watching from the office window.

"Anything out of the files?" Mathers asked.

"Enough to know I'm coming back with a warrant."

"Good show. What's next, Émile?"

"Run his prints. I think he's clean, but let's check. Later on we'll visit the Artinian family. Pay our respects. Share their grief. We were the ones who found their son."

"Sounds like a plan. You must be good at this next part, Émile—how do we write this one up for the department?"

Cinq-Mars smiled. "You're always so worried about the department."

"I don't carry your weight."

"This one's a cinch. We're investigating a stolen car ring. We expect to move in a week or two. We'll make it a department operation. Spread the credit around. Next week, or the week after, when we raid, they'll either be around or gone. That might clue us who planted the bug."

Riddled with flu and an ample dose of self-pity, Okinder Boyle lay in abject agony upon his bed. The city was enduring a horrendous winter accompanied by a virulent Asian flu, as if forces of nature had conspired to mete out retribution. All Boyle wanted to do was moan. Work was out of the question.

Answering the knock on the door seemed more than he could manage.

Boyle coughed on his way to the door. The very act of standing up seized his sinuses in an apoplectic fit.

"Quit faking it!" a voice shouted from the apartment corridor.

His editor. He didn't know how to take a man who was gruff when he was angry and gruff when he was merely trying to amuse himself. One tone pretty much resembled the other. Boyle opened the door.

"Jesus," the man said. His name was Garo Boghossian, and this was his first visit to his columnist's apartment, which he found shockingly modest. "I guess we don't pay you much. Boyle, you look like crap. Blow your nose for shit sake. Whatever you do, don't breathe on me."

"What're you doing here, Garo?"

"Checking up on you, what do you think?"

Boyle held his aching head in his hand and instructed his feeble limbs to keep him upright awhile longer. He wobbled. "You checked. So go."

"So you're not faking. Big deal. Truth is I suspected as much. Figured you for a sniveling sickly sort who catches every germ that comes down the pike. I'm here on business, Boyle."

The young man had to sit down. He waddled to the nearest chair and collapsed. "I'm not up for this. Save it until I'm better."

"I was in the neighborhood. Let me say my piece, then I'll leave." Boghossian leaned over him. He was a man in his late forties with wild fluffed hair that arose at the sides and thinned on top. His eyebrows were substantial, the lenses of his glasses thick. Usually he dressed as though he had slept in his clothes, but today he looked immaculate.

"I might vomit."

"I hate that. Just hold on for a few more minutes, you pansy."

Boyle looked up, but he was too weak to defend himself. "Garo, I'm not kidding. I'm sicker than you think. Help me lie down. I've never asked you for anything before. Help me back to bed or I'll puke."

Boghossian had underestimated his condition. The editor held him firmly as they crossed the floor and assisted him down gently onto his bed. He looked around. This was a one-room hovel, with a hot plate and a refrigerator the size of a typewriter for a kitchen. A side door led to the toilet, sink, and shower. Boyle possessed nothing but a broken-down dresser, desk, a computer, heaps of books piled in stacks, a potential bonfire of papers, and a swaybacked mattress on the floor.

"Have you eaten much?"

Boyle merely groaned.

"What about fluids? Have you been drinking lots of fluids?"

This time the patient managed to shake his head.

"Jesus, man, you've let yourself dehydrate. Didn't I tell you when you came to work for me that I was your editor and not your bloody mother? Now look at you." Boghossian checked the refrigerator and found two juice containers, both empty. He turned on the tap, but the water would not run clear. "Leave the door unlocked," he instructed. "I'll be back in five minutes, give or take."

He returned in less, with a bag full of juices, aspirin, decongestants, and an assortment of crackers and soups. "I won't let you die, Okinder. I haven't given you enough shit yet. You feeling any better?"

"Yeah," Boyle said. He looked yellowish.

"Drink this."

"What do you want anyway, Garo? Talk slowly. Maybe I can concentrate."

"Do you have a story in the works?"

"The best one ever. Can't do the research until I'm over this."

"Okay. That's good. But listen. I've got another one for you. I know—you choose your own subjects, that's the deal. But I'm asking you to look into this one as a favor to me. There's no one else I can turn to."

"That doesn't sound too promising."

The editor's voice grew quiet. "Down the street from you— maybe you heard about it, maybe you've been too sick—a young man was murdered on Christmas Eve. His name was Hagop Artinian. He was wearing a Santa Claus suit. His neck was broken and he was stabbed with a meat hook through the back and heart.

I just visited the crime scene. It was where he lived. Or where I thought he lived. As it turns out, maybe he only died there. The place has no furniture, Okinder. Less than you do. No food in the refrigerator. No clothes in the closet where he was found dead. Nothing. A table and that closet. That's it."

"How'd you get in?" Boyle asked him. He was listening, but his head swam. He brought his chin up when he noticed that Boghossian had not answered. The man sat hunched forward in a straight-backed chair with his wool cap in his hands. He turned it over and over again. "Garo?"

The editor cleared his throat. "I'm a relative, Okinder. Hagop's my nephew. My sister's boy. We don't understand it. What was he doing in an empty apartment? Why was he dressed like Santa Claus? He was a good kid, a really fine kid. Who had any business killing him? And—some sign was slung around his neck. *Merry Xmas, M-Five.* What's that about? I mean, what's that? You know the streets, your specialty is young people when you're not writing about the homeless. I hope this new story of yours isn't about the homeless."

"Sure it is. I'm really sorry about your loss, Garo. I don't know what to say. I wasn't expecting anything like this."

Boghossian waved him off. "Thanks. Don't worry about me. But look. It's your street. Your beat. It's weird enough on the surface to be the kind of thing you do. Help us out. If he was mixed up in something bad, then you'll have to write that story. But we need to know what it is. His mother needs to know. His father. Me—I just got back from the funeral. I need to know, too."

Okinder Boyle had never imagined that he would see Garo Boghossian near tears. The sight was enough to temporarily diminish his own symptoms. "I'll give it my best shot. You have my word on that."

"Thanks." The editor stood. "Now you drink your fluids. The first order of business is to get well. In your present state you're of no use to a flea. I brought you crackers. If they stay down, there's chicken noodle soup at the bottom of the bag."

"What do I owe you?"

"Forget it. I'll take it out of your hide another time. Just get well. I'll look in tomorrow."

"Who do you think you are," Boyle pestered him, "my mother?"

Boyle listened to the man's footsteps echo down the corridor. This was an editor who hated transparent emotion in journalism. He considered it a crock, a cheap coin. This was a man who edited his dispatches from the streets down to their bare bones. In his absence, all Boyle could feel beyond the aches and aggravations of his flu was the wellspring of pain running so deeply through Garo Boghossian he had scarcely recognized the man.

The house on Avenue d'Anvers was a simple working-class home of a style developed in the fifties and sixties and since abandoned, for it suffered three disadvantages in winter. The roof was only gently sloped, so it did not shed snow. The garage was located under the house and the access was steep, often impossible to navigate in winter. The stairs were also treacherous. Broad, without railings, they needed to be shoveled or deiced frequently. In recent days many feet had trod up and down the steps, hardening the snow with sadness, and Émile Cinq-Mars and Bill Mathers joined the brigade of mourners.

Bright light glowed through the broad living room bay window, which hung out over the garage door, and it was obvious, through the lace curtains, that many people were present. Through the diamond-shaped glass in the door Cinq-Mars saw someone approach after he had rung the bell.

Detective Mathers showed his badge, and the policemen were let in by a clean-cut, skinny, sullen boy of eleven or twelve dressed in creased trousers, a white shirt, and tie. They waited in a cramped foyer, touched by the grief resident in this household. Flowers and wreaths adorned every space available. Accentuating the discomfort of the two detectives were the trappings of Christmas. A tree decorated a corner of the living room, a crèche had been arranged across a cabinet, complete with toy sheep and cows. Cards of sympathy stood on the shelves alongside best wishes for the holidays and the new year. The family's season of celebration and religious devotion had been truncated by tragedy, they would not enjoy a Christmas free from sorrow again. The boy returned with his arm in the crook of his father's elbow. Émile Cinq-Mars introduced himself.

"We talk to police many times," the man said with great weariness. "Please, today, no. This morning we put our boy to rest."

"We don't want to question you, sir. We don't wish to disturb your family. I wanted to pay my respects, Mr. Artinian. My partner and me—we were the ones who found your son. We are not with Homicide, we're not investigating his death. But, as I said before, because we found him, we wanted to pay our respects."

The man nodded. "Please," he said. "Come in. Vassil, my son, he will take your coats."

A small contingent of relations had remained through to the late afternoon. The grieving mother occupied an armchair surrounded by photographs of her son and of the family in happier times. Cinq-Mars approached and stooped to have a word, holding her hand as he extended his sympathy. She dabbed her eyes and touched a Kleenex to her nose. She was a stout woman, and the flesh under her eyes had fallen. The strain of her sorrow made her appear a shambles. When Cinq-Mars arose to his full height again, he accepted an invitation to be seated on the sofa. Mathers sat beside him. They welcomed the offer of tea.

"These men," Mr. Artinian explained to those assembled, "they were the last to see our Hagop alive."

Other men and women in the small living room nodded with interest, and Cinq-Mars promptly raised his hand. How could he put this? *You're wrong. We were not the last to see him alive, we were the first to see him dead.* Even that would not be wholly accurate.

"That is not quite so, sir. My partner and myself, it was our sad duty, to discover him. To find him."

"Ah," the father said, remembering that point now.

The room returned to quiet, and in the vacuum Mrs. Artinian burst into tears. For a parent to survive a child, Cinq-Mars believed, was the hardest.

"Mrs. Artinian," the detective began, "I believe that your son was working on the side of goodness, of justice. I believe that he was trying to help out a friend who was in trouble. I believe that he died a hero to his friends."

Her weeping ceased at this news. Everyone in the room was attentive.

Mr. Artinian leaned forward in his seat. "Mr.—"

"Cinq-Mars."

"Mr. Cinq-Mars, the other officers, they always ask us, did your boy do drugs? Was he involved with criminals? Had he been in jail? In reform school? My boy is a good boy! A university student! He goes to McGill! He does not take drugs. I tell them that. They look at me like I am a bad parent who does not know what his boy is doing. They think, he doesn't know. Hagop comes to see us for his dinner every Sunday. He is happy. He is talking of his job, his school, his life, his friends. I meet his friends. This is not a boy who sneaks around to do drugs."

"Mr. Artinian, you're right, and I apologize on behalf of the entire Police Department for that line of inquiry. It is the job of policemen to ask such questions. We have to ask such questions, but I am here today to tell you that they weren't necessary in this case. Your boy was a good boy. He was trying to help others. In his trying to help others, something went wrong. We will try to find out what that was.

"We will want to know who his friends have been," Cinq-Mars advised the boy's parents. People spoke of names and possibilities. They offered also the names of neighborhood children who had been in trouble, and Mathers dutifully wrote down each potential lead. The senior detective looked sternly upon Vassil, the boy who had opened the door. He encouraged him with a smile. "Do you know of anyone who might help us? Did your brother ever say anything to you that might be important?"

The boy shook his head. He was sitting on the arm of the chair in which his father sat and returned the officer's steady gaze.

Although he had specified no questions, Mr. Artinian encouraged them now, urging his relations to proffer possibilities. Until this point, the investigation of his son's murder had felt more accusatory than helpful, more hostile than sympathetic. Suddenly everyone had a theory, and Cinq-Mars fielded them all.

Mathers sensed that it was good for these people to be able to talk like this, to speculate, to offer opinions on the madness that had claimed the life of dear Hagop. Most of their suggestions were not useful, but he too demonstrated a keen interest and treated every comment with respect.

Vassil Artinian offered no opinions. While Cinq-Mars was watching him, he nodded his chin with a hint of aggression. The senior detective took this as his cue to leave. "You have been most helpful. Now I promised that I would not investigate on this sad day. But I will have an opportunity to talk to you again. Thank you for your hospitality, Mr. and Mrs. Artinian. You have my deepest sympathy."

Vassil brought him his overcoat, and again Cinq-Mars took note of his demeanor. He signaled for the boy's father to accompany him into a corner.

"Mr. Artinian, I wonder if it might be possible for me to have a few minutes with your son alone. He's suffered a great loss. He must be very troubled. I'd like to say a few words of encouragement, man to man."

"You're very kind, sir. Of course. Of course." The bricklayer broke from their huddle and signaled to his son. "Vassil, Vassil, come." He led the boy and the visitor down the hall to a bedroom and ushered them both inside.

"I'm sorry about your brother, Vassil. This must be hard on you," Cinq-Mars began.

The boy glared at him without reply.

"You're on your Christmas holidays, I suppose."

"Yes."

"Do you like your school?"

"It's all right."

"Vassil, what is it that you know? Is there something you'd like to tell me?"

"You must think my family is stupid," the boy said, defiance brittle in his tone.

Cinq-Mars had not expected the attack. "I think no such thing. You have a fine family, that's obvious. Why would you say such a thing?"

"You come in here. You say you're paying your respects. All you really do is get us to tell you things."

The detective made a gesture to suggest that he ought to be forgiven. "Sometimes, the policeman in me, it comes out even when I try to behave like everyone else."

85

"Merry Xmas, M-Five," Vassil Artinian spat out.

"Pardon?"

"My mother speaks no French. My father, very little."

"But you do."

"I go to school. M-Five. March Five. Cinq-Mars. That's you. My brother—"

"Yes—"

"Once we were walking."

"Yes?"

"He saw a copy of *Allô Police!* He picked it up to show me. He said, 'Do you see this man? He gets the credit. But I am the one who makes him a hero.' "

"Was I the man in the picture, Vassil?"

"Yes, you. Cinq-Mars. My brother dies and you come here to pay your respects. My ass. My fucking ass."

"I want to know who killed him, Vassil. Just like you do."

"To save your own skin, I bet."

"To see justice prevail, Vassil. That's what your brother worked for. Justice. Can you help us, Vassil? Who did he work for? Who were his friends?"

"He worked for you," the boy spat out. "That's all he said. He said he couldn't tell me more. He did dangerous work and you got the credit for catching criminals. That's all I know."

"Is it?"

"It's all I have to know. Better you don't come back here. If you do I'll tell my father what I told you. You'll see. He will break your neck. I won't upset him today. My mother—" The boy's voice broke. "Better you not come back here," Vassil warned.

In the foyer, Cinq-Mars shook the hand of Mr. Artinian, the firm, powerful hand of a bricklayer, and stooped to accept the man's embrace. The officers departed amid a flurry of condolences and thanks, and once again stood outside in the frigid air. The sun had set, the night was illuminated by streetlamps.

"Well?" Mathers asked.

"Well what?"

"Does the boy know anything?"

"Too much and too little," Cinq-Mars told him. "Always a bad mix."

At the foot of the stairs Cinq-Mars chose a chunk of ice by the side of the curb. He hurled it toward the nearest lamppost, and missed. He bent down to pick up another chunk.

"Now what?" Mathers wanted to know.

"Now? We go back to the station. Then we go home to our dinners and our wives. We try to sleep tonight. We try to get the sadness of these people out of our heads. To do that, we tell ourselves that we were not responsible for the death of their beloved son." Cinq-Mars smoothed his chunk of ice into a rounder shape. This time his throw hit its target. The ice smashed across the post and flew off in shards.

"You're not responsible, Émile. He provided you with information of his own accord."

Cinq-Mars did not reply.

"How about we go get a drink first?" Mathers suggested.

"Maybe we better," Cinq-Mars consented.

6

Concealing his squad car behind a snowbank, Émile Cinq-Mars parked in a space plowed for a driveway and shut the engine. Lieutenant-Detective Rémi Tremblay, looking absorbed and official, as usual, tucked in behind an electrician's van on the opposite side of the road. A third unmarked car took up a position a few spaces behind him. André LaPierre's cruiser found a spot beyond Garage Sampson. Observing radio silence, the squad waited.

Huddled together, the apartments on the street were uniformly squat, embattled, and quiet. Snow had been plowed since Cinq-Mars had last visited but not cleared away, and an overnight fall had added to the street's woe. A few snow piles were mountainous, while the snowbanks that ran along the sidewalk had been gouged out to accommodate cars, the excess dumped onto the walk.

Finishing a walk-by in snow up to their knees, LaPierre and his partner came up to the car and struggled into the rear seat behind Cinq-Mars and Mathers.

"Looks good," LaPierre reported. His smoke jumped between his lips. He leaned to one side to gain access to a pocket, his knees poking deep into the seat in front of him, jostling Mathers.

Cinq-Mars delivered the thumbs-up to his lieutenant, Tremblay, across the street. His longtime colleague and superior appeared out of place away from the battle station that was his desk. Flu and winter holidays had decimated his squad, and the lieutenant was pitching in. He nervously tugged an earlobe to acknowledge the signal.

"Hey, Pepsi!" LaPierre called out. Immediately, he covered half his face in a handkerchief and uproariously blew, sounding like a ship's horn.

The French had names for the English in Quebec, and the English had names for the French. The English were called *tête-carré*, or squareheads, a term that went back to headgear worn by the British military in another century. The term stuck because the French considered the English "square," less spontaneous, more entrenched. They also called them *les maudits anglais*, "the bloody English," and on the French tongue the words carried venom. The English ridiculed the French by naming them after food. With Pepsi the favored soft drink in the province, English youth would call their adversaries on the other side of the language barrier *Pepsi*. They'd shout *Mae West* at French girls after a chocolate-coated vanilla cake, or if they really wanted to be mean, they'd bray *pea soup*, another traditional French food. Cinq-Mars knew that he was not being flattered.

"Heard some news, Émile. You're meddling in my affairs."

"Your affairs? You mean with other women, André?" He watched the lieutenant neatly fold the handkerchief. LaPierre's body was not made for the backseat of a car. He was too bony and gangly, his neck too long. His cold, apparent in his watery eyes and red nostrils, was making him hostile. From the way he squinted Cinq-Mars could tell that the man's sinuses remained plugged.

"They'd never go for you, my women, Émile. You remind them of a priest."

Cinq-Mars was intrigued. "I've never met your women, André."

"Don't be so sure. I know for a fact you've arrested three of them." LaPierre's cheeks were concave, giving him an impoverished appearance, but despite his height and gangly movements he was not a skinny man, not anymore. Cinq-Mars had known him as a rookie—he'd looked like a pencil in a uniform then, his fair head an eraser. LaPierre's skin appeared stretched over his face, as though he wore his bones closer to the surface than other men. The taut forehead, the sunken cheeks, the evident blue veins on his temples, the hollowed cavities for his eye sockets—LaPierre had always looked deprived, or famished, in some ill-defined way. He had an addict's wasted look.

Forced to crack a grin, Cinq-Mars waited for the man's charges to be laid.

"*Pepsi*, you've been interfering in my case."

From behind the wheel, Cinq-Mars twisted around to examine his fellow officer more closely. "What're you talking about?"

"You visited the Artinian family in their home, Émile. Interrogated the younger son."

"André, pay attention. Bill and me, we found the body. We were paying our respects, that's all."

"You're a kind soul, Émile. Your next promotion should be to sainthood. We'll call you Saint Émile, the Patron Saint of Stoolies. You can tell us to say ten Hail Marys and cut the dicks off six perps." His lips were sticky with phlegm.

"The boy misunderstood a few things," Cinq-Mars explained.

"Like what?" LaPierre was filling the car with smoke.

"Cops show up around his house asking if his brother was a drug addict. That you, André? I told him his brother was a good kid who worked with us. No harm in that. I'm just helping out the family."

"You're talking front-page news, Émile. I would've liked hearing it when the case opened up. How about you, Alain? If you were the IO on a homicide, wouldn't you appreciate a colleague letting you know that the victim was his stoolie?"

Déguire merely chewed on his lower lip. He possessed the distant gaze of a man who was daydreaming, who'd rather be on vacation, or playing sports, than working. Given his muscular neck, his broad forehead, and the cavernous crease across his brow, Alain Déguire had the demeanor of a man who could head-butt a door into matchsticks. Cinq-Mars caught his eyes in the rearview mirror. The young man did not look ready to take sides with one superior officer over another.

"Nobody messes with a case of mine, Émile," LaPierre carried on. "Maybe you're the big cheese, maybe you're caramel spread, but you're interfering, withholding information." With smallish ears, and that neck, bare pate, and height, the man's bearing appeared remarkably giraffelike, so that in the car he looked as though he was being shipped to a zoo. If he crouched any lower his knees would be in his teeth. "I want to see you this afternoon. Feel free to tell me every-thing you know about my case. After that, stay the hell away. You—English—I'll talk to you, too."

Neither Cinq-Mars nor Mathers responded.

"Ah, yes"—LaPierre contemplated, smoking and hacking—"we'll have a nice long chat. Send out for pigs' knuckles maybe. A couple of beers. You got an ashtray back here, Émile? This car's so clean it's like a showroom. Smells nice, too. Doesn't anybody ever bleed in your car? Nobody pukes back here, I bet. I got guys puking and bleeding in my car all the time, don't I, Alain?"

"That's right," Detective Déguire acknowledged. The answer came by rote. Cinq-Mars had the impression that he'd respond the same way if he was called upon to confirm that the world was flat.

"Cinq-Mars—he keeps his hands clean," LaPierre taunted. "Take today. This is his case. Who gets to do the dirty work? Me and you and half the department. I'm telling you, Émile, if somebody bleeds we're taking him back in your car. I'm not waiting for an ambulance. It's your car we're taking."

"Toss your butt out where it belongs."

LaPierre did as he was told without comment. "Yes, Saint Émile, we'll have a chat. Bring a rosary, Your Holiness, it'll help pass the time."

Uniforms with rifles crouched behind cars and burrowed behind snowbanks.

Cinq-Mars changed the subject. "Ever been on this street before, André?"

LaPierre peered around both of Mathers's shoulders for a better view. "In my lifetime. Not lately. Why?"

"Tell him, Bill."

Happy for the privilege, Mathers turned half around in his seat. The chubbiest of the four men in the car, he was probably also the most lithe, able to be comfortable while his body was contorted into a twist. "Garage Sampson is where your victim worked."

"Who?"

"Hagop Artinian."

At the end of the block, officers on foot were moving into position.

91

Vans coming from the rear remained out of sight.

"You're really up on your case, André."

LaPierre snarled, "I had the flu. I was off sick. Not to mention I got fellow officers withholding information."

"This should've been your bust," Cinq-Mars baited him. "If you'd come down here, talked to his employer, his fellow workers, you'd've had it yourself."

"What were you doing here, Émile? Paying your respects, I suppose."

"As a matter of fact."

Vans appeared in Cinq-Mars's rearview mirror. Lieutenant Tremblay's voice crackled over the radio. "Front line—ready and close. Go! Squad—on my mark."

They watched as four vans stormed the drive in front of the white-washed garage gleaming in the sunlight. Rifles up, uniforms leapt out and closed fast.

"Go!" Tremblay commanded over the two-way.

"East of Aldgate," remarked Cinq-Mars with a sigh as he removed his pistol from its holster and checked the safety. He climbed out of the car and carried his gun in his hand with his hand in his pocket as he walked at a normal pace toward the garage.

"You ever going to tell me what that means?" Mathers asked him, catching up. He was trying to be calm, and sound brave, but the tension was apparent in his voice.

"You're a detective. Figure it out."

Plainclothes officers stepped out of their squad cars and briskly tramped through the snow. Uniforms guarded the garage doors while others rushed the interior. Cinq-Mars felt the bristles in his nostrils stiffen in the cold. By the time he made the short walk, the building was secure. Inside, secretaries sat wide-eyed and weepy, their hands on their heads. Cuffed mechanics lay bent across the hoods of auto-mobiles. The owner, a burly, neckless man, had had his hands cuffed behind his back.

Mathers asked him his name.

"What's it to you? Why you bastards come in like this?" His bushy eyebrows sloped low on each side of his face.

"Last name first," said Mathers, pen poised.

"Kaplonski, all right? Walter."

"We have a warrant to inspect the premises, Mr. Kaplonski."

"Inspect. You want to look around my place, look around. You don't need guns for that. I sue you for this one, you hear me?"

"The cars are stolen property, Mr. Kaplonski. We're checking the numbers now, so why don't you shut up?"

"This garage legitimate garage! Look, this car—transmission failure!"

"What about the Bimmer? Seven forty-iL. Brand spanking new. What's wrong with this vehicle, sir?"

"The window. We take out glass to fix—"

"While you were at it you happened to remove the windshield VIN. By accident, I suppose." Kaplonski released more invective, and Mathers warned him, "Sir, we'll be down at Headquarters for a while, me and you—I suggest you don't mention my mother again."

Tremblay entered to inspect their progress. Like the two other top officers, Cinq-Mars and LaPierre, he was a tall man. The three had progressed in the department together, and some had suggested that their height had caused them to be noticed. In the early years on the force many had quipped that if they screwed up as cops, they could always play basketball. Tremblay came across as someone equally at home in a boardroom or on a squash court. He was considered a terror in both realms. He praised the effort. "Textbook. Quick and neat." He had a tendency to sound professorial. "Book the works," Tremblay instructed Cinq-Mars, who was standing idly by, his discriminating nose in the air as if tracing a telling scent. "Give us time to browse," he whispered. "If the workers pan out, release them after. Worry them first. See what they give up."

"Okay."

Cinq-Mars and Mathers both noted that the young man they'd interviewed a few days earlier had acted on their advice and relocated. He was not among those filing out into one of two paddy wagons.

A female officer approached Tremblay. "Sir?" She held one hand on her hip and carried a clipboard in the other, with her hat pinched under her arm.

"What've we got?" He was always happy to scan the paperwork. Crooks were not his bailiwick, but put reports, forms, or computer printouts in front of him and he came into his own.

"We've run down the VINs and plates, sir." A smile flickered. She seemed excited by what she had to report. "They're clean. None of these vehicles has been reported, sir."

"*None?*"

"One, sir, that Benz, a couple of unpaid parking tickets, but that's all. I even checked the cars out back."

Tremblay shot a glance at Cinq-Mars, then surveyed the garage. "Feel free to jump in at any time, Émile."

"Odd."

"Don't tell me this place is legit."

"Rémi, look at the cars. Plates removed, dashboard VINs. None of the expensive cars are under repair. Even money, they're hot."

While the evidence was plain to see, the mystery involving the vehicle identification numbers was difficult to fathom.

Mathers shouted out from the rear of the shop, "Émile! Sir!"

Cinq-Mars strode quickly over.

"Check this out." A car prepped for bodywork had been defaced, the hood spray-painted. In smallish letters under the windshield, English graffiti read, "Welcome." Under that, in large, bold, blood red script across the blue hood of the Honda Civic, shone the inscription "M5."

Cinq-Mars stood silent and flabbergasted.

Coming up from behind, LaPierre volunteered an interpretation. "What do you think—English for March the Fifth? Explain this one to the masses, Émile."

"I know nothing about it."

"Émile, buddy, come on, that's what they all say. Who're you talking to?"

Tremblay wandered over as well. "What's up?"

"Only Émile knows up from down. Ask him."

Cinq-Mars offered his superior a weak, worried shrug and watched as André LaPierre stomped away. "We might've overlapped André's side."

"Santa Claus? Good! I want something out of this. Émile, swear to me we didn't bust a clean garage."

"I'll track the owners. Who'd bring a luxury car to this dump?"

"We're holding a barn load. We need a crime in a hurry."

"Give me help," Cinq-Mars countered.

"Name it." Cops were dumping the contents of trash containers. Bits of scrap metal and old auto parts noisily clattered on the concrete floor.

"André wants to gripe about his case, give me heat for treading on his turf. He's pissing into the wind. I've got nothing for him. Let me put him off until I make headway here. Back at the station I'll need additional personnel and telephones."

"Get on it, Émile. So far we look like idiots." Whenever he was displeased or distressed, Tremblay had a habit of standing with his arms crossed. He kept them folded over his chest now.

"Mathers!" Cinq-Mars shouted out. "Let's go!"

In the office area, uniforms were packing files into boxes. Cinq-Mars stopped to request a copy of the numbers on the confiscated cars. He had to wait for the photocopy machine to warm up. "Get the device," he whispered to Mathers.

"The tap?"

"On the double."

The office was crowded. Choosing a moment when everyone appeared occupied, Mathers bent down on one knee, reached up under the appropriate desk, and pulled the transmitter from its location.

Cinq-Mars shouted out, "Where's that list?"

"Coming, sir," a uniform promised.

Privately, Cinq-Mars snapped at Mathers, "Where'd you put it?"

"In my pocket."

"Why? Give it to someone. I want a report ASAP." Cinq-Mars waited for him to leave the room. "Something else I want copied," he commanded.

Advancing directly to a file cabinet riffled through on his first visit, he extracted a folder and pulled out a sheet that he walked back to the photocopier. A uniform ran the page through for him, and Cinq-Mars seized the copy as it emerged. He deposited it back in the file for all eyes to view, and replaced the folder in the well-stuffed cabinet, where it could not be readily located or identified. All files were being packed for shipment back to HQ.

Timidly, the uniform inquired, "Sir?" He could see the detective was on edge, and he didn't want to upset him any further. "The original?" The constable held up the paper for his superior's retrieval as though dealing with a forgetful professor.

"I'll take that," Cinq-Mars declared irritably. Crossing the room again, he snatched the original and headed for the door.

Outside, Mathers ran to catch up with his partner, whose rage was apparent with every step. The older detective bullied himself into the car and cranked the engine as Mathers struggled in. "Shit!"

"Easy, Émile."

He slammed the side of his fist against the wheel. "Who, Bill? Tell me!"

"You're no good like this."

"Somebody's working me. Some fucker's mocking me. Who? Damn it all to hell. When you bent down to retrieve that tap, it hit me then. I know why it was in the outer office, not the inner."

"So they can listen to their staff?"

"You saw their staff. They don't know squat. Hagop Artinian didn't plant the device, Bill. He was around the office night and day, he could have found a better location. The bug was planted by someone in there as a customer. Someone who had to do it quickly when no one was looking. Like you, someone waited for a back to be turned. Maybe he dropped his pen, or bent down to tie a shoelace, then positioned the tap lickety-split."

"Which means—" Mathers pondered.

"Artinian would have done a better job. He had time and access. Eliminate him. Exclude Kaplonski spying on his own staff because he doesn't have a staff worth spying on. Which leaves two choices. Us, or another gang. The fact that the car was there with my name on it—that tells me something."

"Another gang," Mathers assumed.

"A gang that wants to get at me. Or—" Cinq-Mars finally pulled the car out into the middle of the street.

"Or what?"

"Or"—Cinq-Mars considered, looking across to gauge how his partner would take the news—"it could have been planted by one of us. We could be the other gang. When they heard I was coming back they spray-painted the hood. Old news, Bill—inside the department I've got enemies."

Mathers whistled.

They spun their tires on the snow getting onto rue Notre-Dame, and Cinq-Mars drove hard. The street was a tight two lanes here and prone to heavy business traffic. Discount clothing stores by the dozen, fast-food restaurants, fruit stands, and crummy bars contributed to a street commerce that was both hectic and down-market. Cinq-Mars popped his revolving light onto the rooftop to force his way around delivery trucks. Past Atwater the road widened, and Mathers hung on as Cinq-Mars pushed his foot lower on the pedal. Here the shops looked run-down, an appearance that belied their dependence on upscale clientele for antiques and modern art. Another half mile and the street widened again. The extra lanes in both directions gave Cinq-Mars room to speed. As they approached Old Montreal, Cinq-Mars blared his horn at cars and horse-drawn carriages alike. Mathers breathed calmly again only when they turned down into Police Headquarters.

The square stone-and-brick building that served as Police Headquarters could easily pass as a more benign institution, such as a school or hospital. Cops were gathered on the grand stone stairs, chatting, but otherwise nothing gave the building away as a police station.

"What now?" Mathers asked. Their car was in a line to be admitted into the subterranean garage.

"I'll contact the owners of those cars. You find—what's the name of that boy, the one who worked there?"

"Geez, you're lousy with names. It's Jim Coates."

"Find him. Make sure he's alive and healthy. If he's not, don't bother coming back. Just shoot yourself, Bill. That'll be better than what I do to you. Find him and talk to him. See if he has anything more to say."

"Meet you back here?"

97

"Could be." Cinq-Mars parked between squad cars close to the garage elevator.

Bill Mathers climbed out of the car, then back into it, this time on the driver's side. He watched as Émile Cinq-Mars marched over and punched the elevator button. The man was fuming, taking this personally. Which, Mathers intuited at that moment, was exactly how those working against him wanted him to react.

He checked his notebook for the address of Jim Coates. Mathers was anxious to prove himself and glad to be assigned a job to do on his own.

New Year's resolutions had a habit of getting away from Julia Murdick, and this year's were proving the rule. She had promised herself to turn Selwyn Norris down flat—whatever he wanted she would not deliver—and she was committed to showing up for a doctor's appointment she'd been putting off forever. Julia had sworn a third and solemn oath to maintain the first two vows. All three were suddenly in jeopardy.

"I'll say this again, Selwyn, because I don't think it's sunk into that Neanderthal skull of yours. I'm doing this one teensy little favor for you and that's it. Nothing more. Nada. Never again. *Tout fini.*"

"You do get hyper when you're excited, Snoop."

"Don't tease me if you know what's good for you. I can still back out. *Christ!* How did I let you talk me into this? It's like some weird sorority initiation."

Talking Julia into this tidbit of an operation had not been difficult, although Norris guessed he'd be better off keeping the opinion to himself. She was right. In the twinkle of light on a snowflake she could change her mind—something he was keen to prevent.

He made the turn off Sherbrooke Street, the busy thoroughfare that cut through the heart of downtown Montreal, onto University Avenue, which ran alongside the congested campus of McGill University. Catching sight of a van pulling out from the shadow of the engineering building, Norris slowed to claim the spot. Beside him, Julia was growing more fearful.

"Piece of cake, Jul. There's nothing menacing or scary or dangerous about today's operation."

"The more you repeat yourself the less I believe you, Selwyn."

"I won't mention it again. I'll expect you back in two shakes of a lamb's tail."

"You better be around, Mister Buddy. I will not give up my doctor's appointment. Six weeks I had to wait."

"I'll drive you over."

One hand on the door handle, Julia looked across at him. "You're something else," she summed up. "I don't know what, but you're altogether strange."

After an overnight blizzard, the day had turned sunny and frigid. Julia tucked her collar up around her neck and trudged into the wind. This was such madness. She located the address that Norris had provided and tramped straight inside to elude the cold. In the small foyer she knocked snow off her boots and shook the cuffs of her jeans dry. Julia removed her mittens and hat, unfastened her coat, and blew warm air across the tips of her fingers before giving them a brisk rub. She had made it inside. Now all that she had to do was walk up the stairs and knock on the appropriate door.

She hesitated. Butterflies swarmed and her knees felt knocky. She wanted to protest against this predicament. The harder she tried to pin the blame on Selwyn Norris the more she inwardly protested. She was a grown-up woman. Perfectly capable of making her own decisions. She'd consented to going through with this charade, and since she'd done so the only option was to proceed. Julia found that she couldn't be angry with Norris without becoming more virulent against herself. If only one giant part of her wasn't so *excited*. If only one part of her wasn't so damn *interested* in what she was about to do.

She climbed the stairs of the rooming house.

The quarters were dark, poorly lit, dank. Doors filtered the familiar sounds of student life. Rock'n'roll, laughter, a soap on the tube. She had read that Santa Claus had perished with a meat hook in his heart and wondered if it had happened in this very house or one of the identical ones nearby.

She climbed a third set of stairs, her heart hammering. The excitement felt akin to sex. If she wasn't having the other at least she had this.

Julia knocked on the door marked twenty-six. Inside a chair scraped against the floor followed by the soft pad of steps. Bedroom slippers, she bet. The latch was undone. She half-expected a pistol to poke out at her as the pale face of her target moved from the shadows into view. Dressed in a robe loosely gathered over a black undershirt, the young man before her had a mop of wild and stringy dark brown hair. His nose was Rudolph red with a drip, and his eyes looked glazed.

"Hey," Julia Murdick said.

"Yes?" the young man replied, then coughed, covering his mouth with a fist.

"Are you Okinder Boyle?"

"Guilty as charged. Who are you?" He turned his head away to cough.

"You talked to my father, Carl Bantry. In his present circumstances, I guess you know him as the Banker." She sucked a breath, breathed out, and told him, "My name is Heather Bantry."

The jaw went slightly slack, the head-cold eyes agog. The door had opened a tad wider, which Julia accepted as her invitation to enter. She stepped into the drafty, shadowy room, confident, in command, a walking tower of secrets, and scared half to death.

A bit of a mumbler, this Boyle, not that the flu helped. He had to repeat himself twice before she understood that he was offering a chair. Julia sat down.

The young journalist gave her a searching look then, one that assessed her attitude and body language and not merely her healthy good looks. She could see him swimming upstream, battling the currents and rising—*come on little fish, come on*—to the bait.

"Your name again—" He scratched his unkempt head and tried to think.

"Heather," she told him. "Bantry. I just transferred to McGill for the new semester. I'm hoping I can help Dad."

"That's good news. He needs someone looking after him." Boyle gestured in a way she found charming, the hands a nervous dance of activity.

"If he wants to live in a tunnel, what can I do? I don't have resources. I'm only a poor student who's been written off by her mom."

100

Boyle nodded sympathetically.

"Dad said you were going to write about him. But unless I missed it, I haven't seen any article written about my father."

"I got sick," he explained. "Bad flu. Couldn't work. I'm only getting back to it now. I'll need to research your dad before doing the story."

"Research?"

"Talk to the bank, that sort of—"

"Those scumbags! They had to be dragged into court and made to cough up!"

"Heather, that's what I don't understand. If the courts directed the bank to pay your father a disability pension, why didn't his circumstances improve?"

Bingo! She had him. "What the court gives the court takes away. The judgment stipulated that the bank's insurance plan pay my father an allowance. Which they did. But welfare cut him off because now he had this other income."

"You don't think that's fair?"

"It would be, except by this time my mother had her divorce decree, which clearly stipulates that as my father's income increases, the *rate* at which he pays alimony also goes up. His disability payments were added to the welfare payments, even though the welfare was to stop shortly, and the disability was garnisheed by my mom. So he actually receives less money on the bank's disability than he was getting on welfare. Go figure."

"What does your mother think about this?"

"She grabbed the cash and looked the other way."

"It's nuts," he commiserated with her.

"Will you run the piece on my father?"

"Are you kidding? It's an amazing story. I take it you don't object."

"*Object?* I'm *desperate* for people to know what happened. Maybe friends from the old days will hear about him, maybe they'll help."

"The community could be moved by this story, Heather. Here's a man at the pinnacle of success, vice president of one of the largest banks on the continent, and one day—"

"He can't get off the train."

"—he can't get off the train. He goes to work in the morning, he's the kind of man who enjoys taking the Metro, but at his stop—"

"He stays on."

"—he stays on. Then spends the entire day going back and forth on the subway. At the end of the day, he finally gets off and goes home."

"That was the first time but not the last."

"Four days in a row. Finally the bank calls his home to see why he hasn't shown up for work, and his wife finds out that he hadn't been to the office all week."

"He broke down in front of Mom," Julia improvised. "He said he couldn't get off the train. Mom freaked."

"He went into therapy," Boyle said, repeating the story for the sake of the corroboration he was receiving. As research went, this was a breeze.

"Right. Tell me about it. Therapy. Empowerment. Getting in touch with your feelings. He walked out of therapy a sick, confused man and went straight to his boss's office and resigned. Just like that. No severance pay, no disability, no unemployment insurance. In-your-face quit. It would be heroic if it wasn't so damned pathetic."

"A year later his wife leaves him," Boyle says, guiding her to fill in the details.

As Heather Bantry, Julia was only too willing to oblige. "A year after that he's on welfare, sick, disoriented, on the streets, a case. Next came the court fiasco declaring he'd been mentally incompetent when he quit, so things looked rosy. But he ended up poorer than ever. In three years a vice president of the First Canadian Bank goes from middle-class comfort to spending Christmas in a tunnel."

"That's a story." Boyle was elated. He could easily forget his professional detachment on this one. "It says—this could happen to me. This could happen to anyone!" He stopped to cough and blow his nose. "Here we have the justification for a social safety net the rich can understand. A mental breakdown, and no matter how well you've planned, no matter how safe and secure your life, with bad luck you can be shoved to the bottom of the ditch."

She could imagine her instructor urging her out the door. She had gained the information she needed—he still planned to write the story—now was the time to depart gracefully. "I'm really pleased. Good will come of this, I'm sure of it."

He pushed himself to his feet as well. "Listen, in case something comes up, can I have your number? People might be calling the paper to help, stuff like that."

Without skipping a beat, Julia shook her head. "I'm just getting settled, I don't have a phone yet. No permanent address either. I'll have to call you later."

"Here." He handed her a business card from his desk. "How did you find me in the first place?"

She suffered a lapse. Not having a ready reply made her mind race. "You're famous," she answered quickly. "I asked around. You weren't so hard to find." She could hear Selwyn's voice, *Good, Julia. Good good!*

"Thanks for dropping by, Heather. Keep in touch, okay?"

"I will. So long."

Julia Murdick flew down the stairs and sailed out the door to the windy arctic street. She ran through the light scuff of snow on the plowed sidewalk, and by the time she turned the corner her lungs hurt from breathing frosty air too rapidly. She caught hold of herself. Slowed herself down. She did not want Norris to detect her excitement. This was going to be her more difficult challenge for the day— concealing her euphoria.

Detective Bill Mathers traveled into Verdun to locate Jim Coates, but no one answered his door. This was an old, run-down community, originally populated by Irish who'd come to build the bridges onto the island and stayed to labor in the railway yards or on the docks. All that was gone now, the area mostly French. Steep stairs led up to drafty flats. Mathers teetered on the top step, trying to see in the window. He looked down at the crowded street below. A dog barked up at him as though he emitted a foreign smell. The street looked like a tinderbox. Verdun was notorious for its fires. In winter the desperately cold made mistakes and set their homes ablaze. In summer, the back alley sheds were kindling to bored kids and firebugs and those

103

out to cheat insurance firms. Mathers shivered and went down to the
flat below, where the landlady revealed that the young man had
moved without leaving a forwarding address.

"I asked the scalawag where he thought he was off to. The scamp
didn't know." A diminutive, frail woman in her eighties, wrapped in
a piss yellow housecoat, she stood with the aid of a cane and spoke
with the voice of a cranky despot. "He paid for January and a month
extra, to break his lease, then he packed off and left."

"Have you rented the apartment? Can I see it?"

"Nothing to look at but dirt. Take the Hoover up if you go."
Mathers waited while she engineered her creaking form off in search
of the key.

Not much of an apartment. Junk mail had tumbled through the slot,
a Monday morning's worth. Dust bunnies procreated. The telephone
had been abandoned on the floor, yanked from the jack. Mathers
plugged the phone back in, but there was no dial tone, the line had
been disconnected. A lonely coaxial cable slipped out from one wall like
a rat's tail. Mathers departed, dropped off the key, and headed for the
corner deli, where he ordered a bowl of soup. He sat in a booth that
had been slashed with a knife and never repaired, and made a phone
call while the can of Campbell's was warming. After lunch he called
the office a second time. He was told that Jim Coates had discontinued
his telephone service and paid the electric bill but had advised neither
utility of a forwarding address. Nor had he contacted the Post Office.

"One last try," Mathers suggested. "Call the cable companies."

Five minutes later Bill Mathers was on his way to the new address
of Jim Coates. Dispensing with mail and telephone, the young man
had been unable to cut himself off from his favorite shows. He'd
moved to a small apartment eight blocks away, where utilities were
probably included in the rent, and Mathers wondered if that had
been intentional to avoid being traced. Good thinking if it was. He
rang the doorbell and was buzzed up. Waiting on the third floor, the
young man was not pleased to see him.

"How're you doing, Jim?"

"How'd you find me? I just moved."

"Can I come in?"

Coates considered his options a moment, then stood aside. "So how'd you find me?" he asked again.

"Were you trying to hide?"

The mechanic moved across the room and turned off the tube.

"You quit your job, Jim. Changed residences. You've been on the go in a hurry. We were wondering why."

"You suggested it."

"I suggested finding another job, giving Kaplonski notice. I didn't say move."

"Whatever," the young man muttered. "Time for a change. It's no big deal."

"Why the fast tracks?"

Coates paced nervously around his living room, rubbing his hands as if they were cold. "Like you told me, they're crooks. I wanted the hell out."

"Why so fast?"

"You scared me, all right? Look—what is this? Since when is it a crime to quit my job? Can't a guy move?"

Mathers stepped closer to him, inhibiting his restless wandering. "You didn't give the Post Office a forwarding address. You don't have a phone. If something's going on I should know about, I want to know about it."

"Nothing's going on, all right?"

"We raided Kaplonski's place this morning. Took everybody in."

"Everybody?"

"The works."

"Now you're here for me?"

"We noticed your absence. Wanted to make sure you're all right. Are you all right, Jim?"

"I'm fine." He did not look certain.

"Yeah?"

This time the mechanic hesitated.

"What's the trouble?"

Mathers had maneuvered him into a corner of the room, and the young man could only flap his arms in a gesture of worry. "It's probably nothing."

"Tell me anyway."

"I was having lunch the other day, okay? Near Garage Sampson. I used to go around the corner to this greasy spoon. A guy walks in. I'm at the counter. He sits down beside me. There's other places at the counter but, you know, he sits down right beside me. Then he's talking to me. The weather. Hockey. Politics. He's reading the paper, whatever's on the page he talks to me about it. He starts asking what I do. So I tell him. By now I'm ready to leave. Then he wants to know if I'd like to make a few."

"What did you say to that?"

"I'm leaving. I mean, I'm not talking to this guy. I don't know if he's a creep or what, but I've seen him before, so I'm leaving."

Mathers took another step forward, and the boy was blocked off now without hope of escape. "You saw this man before, Jim?"

"Yeah. In the same place."

"So maybe he's a regular, something like that."

"Maybe. But the only time I saw him there he was talking to Hagop. And, you know, Hagop's dead."

Mathers nodded, and took a breath to control his own emotions. "So you just ran out, or what?"

"I told him I wasn't interested. He laughed, he said I didn't understand. He leaned into me, you know, he whispered. He was creepy. He said he had a business proposition. I asked him, what proposition? He's talking differently now. His accent's changed. Like this was his real voice and that other voice was fake. He said he wanted me to talk to Kaplonski. Say a few things. He said he wanted me to put a bug in his ear."

"His exact words?"

"A bug in his ear, yeah. I was scared on account of Hagop. So I told him I couldn't do that. I never talk to Kaplonski. He said he'd pay me five hundred bucks to have one conversation. I jumped out of my skin, man. I mean, Hagop talked to this guy and Hagop's dead. Here's some creep offering me five bills to talk to my boss and I'm supposed to believe that's not dangerous? I don't know what's going on, but I don't want to know either."

Mathers scratched himself under his collar. "Let's sit down, Jim.

Give me a description of the guy. Everything you can think of. Take your time. Try to remember every little detail. You did a good job covering your tracks, but I'll fix it so nobody follows you the way I did. First, tell me everything you remember. Height. Hair color. Hairstyle. Eye color. Clothes. Jewelry. What kinds of accents he used. Distinguishing marks. Everything. Talk to me, Jim."

Detective Mathers sat back on the lumpy sofa. Opening his notepad, he began to write in earnest. He wrote down the details, such as they were, and coaxed more out of his witness, as though he was an artist lovingly crafting a portrait. He wondered who was forming on the page. The detail that he underlined three times was mention of a scar, about the size of two fingernails, that shone on the man's cheek as a patch below his right eye.

As instructed, Julia Murdick undressed in the narrow confines of the examination room. Her doctor did her best to keep the heat cranked up, but the room felt chilly nonetheless. Julia donned the thin robe provided and climbed onto the examining table, fitting her feet into the stirrups, convinced that contrary to graffiti she'd seen on campus God was not a woman. Had God been female She never would have equipped women with such complicated sexual plumbing. And the speculum! God had to be a sexist to permit the invention of that device. Surely the contraption traced its origins to torture chambers.

Dr. Melody Weesner entered a few minutes later wearing a bright, earnest smile. "Let's have a peek," she chimed.

She'd warmed the speculum first, at least. Julia grunted as the instrument opened her wider. Perspiration broke across her forehead. *The indignities*, she chanted to herself.

"You already know about the retroverted uterus."

"Inherited it." Julia waved off the doctor's protest. "All right, not exactly, but my mother has one too. Is that my problem? Mom says she manages, but I can't."

"We're done here," the doctor reported, and she removed the instrument and peeled off her rubber gloves.

"What's the verdict?"

"Julia, you have an unusually high and narrow opening, what is frequently referred to as a steeplechase arch."

"What does that mean?" She was jolted back again.

"The pain that you have experienced with intercourse, the discomfort——"

The doctor went mute.

"So it's not some residual part of my hymen?" Which had been suggested during a preliminary discussion. Julia was extricating her feet and legs from the stirrups and climbing down from the table.

"There's no scarring or tissue problem."

"The uterus thing, that's not it?"

"When you have intercourse, because of the position of your uterus, the cervix is likely to be in contact with the penis, and that can hurt."

"Does it ever! But the rending, this feeling that I'm being——it's hard to describe——a penis isn't much more comfortable than that speculum." With her feet on the floor again, she felt that she had a better perspective to figure this out.

"The pain that you experience, Julia, the discomfort, will likely persist."

"The *pain* will persist? You make it sound like the *pain* should win a prize. Should earn merit points for perseverance."

"Julia——"

"No! What are you telling me? That sex is *always* going to hurt me? And if I go through the pain and get pregnant, my kid has to be sawed out of me, my belly sewn up like I'm Frankenstein's mom, is that what you're telling me?"

"Julia——" The physician did not want to speak in such terms.

"Is it?" Julia Murdick was tall and square-shouldered and forthright when she had a mind to be. Dr. Weesner could not back away from her clear demand.

"It's probably going to hurt to have intercourse. A woman's pelvic muscles relax during pregnancy, the channel is apt to expand, but in your case, it's unlikely to be enough. Birthing will require surgery, but that's not uncommon."

"Shit!" she called out. "Fuck!"

"I'm sorry, Julia."

"Damn it!" she cried.

"There are other possibilities."

"Such as?"

"You never know. You might fall in love with a man who—how can I put this delicately? Who is rather small in that area. That might solve the problem."

Dr. Weesner left her alone to spew in private.

Julia Murdick was twenty-one years old and feeling cheated. A sadness welled within her, the premonition of depression. She leaned against the examining table, unable to stem a rising wave of distress.

What will I do with my life now? What will I do?

Outside, Selwyn Norris was waiting to drive her home.

Fuck it.

Fuck it, I'll do it. I'll do it, Selwyn.

Émile Cinq-Mars was the last person to arrive at the meeting on the top floor of the station. Tremblay was there, as were LaPierre, Mathers, Beaubien, and Déguire. The men sat slumped in the hefty furniture of the lounge, their legs stretched out before them, as though their bodies were prone to simulating sleep. Midnight had passed. Everyone was pulling long hours. "Nice of you to join us," taunted André LaPierre.

"What've we got?" Lieutenant-Detective Rémi Tremblay demanded. He raised himself upright, seemed prepared to stand, as though rank and responsibility required that he assume a certain posture.

LaPierre blew out a gust of air as a signal that he was willing to start.

"Shoot," Tremblay told him.

"Kaplonski gave up zilch. He's a wild man who knows a few things, but he lawyered up and the Great Wall of Silence came down. The most interesting thing was his choice of lawyer—Gitteridge."

Of those in the room, only Mathers was at a loss. He asked the question by lowering his eyebrows and holding open his palms.

"Old Mafia connection," Cinq-Mars told him.

"No longer just the Mafia," Alain Déguire piped up. Like Bill Mathers, he had never sat in on a meeting attended by rank, and he was anxious to prove himself. He frowned with the seriousness of the situation, which caused the upper fold in the crease along his brow to slump over the lower one. "Hell's Angels, too."

"Same difference," Captain Gilles Beaubien put in. A hefty man who seemed proud of his paunch, the captain rested his hands on his stomach.

"How do you mean?" Mathers asked. He wanted to appear attentive.

"The Mafia hired the Angels to do their dirty work," Déguire told him in a grave tone. LaPierre was nodding beside his protégé, proud that he had taught him well.

"Since when does the Mafia need help?"

"Since we busted their balls," bragged Beaubien. "We put a few big boys away ourselves. The rest got nailed in Florida. They're all doing time now."

"A remnant remained," Tremblay stated sharply. He was impatient with the discussion and would rather have called the meeting to order. He believed that his superior, Beaubien, always preferred amiable talk to getting any real work done.

He had a point. Beaubien was obviously in a jollier mood than the others, less weary, and was now leaning toward Mathers, delighted to have a junior around to instruct. "The remnant fought among themselves. Some splintered off and became the backbone of the Rock Machine. The rest picked up their balls if they still had any left and tossed in with the Angels."

Standing to refill his coffee cup, LaPierre exercised a personal grievance, also addressing Mathers. "You know how it is, English? The Mafia do what the English do, they hire French lackeys for their dirty work. What's new about that?"

Mathers was unsure if he should believe him.

"Bill, Hell's Angels divide into chapters," Tremblay broke in, wanting to get the lesson finished so they could move on. He spoke in a clipped manner that defied anyone to interrupt or question his opinion. "Each chapter's a franchise, like McDonald's. There was a time when any group could come along and take the franchise away by proving it was tougher, meaner, more brutal. In Montreal, in the old days, there was competition. The gang that finally won was tough, generally regarded as the most brutal on earth. But they left Montreal, mostly due to pressure from us—we were attacking back then, we had them on the run."

"They left the city because they were doing so well elsewhere, that's the real reason," Captain Beaubien interjected. "More money, less hassle, out of town. We never bust *their* balls. I would never say that."

Cinq-Mars was smiling and shaking his head.

"You don't think so, Émile? You're an expert on the gangs now?"

The detective looked as though he was about to speak, but he ended up shaking his head and folding his hands in resignation.

"Come on, Your Holiness," LaPierre encouraged him, "give us the Sermon on the Mount. Why did the Angels leave Montreal for the countryside?"

"You want the sermon?" Cinq-Mars challenged him. "I'll give it to you then. They left because they were buying time. They needed time to undermine the police. They needed time to undermine the judiciary. They needed time to put their own house in order, to undertake new alliances, to develop an intelligence network, and to secure the countryside so they'd have a stronghold from where they could return and *successfully* assault the city, in spite of any resistance from us. It was a *strategic* retreat, gentlemen. A retreat that probably won them the war."

Each man mulled that perspective, perhaps surprised by both its force and its logic. Tremblay cleared his throat, making a bid for control again. "Everybody's right. There's truth in what everyone says. What we know for sure is, the Angels took up residence in the countryside. Now they want back in but the Rock Machine has other ideas. Yesterday a boy was killed, so the Wolverines have been set loose. We'll see how that shakes down."

Mathers nodded, his head bowed, feeling rather sheepish that his presence had necessitated an elementary lecture. He had more questions but wasn't going to ask them here. Tremblay had called the after-hours meeting, and everybody, himself included, wanted to get through it and head home. They'd been run off their feet all day, and each man faced more drudgery tomorrow.

"Not your favorite subject, is it, Émile?" Tremblay added. "I know you feel we overemphasize the gangs."

"Émile's an idealist," LaPierre intervened. "He likes his crimes straight up. Nothing too complicated. I'm surprised he had an opinion tonight. Conspiracies addle the brain, he told me once. Does gang talk addle your brain, Émile?"

"Catch the criminal," Cinq-Mars answered evenly, "solve the crime. It's a simple philosophy, André. You're welcome to your conspiracies. The Angels are back, so let them fight the Machine. While that's going on, I'll catch the crooks. We'll see who gets arrests in the long run."

"All right, you two," Tremblay interjected. "What else do you have, André?"

The giraffe of a man used his long legs to step easily over an ottoman and seated himself again, mug in hand. "The secretaries, the mechanics, Kaplonski, everybody tells the same tale," LaPierre continued. "Some believe the gospel chapter and verse, some know better. They say Garage Sampson is in the business of buying luxury cars secondhand, to ship them overseas, where they sell for more. They have records to show they've done that every so often." He took a long gulp from his coffee. "They know how to cover their ass. The secretaries believe they're not breaking any laws, only loopholing a few. Garage Sampson makes it look like their cars are being shipped by private owners, which would turn the whole thing legit. Kaplonski's been around as an owner. Two priors for installing hot parts. Reduced to time served and fines. Legally, our people say he has a case if the cars aren't hot. Beating him will be a battle."

"We have the name of a ship waiting to load, and that's it," Tremblay mentioned.

"What country?" Cinq-Mars spoke up. He seemed unusually meditative and distracted, as though he'd been sidetracked by more urgent matters.

"Russia," Tremblay said. "There's a Russian freighter in the harbor waiting to pick up Kaplonski's cars."

Cinq-Mars stood and crossed the room to the coffee machine.

He'd been running on adrenaline and caffeine most of the day, and exhaustion now moved through him like a flu. He hoped he wasn't coming down with something. "I talked to the vehicle owners. Every one of them. The cars are hot. Nobody sold to Garage Sampson."

"Thank God," Tremblay declared. "At least we have a crime!"

"Mmmm," Cinq-Mars murmured, tearing the edge off a Sweet'n Low. "That's not all we've got. We've got trouble, Rémi. Big time. I ran down the cases. A stolen car report was filed for every theft, but only the paper files still exist. No records, and none of the plate numbers or VINs shows on our computer."

"An access problem this morning, it happens," Captain Gilles Beaubien speculated with a grin, as though all the world's riddles could be summarized as neatly.

Cinq-Mars shook his head. "I wish. The files are entered into the computer, I've been assured of that, but some files don't stay there for long. We have to assume that certain files are systematically being deleted. Consequently, a uniform phoning in a plate number would never get notification that the vehicle was hot."

"What are you saying?" Tremblay asked, leaning forward.

"A glitch. It happens," Beaubien analyzed, still smiling. "I'll get our software people on it."

"No glitch. The records of certain hot cars have systematically been deleted from our computer records."

The room was quiet awhile digesting this news.

"Are we talking a hacker?" Beaubien asked. An essentially sedentary man, he was given to extended lunches, naps, and considerable liquid refreshment through the course of the day. Years of service and a willingness to work with the top brass counter to the interests of the Policeman's Brotherhood, the cops' union, had earned him his rank. Whenever there were issues of income or pension, Beaubien came down strictly on the side of management. He didn't care that everybody knew it, and as he rose through the ranks that attribute had made him both despised among his peers and exceptionally valued by the brass.

"Not likely," Tremblay had already determined. Sometimes it was best not to humor his superior. "Sounds like an insider to me."

"Top priority!" Beaubien bellowed out. "Find out who!"

Although he was the senior in the room, nobody jumped to do his bidding.

"Let's say bikers are doctoring our computer," Tremblay summarized. "What do we do about it? First, nobody mentions this to anybody. If it's internal we might set up a sting, and I don't want a leak. Any leak, I'll know it came from this room. I'll take charge of this myself. What about the Russian freighter?"

No one was quick with a thought.

"Talk to the ship's captain," Mathers suggested, anxious to redeem himself. "Maybe get a lead off him. Maybe a shipping broker's dirty. Maybe a union local on the docks is involved. We can see where that leads."

"Émile, you and Mathers jump on it. André, don't give me a hard time, I know you're Homicide, but I've got more detectives down with the flu than I've got uniforms. Anyway, this case is related to Santa Claus. I want you to keep tabs on Kaplonski. Find out who his friends are. Okay. Let's run down what we've got. You, Mathers, fill us in."

Bill Mathers cleared his throat and sat a little straighter. He was anxious to prove his mettle but had not expected the limelight. He swallowed hard. "We've intercepted a stolen car ring that delivers automobiles to the former Soviet Union. Connections indicate Hell's Angels involvement. Kaplonski is dirty but a small piece of the puzzle. Probably so small you'll need a magnifying glass to figure out his place in things. But an Angels lawyer, Gitteridge, formerly with the Mafia, is in his corner. An employee at Garage Sampson, Hagop Artinian, was found dead on Christmas Eve wearing a Santa Claus outfit. We have to presume the murder and the stolen cars are related. Messages to Sergeant-Detective Émile Cinq-Mars were part of both the Santa Claus killing and the raid today. In both cases the perps knew in advance who'd appear on the scene. To top it off, the police computer has been infiltrated, compromised by an unknown mole with apparent connections to Garage Sampson, stolen cars, the Russian freighter, Artinian's murder, the Hell's Angels, and the Mafia."

Perhaps no one in the room had put everything together before. The officers were quiet, having difficulty deciphering the implications.

Mathers shot a glance at Cinq-Mars. He had deliberately held back mention of his conversation with Jim Coates. That seemed to be attached to their rogue investigation, not this department overview. As Cinq-Mars was issuing no objection, he presumed he'd done the right thing.

"Tomorrow, gentlemen," Tremblay summed up. "Tonight we sleep."

"Hang on," Cinq-Mars requested. His body had settled so deeply into the cushions that he had to rouse himself with considerable exertion. He put his coffee cup on the floor and remained leaned forward, hands on his knees. "I want to discuss jurisdiction." His tone conveyed a challenge.

"I don't follow," Tremblay said.

"We have a stolen car ring. That's me. We have a homicide. That's André. We have possible gang involvement, which means the Wolverines. And we have internal espionage. I guess that's you, Rémi. What we don't have is coordination of this investigation. I want to propose a solution."

"I'm op leader," Tremblay declared. "Do you have a problem with that?"

"I'd prefer it was me," Cinq-Mars told him.

The officers made eye contact. The senior detectives had never heard Émile Cinq-Mars undertake this sort of initiative. He scorned political aggressiveness in others. Cinq-Mars and Tremblay stared at each other calmly, intently.

"I see no reason to step down," Tremblay challenged him. "I'm curious, Émile. What's up? Why do you want this?"

"Rémi, twice the perps left messages for me at the scene. Two signs. *Merry Xmas, M-Five* and *Welcome, M-Five*. That tells me I'm already involved with them, somehow, some way. My contacts can probably help in this situation. To be frank, I don't wish to be impeded."

"I see. Bottom line, I'm op leader. Live with it." Even at this hour of the night he was well groomed, not a hair out of place. He was the only one among them to have shaven since dinner.

"You are about to head a crucial internal investigation that could burn the bulk of your time and then some."

"I'll manage, Émile, now drop it."

"At the very least we need a field op leader."

"That'll be me," André LaPierre spoke up. "What's another stolen car? The major crime here is homicide. I work with the Wolverines on a regular basis, since half the killings in this town are gang-related. They don't even know you, Émile."

"I have the contacts to break this case. You don't. Today we raided the garage where Hagop Artinian worked and you didn't know why you were invited along."

"Fuck off, Émile! I had the flu, okay? You know that!"

"André's right, Émile," Tremblay decided. "It's the Santa Claus murder we want to break. Why put somebody away for car theft if we can nail him for murder? The fact that you're involved, that the perps took the trouble to scrawl your initials at the scene, that's good enough reason to work behind André. Keep your distance. Let him do his job without interference. As for your contacts, I assume and I expect that you will share any information that comes your way. Which brings up the next issue, Émile. Why didn't you tell André about Hagop Artinian being a snitch?"

Cinq-Mars shrugged and retrieved his coffee off the floor. "André was home sick. I was planning to tell him when he looked less green."

"That's a crock!" LaPierre fired out.

"Tell me something, André. Did you raise Artinian's murder with Kaplonski? Or just the car thefts?"

"Just the cars."

"Why? Shake him up. A good Mafia lawyer will take care of the cars, he knows that, so he has nothing to worry about. If he talks, he has to figure his pals will whack him, so where's the incentive to speak up? Go after him for the murder, make him think twice."

"I'm holding back on that," LaPierre stated.

"Crap," Cinq-Mars muttered.

"Excuse me, gentlemen." They had assumed that Gilles Beaubien had either fallen asleep or been left so far behind by the conversation that he'd been rendered mute. His round form appeared Buddha-like as he lifted his head slightly to speak. "I just had a thought."

This news stirred no one's interest given the lateness of the hour, the weariness of the men, their testiness and general disrespect for the speaker. Limp and bored, they waited. And looked up only when the captain's silence was prolonged.

Finally confident of their notice, Beaubien announced, "I'll take charge of this investigation myself."

Tremblay responded quickly, virtually throwing himself into the breach. "Gilles, you've been at a desk a long time—"

"That's a good reason to undertake the challenge, Rémi. Émile's right. You'll be wholly consumed by the internal investigation. We have different departments to coordinate. The Russian involvement, that's RCMP. We'll need someone with rank to talk to the Mounties. In fact, Cinq-Mars and Mathers will *not* talk to the Russian captain. I'll ask the Mounties to do that."

Mathers, not knowing what all this meant, noted that LaPierre and Déguire seemed apoplectic, Tremblay panic-stricken, Cinq-Mars merely bemused.

"You've been behind a desk a long time, Gilles—" Tremblay started again.

"I'm still behind a desk. Everything goes through me. That's final. It's not up for discussion. In case you have other ideas, Rémi, try to go above me and I'll bust your balls. That's solemn."

"Gilles," Cinq-Mars began, "don't get us wrong. We appreciate your offer. We value your leadership. But, you know, your heart—"

"—is ticking, Émile. Thanks for asking. So's the clock. First meeting of the task force will be tomorrow morning at eleven sharp. Be here."

"Here?" LaPierre asked him.

Beaubien had committed his first blunder. "My office," he corrected himself. "Eleven sharp."

He slapped his hands on his knees as he stood and quickly departed, a marked spring to his heavy step.

"You had to bring up the issue, eh, Cinq-Mars?" Tremblay said. "Now we're screwed."

"Do you realize the paperwork with this guy?" LaPierre complained. "Five hundred words a day in triplicate. Déguire!"

"Sir?" Like the other junior detective in the room, Alain Déguire had chosen to keep his head low and try to follow the conversation. His misfortune was to be singled out while in midyawn.

"Tomorrow morning. Eleven o'clock. Walk into Beaubien's office and shoot him dead. You'll be declared a national hero."

No one laughed. They rose and silently left the lounge. The elevator was a strained space, each man relieved when one of his colleagues departed or he stepped off himself. Only Mathers and Cinq-Mars already had their coats with them and journeyed all the way down to the garage.

"I guess we're in a bad situation," Mathers probed. "With Beaubien."

"Think so?"

"You don't share everyone's opinion?"

"Ask yourself, who invited him to the meeting in the first place?"

Mathers detected a sly grin lurking below his partner's placid surface. "You?"

Cinq-Mars bopped his chin. "Tremblay—on our tail all day. LaPierre? He'd have us at our desks, sharpening pencils for life. Which of those two would voluntarily let me be in charge? When you're stuck, Bill, you look for another option."

"Beaubien's an option?"

"He'll never know what's going on." In a manner that Mathers found strikingly fraternal, Cinq-Mars put a hand on his near shoulder. "I just finessed our freedom on this case. I'm proud of myself. By the way, that wiretap? At the garage? Cop issue. An obsolete model, at least a decade old. Good night, Bill. See you in the morning. Don't forget now. Big meeting. Come prepared. Bring donuts. Beaubien will love you for it."

"Eleven sharp," Mathers said as he watched his mentor move through the cold damp of the garage. He surmised that he might never learn the secrets that had made Cinq-Mars top cop, but no doubt the man could teach him a few things.

7

A van blew in the early morning hours, shattering windows across a three-block radius. Wearing nightclothes and boots, and huddled in blankets stripped from their beds, residents fled to the streets fearing gas leaks, the end of the world, earthquakes, a comet. Details were slow to be processed. Policemen stomped their boots in the frigid dark. The driver's wallet and its contents had disintegrated in his hip pocket along with most of his gluteus maximus, but the vehicle registration in the glove box had been spared. If the driver was the van's owner, then he was a known member of the Rock Machine, a former B & E specialist conscripted into the gang while in prison. Upon release, Jacques "Ladder" Dufour had taken a driver's ed course to learn to ride a motorcycle. When he showed up for his road test the Motor Vehicles Bureau officer glanced at him and at the four bikers at his side and passed the exam paper across the counter along with the answers. The officer later declined to test the prudence of his driving habits on the street. Instead, he issued the driver's permit valid for motorcycles. Ladder had enjoyed the perks of being a gang member, especially the extraordinary access to women and the gaming rooms of Las Vegas—now he had paid a common consequence. In the Gang Room, André LaPierre pinned his name to the history board. "Jacques Dufour," he wrote down. "Known as Ladder. Bomb blast. January 7. 3:52 A.M." In the margin he scribbled, "Burnt cherry pie. We'll miss his cute ass. So will he."

At the first ring of the phone, horses whinnied and stomped lightly, as though the sound was threatening. Brushing a gray colt, Émile Cinq-Mars spoke soothing, wordless utterances as dust flew off the animal's back to settle on the frosty concrete floor.

He had been in the stables since dawn, feeding and watering the animals and participating in a major muck-out of the stalls. He and Sandra owned two dressage horses, a pair of show jumpers, and six polo ponies, and boarded another eight mounts. By the phone's second *brrrr*, most were contributing to the racket, talking back, their breath puffing in the brisk, damp air like a remnant of dragon fire. Either they knew that calls to the stable were ominous or they picked up on the dread the humans felt.

Sandra answered. Cinq-Mars allowed himself to hope, but she called out, "It's for you." She held the receiver as she might a dead rat, waiting for him to take it off her hands.

Cinq-Mars feigned reluctance. "Who is it?"

"He won't say."

For the sake of his marriage, he suggested, "Take a message."

Sandra and Émile had met while he was in New Hampshire buying horses for a friend. For Sandra Lowndes the combination of a big-city, French-speaking detective who knew horseflesh, traded with the cunning of a poker player, and carried himself with the bearing of a president was too exceptional not too warrant an extended look. They hit it off. She learned that his first wife had died seven months into the marriage, when Émile had been twenty-nine, and that his second wife had persevered for five years before crumbling from the long absences, her worry about violence, her infertility, and recurring, prolonged bouts of depression. While the marriage had never been a happy one, divorce did not come easily to Émile's strict Catholic upbringing. In the end, an annulment was procured and he adjusted to both the edict and its inherent hypocrisy.

Watching as she spoke into the phone, Cinq-Mars was nicked by a sense of admiration. Here was a woman out in the cutting cold of a humid barn tending to her animals, working tirelessly until each horse was watered and fed, warmed and soothed. When they had first met, they talked horses by day, American politics through the evening. Sandra was fiery and opinionated, invigorated by her feel-ings for him. They discussed the impossibility of forging a life together and jointly chose a long-distance relationship, with visits. Another two years of delightful romance passed before the notion of marriage began to evolve.

While the reality of life together had proven more problematic than the courtship, they were both giving themselves and each other time to adjust. The majority of Émile's closest friends spoke only French, and Sandra had difficulty getting her tongue around the lan-guage. Given their age difference, she shared few of his interests. While she had enjoyed life in the city, Sandra had been ambushed by loneliness and by how much she missed horses, and with their hap-piness deteriorating she'd proposed the purchase of a hobby farm. She wanted a stable again and argued that he would welcome the activity at retirement, that in the short term they could make it pay. Cinq-Mars saw the enterprise as marital glue, consented, and they embarked upon the adventure.

"The Russian freighter is the key," Sandra said. She held the phone now against her shoulder, awaiting his response.

"All right. I'll get it."

He accepted the receiver from her and spoke into the mouthpiece. "Who are you?" Sandra went back to her labors.

"The Russian freighter is the key."

"Yeah, I got that message. Now who are you? I'm tired of this."

"I'm not at liberty to say."

"Give me a code name, then. At least that. I need to refer to you in some way. When you leave messages I need to confirm who's calling."

His source chuckled lightly on the other end. "You're looking for a clue. You're hoping I'll give something away. All right. I'll go along with that. Give me a second. Okay, let's name this operation Steeplechase. You can call me Arch. Any messages left from Steeplechase Arch refer both to me and to this operation."

"What operation?"

"Don't patronize me, Cinq-Mars."

The detective squeezed the phone in his hand, as if information might squirt free. "Tell me about the freighter then."

"I already have. The Russian freighter is the key. Take it from there. Good luck, Cinq-Mars."

Steeplechase Arch hung up.

Cinq-Mars mulled over the message, then crossed to where his wife was sweeping dust and asked without a word of preamble if she had ever fired a rifle.

"Émile, what's going on?" She leaned on her broom and explored the intensity in his eyes.

"East of Aldgate," he murmured, looking away.

"Excuse me? Émile? What does that mean?"

"Sandra, you were raised on a farm. You must've fired a weapon."

"Rifles, sure. Shotguns in duck season. I'm American. Don't we all blast away at each other? It's our constitutional right."

"I'm going into the village. I'll buy a shotgun. I want you to keep it with you whenever I'm gone. Especially out here. When you ride the trails, take along the cell phone. From now on when you're in the house, I want you to keep the doors locked. I don't mean to scare you, but this might be a good time to be prudent."

"Émile?" She searched his eyes but found no solace there, no humor, no retraction. She turned her head away. Cinq-Mars moved to enclose her within his embrace, but she twisted out of his grasp and returned to the horses.

"Sandra," he said, coming up behind her.

She faced him again. "Émile, what next?" When he could not answer she shook her head. "Go," she said. "Get the gun. Don't worry about me. I can shoot straight."

"It's probably nothing," he said.

"It probably *isn't* nothing," she corrected him. "But how am I sup-posed to know when you won't talk to me? Out of the blue you ask me to arm myself. Will you ever tell me what's going on, Émile? Ever?"

How could he convey his gut suspicions when they made no sense?

"This isn't about cops and robbers, is it?"

Cinq-Mars nodded. "People don't realize it yet, but there's a war on. No one knows I'm involved, but when they do. . ." He let his voice trail off.

The couple stood silently next to each other, and Sandra at last consented to his embrace. In the cool damp of the barn, they kissed. Breaking it off, she bent to resume her labors, sweeping, tirelessly sweeping, and Cinq-Mars turned and through the small side door walked out into the brilliant sunlight of that fine winter morning.

With Detective Bill Mathers in tow, Sergeant-Detective Émile Cinq-Mars traveled to the city docks before noon and drove down to the commercial gate, expecting his badge to ease entry onto the property. Instead, a security guard, looking down upon him, recited a litany of procedures. Mathers got out of the car and went around to the cubicle. With his face to the frosty glass, he demanded to know what the old fart had against cops. Cop and sentry had a few bad moments. Finally, the guard made a phone call, authorization was granted, and Mathers signed the visitors' book. At that point Cinq-Mars heaved himself out of the car, barged into the guard's hut, and demanded to see the book.

"I'm not authorized to show you that," said the man, a wizened churl with a gripe against the living who did his best to make the world conform to his rules.

"I don't have the authorization to arrest you for impeding an investigation, but I could be induced," Cinq-Mars warned him. He was hoping the man would laugh, but instead he put a hand on his holster, straightened his back, and looked grim. "Hey. I'm kidding."

"I don't have authorization."

He was finding the guard's bullying meekness mildly endearing. "Go ahead. Request authorization. I'm happy to wait." He tapped him on the shoulder as if they were old comrades-in-arms and stepped outside. The moment the guard concluded his call Cinq-Mars barged back inside while Mathers stepped up to the glass, and together they examined the book with the window of the cubicle between them. "There!" he announced. The mother lode.

"Lordy be. How about that?" Mathers whistled.

"Day before Christmas, were you on duty?" Cinq-Mars asked the guard.

"I got seniority. Took five days off around Christmas. Two before, two after."

"You'll have to make another inquiry. I want you to request authorization for me to confiscate this book as evidence."

The guard looked from one man to the other to determine if he was pulling his leg before consenting. "Somebody better send me a replacement book." He'd decided the two detectives appreciated the value of procedure. Minutes later the officers departed with the book sitting on the backseat of their squad car, following the guard's meticulous directions along the docks to the Russian freighter.

Dilapidated grain elevators stood alongside the freighters belligerent against the wharves. The Port of Montreal wasn't busy in winter, although icebreakers kept the river open to the sea. The scarcity of ships and the quiet made the docks an eerie place.

Clambering out of the car, the detectives stared up at the rusty black behemoth that was the Russian freighter. Shared knowledge passed between them. This was no three-bedroom apartment. What could be concealed within that frame was beyond their ability to discover. Snow and ice hung from the upper decks. Spring lines binding the ship to the wharf were rimmed with icicles that glittered in the morning sun. The ramp leading to the main deck looked flimsy. Wind had blown snow across the ship's name.

"Kind of makes a needle in a haystack look like a snap," mused Mathers.

"At least in that situation you know you're looking for a needle."

"I could ask what we're doing here," the junior partner hedged.

"You could, but you don't want to waste our time."

They proceeded to the base of the ramp, and Cinq-Mars made room for the more agile man to go first. They ascended, their gloved hands clamped to the frozen rail, resisting the urge to glance down. Halfway up, Mathers stalled, his breath puffs of steam. "Are you sure we can't leave this to the Mounties?"

He had such a baby face, Cinq-Mars noticed. With that mug he was a choirboy for life. "They've been here. Didn't find a thing. Mush, Bill. Don't leave me out here to freeze."

They were ignored on deck. Political change in Moscow had not altered the disposition of these sailors, a sullen, uncommunicative, accusatory lot. The detectives climbed an exterior companionway to the high wheelhouse, where a hostile officer informed them that the captain would be summoned. He made them wait, nattering in Russian, before he put the call through.

Activity on the decks was lethargic, and the noise of the ship reverberated through the steel hull, the low murmured burr of the ship's systems interspersed by a rhythmic clanging. The wheelhouse was dreary. Despite a continuous blast of warm air, the steel walls caused the men to feel damp and chilled. They waited in the company of wary junior officers who were inspired to stare, and by the time the ship's captain arrived both policemen believed that they were the ones under official scrutiny.

Captain Vaclev Yakushev was no more than five feet, six inches, a hundred and twenty pounds. Heavily accented, his first words showed a rudimentary command of English, and he promptly dismissed the three crewmen present.

"You are not the police here before."

"Probably you were speaking with members of the RCMP," Bill Mathers told him. "We're MUCPD—Montreal Urban Community."

"What business you have here? City Montreal Police—what I have do with you?"

"What's your name again, sir?" Cinq-Mars shot out in a hard voice. He would not be reduced by this man. He was anxious to intercept any drift the conversation might take toward challenging his right to be there.

"Captain Vaclev Yakushev. This I told to you. Who are you?"

"Sergeant-Detective Émile Cinq-Mars. My partner, Detective Bill Mathers. How long have you been in port, sir?"

He screwed up his face to indicate that the question was difficult. "Little while."

"Be more specific, sir. Check your log if necessary."

"We come here, it was eleven October."

"You've stayed awhile."

"That's what I told to you." He shifted his shoulders around to put his rising impatience on display.

"What has kept you in port so long?"

"This is known. We have difficulties."

"Excuse me?"

The man expressed his irritation. "This is known."

"Not to me."

The captain heavily sighed. "Ownership is problem. Until owner-ship of vessel is resolve, we cannot sail."

"Why do you continue to load and unload?"

"We have no hurry. Sometimes we are told to us hold shipment. After that we are told to us unload. Once we are told load what we are told unload three days before. Of course, all is nonsense. What can we do? We load, we unload. We are here stuck."

"On the twenty-fourth of December, the day before Christmas, what were you doing?"

"I do not know what I do on that day."

"Check your log, please, sir."

The man hadn't shaven in a few days and his beard was gray with black bristles mixed in. His gray hair was cut short. He wore a blue sweater with an elbow in need of darning and flipped through the pages of the ship's log with evident disdain for the process. "A day the same as every day," he concluded.

"Was it? On that day a man by the name of Mr. Walter Kaplonski visited your ship. Do you recall the visit, Captain?"

"Mr. Kaplonski, yes. I have done business with this man. As I said, it was a day like every day."

"Was he accompanied?"

"I'm sorry?"

"Did he come alone or was he with someone?" Cinq-Mars gazed out across the broad decks of the freighter as though he was taking only a token interest in his questions now.

"This I don't remember. I would say that he come alone here."

Cinq-Mars turned. "That's odd, because on the day in question Mr. Walter Kaplonski signed in at the gate in the company of Mr. Hagop Artinian. Did you meet Mr. Artinian, Captain?"

The captain gestured with his hands to indicate that he was at a loss. "I do not know this name."

"You don't."

"I do not."

"He was not aboard your ship?"

"I would say no."

Cinq-Mars found the man's impenetrable mien suspicious in itself.

"The record at the gate says that Mr. Artinian and Mr. Kaplonski were on the docks for about five hours before they passed back through the gate."

"Maybe this other man he was waiting on dock. Maybe he did not come aboard my ship."

"Thirty below zero that day. He would have frozen to death."

"Perhaps he waited another place. On ship. On dock. I have no memory that name. I have no recollection Mr. Kaplonski arriving himself with another man."

"Your English is improving, Captain. Your accent is losing its hold." The captain stared back at him. "I have your permission to speak with your crew?"

"No, not. My crew has duties. I have spoken to police one time before. You have no place here."

"We understand that you are loading stolen cars for shipment to the Soviet Union," Cinq-Mars told him. Here was a man not unfamiliar with interrogation, he believed, and he wanted to keep him guessing.

The man smiled thinly. "You make errors. Three. One error is, no cars aboard my ship. Other police check for that. This is false accusation. Another mistake, this ship does not return my country. We sail from here go Boston, New York. I understand this, but must wait for to resolve ownership. After, I am told, we go San Francisco through Panama Canal, or we go Buenos Aires. To be decided. We take no cars back my country. One more error you make say is Soviet Union. Perhaps you do not know this but Soviet Union is no more existing."

Émile Cinq-Mars walked slowly across the steel floor. Bits of black rubber mat clung to the surface, although most had worn away. He came up very close to the steely-eyed captain of the Russian freighter, and the smaller man held his ground. "How long do you intend to remain in port, Captain?" he asked him quietly.

"This is not known."

"Approximately."

"Many weeks."

"I'm glad to hear it. Sufficient time for us to conduct our investigation."

"Then everyone is pleased. I hope you to find your cars, Detective." He craned his neck to look back at Cinq-Mars, to meet his challenge. Clearly he was not about to be intimidated by mere height. He had stood up to large men before.

"Mr. Hagop Artinian, the young man who was on your ship, the man you have no recollection of seeing, was murdered that very day. The time of death puts him aboard your ship, Captain."

"This is not possible—"

"No? A question's just been answered for me. Now I know why he was dressed as Santa Claus. You could not risk having the security guard check the car trunk, which they routinely do, and yet you had to get Mr. Artinian out of here and you had to have him check himself out at the gate. So you dressed him and Kaplonski as Santas, as if they were off to do some good, and you drove them out, the living beside the dead. Now all I have to do is figure out what interest it is that you and your people have with me, to go to the trouble of placing a sign around his neck with my name on it. That is the next mystery, Captain. Like the last, it shall be revealed. Good day, sir."

The Russian captain was unyielding, unflinching in his reaction. He seemed to be breathing normally, the smile remained taut, the eyes steady. Cinq-Mars left him and held the door for Mathers to pass through first. He nodded to the captain as he took his leave.

On deck, Mathers arched an eyebrow at his partner.

"You think I said too much, Bill?"

"I wouldn't mind hearing your theories before you try them out on the bad guys, that's all. Sometimes I wonder if you trust me at all, Émile."

"More than you realize. Captain Ya—. How do you say it? You're good with these foreign names."

"Yakushev. Come on, it's an easy one. It's a common Russian name."

"Ah, but is he a common Russian? That is what we must find out. Something tells me that our Captain Ya—. Yaku—."

"Yakushev." Mathers sighed.

"Something tells me that he's quite uncommon among his fraternity."

Mathers nodded and clapped his hands against his sides as a cold wind caught him head-on. "Are we through here?"

"We have some legwork left. I want the ship's manifest. I want an itemized account of everything that has been loaded and unloaded while it's been in port."

"Anything else?"

"Where do you think the killers found Santa Claus suits on Christmas Eve? Did they steal them, buy them, rent them? I'll run down the costume and novelty stores, see if anything turns up. If they killed the boy onboard this ship, and got him back through the gate dressed as Santa, they must have had that suit ready for him. They must have known they were going to need it."

"They let Artinian sign himself in. He had to. He had to show ID. How could they have been so stupid? They let him write his name in the gatekeeper's log! Then Kaplonski signed him out. That I can understand, they don't care who signs out as long as the count is right. But with their names together in the logbook, it's like announcing that Kaplonski did it. They gave us the time and place! I can see it if they hadn't planned to torture and kill him, but if they had a plan, it wasn't much of a plan."

Cinq-Mars disagreed. "Who would look for Artinian here? They never expected us to show up on the docks."

"Why did we?" Mathers wondered aloud. "We were told not to."

"We were told not to. That's interesting by itself. Drive me back to the station, Bill. Come back here after that."

Okinder Boyle hung about the school yard during morning recess until he realized that that was perhaps not a smart idea. His lurking, sulky reporter act might carry leverage in certain crowds, but in the vicinity of children the look promoted him as dangerous. He retreated and chose to wait for noon within the foyer of a small apartment building kitty-corner from the Artinian house. After

Vassil had come home for lunch, Boyle maintained a close watch, following him back to school the moment he reemerged.

"Vassil!" he called out. "Vassil!" Keeping up in the snow was difficult.

The boy stopped and eyed him warily and, before he got too close, issued a challenge, "You a cop?"

"I'm a friend of your uncle Garo's," Boyle told him. "He's my boss. I write for *The Gazette*."

The boy continued to eye him closely. "*The Gazoo*, my uncle calls it."

"I'm one of the animals."

"Uncle Garo says you're pretty good."

"Does he? I'll remind him of that sometime. He never tells me."

"No?" The boy seemed genuinely surprised.

"Your uncle Garo is a good man to emulate, if that's what you're doing, Vassil. But don't tell him I said so, all right?"

They continued walking along the plowed, sanded sidewalks.

"I liked today's story, the one about the Banker. Did you really go into that tunnel?"

"Guilty as charged." It pleased him to be recognized.

"Cool." They crossed a street. "Is this about Hagop?" Just saying the name caused his lip to quiver slightly.

"Garo asked me to check things out, maybe do a story. Some things are unexplained about Hagop. Why the Santa suit? Why did it happen at all? He was a good kid, everybody agrees on that, what was he doing with the wrong people?" Boyle wanted to keep talking to let the kid pull himself together. He was obviously fragile when discussing his brother. "Maybe your uncle has more confidence in the press than the police, I don't know, but he loved Hagop and wants to know what happened."

The boy walked on beside the reporter in silence. At the corner nearest his school he stopped. He moved his feet around to warm them and gazed intently at his boots.

"As reporters, we have to blow off the smoke," Boyle told him, "see what's really going on. If there's anything about your brother, any angle that might shed light, I hope you'll tell me, Vassil. Let's uncover the truth no matter what it is, but I have a feeling the truth will honor Hagop's memory. Do you think that's true?"

Vassil Artinian nodded. Boyle could not be certain, but he thought he detected anger on his face underpinning his grief. The boy's cheeks were flushed.

"Can you help me out here, Vassil?"

Again the boy nodded, only this time he raised his head. "Yeah," he said. "I know a few things. But I promised Hagop not to tell anybody." He had to wipe away a tear from the corner of one eye.

"I know," Boyle told him in a soft voice. "Think about this. Maybe Hagop said a few things to you just in case. He probably knew he was in danger. Maybe he wanted you to know a few things in case something happened to him."

A friend shouted and waved to Vassil and the boy idly waved back. "I gotta go," he said.

"I can meet you after school."

The boy consented with a nod, and it seemed to Boyle that he had grown eager. "A block up, there's a hangout, corner of Jarry. If you want I could meet you there."

"Thanks, Vassil. I'll be waiting. You have a good afternoon now."

Puffed and bothered, Sergeant-Detective André LaPierre led Émile Cinq-Mars into Interrogation Room 9 in the late afternoon. Bill Mathers slouched behind, hands in his pockets, shoulders slumped, followed shortly by Captain Gilles Beaubien in uniform and Lieutenant-Detective Rémi Tremblay. Cinq-Mars carried in a briefcase that had heft. With Mathers, he chose to seat himself on the side of the table normally reserved for felons. The trio of officers pulled up chairs on the other side.

"His Holiness is in the confession box," LaPierre derided, his fury apparent.

"You contravened a direct order, Cinq-Mars," Beaubien declared.

"What's that, sir?" Cinq-Mars was wearing a look of sublime innocence.

"I gave you an order to stay away from the Russian ship!" Beaubien exclaimed.

"Why was that, sir?" For a moment it appeared that Beaubien

would burst a gasket, if not a heart valve. Tremblay intervened on the side of diplomacy.

"The point is, Émile, you boarded the Russian vessel without permission from your op leader who had issued a contravention."

"Ah," Cinq-Mars acknowledged, as though this was all coming clear to him for the first time. Next to him, Mathers slid down another notch in his chair. He was hoping that his partner intended to take all the heat, and not merely the lion's share, upon himself. "How is it that André reacts so quickly to that and yet so slowly to matters of importance?"

LaPierre raised both hands. "Hang on a second here. This is my interrogation. We agreed. You two are along to supervise and witness, remember?"

"They're here to keep you from killing me, André." Cinq-Mars chuckled.

"I ought to," LaPierre told him plainly. "I should blow your brains out."

"Gentlemen, this is not productive," Tremblay warned. He carried a briefcase of his own and sifted through it for his tape recorder. He placed the device in the center of the table and punched the record button. "This meeting's called to order. Present in the room, Mathers, Cinq-Mars, LaPierre, Beaubien, and Tremblay. Sergeant-Detective André LaPierre has issued a complaint against fellow officer Sergeant-Detective Émile Cinq-Mars. For the sake of expediency, he has consented to an informal inquiry. LaPierre has requested that Captain Gilles Beaubien be present, and Cinq-Mars has asked that myself, Lieutenant-Detective Rémi Tremblay, moderate. In my capacity as moderator I have asked that Detective Mathers be present as an interested party. André, ask your questions and, if you wish, make your charge. Be advised that we are going to conduct this inquiry in a civil manner. Also, I remind everyone that what we say here stays within these walls."

Nodding, LaPierre took a moment to gather his composure. "It's simple," he declared, his rage apparent. "This is my case. I cannot accept interference by another officer, *especially* by one who isn't Homicide. On the night of the murder, Cinq-Mars had the body of the victim removed from the scene of the crime. He has interviewed the Artinian family, he's interrogated the victim's eleven-year-old brother, and revealed to that boy that the victim had been a police informant—*information* that he failed to disclose to the IO. As well, Detective Cinq-Mars visited the premises where the victim had been employed. I have yet to learn the results of that visit. Subsequent to these events—and *after* I had reminded Detective Cinq-Mars to stay the hell away from my case—*against* the specific command of the op leader, Detective Cinq-Mars boarded the Russian freighter and came *this close* to accusing the captain of committing murder. The captain's complained to us. I want this man reprimanded, and I want him to stay the hell away from my case and stop screwing it up!"

Tremblay allowed the dust to settle. When the two combatants locked eyes again, the lieutenant indicated that it was time for Cinq-Mars to respond.

"You forgot to mention, André," Cinq-Mars began, opening his briefcase and removing the gatekeeper's log, "that I also checked with security down at the docks. I confiscated an entry and exit record that puts Hagop Artinian on the docks at the time of his death—"

LaPierre was on his feet. "Damn you, Émile! This is *my case!*"

"—and in the company of Walter Kaplonski. This is your case?" Cinq-Mars asked over LaPierre's bluster.

"Yes, it's mine, *tabernac!*" Whether he was speaking English or French, LaPierre had a tendency to mix in swear words from both languages.

At that rebuke, Cinq-Mars jumped to his feet and slammed the logbook hard upon the desk. "Why aren't you on it, then? Where the hell've you been?"

"*Taberhuit!* You've been withholding and interfering!"

On his feet as well, Tremblay held an arm across LaPierre's chest. "Both of you, sit down and shut the fuck up!"

Reluctantly, both combatants sat, struggling to breathe calmly.

"It's still my turn to speak," Cinq-Mars pointed out.

"So speak."

"On the night of the murder, Sergeant-Detective LaPierre was in the john puking and shitting his guts out. It was always one or the other. During the entire time that forensics was there, LaPierre was nowhere to be seen. We heard him, but we never saw him. I did not remove the corpse, it was not done on my order. Forensics did that. Now, my partner and I were the first to discover the body, consequently it was only fitting that we pay our respects to the family. I had a chat with the boy because he appeared troubled. He had just lost a brother, after all. As far as Hagop being an informant of mine, that's not something I talk about to other officers. My informants are my informants. I don't say who is, I don't say who isn't. To the family, however, I let them know that their son was a good boy, someone who worked on the side of justice. I was being *nice*.

"Now, I visited Garage Sampson because I was looking to break a stolen car ring, which happens to be within my jurisdiction. If André has a problem with that, he should look to his own performance. If he never visited the victim's place of work, that's not my fault."

"What about the ship?" Beaubien interrupted. The edge to his voice indicated that he cared about little else. He stabbed the table with a forefinger, knotting his brow in combat. "Tell me about the ship. I gave that order myself."

"I respect your orders, sir," Cinq-Mars obliged him. "But I wasn't actually visiting the ship, sir. I was visiting the gatekeeper's cubicle. That's where I recovered the logbook which puts Artinian on the docks, with Kaplonski, at the time of his death. Once I had that information, it was only fitting that I confront the ship's captain—"

"How's that fitting?" LaPierre wanted to know.

"A direct violation of my order," Beaubien insisted.

"Sir, your order, with respect to the ship, had to do with the investigation of stolen cars. I wasn't investigating stolen cars onboard that ship. I merely inquired how long the ship had been in port and how long the captain expected to remain, so that when I passed the information about the logbook along to André he would know the situation. I couldn't just walk away with the book in one hand if the ship was about to set sail, now could I?"

"You've been raising horses too long, Émile. All you do is shovel shit."

Tremblay held up his hand. "Do you have anything more to add? Either of you?"

The litigants chose to keep their peace.

"All right then. This is my decision, and there will be no further discussion and no bitching. Cinq-Mars, I'm giving you the benefit of the doubt. No reprimand. However, I am issuing fair warning. The homicide is André's case—"

"Then why doesn't he do something with it?"

"Shut up. André is the IO on the Artinian murder. Period. End of sentence. You, Cinq-Mars, will not withhold a stitch of evidence. You will not interfere with his investigation. Nor will you conduct your own sideline. You will stay one hell of a distance away from this case. Is that perfectly clear?"

Cinq-Mars nodded.

"André, you will not be bothered by Émile again. But get cracking. I want to see some results."

LaPierre extended his hand across the table.

Cinq-Mars studied the proffered palm. "You try to get a reprimand against a fellow officer and now you want to shake on it?"

"Heat of the battle, Émile. No hard feelings."

Cinq-Mars reluctantly accepted his hand.

"One more thing," Captain Beaubien announced. The four other men in the room settled back into their chairs, expecting something less than pertinent. "Detective Mathers."

"Yes, sir?"

"You're junior to Cinq-Mars, and you will report any discrepancies or you will be demoted to foot patrol quicker than you can say Jackie Robinson."

Cinq-Mars wanted to ask him what he knew about Jackie Robinson, who had begun his professional baseball career, as a black man in the white man's leagues, in Montreal, but he checked himself in time.

Mathers said only "Understood."

"Another thing," Beaubien continued. "As op leader, I'm removing both of you from any further involvement with the operation. Your contribution so far is appreciated. But both of you need to be reminded what it means to have a chain of command. Cinq-Mars, you're gone."

The two men glared at each other.

Tremblay clicked off the tape recorder. "We're done. Remember, within these walls."

Satisfied, LaPierre scooped up the logbook.

"You'll want to check who else was onboard that day."

"It's my case, Émile." He led the brigade out. Cinq-Mars remained seated, and Mathers dutifully stayed behind as well. They listened to the silence.

Finally, Mathers stated the obvious, because he wasn't sure if it was true or not. "I guess we're off this case."

"Are we?" Cinq-Mars asked.

"Émile." He wanted to protest further but didn't dare.

On his feet, Cinq-Mars came around behind him. He bent low to whisper in his partner's ear. "Within these walls."

He straightened sharply, reverted to restless pacing, then leaned close to Mathers a second time. Rage made him pant.

"We had weight in this room, Bill, but don't be intimidated. I have a line open to weight heavier than what you saw here. That's why they consented to make this informal. That's why they insisted on doing it within these walls. Because an official tribunal would expose them to the real power in this department. They know it, and I know it. It's only fair that you know it also."

He paced again. Mathers could feel his partner's ire.

"I get information, Bill. The good stuff. Prime stuff. I get arrests. Flesh traders shipping young girls to foreign countries. Asian connections importing girls. Hot car rings, drug pushers, jewelry thieves, I get the busts. Why? Because my phone rings. I pick up the phone, and I act on the information I receive. I don't pay for it, in cash or in favors. All I do is receive it, and arrest the bad guys. I never had to pay until Christmas Eve."

Again he broke off. Mathers waited.

"My information cost the life of that boy. Hagop paid with his life for doing our job. That's a higher price than I ever agreed to. That's a bargain with the devil I want to rescind. Nobody can tell me that

I'm not on this case. I am on this case because I am implicated in this case."

Cinq-Mars pulled away again, and Mathers did his best to console him. He spoke quietly as well. "It's not your fault, Émile. Who wouldn't accept that information? It's prime. What choice did you have? You can't ignore solid leads."

"I took the information and that boy died. Okay, I've made my peace with that. But somebody ran that boy. Somebody guided him. Who that was, I don't know. I call him my source. His code name, between us, is Steeplechase Arch. He's not the one who killed him, but he is responsible for involving him, and therefore he's responsible for that boy losing his life. He's the one I'm after, Bill. I am involved in this case, and nobody, nobody, can tell me otherwise. If you don't want to be my partner, say so now."

"I'm your partner," Mathers stated simply. "I bust my gut to get the chance to line up with you. I'm not bailing out now, Émile. This is my chance to prove myself. I hate being treated like some English kid who's lucky he's not been assigned to traffic patrol. I'm a good cop. But I'm English, and I'm young, and I look like I should be coaching the swim team. I'm in. I'm in because this is my one chance to make something of my career. People think I'm the do-gooder, that I won't bend the rules. Well, give me a reason, give me a good reason, then see what happens."

Cinq-Mars sat down beside him and exhaled down to his toes. "I don't know where to start," he confessed. "I don't know who he is, I have no links to him."

"Sure you do," Mathers chirped.

"Excuse me?"

"*You're* the link to him. Do you think he chose you out of the phone book? Hardly. Your source knows you. He must've known who he was choosing to be his conduit. Either he knows you or he knows people close to you."

Cinq-Mars looked sternly down his impressive nose at his colleague. "You've given this some thought," he noted.

"Have you heard from him lately, since the murder?" Mathers asked.

"Early this morning," Cinq-Mars conceded.

"And?"

"A cryptic message. *The Russian freighter is the key.*"

Mathers nodded. "That's why we raided."

"Raided!" Cinq-Mars ridiculed. "It was a promenade."

"Whatever. You were lured there, in any case."

"Bill," Cinq-Mars said, leaning forward and placing his index finger gently upon the other man's wrist, "listen to me. This is my fear. Steeplechase Arch, whoever he is, whatever he's up to, was trying to run an agent inside the Hell's Angels. That agent was Hagop Artinian. That agent is dead. Whoever he is, whomever he represents, I have no reason to believe that he will quit now. I believe he will try to run somebody else. And if that doesn't work, somebody else. The life expectancy of an informant inside the Angels is brief, the method of death, brutal. Hagop Artinian was tortured and murdered. Whoever his replacement is, that's whom I want to protect. I don't want another young life on my conscience. Whoever is next must not die. This is our job. Now you understand why we're involved in this case? This isn't some personal thing. This is urgent. This is necessary."

Mathers met his gaze. He granted his consent with an imperceptible bob of his head. "Understood. But let me ask you something. I have a wife and kid to support. What about Beaubien and LaPierre?"

"Leave them to me. I'll deal with those two. Their days are numbered." Cinq-Mars smiled slightly. "Within these walls, Bill. Remember that."

"Yes, sir," Mathers answered quietly.

Julia Murdick skipped through the snow to La Magique, a nightclub, hurrying to escape the cold. Inside, down a long entry corridor, she was met by a bouncer, a graduate of the weight room, who gave her a long look but admitted her without charge. "What is this," she asked, "Ladies' Night?"

"Every night," the thug told her, "is free for you."

Julia smirked, to let him know that she felt less than flattered.

She was the only woman in the place wearing clothes.

She sat in the dark club and ordered a beer from a bare-breasted teenager who looked at her a little coyly. Julia was either a customer or a job applicant, and either way the waitress was curious. Two women danced seminude onstage, slowly removing each other's clothes, while others stood on plastic milk crates and displayed themselves inches from the eyes of patrons. Close enough to be licked. When the waitress returned Julia asked if Max Gitteridge was around and the girl pointed him out.

Gaining liquid courage, she walked across to the lawyer's table. Selwyn had told her not to delay. She had to arrive early so the place wouldn't be busy, and she had to act quickly before a patron got up the nerve to hit on her. Gitteridge had a phone pressed to one ear, and in the other he'd inserted a finger to block out the music. He was a small man with black, slicked hair and a narrow, pinched face. The features were generally weak, the nose narrow, the chin pointy. He was wearing a double-breasted suit over a black turtleneck, and Julia thought the shoulders had been bulked up. She put him in his late forties. She sat down opposite him in the booth. She didn't know what to make of a man who still greased his hair. Hard to believe. He regarded her without courtesy, and that made her squirm. His pupils were large and dark. When he hung up, he took the finger out of his ear, and said, "Say what, sugar?" as if he was trying hard to be a cool dude.

She had to lean in, on account of the music. With her jacket open, the tops of her full breasts were revealed at the neckline to her sweater. He was noticing.

First she slid a newspaper article written about Max Gitteridge across the table. He took a quick glance, enough to recognize the headline in a revolving light from the stage. "Lies," he told her, raising his voice to be heard. "I intend to sue."

"So you don't represent the Hell's Angels and the Mafia?" she asked him.

He signaled for her to lean forward again, and he moved toward her. He stared at her breasts while speaking near her ear. "I don't ask clients to list their memberships in social clubs. Who are you and what do you want?" He leaned back to wait for her answer, forcing Julia to shout.

"My name is Heather Bantry. I want to propose a business deal."

"You don't want to dance?"

She thought she'd love to take a tube of his hair grease and smear it across that leering smile. Instead, she slid a newspaper column on the Banker across to him. "Have you read this?"

"What is it?"

"It's about my father. He's looking for a job."

Gitteridge gave the clipping a glance, holding it up to catch a bit of light. "This is about some guy who lives in a tunnel."

"Yeah," Julia agreed, shouting to be heard. "Some guy. Who just happens to be a former vice president for international commerce at a major bank."

Gitteridge read a little further. "Says here he's nuts."

"That's where I come in. I know how to take care of him. I can keep him level. I have that effect." Julia caught sight of a woman removing her bikini bottoms inches from the glare of a customer. She was momentarily shocked that the woman was shaved, and when she glanced up at her face, the woman was smiling right at her. She jerked her eyes away, facing Gitteridge.

The man separated his hands and brought them together again. "Do I look like an employment office to you?"

"Read the piece. That's all. My phone number is at the bottom of the page if you want to get in touch."

She stood up, but Gitteridge quickly waved her back. He motioned her to sit down beside him. "What did you say your name was, sweetheart?"

"Heather."

"Why'd you come to see me, doll?" He ran his fingers up the inside of her thigh.

She resisted clamping her legs together and instead leaned closer to Gitteridge. Julia tucked her hands in her leather jacket. "My father's had a mental breakdown. He's been on welfare, he's living in a tunnel. He's broke. Ruined. He's destitute. He can act funny sometimes. The goddamn Royal Bank isn't going to hire him, now is it?"

With that, she wriggled free of his grip, jumped up, and walked through the gloom of the nightclub, doing her best to keep her eyes off the tempest of dancers and the avid, entranced faces of their admirers. Selwyn Norris would not be waiting outside to give her a lift home this evening. She'd have to make her own way back. He had warned her that she might be followed.

Buried in his cubicle through the dinner hour, Émile Cinq-Mars was disturbed by a call from downstairs. A reporter was asking to speak to him. "What about?"

He waited while the officer addressed the visitor again. Then she said, "Santa Claus."

Minutes later, arriving at his desk under escort, the reporter introduced himself as Okinder Boyle. After nodding thanks to the uniform, Cinq-Mars stood to shake the young man's hand and assumed that he would be blowing this off quickly enough.

"I have nothing to say about the Santa Claus case," he advised him. "The investigation is ongoing, the responsibility of Homicide. Perhaps you'd like to speak to Sergeant-Detective André LaPierre?"

Boyle sat down, folding his coat across his lap. "I'd rather talk to you."

"It's not my case," Cinq-Mars said in a switch to English. "I appreciate your interest, sir, but I have nothing to say. The investigation is ongoing, the responsibility of another department."

"I spoke with Vassil Artinian today."

Cinq-Mars gave him a closer look. "Did you now?"

"He told me his brother was working for you."

Émile Cinq-Mars finally sat down. The beginning of the night shift had brought boisterous officers into their vicinity, but even in the rising bedlam he feared prying ears. "Would you like some coffee, Mr. Boyle?" he asked quietly.

"Thanks. I would."

"The coffee here tastes like sewer water. Let's go out."

Cinq-Mars led him outside Police Headquarters and up the hill on rue Bonsecours into Old Montreal. At this time of year the sun set a little after four, and at six-thirty darkness had settled in as deeply as the cold. They faced a bitter wind along rue St. Jacques past City Hall, where late rush-hour traffic still managed to work itself into a snarl, and at Place Cartier they walked downhill a short stretch past the old stone buildings that now housed restaurants and bars to cobbled rue St. Paul. From here, the early settlers of the city had believed, they'd convert the savages. Cinq-Mars guided the younger man into a coffee shop. They were both mute, conversation stifled by their cold lips and stiff cheeks. "Are you a Montrealer, Mr. Boyle?"

"I'm from Grand Manan," the journalist told him, and explained that he'd been raised on an island off the coast of northern Maine that belonged to New Brunswick. "I'm descended from a long line of fishermen."

"Now you catch different fish in different nets."

"No, sir. That's what you do. I just write about those fish."

"Ah." Cinq-Mars took a table in the rear, sitting with his back to the wall. He ordered coffee and Danishes for them both and was contemplating a way into the conversation when Boyle seized the initiative.

"So far you haven't denied Vassil's claim. Hagop worked for you."

"He did not."

"Vassil lied?"

"He misconstrued the facts."

"How so?"

"Mr. Boyle, I'm not about to surrender confidential information. You must have known that coming in."

"Then I'll print the facts as they've been construed."

"I was afraid you might think that way," Cinq-Mars admitted. "I'm advising against it."

Their pastry and coffee arrived. Boyle observed Cinq-Mars stir in his Sweet'n Low. "Why's that, Detective?"

"This is all part of an ongoing investigation. You could jeopardize the case, put other people in danger."

"So you concede that Hagop Artinian worked for you?"

"How could he have worked for me? I never knew his name until the day he died. Did I ever direct him, or ask him for information, or give him money or favors in exchange for information? Categorically, no."

"Detective, I'm a journalist." He struggled to chew and swallow quickly. "I write about events that interest me. The death of a student a few doors down from where I live, while wearing a Santa Claus suit, that interests me. This is not a story I walk away from. That dead boy

142

was wearing a sign, *Merry Xmas, M-Five*, which apparently refers to the city's most famous policeman, the legendary Cinq-Mars—now that's a story. I'm itching to break it. If you want to convince me otherwise, you'll have to do a better job."

Cinq-Mars took his point. He quickly gathered his thoughts, for he was learning not to underestimate this man. "Sorry to have to put it this way, Mr. Boyle, but I may be obliged to speak to your editor."

"Detective, before you go any further—"

"Allow me to finish—"

"No, allow me. My editor is Garo Boghossian. Do you know him?"

"I'm sure he's a man of some influence—"

"He is. He's also Hagop Artinian's uncle. Do you really think he'll ask me to back off?"

From the moment that Okinder Boyle had arrived, Émile Cinq-Mars had been losing one minor debate after another to him. What he had counted as insignificant setbacks were beginning to multiply.

"I think we can help each other out," Boyle continued. "Provided that you're willing to answer a few simple questions. Are you working on this case?"

"It's not my case." He was willing to play along with him for a bit. "Cinq-Mars—"

"Have I taken an interest? Yes. After all, I found the boy's body."

"Did Hagop Artinian, at any time, work for you—or failing a definition of what that means, supply you with information?"

"It's my understanding that, on rare occasion, Hagop Artinian lent a hand with law enforcement. Perhaps more often than rarely."

"Do you know why he died?" Boyle asked bluntly.

"No. Do you?"

"No. Do you know why he was dressed in a Santa Claus outfit?"

Cinq-Mars hesitated longer than he would have liked. That alone required an explanation. "I have a theory. Perhaps—we shall see—perhaps I can offer it up as trade."

"One more query first. How do you respond to the theory that Hagop Artinian was working for the CIA?"

In an instant, Émile Cinq-Mars knew that there would be no camouflaging his surprise. "Who's been floating that cockamamie tale?"

Boyle did not respond, regarding the detective with a steady gaze. "Vassil said that? His brother told him that?"

Again, the young man did not respond.

"It makes no sense. If Hagop helped us, his work had to do with relatively minor crimes. Crimes within my jurisdiction. The CIA? What possible link could there be? Either Hagop was fabricating a story for his brother, or—"

"Or?"

"—or somebody strung him a line."

"The theory doesn't interest you?"

"I have to dismiss it. I consider myself an open-minded person, Mr. Boyle, but until there's a link—"

"But it does interest you, Detective. I can tell." Boyle scratched the side of his throat where his scarf irritated the skin.

"Why are you telling me this?" Cinq-Mars asked.

"To gauge your reaction. I can't print the story without verification. I can't go on the word of an eleven-year-old even if I do think he's credible. Like you, I'm not sure what motive Hagop would've had to tell his brother. A silly boast? An idle fantasy? It's possible, but it doesn't jibe with what we know about the guy. Was he speaking the truth? I can't say that either."

Cinq-Mars regarded the young journalist with intensity. "I still wonder why you told me."

Boyle nodded, conceding that he had avoided the question. "I'm not entirely neutral in this tale. I told you on the chance that it was something you needed to know. I'm hoping that you might consider telling me a few things sometime. Maybe not now, but someday you might choose to say something to me first. You were moving toward proposing a trade. That's too mercenary, Detective. What I want is the real dope on Hagop. I'm interested in how he'll be remembered. I'm interested in how he died. Not official versions, the real stuff. You might be the only person who finds that out. I'm not looking to establish an adversarial relationship. I'm hoping we can help each other out."

"What will you publish, Mr. Boyle?"

The journalist shook his head. "I'm probably as far from publishing as you are from solving the case."

144

Cinq-Mars drank his coffee. "I take it that I won't be reading in *The Gazette* tomorrow that Hagop Artinian worked for me."

"You got it. Now. May I test our new friendship? Is there any possibility—however remote, no matter how unlikely or illogical or far-fetched—is there any possibility that Hagop Artinian was working for the CIA? Can you, with what you know, imagine such a thing?"

Émile Cinq-Mars sipped his coffee. "Let's put it this way," he said, choosing his words carefully. "Now that you have raised the issue, I'll keep it in mind. That's all I'll say."

"That's all you need to say, Detective. But if anything breaks along those lines, remember who you owe."

Cinq-Mars tapped behind his ear. "I'm not sure about that. On the other hand, if there comes a time when I can make a contribution to the memory of Hagop Artinian, for the sake of his family, I shall do so."

"Fair enough. Now. What about the Santa Claus suit?"

Cinq-Mars smiled, quite warmly for him. "We are beginning a friendship, Mr. Boyle. Nevertheless, we work in competitive fields. We both gather information. If we trade, it should be equitable. You've given me a thread. A loose thread that may have no significant value. In exchange, you're expecting a considered and plausible theory from me. Is that a fair exchange?"

"Then give me a thread, if that's all you're up for," Boyle pressed him.

"I have a better idea. I'll give you a story. You print it. Every tangent cannot be confirmed, but the facts can be verified. I have the documentation. You don't have to diverge from the facts. I was going to give this to my friends in the francophone media, maybe to *Allô Police!* But since you're here, I'll tell you a story if you'll print it."

Boyle tried to laugh him off. "Come on. If I came to you and asked that you make an arrest in exchange for information, what would you say?"

Cinq-Mars preferred not to answer. "Show me the evidence first."

"Same here."

The detective thought a moment. "You have an odd name. Odd for me anyway. What did you say your first name was?"

"Okinder."

"Yes." Excited by a connection, Cinq-Mars shook his right fore-finger in the air a moment. "My partner—he's English—reads your paper. It's part of his job, in a way, to tell me what's in the English media. It helps pass the time, and I don't like to be blind to what's going on in half the city. He mentioned your name, Okinder. I remember because it sounded strange to me."

"You should talk. Your name's a date. I've never heard of Johnny the Fourth of July. Or Wanda August Ninth."

"I'm from either corrupt or sturdy stock." Cinq-Mars shrugged. "My surname could be a corruption of Saint Marc, or else the name derives from the fifth son of a family out of a village called Mars. The legacy of the first four sons didn't survive." A memory dawned and Cinq-Mars waved a finger. "Okinder—so you're the one who walked into the Mount Royal tunnel on Christmas Eve and talked to the banker who had lost his mind. Okay, I've got you pegged now. All right, you can have the story. I'll tell you why Hagop Artinian was dressed as Santa Claus. Get out your notepad."

"May I use my tape recorder?"

"Absolutely not. Nor can you attribute anything I say to me."

Okinder Boyle complied, and sat waiting with pad and pencil poised.

Cinq-Mars told him about the Russian freighter, and about the gatekeeper's log that put Hagop Artinian on the premises, and prob-ably on the ship, at the same time as his estimated moment of death. He told him why he thought the Santa Claus uniforms were deployed, that that was how the killers had smuggled a dead body off the premises in full view. He told about his discovery that afternoon, that Walter Kaplonski had rented two Santa uniforms a day before the murder, and had not returned them, but had gone back to the store and reimbursed the merchant for the loss, explaining that the suits had accidentally been damaged beyond repair. Clearly, he had not wanted the store to call the cops about missing costumes. He told Okinder Boyle what Bill Mathers had uncovered through a study of the ship's activity in port, that luxury cars had been loaded onto the vessel, and that luxury cars had been off-loaded, and that an inspection by the Mounties that very day had shown no vehicles onboard.

"I don't get it."

"A Mercedes, let's say, is loaded onto the vessel for shipment to Russia. Days later it's off-loaded with European registration for use in this country as a legitimately imported vehicle. Who's buying we don't know, but I have my guesses."

"Such as?"

"The process is organized. The usual suspects."

Boyle could not believe this golden platter of information. "Somehow Hagop Artinian got involved in this. Was he doing undercover work?"

"I'd appreciate it, Okinder, if you never raise that possibility. Hagop worked for Walter Kaplonski, as a part-time mechanic in his garage."

"Garage Sampson, yes. That's Kaplonski's place?"

"We raided the garage."

"And?"

"A document was found. I can fax you a copy sometime."

"What does it show?"

"Police officers using Mr. Kaplonski's garage for free repairs to their personal automobiles."

"No shit. You're telling me this?" Boyle wrote furiously.

"One of those officers was André LaPierre, who's the IO into the murder of Hagop Artinian. The other is Gilles Beaubien, a high-ranking officer in this department."

"How high?"

"Captain. He's the operations leader with respect to this investigation."

"Whose guts you hate, right? I thought cops didn't rat on cops?"

"Who's ratting? You're not hearing any of this from me."

"You got that straight."

"Off the record?"

"Sure. Absolutely. No problem. What?"

"Off the record, I made sure that LaPierre came along on the raid of Kaplonski's garage. You know, a cop may find out he can get repairs to his car at a garage for free. Of course, he shouldn't do it.

But am I going to be appalled by human nature to find out that some cops do? LaPierre's a street cop. A womanizer, a night owl. He works the dark side of the alley. So, I'm not appalled, and I won't hang him by the balls because he gets a free brake job. He told me he hadn't been on the street where the garage is located in years. Okay, he wants to cover his ass. But, he made it look as though he had no clue that Hagop worked there. He interviewed Kaplonski. Never scratched him. Says his lawyer saved him, but you can work around lawyers. LaPierre's done nothing but crap on this case, and I don't protect other people's crap—cops or no cops. I made sure that Beaubien got wind of the facts. He took over the case. Which could be seen as commendable or as contemptible, depending on how he handled it. I wanted to find out."

"How'd he handle it?"

"He kept me away from Kaplonski. Then he tried to keep me away from the Russian freighter."

"But you went anyway," Boyle noted.

Cinq-Mars stretched. "Which puts me up Shit Creek. I want to go after Kaplonski without my hands being tied. There's something else. LaPierre gets wind of a garage that makes deals—I understand. He has his nose in the dog poo on the sidewalk. But Beaubien? He doesn't step in shit. He's an ivory tower cop. He's delicate. He never hangs out with cops. How does he find out about a convenient garage? How does he know where to go or what to say, how does he get in the door? He can't ask around the department, who'd confess something like that to him? Since when is Beaubien connected? That's a puzzle."

"In a nutshell, you need LaPierre and Beaubien out of your way. Beaubien might be dirty, LaPierre might have smelly feet, but otherwise you're not sure about them. That's where I come in."

"You're a quick study, Okinder. Call me Émile, by the way."

"Émile, what can I say? I know you have your reasons, but thanks anyway."

"You're welcome. You understand, it's only the garage and police connection that should be printed. The matter of the Santa Claus suit is for future use."

That both their hands rose above the table, that they shook, seemed a simultaneous, mutual, and solemn agreement.

"Shall we brave the cold again, Émile?"

Cinq-Mars smiled, stood, and buttoned his coat. "Not together, Okinder. You and I shouldn't be seen in public. Nor should you ever say anything important over the phone. Never leave a message with substance. In fact, you'll need a code name."

"Cloak and dagger. I love it. So what's my name? Deeper Throat?"

A possibility popped to mind. "Steeplechase B," Cinq-Mars told him.

"Cool. So tell me, who's Steeplechase A?"

Cinq-Mars shot him a cutting glance. "I have to remember to watch myself around you, young man. B for Boyle," he explained to him. "Don't you worry about Mr. A."

Alone and grim, Émile Cinq-Mars headed into the blustery night. Time to return to the country and a warm, crackling fire, to snug down with a book, his wife, and a Glenmorangie and soothe his weary brow. Tonight he'd forget about villains and dead youths. Instead, he'd dwell upon the news that Okinder Boyle had brought him, that his source, Steeplechase Arch, for reasons beyond his ken, was connected to the CIA. The notion had validity. How else had he successfully camouflaged phone calls so they could not be traced? How else had he recruited others except through training, skill, and good connections? How else had Arch secured a catalog of information, the good stuff, except through the cunning of an international intelligence agency? But if true, why was the CIA in contact with him? Why had the CIA bolstered his career, with what ultimate purpose in mind? What, essentially, was going on?

Cinq-Mars returned to Headquarters, took the elevator down to the garage, climbed into his Taurus, and turned the car for home. He needed rest. He needed to relax. He needed a drink. He wanted to soothe his bones.

Out of the city, across the highway, the wind was picking up.

A blizzard was about to begin.

TWO

MALICIOUS MALALIGNMENT

8

Conversation around the coffeemaker petered out whenever Émile Cinq-Mars came by, his colleagues drifting away. He retreated to his cubicle. His dismissal from the company of cops was connected to a column published in *The Gazette* the previous morning alluding to police graft. Cops didn't read the English paper as a rule, but nobody missed this one. They didn't cry over seeing Captain Gilles Beaubien slapped down a peg, but André LaPierre was one of their own. The word traveling around Headquarters was that Cinq-Mars had sold out one of their own.

Fuming, preoccupied, busy with the paperwork on an old case that was coming to trial, Cinq-Mars failed to notice Rémi Tremblay step into his cubicle. The lieutenant put down a sports bag.

"You're deep in concentration, Émile."

"That look. Something's on your mind I don't want to hear."

Seated, his posture erect as usual, Tremblay did a quick, nervous scratch of his pointy chin, as though he dreaded this conversation. "We need to talk. A story's circulating that you gave up LaPierre and Beaubien to the press."

Cinq-Mars rubbed the back of his neck. "Rémi, first off, ask yourself who's doing the circulating."

"The thing has a life of its own. I'm thinking the same way myself." This was one of his favorite moments, talking to a colleague about his conduct. He'd rather do that than sit on a perp any day. "Émile, you were down there. Busting the place was your idea. Files we took out

153

of that garage contain a photocopy of cop names—only the copy. It wouldn't surprise me if the original ended up on your desk. From your desk to the newspaper."

"You have nothing to go on here." Cinq-Mars stabbed his desk with his left middle finger.

Wearily, Tremblay sighed. He moistened his lips. "At the garage you photocopied a document and kept the original. I talked to the cops on duty. You were the only officer who helped himself. We went through that same file, and retrieved the only document that was a copy. It contains a list of seventeen names, Émile, including two mentioned in the article, who also happen to be the same two who reamed you out last Friday."

"The names mentioned were involved in the raid on the garage," Cinq-Mars protested, gathering force. "That's the writer's point. Which brings up a few questions. Such as LaPierre's conduct, and why Beaubien chose to muddle in."

"You've revealed yourself, Émile. You're on the side of that English writer."

"He raised certain issues, that's all I'm saying."

"I'm up against a different issue."

"What's that?" Cinq-Mars asked quietly. He decided that no cop in the department paid as close attention to grooming as did Rémi Tremblay. His hair was carefully blown dry, and he probably made a trip to a stylist for a trim once a week. He shaved his jaw so closely that the skin was milky, waxy smooth.

"Who's next?"

"What do you mean?" Cinq-Mars asked him.

"I wasn't born at noon on Sunday. You wanted this project and Beaubien butted in. Now he's under suspension. For him, paid leave. You've been sparring with André. Suddenly, he's on the mat, down for a mandatory eight-count. He doesn't have the same leverage as his boss—the union will have to petition for his pay." Tremblay picked infinitesimal specks off the fine crease of his trousers. "Now what? If I become op leader, do I wash up onshore?"

"Rémi—"

"You're playing a dangerous game. Wish I knew the rules of combat."

Cinq-Mars tried to laugh him off. "The law of the jungle, Rémi. Every man for himself."

"That's about the size of it. I'm going to direct this operation."

"I would expect nothing less," Cinq-Mars told him. "You have my support."

"Do I? Then tell me, what will it take to keep you happy? What do you need?"

Émile Cinq-Mars leaned back in his swivel chair to observe his fellow officer. For years they'd held the same rank, moving up together, although from the outset Tremblay had been the more astute political insider. When the time came for only one to advance, Tremblay had been the logical choice.

"How's your internal investigation going?" Cinq-Mars inquired. "What do we know about the computer leaks?"

The lieutenant lightly scratched his chin again, which tipped Cinq-Mars off that the man had again grown anxious. "The investigation is ongoing. A few signs are pointing to a clerk in data entry—she was one of André's flirtations. I'm not saying the two things are connected."

"That's why you're not reaming me out about André, even though you think I gave him up."

"I'm not saying he's dirty. Not yet. If he is, I don't know if it goes under the skin."

"Not yet."

"Maybe never."

"You asked what would make me happy."

"Will I regret it?"

"I'll do what you ask me to do. Just don't tell me what I *can't* do."

The two men looked hard at each other and neither broke off. "Just stay inside the legal bounds. What are you after, Émile?"

"The bad guys," Cinq-Mars divulged. "Just like always. Like in the old days."

Rémi Tremblay sighed heavily. He stood, turned, and twisted half around again. "You have a nose for the bad guys, Émile. I respect that. I hope you also know who your friends are."

Julia Murdick crossed Park Avenue to walk along the eastern slope of the mountain to McGill University. The avenue was wide here, eight lanes, and as usual in Montreal, if drivers were given any room they dispensed with speed limits. North of the mountain Park narrowed to four lanes that ran past miles of ethnic shops and restaurants. South of the mountain, Park narrowed again, with commuters veering west along the mountainside to choose a street for the steep descent into downtown, or they carried on into the student ghetto. The avenue took its name from this short trek across the mountain park.

The ancient volcanic hill veered upward in a graceful white incline while the avenue she walked, near the base, rose as well, swelling to a modest rise before swerving downward to the city's core. Julia loved Mount Royal Park, which, she discovered, had been designed by Frederick Law Olmsted, who counted New York's Central Park as another of his achievements. During the warm, late summer months, she had walked the old horse-riding trails and climbed the steeper rock pitches, idled through the cemeteries, checking out the names and dates on tombstones and crypts, looking for signs, for no particular reason, of plagues. As did so many others, she walked the mountain at night, cutting through the woods after an evening class, sensing safety in numbers. Part of the pleasure, though, had to do with the component of risk. Back then, the mountain had conveyed a different mood. Who else lurked among those shadows? She stayed fairly close to couples, keeping their pace for her own security although she was curious about them too, observant. Their kisses sometimes touched her, it seemed, as though they were moist upon the humid air. She realized at a point that she was lonely, achingly lonely, loving her new city but terrified of it, and on one of those nocturnal rambles she first encountered Selwyn Norris.

He had been waiting for her, his long legs stretching out across the path from a park bench, and as she stepped over his shoes he had commented, in a throaty voice, on the soft fall of the evening light. Norris asked, louder now as she walked away, if she had detected the mournful sunset song of the hermit thrush, rare on the mountain. She walked on, amused, wanting him to continue in that vein. But he pulled a tired line, calling out, "Don't I know you from somewhere?"

and so she spoke for the first time, crudely comparing him to an unsavory body part. He came back with, "Julia, isn't it," ending her retreat, "Murdick?"

Right off the top with the intrigue. She'd become the mule who followed his mystery carrots, lugging behind her a cart weighted with psychological baggage. At the time she'd been astonished by her willingness to be picked up. His charm was thin, but if she was going to fall on a whim the guy had to be well dressed, older was better than some gloating college boy who'd spread the story around, and he'd have to hold up his end of the conversation to cover her nerves. Selwyn Norris held up his end. She hadn't needed to speak at all. That first night she consented to entering his Infiniti, a sumptuous car, expecting a ride to his place, maybe to a downtown café if she was lucky. Instead he had driven to her apartment building, although she had never given him the address.

"I don't get it."

"My way of letting you know that I've had my eye on you."

"What, you're some sort of stalker?"

"Who will never take advantage. Sleep tight, Snoop. Don't let the bugs bite. From now on, accept no rides from stray men."

Yeah, right, she thought these months later. *Unless they happen to be Hell's Angels. In that case, jump right in.*

She hadn't had to give him her phone number. He already had that too.

Why did he call me Snoop? And—why did I like it when he called me Snoop? As though, she thought, Selwyn Norris had renamed her on their first meeting, and subsequently re-created her to suit the christening.

Near the crest of the rise an underground pedestrian walkway traversed eight lanes of traffic. Proper lighting and mirrors to peer around the corners failed to assure Julia that the tunnel was safe for women, and she avoided the route always. A female student emerged on her side, another skipped down into the tunnel as she approached, and she was idly questioning their judgment when a car skidded to a stop along Park Avenue. Two burly men in winter coats struggled out on the same side. The doors were slammed hard and the vehicle carried on, earning blares from drivers. Julia cast the men a look. They qualified. Large, beer-bellied, bearded, scruffy, long-haired. If not for the season she could picture them astride Harleys. If someday bikers really did come for her, would she get the spruced up bunch that Norris kept telling her about, or warmed-over scruff like these? Picking up her pace she passed them before they ascended the grade to the sidewalk.

Immediately she was aware that they were bearing down on her, or was this nonsensical panic, nerves? Julia breathed deeply and stopped short, turned to face them, to stare down her fright. Pedestrians were afoot, automobile traffic was steady, she was out in the open, logic decreed that she was safe. Neither man looked at her, and they walked at a fast clip as if they had a destination in mind. She turned to carry on again and took four strides before the men were closer and she panicked again and turned again and this time the man in the beaver coat opened it as though to expose himself and she caught her breath and looked, expecting a penis stiff in the chill and there, tucked in the belt of his jeans slung low under his belly, hung a limp pistol. She looked up at him and the man was ugly and splotchy-skinned and his teary eyes were small and he said, without moving his lips, "Be cool, bitch, or I'll shoot your ass." Confident that she had seen his weapon, that she had studied it a second time, that she was scared half numb, he closed his beaver coat. "Come on," he commanded.

"Get off me."

Each man had clutched an elbow. They had timed their intercept with the entrance to the tunnel and led her and partially lifted her in that direction.

"What do you want?" she demanded, her voice faint, unconvincing. Her feet scarcely touched the steps down into the tunnel, and the moment they were inside one man held her against a wall and covered her mouth and he was saying quietly, "Bitch, don't move. Don't say nothin'." She was terrified then, frightened that this might be random, that they had not come for her, that this had nothing to do with the Hell's Angels. She was in danger of hyperventilating and the man holding her continued to talk and he spoke slowly and this wasn't a rape she began to believe and calmed down enough that the man removed his hand from her mouth. She shot a glance through the tunnel. No one was coming, but the young woman who had preceded them remained inside, walking away. She had that option. To yell for help. To hope that help might arrive before real damage could be inflicted.

The man with the beaver coat took out his gun and Julia panicked again and the other man covered her mouth again and the man with the gun spoke with a softness and a calm that scared her. "We won't hurt you, nothin' like that. Don't get scared. Some buddies of mine wanna meet up with you, we're providin' your limo service, that's all, like you're some kind of movie star." His English was firm and the accent faint, but he was French, which improved her odds that he was from the Angels.

She nodded that she understood. She could not speak.

"You gonna do what I say, bitch. Be on the safe side. We're takin' care of you. You gotta understand that."

She nodded to indicate that she was listening.

"I'm gonna point my pistol at your eyeball. You look up the barrel. Look right up it. The whole time you're looking up it, you listen to me, bitch. You don't interrupt. You don't miss a word I'm sayin' because I won't repeat myself."

The man had not asked for her consent this time and he raised the gun above her head and she had to look up to stare into the black hole of the barrel and she stared at it and told herself that she would not go berserk here, she had expected intimidation, and she understood that she was supposed to imagine her death here and the bullet approach and the spatter of her brains against the wall but saw instead the cold metal and Julia was speculating on the color, not silver, not gray, not gunmetal, and she felt a calmness then, a peacefulness, and she believed that she would be all right, that she would neither wail nor rant.

"You will walk with us. You won't run off, you won't scream, you won't talk. You'll do what you are told. Behave like everything's normal here because that's how it is. Everything's like normal."

He took the gun out of her face then and hooked it in his belt again and wrapped himself in the beaver coat and she could breathe properly once more, almost.

"Let's go," the other man commanded in French. He also spoke quietly but in a snarly tone. They walked on through the tunnel, Julia between her escorts, the sounds of their heels echoing in the narrow enclosure. She looked at their boots making all that noise. She couldn't feel her own feet or sense her steps, her knees failed to work, something was wrong with her, it wasn't peacefulness that had overtaken her, something else, she was in a state unknown to her. Both men, she noticed—and that was all that she knew for certain, all that occupied her consciousness—wore motorcycle boots.

Out of the tunnel Julia stood on the sidewalk between the two men, the sun in her eyes. They were waiting for someone to arrive. "Stay cool," the one who spoke English warned her. Duluth Avenue cut through the lower section of the park. Suddenly a van turned off Park Avenue and braked and the side door slid open and she was bundled into the vehicle. She fell upon the brown shag carpet on the floor. No seats, no windows in the back, and she rolled as the vehicle sped on and gripped fistfuls of shag to support herself. A man clutched her ankles, moving them out of his way. She lay partially on her side and the man with the pistol in his belt crouched over her and she feared being beat up or raped or killed, and he said, "Take that pack off."

Julia managed to get to her knees to slip the backpack from her shoulders. The movement, the activity, helped restore her. She'd been in shock and she was coming back to herself now and she was trembling and vaguely nauseous. The van stank of randy cat. The man with the pistol searched through her sack and she was glad that Norris had taken infinite precautions.

Each of her books carried the name of Heather Bantry. A couple had been purchased brand-new in order to inscribe her name. In one he'd crossed out the identities of previous owners, including that of Julia Murdick, and added Heather Bantry's. For two others he had merely ripped out the page inscribed with her real name and had her sign again as Heather. The biker went through her wallet. How Norris had been able to do so she did not know, but he had provided her with a social insurance number, a health insurance card, a student ID with photo, an Ontario driver's license, a credit card, the works, all in the name of Heather Bantry. She was glad now that he had not trusted her to go through her apartment alone. He'd explained that the Angels

160

wouldn't explore her place with careful attention, that they'd restrict themselves to a primitive ransack. That was their style. They were probably inside right now. Norris had found several bits of evidence linking her to the name of Julia Murdick, including a postcard magnetized to the refrigerator door. If the name of Julia Murdick came up, she was to refer to her as a previous roommate who had moved out. If the fact that she had a one-bedroom apartment, with one bed, was ever raised, she'd reluctantly confess that Julia Murdick had been her lover. "They'll like that. It'll make sense if they think you're an outsider. It'll explain why you're not down at the latest dance. It'll explain anybody who might phone for you, the real you. It'll explain a lot." Having riffled through her possessions, her abductor did her the courtesy of replacing everything.

"College girl," he mumbled.

"I hope you are who I think you are," Julia responded, pleased to finally find a voice. She quavered, the sound was faint, which was okay. Norris had forewarned that she might become frightened. He had instructed her to use fear to her advantage. *Better to be frightened than not. You're less suspicious if you're scared. The Angels like to be scary. You'll offend them if you don't show fear. Allow your natural fear to shine through along with your natural feistiness.*

Julia made herself as comfortable as she could in the rear of the van. No one stopped her from doing otherwise, but they indicated that she had to face the back, not the front windows. They drove on, and she rehearsed her position and prepared herself for the interrogation ahead.

Be who you are. There is one safe course—be Heather Bantry, and know what you want.

Okay, Selwyn. Gotcha.

Along the way the van stopped and both men in the rear jumped out. They were replaced by a man and a woman and the door slid shut violently and they drove on again. She had not anticipated the gender mix. The woman wore a black leather jacket and jeans and boots, her hair shorn around the ears. She seemed malnourished, pale, weak. Slender and sullen, the moll did not look at her and did not move toward her until the man who had boarded the van signaled that it was time to do so.

When she spoke her accent was heavy, the words tentative and slurred. "Me, I search you."

Julia switched immediately to French. "Go ahead."

The protocol lifted her spirits. They had not allowed any of the men to rub her down or touch her breasts or squeeze her buttocks in a hunt for weapons or a wire. They had obliged her by getting a woman for the job. The biker's moll was thorough, looking and probing and running her hands over Julia's body so that she did not know whether to giggle or kick her off. She yelped once, and even the driver looked at her. Julia apologized. After that the search went quickly.

The van pulled over again and the woman got out and the man with the pistol and his companion got back inside. They drove on, four of them in the rear now, and Julia could not help but believe that she had passed an important initiation. Her body tingled all over as if she'd been sleeping on grass.

The driver lit up a cigarette and the others moved forward and helped themselves from his pack and Julia was offered one but she declined. The van filled with their smoke and her eyes watered and she promised herself to have a word with Norris. This was one hazard he had neglected to mention.

"I don't suppose we could declare this a smoke-free zone for as long as I'm in here," she said. Her captors scowled at her. "Just checking."

Saying something had felt good, her courage and natural lippiness returned. If these men were going to buy her incarnation as Heather Bantry, she'd have to sell them on a persona, a wit, a gaminess as though she was wild and irreverent and sassy while also being smart and controlled, cultivated and middle-class. She told herself these things and realized that she already lived the part—Selwyn Norris had chosen wisely. That thought prompted her first cynical doubt. She was sitting in the back of a smoky, cat-stink van with gang members, suffering the notion that Norris had solicited her not because he thought that she could play a role but because she suited his requirements for a certain type. She felt lonely then, duped. Had his attentions been not personal but calculating? Wasn't he concerned for her, didn't he marvel, wasn't he enchanted? *He could be so infuriating!* He had forewarned that she'd come to doubt him, that she had to hold fast, she had to stick to who she was, Heather Bantry, and what she wanted, rehabilitation for her father, that any other course was treacherous. *All right!* she shouted within her head to alleviate her own anxieties, *I'm Heather Bantry. I'm Heather Bantry. I'm on my own now. No one's around to help me. Are you satisfied, Selwyn? I'm Heather Bantry!*

She slumped lower in the van to elude the thicker tiers of smoke and in doing so saw, on occasion, the tops of duplexes and apartment buildings and patches of sky through the front windshield. The sky seemed promising, lustrous, as though of another world and her view from inside a prison. Julia concentrated on the sky and tried to catch bits of shadow and from those calculate the angle of the sun and the direction in which they were traveling.

The driver only stopped in a hurry, never gradually, and repeatedly Julia was thrown forward and the vehicle wiggled on loose snow. The man with the gun, who was probably along, she guessed, for his command of English, told her to face the back. "Look out the window once more I'll shoot your butt."

They stopped. One rider stepped out, two others climbed in. One was Max Gitteridge.

He made himself reasonably comfortable against the back of the passenger seat. "We meet again."

Julia asked, "Can I face the front now?"

"Face forward," Gitteridge allowed. "I was reading about your father like you said. I've done my research. He had a breakdown."

"That's right," she told him.

"I don't want to offend you, but I'm interested—is he whacked out or what?" Gitteridge was speaking English.

She tried to sit up as he did, with her back against the rear door. "He's not whacked out. He's good. But it's important how he gets treated. Dad's delicate. Put him in the back of a van, make him stare down the barrel of a gun—I'm not saying anybody here would do that—if something like that happened to him, yeah, he'd go funny again."

"What happens when he goes funny?" the other new arrival asked her. He was wearing a cashmere overcoat, which he unbuttoned in the cramped quarters, revealing a sharp beige suit. She decided he was one of those snappily dressed bikers Norris had told her about. In all, he wore four rings on his fingers. His black hair was combed straight back and greased down. She figured him to be around thirty, not much older than that, and he had scaly skin. His eyes were penetrating, steady, dark.

"Sometimes he takes a ride on the Metro."

"So?"

"Trouble is, he won't get off. He'll stay on the Metro, going around and around until somebody kicks him off. Sometimes when he's sick he'll sit in his chair and if you ask him to do something he'll get all excited and prepare himself. Then he'll stand up, cross the room, and go sit in another chair. If you coax him again he'll get all excited again, like the first time never happened, and go sit in another chair. If you left him alone, he'd just sit in the first chair and never move. My dad gets into a loop where he can't turn off the switch. He cycles. It's like he goes around in circles in outer space."

"So he's wacko, that's what you're saying," Gitteridge surmised.

"We're supposed to take care of this guy?" the other man wanted to know. He was studying her with a hard gaze. His clothes were the finest she'd ever seen on a man, but he looked alien to her, whacked-out or something.

The operation might depend on the issue he had raised. Selwyn Norris had drummed the matter into her head. She had to portray Carl Bantry as a flipped-out banker, one too loony to be accepted back into his profession, yet he had to be manageable, a man whose knowledge and talents remained sufficiently intact to benefit the financial prowess of any organization.

She had to be strong here, defiant. "My father is *not* a charity case," she told him, and she matched his glare. She matched it and she reveled in her tone and the sinew of her conviction. "*I* am not a charity case. My father is talented. He's capable. He can work as well as anybody, and when it comes to banking, when it comes to international finance and currencies, he's one of the best. I know because in the old days some of the world's biggest companies came to him for advice. *Countries* came to him. He knows his stuff and his illness hasn't diminished that one bit. Okay, so he's fragile. I have to take

164

care of him. You can't pressure him or bully him. He loses his mar-
bles then. But the goddamn banks screwed him and they won't hire
him back, they won't admit to making a mistake. But if somebody
needs a financial expert, if somebody needs to move money around,
or if somebody needs to know how to work money on an international level, they couldn't do better than to hire my old man."

"But he's a nutcase, Heather," Gitteridge reminded her. "So who's
going to hire him?"

She could not pretend to be a tough girl here, not in this company.
She was a banker's daughter negotiating for better terms from the
world in which she found herself. "Someday my father will be hired by
people who don't care that he's lived in a tunnel. They'll see he's a
financial expert who rose through the ranks way quicker than most. My
father will be hired by someone who appreciates that he doesn't have
options in life, so he'll be loyal to anybody who gives him a chance."

"No matter who?" the man in the high-gloss beige suit asked her.
He had acne scars around the rim of his jaw. Although the hands in
his lap looked like they'd been given a manicure recently, he had
hood features, a generic hardness, a menace.

"No matter who."

The two men up front shared a glance. They responded favorably
to the way she talked. She didn't lead them into conversations they
had no desire to indulge, didn't ask them to compromise a thing. *A
good start*, Julia thought, *to any relationship*.

"Let's say somebody hires him," Gitteridge put forward. "What
happens if he goes nutso?"

"I'll be around. I'll see to my father's needs. Keep him on top of
things. I'll protect him from anything he can't handle. In the first
place, he's not nearly as sick as he used to be. He's almost cured.
What's past is past. It'll be my job to keep him content in his environment. I can pull him out of his cycles. I have that effect. If he does
flip, a little delay and I'll have him back on track. No big deal."

"Let's go see your old man," Gitteridge proposed.

"Hang on," Julia declared. "Not so fast."

"You've got a problem with that?"

"Sure do. We haven't worked anything out. I'm not going to

introduce you to my father until we understand each other."

Gitteridge smiled. She didn't like his smile. He was a handsome man otherwise, but the lowlife in him showed when he smiled, as though the gesture was unnatural. "That's not exactly how it's going to work, Miss Bantry. You are going to introduce us to your father—now—and that's that."

"No way."

"I'm not going to argue the point."

"Neither am I. I know where he lives, you don't. My father is stable, he's okay, but he might flip if a bunch of rowdies barge in on him. Tell me if you want to hire him first. Make an offer. If the terms are acceptable to my dad, I'll make the introductions."

Gitteridge issued that bony, pinched sneer again. "You know, Miss Bantry, if I was a lawyer for the Hell's Angels or the Mafia—which is a fantasy, but if I was—I'd be pretty much dumb to get involved in my clients' dirty work. If I was such a person and I found myself in a situation where dirty work seemed the only answer, I'd ask the driver to stop the van at the next intersection. I'd get out. You wouldn't. Now, do I get out at the next corner, or what?" He raised his hand as though to signal.

"Yeah, yeah, you win. I'll take you to see my dad. But don't hurt him. He can't suffer duress."

"What's that?" the man in beige asked.

"Don't upset him," Julia explained.

Gitteridge said, "Miss Bantry, I'm a lawyer. I'm not a goon. I have been asked to visit a potential client, and I will do so. After the visit, we'll talk."

"I have your word my father won't be harmed?"

"I don't give my word to you on anything. But we are going to meet your father and that's that. Now, tell me where he lives."

Julia realized then that they weren't moving, nor were they stopped at a light or stuck in traffic. She gave up the address. Gitteridge slid the side door open, bent low, and stepped out. "See you there," he told her. The biker in the dandy clothes followed him out.

The van spun away from the curb and Julia Murdick hung on.

Julia stepped inside the shabby apartment block, heading for the buzzers, when the man in the cashmere coat and fancy suit restrained her, demanding, "Which one?"

Coded signals would not be permitted.

He rang the buzzer at length, and inwardly she smiled. She couldn't have signaled their arrival in a more deliberate fashion.

The bell rang back and they entered through a second set of doors.

"Which way?" Gitteridge asked.

"Top floor."

"After you."

Four of them followed her up. Gitteridge and the other guy in a suit maintained her pace with ease. The two big bikers who had abducted her were back, and they found the ascent difficult.

She was rattled by nerves as she gained the top floor. *Please, please be in character. Please please please. Lordy, I'll be wearing concrete pumps.*

"Which door?" Gitteridge demanded.

She led the men there. The sleazeball in the suit rapped his knuckles against the wood. She wanted to touch his lapels, feel the material.

They waited, and heard a shuffling motion before a peep of a voice inquired, "Who is it?"

"Daddy, it's me," Julia chirped. Her temples throbbed, she was parched, but she had found her voice and it had sounded true and confident.

The chain lock was detached before the dead bolt was unfastened. The hood in the fine threads stepped to the door with the demeanor of a man about to charge through, and one of the panting fat boys joined him.

"Remember," Julia warned, "be gentle. He's fragile."

The door opened and Heather Bantry's daffy, brilliant, frail father stood before them in a ratty housecoat and pajamas three sizes too long. Unshaven, his hair disheveled, the Banker appeared passive, almost comatose. He smiled at Julia and at the men with the same insipid grin. "Been up since the crack, waiting for the morning trains," he said dully. "Would you like a cup of tea?"

"We'd love some, Daddy."

"Better come inside."

"Where's he going?" the well-dressed gangster asked as the Banker did a quick turn and headed down the hall to his kitchen.

"To make the tea."

Gitteridge held out his hat. She looked at it. The rough-looking bikers were visiting rooms, checking the windows. Julia decided to accept the hat. She took their coats as well and hung them up beside her own. The two fat guys remained dressed as they were because they weren't staying. They returned to the corridor, presumably to guard the doors, inside and out, and Julia was glad to be rid of their smell and menace.

She and Gitteridge and the tough guy walked down the hall, their steps echoing in the narrow enclosure. In the kitchen the man in fancy dress lit a cigarette. "I don't drink tea," he announced.

"Nice cup of tea," the Banker stipulated. He was tousled and quaint, old womanish in his mannerisms and given to sudden, slight, involuntary twitches. He was shorter than the coed claiming to be his daughter. A square scar shone below his right eye. "What can be finer in the middle of the day? The trick," he declared, "is to warm the pot first."

"Everybody knows that, Daddy." Julia expressed the impatience of a child for parental babble.

"The secret's out, is it? Well well. What can I say?"

The daffy financial whiz busied himself with teacups and saucers and boiling water. He had scarcely acknowledged the presence of the men, and when he turned and wiped his hands on his housecoat he grinned at them in that flat, strange way and offered a hand. "Who're your friends, dear? Professors from the university?"

Reluctantly, Gitteridge shook the Banker's hand. "Mr. Bantry," Gitteridge said. "I've been reading about you. It's nice to see you're out of the tunnel."

"These are businessmen, Daddy. They're interested in your services."

"What can I say? I'm not at my best. If she told me you were coming, I would have dressed. Put on a suit. With tie. But I don't have one or the other. I would have prepared a pot of tea."

"Do we have four cups, Daddy?"

"*Four* cups? Yes. Four cups. Four."

"I don't want no tea," the suit said.

"Oh, dear," the Banker fretted.

"Don't upset him."

"All I said was—"

"What's your name?" Carl Bantry asked. *Good,* Julia was thinking. *Get information. I keep forgetting.*

"This is Jean-Guy," Gitteridge mentioned.

The hoodlum wandered off into a corner, where he used his index finger to draw circles around his right temple, and Gitteridge gave him a nod. They had made it obvious that the Banker was daffy. Now they had to convince their guests that he was also savvy.

"Daddy, these gentlemen are interested in offering you a job. They're looking for someone with banking experience. Someone with expertise in international finance."

"Sounds like me!" Bantry whooped.

"You'd be perfect for the job."

"You understand," Gitteridge cut in, "we'll be the judge of that."

"That's the problem," Bantry argued, and his voice sounded serious, direct. "Now! Who takes milk and who takes sugar?"

"We're wasting our time with this guy," Jean-Guy murmured. "He's nutso."

Julia pleaded to give him a chance, unaware that Gitteridge was prepared to do exactly that. "What do you mean, sir? What's the problem?"

Musing, Bantry patted his light down of whiskers a moment. Julia prayed he understood that this was his audition, that there was no time for further nonsense. The men were halfway out the door, and she doubted that patience was a virtue with them.

"A cup of tea," Bantry chanted quietly. He studied the floor. Julia wanted to scream. "A cup of tea. A cup of tea in the wintertime. Tea. I was up at the crack. Waiting for the morning trains."

Suddenly she understood. Julia stepped forward and gently cradled her make-believe father in her arms and touched his forehead lightly. "Daddy?" she said very softly. He had created an opportunity for her to demonstrate her worth.

The men watched.

"Tea," Bantry said. "Yes."

"Daddy, you told this man that it would be a problem if he judged your ability at international finance. Why did you say that?"

He surfaced from the particular rhythm of mind that had trapped him. "Balderdash!" he shouted, so forcefully that his words threw Julia off. Suddenly she was standing to one side. "I know the ropes. I have the contacts. I know the economies of scale, the deceptions of arbitrage, the finesse necessary to negotiate currencies and to traffic in cash. I know how to harvest money and invest it, and move it, and who will judge me? Who will judge my worth?" He looked straight at Gitteridge to answer his own question. "A dolt who probably thinks buying an automobile is a good investment."

Bantry continued to stare down the lawyer, and Gitteridge glared back, attentive to any signal of madness. Bantry held his gaze, and Gitteridge was obliged to speak. "My associates, my clients, have certain financial concerns and needs."

"Yes yes," Bantry said.

"They are particular and sensitive."

"Of course."

"We would like to ascertain if you can be of service to us."

"Sir, you are welcome and I would say entitled to one freebie."

Julia had to rescue the whistling kettle from the stove. In his current frame of mind Carl Bantry had forgotten entirely about the tea.

"Excuse me?"

"Give me a problem. I shall provide you with a solution."

Gitteridge gestured with his hands. "That's a difficult proposition on such short notice—"

"Hypothetical, of course."

"Well—"

"Sir, let's have it."

Gitteridge flashed a grin and moved off to one side. "All right. Let me think. Let us suppose, hypothetically, that a client possessed, say, ten million dollars, and, hypothetically, this client was unwilling to declare how the money had been acquired. Not to say that the money was garnered through anything but legitimate means, but let's say that that particular client would rather keep the information to himself. In what country should these funds be deposited, if a short-term deposit is what the client has in mind? Would you suggest the Bahamas, the Cayman Islands, or Switzerland?"

"None of the above."

"Say again? Then where?"

"Ha! You see, you posed the wrong question, sir. Now you are asking for a second freebie. All right, this is your lucky day. I shall be generous. Poland."

The lawyer stared at the man who, despite his attire, now looked the essence of forthright determination. "Poland?"

"Now I suppose you expect me to explain myself."

"That would be interesting."

"Where ten million dollars can be deposited is of no consequence. Hire Bozo the Clown and he will set your client up with a secret numbered account. How to get the money to any of the places you mentioned is a surmountable problem, but a nuisance nonetheless. Usually it has to be carried in a sack. A million in twenties weighs five hundred and fifty pounds. A problem. Set up an offshore company with a Polish name and establish a bank account, run the funds through a series of blind accounts for numbered companies, each one receiving a modest sum—say, half a million over a couple of months, then collapse those accounts after the money has been harvested by the Polish account, then wire it—wire it—to Poland to assist with a development project there. While you're at it, invest in Polish enterprises to a minor degree. You will lose a little, or you'll gain a little. It is of no consequence. Pull out and no one's the wiser, the money now has a country of origin, no bank is suspicious of extraordinary sums coming out of the Eastern Bloc, and that money is now not only hidden and accounted for but also freshly scented, crisp, clean, impeccable, what the criminals call laundered. Of course there are complications, sir! But do not expect me to yield all my secrets. You have had enough freebies for one day."

A silence consumed the room, with all eyes but Julia's intent on Carl Bantry. She surveyed Gitteridge's reaction. He showed nothing, although his silence suggested respect. "How safe would the money be?" he asked at last.

"If your client is primarily interested in safety, may I suggest the Royal Bank of Canada? Term deposits? If your client is interested in limited risk to capital with the benefit of exceptional periodic gains that are bound to offset the occasional downside, tell him to invest the money wherever I happen to be employed."

"Daddy," Julia said quietly, "tea?" She held up his cup to him.

"A cup of tea," Bantry said, suddenly subdued and lethargic again. "A cup of tea. On a winter's day, a cup of tea." He addressed the cup he was holding in his hand without drinking from it. "Why'd I get up so early?"

"Daddy," Julia encouraged him. "Drink."

He sipped his tea, neglecting to serve his guests, and Bantry never glanced up as Julia ushered the visitors to the front room.

"If you want him, my father will discuss a contract with you himself. We'll need up-front money to get him dressed properly and groomed and all that. He can set up an office right here, but we'll need phones and extra lines, a computer, a modem, a fax, a printer, yada yada yada. He won't keep paper records, you can see for yourself that he'll never make a reliable witness, so you have nothing to fear on that side of things."

Jean-Guy interrupted her. "Who says anybody needs this guy?"

"You do, by being here. And by sending down your lawyer." Their performance had gone so well. She hoped that her exultation, her joy, didn't show too much.

"We'll be in touch, Miss Bantry," Gitteridge told her. He had opened the closet that contained his topcoat. "We have your number."

"Great."

The men collected their outerwear and stepped through to the corridor. With a mere nod, Julia closed the door on their visit and promptly skipped down the hall to the kitchen to celebrate. She was virtually running by the time she spun through the door, reaching out to grab the doorframe to slow herself down. In the kitchen, the Banker held an index finger firmly to his lips. His eyes conveyed a fierce demand for caution. Julia was hushed before she spoke. Then he nodded for her to come forward. She leaned way over to gaze at the spot he indicated, and saw what she took to be a listening device wedged beneath the rim of old countertop.

The Bantrys straightened up, and the daughter gave the father a rugged hug. "I think they're going to hire you, Daddy. You did good, Pops. I knew you could do it! If they have any brains at all they'll hire you."

"That would be nice, dear. Would you like a cup of tea?"

"Yes, Daddy. Yes! I'd love a cup of tea!"

9

North of the mountain, in the affluent, largely French-speaking neighborhood of Outremont, Émile Cinq-Mars waited with Bill Mathers in an unmarked car six doors up from Walter Kaplonski's. The house stood high off the curb, narrow, semidetached, approached by a steep double tier of concrete stairs. Although the building required a general sprucing up, trim paint especially, the three-story elegance of fieldstone and brick, leaded glass and time-darkened mahogany clearly marked a rich man's abode.

"Nice digs," Mathers mentioned.

"Crime pays." Today they spoke English, as though adopting the language of their prey.

"Keeps me employed," Mathers concurred.

Cinq-Mars had made it clear that he alone would choose the timing for the bust and had positioned a uniform and Detective Alain Déguire, André LaPierre's orphaned partner, around the corner in a blue-and-white. Mathers scrunched down in the front seat and took a chance on thinking aloud. "His kids are in school. His wife's taken a drive—to meet a lover if she has half a brain. We know he's inside. We know he's alone. I say there's no time like the present."

"Where's his lawyer?"

"What difference does it make? Kaplonski will clam up and call him. After he talks to him he'll go real quiet."

"He can try," Cinq-Mars demurred. "It's not so easy to say nothing."

The sun on the windshield warmed them.

The cellular phone rang, and Cinq-Mars retrieved it and uttered his own name and no further word. He powered off and smiled at Mathers. "Golly gee, Bill," he said, with mock surprise. "Kaplonski's lawyer just went into court. Gitteridge has a trial—judge and jury. He could be incommunicado for hours."

Chuckling, Mathers shook his head and sat up straight. "Émile, we can't talk to Kaplonski. He lawyered up. You know that."

The argument evoked little more than a shrug from Cinq-Mars as he called on the two-way for Déguire to come around. He and Mathers clambered out and strolled down the block, taking their time.

"Seems to me we picked him up on suspicion of car theft and possession of stolen property," Cinq-Mars mentioned. "That's my recollection. Now I'm arresting him for murder. Different story. He never lawyered up for that."

"You're splitting legal hairs."

"Too bad for him his lawyer's in court. Gitteridge could've guided us through the hairsplitting, given us a few pointers. Unless you're offering to be his counsel?"

"Émile, he won't talk to us."

"At the station? Never. Kaplonski values his life too much. But HQ's a distance—who knows?—we might get to chat along the way. A little human discourse, Bill—it's rumored to be good for the soul." Cinq-Mars stood at the foot of the stairs, gazing up. Yard space was precious and sloped. Children, sliding on their fannies, had plowed troughs through the snow on the lawn down to the bare sidewalk.

"Straight on, Émile? Murder won't stick to this dope. Accessory, maybe. Material witness, good chance. Homicide? Never."

"I doubt he did it myself—but does Kaplonski need to hear that from me? Follow my lead, Bill."

"Once in a blue moon, it'd be nice to know what's going on ahead of time."

Cinq-Mars cracked a wide grin. "Simple as pie, William. LaPierre gave this man a gentle rubdown and a manicure, trimmed his hair. I don't plan to sprinkle him with talc. I'd prefer to see him itch. I want Kaplonski to feel an insatiable urge to scratch himself."

The squad car braked at the foot of the stairs to Kaplonski's place, driving a front tire onto the sidewalk, narrowly missing a hydrant. Déguire and the uniform jumped out, and the four men leisurely climbed the first set of stairs in the morning light with the rhythmic flash of the car's rooftop cherries reflecting off the brick. Déguire looked peeved. His partner's archrival had selected him for this duty, and he looked worried about that, his heavy forehead sinking lower over his eyes. He seemed lost in troubling thoughts. At the initial landing Cinq-Mars signaled him and the uniform to circle around through the snow to the rear as he and Mathers carried on.

"So why's Déguire here?" Mathers asked quietly.

"No special reason."

"You expect me to believe that?"

Cinq-Mars gestured with his chin. "It's a test."

"You test us all, don't you, Émile?"

Cinq-Mars removed his revolver from its holster, pocketed it, and with his free hand rang the bell. "East of Aldgate," he stipulated.

"East, west, north, south—makes no difference to me. Who knows what you're talking about?" Mathers knew enough to take out his gun and snap the detective shield off his belt.

"I've been meaning to ask you, Bill. Anything on for the weekend, you and your wife?"

Mathers shrugged. "No plans, no. Why?"

"Come out to the farm Saturday night for dinner."

The interior door opened. "You're kidding me."

"Why would I? Our wives can meet. I'd like to show you the place."

Wrapped in a bathrobe and smoking a cigar, Kaplonski answered the door. He snatched the cigar out of his mouth to more effectively sneer. "What's this?"

Cinq-Mars ignored him and pressed his partner instead. "What do you say?"

Mathers sputtered, "Sure. Thanks. Look forward to it."

"Sevenish all right?"

"Fine." He couldn't fathom his partner's timing.

Turning, Cinq-Mars inquired, "Mr. Walter Kaplonski?"

"Dickface, you know me."

"Police."

"I know who you are, Asswipe. You got a warrant?"

"Sir, I am placing you under arrest for the murder of Hagop Artinian."

Kaplonski was shaken. He visibly paled.

"May we come in?"

"What for?"

"So you can change your attire, sir," Cinq-Mars pointed out. "Otherwise, we're obliged to take you downtown dressed as you are."

Kaplonski checked his bare legs under the housecoat. "You limp dick," he seethed, looking up again.

"Thanks for the invitation." The two policemen followed Kaplonski into the house, and before they'd gone ten feet he had his hands on a telephone. Cinq-Mars stepped up and clicked the line dead. "No calls," he informed him.

"Hey! I got a right to talk to my shyster!"

"Sure you do." Cinq-Mars took the receiver from his hand. "Your guy's in court, I'm just saving your breath. Make the call downtown."

"Pig Pussy," Kaplonski muttered.

"Put out that cigar, sir."

A blustering Kaplonski suggested to Cinq-Mars that he preferred carnal relations with swine and goats.

"True, but you'll do in a pinch. Now put out that damn cigar."

Kaplonski shot a look at Mathers, who merely grinned, his pistol in evidence at his side. Taking one last contemptuous drag, the prisoner crushed the cigar in an ashtray on the telephone table and glared back at Cinq-Mars.

"Don't even think about it."

Despite the prohibition against the pastime, Kaplonski seemed wrenched by thought. He considered his options carefully, and chose to blow his smoke away from the detective's face.

"Where're your clothes at?" Mathers asked.

"Pig Puke."

"Where?" Sticking an edge of his gold shield up the man's nostril, he lifted.

"Upstairs."

"So let's go there."

On the way up, Mathers wiped his shield on the shoulder of the man's robe.

In an untidy lump, Okinder Boyle lay on his bed, the knock reverberating in his head like pistol shot. "Who's there? What the hell do you want?"

A young woman's voice replied, "I'm looking for Mr. Boyle."

"Can it wait? I'm not up."

"It's important. I need to speak to Mr. Boyle."

The act of swinging both feet off the mattress onto the floor started his head spinning like a wonky gyroscope. Groggily, Boyle hoisted himself upright and tied the sash of his dressing gown. "Are you a bailiff, a rent collector, a bill collector, or an employee of any government branch whatsoever?"

The pause intrigued him, as though the visitor needed a moment to reflect on her choices. "None of the above. It's urgent that I speak with you, Mr. Boyle. Whether it's right this instant or in five minutes won't make or break me."

Urgent. The need to talk had been moved from *important* to *urgent.* Boyle dressed hurriedly and did his best to tame his morning hair. About to admit his guest, he decided that brushing his teeth and gargling with mouthwash might be prudent, if for no other reason than to oil his Sahara tongue, the result of a wretched hangover.

He checked his look in the mirror again. *Life is hard and then you die.* He was the author of his own calamities. He just couldn't come up with enough good daytime stories. The interesting people came out at night, and he hung out where they did. He knew why so many of the older reporters down at the paper were drunks. He was determined not to follow that path, believed he didn't have whatever it took to be a real drunk. But he was a night owl, and loved that part of his life. Finally prepped, he flung open the door.

Before him stood an attractive, severe young woman, fair, trim, with delicate features, a large mouth, and smallish green eyes.

"Mr. Boyle? Okinder Boyle, the reporter?"

"Half in spirit, barely in body." He held on to the door for support.
"My name is Heather Bantry."

"Who?"

"You wrote a story on my father, Carl Bantry. You said he lived in a tunnel."

"I wrote a story on Carl Bantry—"

"The Banker, you called him."

"That's right."

"I saw your piece a couple of weeks ago. A friend sent it to me. My mother and I live in Seattle now, but I go to school in Vancouver. Since I was coming to Montreal with my debating team, I waited until now to get in touch."

"I know who Heather Bantry is," Okinder Boyle told her.

"Excuse me?"

"I've met her. I've met Carl Bantry's daughter."

"Mr. Boyle, I'm sorry. I'm Heather Bantry. We've never met. I'm Carl Bantry's only daughter."

He suffered her accusatory gaze a few moments longer and found that the uncompromising nature of her regard obliged him to be civil. "Come in for a minute," he invited. "We'll talk about this."

The night had been feral, a fact that was evident as he viewed the detritus of his room. Boyle scooped underwear off the chair he offered his guest, raked clothes from the desk and floor. Part of the mess he bundled up on his bed, and the rest he chose to ignore.

"Mr. Boyle—"

"Call me Okinder."

"—my father does not live in a tunnel."

"Few fathers do. However—"

"Why would you write such unadulterated crap?"

Time to sit up and take notice. The young woman's rage was becoming apparent, her ability to fight equally obvious.

"I have to tell you, I had a rough night. You've taken me by surprise." He grinned in his best sheepish, teddy-bearish manner.

"I don't give a shit." She sat pin straight in his office swivel chair. "You've caused my family embarrassment, pain. We've suffered on account of my father's illness, then you come along and exploit it. You embellish what he's gone through. You take a grain of truth and out of that concoct ridiculous lies. Who the hell do you think you are?"

"Wait a minute. Hang on here. I don't know who *you* are—"

"My name is Heather Bantry—"

"I *know* Heather Bantry. I have *met* Heather Bantry!"

In a trice the young woman was on her feet fishing through the pockets of her coat. She pulled out a billfold and scattered several pieces of identification, many with photos, across his desk.

"There is only one Heather Bantry who has a father Carl Bantry who was a banker in this city and that's me. I don't know what you're trying to pull, but let me tell you something, if there's any way I can sue, I'll do it. You can't get away with this crap."

She was up and headed for the door with her bits of identification in hand.

"Stop," he urged.

She opened the door.

"Heather!" he called. She paused, turned, a hand on the door. "Hey, look, I'm confused. If I made a mistake, it was out of ignorance. Please. Stay a minute. Help me understand this." The young woman wavered for only a moment longer before venturing back into the room.

She returned her identification to her wallet. "Why did you write that my father lives in a tunnel?"

Her razor anger impressed him. He could detect no guile in her. "Tell me something, Miss Bantry—Heather—how did you find me?"

"I asked for you at *The Gazette*. They said you're not usually in the office, and they don't hand out home addresses. I asked around but nobody could help. Then I found out you used to work for another paper, that alternative rag thing? They had no qualms about passing out your address."

A better story, Boyle considered, than the one provided by the first Heather Bantry, who had merely followed her nose and been guided by strangers on the street. "Heather, why do you think your father doesn't live in a tunnel? When's the last time you saw him?"

"Yesterday. I come up from time to time. He lives outside the city, way out. He's in a nursing home on the south shore."

He sat back to absorb the news. He needed help here, guidance. If the woman proved to be who she claimed to be, he might have been responsible for a serious breach of conduct. He'd have to own up, and the potential for public embarrassment was extreme, but a different concern contested for attention. If he'd been duped, the question arose, why? Who had claimed to be the tunnel-dwelling Carl Bantry? And why? Who was the woman who had posed as Heather?

"The nursing home—who pays the bills?"

"His old bank. The one he worked for."

A contradiction, as the bankers he'd consulted to verify the original story hadn't mentioned supporting Carl Bantry. Still, neither her conviction nor her identity could be readily dismissed.

"Miss Bantry, do you have a number where you can be reached?"

She did. She was staying in nearby Westmount. The original Heather Bantry had made an excuse not to offer an address. She had promised to keep in touch but had not.

"If what you say is true, I've been duped. I'll apologize in print, submit to a stoning, jump from the Jacques Cartier Bridge, whatever you decide. Suing me, well—look around you. Not much future there. Suing the paper means fighting lawyers who win those suits every day. If you can give me a little time, a little latitude, I'll get back to you."

Mollified, the young woman scratched out her address in Vancouver, her numbers there and locally, and provided the address where her father could be found. After she said good-bye, Okinder Boyle turned back to the cramped, dreary confines of his room. "What the hell?" he whispered aloud, and shut the door. "What the *hell*?"

Kaplonski came down the staircase dressed, cuffed, and grim. The uniform held his arm above the elbow, Mathers followed, and as he reached the bottom step Cinq-Mars sauntered over to the front door, hands in his pockets, jiggling his change. He peered around the lace curtains. A few curious Nellies were milling about outside, attracted by the squad car. Turning back, the policeman regarded his captive.

"Pig Fart," the man said.

"Mind your manners," Cinq-Mars warned him. "You're better off if I'm in a good mood. I mightn't do you any favors otherwise."

"What?"

"People are on the street. I bet your neighbors assume you're respectable. Probably young girls baby-sit your children. Now we can lead you down those stairs in cuffs, Mr. Kaplonski, wreck their illusions about you, or we can protect your public image."

Kaplonski looked at Cinq-Mars. "Like how?"

"Déguire," Cinq-Mars directed. "Take your uniform and drive the car away. Straight down. Two blocks. No siren, no flash. Wait for us there."

Déguire hesitated, his bulky forehead knotted in a frown, then he left with the uniform.

"We'll give that crowd time to clear," Cinq-Mars explained. "I'll take the cuffs off before we leave. I'm guessing you're too fat to run."

"What do you want from me?" Walter Kaplonski asked, his anxiety apparent.

"Peace and quiet. I have a headache. Don't give me a hard time."

The prisoner still could not believe his good fortune and remained stiff at attention, his cuffed hands in front of him. Mathers checked the window after a few minutes and nodded to indicate that the bystanders had dispersed. Cinq-Mars unsnapped the cuffs, and Kaplonski rubbed his wrists.

"We're going out now," Cinq-Mars prepped him. "Put your coat on. Check the pockets, Bill."

Mathers went out first, looking in both directions. After giving the all clear he walked on ahead, and Cinq-Mars opened the door for his captive. They strode down the steps and along the sidewalk in tandem toward his car.

"How come you do this for me?"

"That's my business, Mr. K. I'll tell you something. I don't think you have a clue what I'm really doing for you."

They kept walking.

"What you mean by that?" Kaplonski asked.

"I have a job to do. Today it's my job to arrest you. But when your friends find out the charge, I wouldn't take a bet on your chances."

They reached the car and Kaplonski crawled into the rear.

Cinq-Mars went around and surprised the other two by climbing into the back as well. Mathers, flummoxed, wedged himself behind the wheel and turned the engine over. "Straight down?" he asked. "Pick up Déguire?" Enough oddities had accompanied the arrest that he was not about to assume anything, least of all the obvious.

"Call him on the radio first. Tell him to fall in behind when we pass by. Don't let any cars between us. Tell him to keep an eye out. Tell Déguire to write down everything he sees. If Kaplonski gets his head bashed in, tell him to write down the details."

"What?" Kaplonski asked.

"If he gets bumped, tell Déguire to write everything he sees. It's for your own protection," Cinq-Mars assured his passenger. "I'm not betting on your chances to live a long life. If you go down, I don't want anybody saying I had something to do with it. That's why you're not cuffed. In case you have to run."

The detective did as instructed, then started driving.

"I don't got to talk to you," the man declared.

"After I do you a big favor?"

"We didn't make no deal."

"Hey, you got me there, Kaplonski. At least you're not calling me Bacon Breath to my face or any of those ugly names. I guess if I'm civil to you, you'll be civil to me. Is that how it goes, sir?"

"Sure," the man said. "Why not?"

Cinq-Mars smiled in such a way that his prisoner was curious.

"What're you grinning at?"

Cinq-Mars continued to smile. Déguire's car tagged in behind them, and they stopped at a red light. This was the start of the commercial district for the area, with a bank and a pharmacy on two of the corners, and competing small grocers on the others. "Go west, Bill. Take the expressway. I was just wondering," Cinq-Mars said.

"About what?"

"About what you know."

Kaplonski smiled himself. "I don't know nothing."

"Maybe you'd like to rephrase that, sir. Think about it."

Kaplonski qualified his statement. "I don't know nothing special, is all."

"How come you rate a Mafia lawyer?"

He rocked his head from side to side. His breathing was raspy, as though anxiety aggravated his windpipe. "He's my lawyer, is all."

"You're a big shot?"

Kaplonski shook his head. "I'm not talking to you."

"Course not," Cinq-Mars agreed. "Nobody says you are. Hey, Bill, do you hear Kaplonski talking to me?"

"Sorry." Mathers tapped one ear. "I'm stone deaf."

"You see? You're not talking to me and I believe you. Let's hope your friends believe you. That's another matter, but I'm here and I believe you."

Kaplonski maintained silence, but he was looking at Cinq-Mars, hoping the policeman would continue.

"What do you say me and you reach an agreement?"

The prisoner shook his head. "I can't do that."

"You don't know what it is yet. It's simple. I'll talk, you'll listen. How's that? You don't want to talk to me? Fine. Don't. All I ask is that you pay attention all the way down to HQ. Do you have a problem with that?"

He shook his head and put his fist to his mouth to cough.

"Good. This is how it looks to me. You're running a stolen car ring. No, wait. It's not my intention to offend you, sir. Stolen cars were discovered on your property. How's that? That's fair. I haven't accused you of anything, just restated the facts as they're known. Okay, so, in the blink of an eye, you bring in a Hell's Angels slash Mafia lawyer to plead your case. Now, why's that? I have to ask myself. How come the Mafia cares about you? You're not Italian. You're not one of the Angels, are you? I don't see any tattoos. You don't ride a Harley. Maybe you contribute to their enterprises, you're a cog in their machine, who knows? What I do know is that the company you're keeping interests me more than you do."

Kaplonski turned back to face him, but Cinq-Mars had looked away.

"Now, they'll defend you on grand theft, auto, charges. They might even back you up on the murder rap. The question sticks, though—how come? You must know something. They're not protecting your ass because they find it cute. They don't give a royal fart if you go down for murder one. Better your ass than one of their own. What is it you know, sir? Why are you so important?"

Kaplonski had returned his attention to life on the street.

"I just hope you don't know too much," Cinq-Mars added.

Kaplonski did not respond, so Mathers asked the question on his behalf. "What do you mean, Émile?"

"It's like this, Bill. If he knows too much they'll blow him away. That's what they do to anybody who gets too close to their business. If I were you, Kaplonski, I'd be worried they're defending you to make sure you stay dumb. Show any inclination to strike a deal—*kaboom!* If I were you, I'd get somebody else to start your car in the morning."

"What you're saying is," Mathers interjected, "the Mafia and the Angels will look like they're on his side, they'll put up their lawyer for show, to keep them informed, but they won't really stick their necks out for him. In fact, they might be happy to see Mr. Kaplonski's chopped off."

"You might have something there, Bill. You might be on the right track. All along he'll mind his manners, talk to no one, thinking he's got this power lawyer, then—*whoosh!*—the rug's pulled out. In a wink he's down on all fours doing serious time with a bat sticking out his rump."

"You guys," Kaplonski said.

"What?"

"You think you break me? Don't make me laughing. You're Boy Scouts to me. You're Girl Guides. You should be wearing the dresses."

"Now, that's what I don't understand, Mr. Kaplonski. That's what I don't get. What's with the cracks? Here we are, enjoying a pleasant conversation, going over the facts as we see them, and you start with the cute remarks. Sir, I think you have a serious problem. I think you're incorrigible. You know," the detective ruminated, "it's too bad about cops going down to your garage and getting their cars fixed for free."

"That's how it goes. I don't see nothing wrong with it. Me, I like to help out public servants."

Cinq-Mars chuckled along. "Hear that, Bill? The man's a philan-thropist. He's a generous soul. I was surprised LaPierre had his name on that list, weren't you, Bill? That disappointed me. I always thought he was a good cop. I guess when he interrogated you, sir, he remem-bered favors you'd done him in the past. I guess your lawyer was counting on that."

Kaplonski stared straight ahead.

Cinq-Mars jerked his head toward the rear. "Guy in the car behind us was his partner. Do you think he's dirty too?"

Kaplonski wasn't interested.

"Yeah, I don't know either. I'm pretty sure he talks to LaPierre on a regular basis. Who knows what he tells him? Does that bother you?"

"No skin off my nose."

"Mine neither. Be interesting to find out, though, don't you think? If he told the wrong people that you and me had a conversation in the backseat of a car, that we looked friendly, what do you think the wrong sort of people would think about that?"

The prisoner looked back at the squad car and then at Cinq-Mars. "What you talking? You arresting me. That's all. I didn't talk to you. I never said nothing."

"That would be true except for a couple of things there, Walter. You don't mind if I call you Walter, do you? You can call me Émile. You've been talking a lot to me this morning, that's pretty obvious to the guy behind us. On top of that, I've decided that you're not worth arresting."

"What?"

"It's like my partner told me earlier, I don't have enough to make a murder charge stick. Even though it was you dressed up in a Santa Claus suit—"

Kaplonski turned quickly to face him.

"—ah, you didn't know I knew that? Now you do. Even though I know for a fact that you were involved, that you rented the Santa suits, that you paid for them when you couldn't bring them back, that you went into that rooming house ahead of me, even though I know all that, I'm going to let you go."

"What's he talking?" Kaplonski asked Mathers.

"I think I've got it figured out," the detective answered.

"Sir, it's simple," Cinq-Mars explained. "Pay attention. This is important. You have to hope for three things. You have to hope that neither of the two cops behind us is dirty. What are the odds on that? And if they're clean, you have to hope they don't go blabbing around the station about what happened today, because a dirty cop would pick up the news that way. And third, whatever it is you know about the Angels, you better hope it isn't all *that* important. If it is, and they find out we had this friendly talk, well, good luck to you, Walter, because you're going to need it. Now, sir, you're free to go. Pull over, Bill."

"Wait a minute."

"Sorry, Walter. I've got places to go and people to see. Get out of my car. And, sir, let me give you fair warning. Don't call my partner Pig Puke again. I am the only one authorized to call him that. By the way, why do you think the tough guys put you on the scene in that Santa suit? Why do you think they had you rent the Santa costumes under your own name? That's all so dumb. Unbelievably dumb. Makes me think they were setting you up all along. Have you thought about that? I would if I were you. Did you think things through, Kaplonski? Or are you just a man of action? Why do you think they had you sign in with Hagop Artinian down at the docks, putting the two of you together at the time of death? You didn't know I knew that? Tell you what, give me a buzz if you come up with something interesting to say, or, who knows, if you suddenly get the feeling that you might be worth arresting. In the meantime, Walter, get the hell out."

His cutting words were uttered with a smile, and Cinq-Mars climbed out of the car with Kaplonski, arched his lower back, and yawned. He patted the freed prisoner on the shoulder and clambered into the front seat. "Go," he told Mathers in French. "Quickly."

The younger detective peeled away from the curb. Before those in the trailing squad car could comprehend that the prisoner had been granted his freedom, they followed, and dispersed only after Cinq-Mars called them on the two-way and told them to do so.

"Amazing," Mathers said.

"God bless Walter Kaplonski."

"So you think Déguire's dirty?"

"Haven't a clue," the senior detective admitted. "We'll wait and see on that."

Arriving late for the evening rendezvous, Cinq-Mars was perplexed. The restaurant was nondescript, a notch above a dive, glaringly bright and, at eleven o'clock, sparsely populated. Bottles sparkled on the mirrored bar. Domes displayed tall cheesecakes topped with a strawberry glaze, tasteless concoctions for which he had a profound weakness. As the waitress came over he ordered coffee only, patting his belly while LaPierre knowingly chuckled.

"So, André," Cinq-Mars began, although the other man had called the meeting, "how's your vacation going?"

"You're hilarious." Two thin Band-Aids covered shaving cuts over his Adam's apple, which was startlingly protuberant. He looked wan, as though his height was a liability when he was under duress and his heart had trouble pumping blood to his extremities. Cinq-Mars hated to think what would happen to LaPierre if he ever really got sick. He was no longer so thin around the middle, but his bones appeared to push through his skin. If he lost any weight he'd look skeletal.

"You should've paid for your repairs, André."

"Émile, you're such a saint. When you die we'll build a shrine in your honor as big as the Oratory. Penitents will crawl up the stairs on their knees for a glimpse of your heart." He lit a smoke.

"That's right. During pledge week students will steal it and hide it in their dorms. What else is new? You can't get away from crime, André. That's why I pay for my repairs. To give myself a break from the bad guys."

"That's not how it is," LaPierre said quietly. He had a distant gaze in his eyes, and Cinq-Mars noticed a slight quiver to his right lower eyelid, something he hadn't noticed before. They were all aging. He wondered if he developed tics of his own whenever the nights were long and his bones were exhausted.

"That's how it looks. How is it, André?"

"Émile, you sit in your chair all day. Stoolies phone you. You make arrests. The rest of us, we have to work for a living." He took a long, deep drag on his cigarette.

"I didn't always have it so good," Cinq-Mars objected.

"That's right. You used to work for your busts, like me. You were a good cop. I admired you. Know something? I'm just as good a cop as you, maybe better." When he wasn't wearing a jacket the bones of his shoulders poked through his shirt.

"You were, until your car got fixed for free."

"That makes me a dirty cop?"

Cinq-Mars raised an eyebrow, as though to suggest that he was unwilling to go that far. "A dumb one."

LaPierre rapped his knuckles on the table. "I work for my arrests. I don't sit on my ass while murderers beat down the door to beg me to arrest them. The criminals I know try to get away from me, they hide. Only you have it so lucky. Me, I work the streets. I drink in the bars, take my girlfriends to rooming houses that charge by the quarter hour. Ever been in one of those? I never made an arrest by going to mass, Émile. I live where the criminals hang out. Go to church where they do. I socialize, I dance with the brokenhearted. That's how the job gets done."

Cinq-Mars bobbed his chin, to show that he understood the merit of his colleague's stance. "That philosophy can excuse many sins, André."

"We're not in the sin business, Émile," LaPierre corrected him. His jaw was trembling now, as he forcibly held back on the passion that ignited this response. "We're in the crime business, and for me that means homicide. If I have my car fixed at a garage where killers sometimes go, that doesn't hurt my chances to catch bad guys."

"Are you telling me—"

"I'm telling you how it is."

"So you had your car fixed for free—"

"—so I could move in certain circles. So I could be seen there. So people won't think I'm a priestly cop like you. I need tips. Information. I need to bump into people who can give me tips and information."

Cinq-Mars sipped from his steaming cup. "It's a good argument, André. If I were you I'd take it before the panel. It might work there."

"I know I can't talk you onto my side, Émile. You and me are alike that way. We've heard every story. Like me, you only want the facts."

"It gets worse, André," Cinq-Mars reminded him.

LaPierre understood. "Céline, in data processing. I didn't know she was connected, Émile. You don't believe that, but I'm saying it anyway. Sure, I screwed her. I'm a man not a priest. I screwed her, and I had a good time, too. Tremblay tells me she keyed the entries, deleted stolen cars from the computer log. That was her. That wasn't me. I know nothing about it. Nothing, Émile."

"Your investigation of the Artinian case was shoddy."

"I had the flu!"

"So you say. But you didn't call in sick. You were on standby for Christmas Eve. So how sick were you?"

"*Taberhuit.* It was just coming on me. *Maudit calice.* You know how it is, Émile. You're on standby for a holiday, you figure you might get an easy night. Why should people kill each other on Christmas Eve, *tabernouche*? Better to be sick on standby, save your days off for when you're healthy. Don't tell me you've never done that. You're a saint but don't tell me you're ridiculous. I figured I'd get away with that one night, that way I'm safe for New Year's. If I phoned in sick, for sure I get booked on for New Year's, and you know what a shit ride that is. Anyway, Émile, I don't have kids. I was doing some daddy-cop a favor, *tabernac*."

When the English swore they used sexual references or bodily functions to get their rage across. If Cinq-Mars really wanted to let loose a profanity he chose English. The French swore by being sacrilegious, denigrating religious relics. So they would say the French word for *tabernacle*, and add embellishment, or the word for *chalice*, and call it bloody. Cinq-Mars figured that LaPierre was into a swearing spree because he knew how the use of religious words irked him. Unconsciously or deliberately, he was trying to cut him. "Afterward you stayed on the case. You didn't call in sick then either."

"I wanted the case, Émile! I waited for the flu to run its course, that's all. I didn't want to give this one up."

"Why not? It's just another case."

LaPierre seemed unprepared to answer. He held the heel of one hand on the table with his elbow upraised and he stared at the saltshaker. "When I saw the message on that sign, M-Five, I didn't mention it, but I thought it was connected to you. March Five. If something was going on, you know, to bring you down a notch, I wanted to be in on it. That's all."

"Gee. Thanks."

LaPierre derisively waved his hand in the air. "I'm no saint. When have I pretended? I'm a competitor, and I'm tired of being in your shadow. It didn't used to be that way."

Cinq-Mars continued to watch him, and he said nothing.

"Lately, it's not been so good. So many homicides are bombings. The Rock Machine blows up somebody from the Hell's Angels. We know it's the gangs, we know it's a settling of accounts, do we catch the perp? No. Maybe down the line an asshole turns and we find out who did what to whom, but those cases never come to trial. Half the time the shits don't live long enough. If they do, the Wolverines handle the investigation. I get a case that doesn't look gang-related, not especially, not at first, well, I want that case, Émile. I want that opportunity. I'm not going to hand it off because I got the flu."

Cinq-Mars conceded, "I can understand that, André."

"Some people think I'm sliding into retirement. Maybe I'm not as young as I used to be, but I got fire in my belly, Émile."

"My partner told me you interviewed Artinian's girlfriend. That shows you were on the job. Did you get anything out of her?"

LaPierre thought about it as he drank his coffee and smoked. In the end he acknowledged that he hadn't learned much. "She confirmed what we knew about the boy."

"Anything you can give me, André? I know you're a competitor, but it's your career on the line. If you found something in your investigation, anything, give it up now. If something good pans out, I'll go to your hearing. I'll let the panel know you helped us out."

Sergeant-Detective André LaPierre appreciated the news. He thought hard, pressing his thumbs to his temples as though luring memories of the investigation from their mental sockets. Cinq-Mars doubted that whatever he had to say was as deeply entrenched as the motion implied. "One thing," LaPierre said.

"Yes?"

"Maybe it's nothing, you know how it goes. There was an employee at the garage, his name was Jim Coates." Cinq-Mars took out his notebook, and LaPierre spelled the name for him.

"What about him?"

"He's disappeared."

"What do you mean?"

"Soon after the murder, he vanished. Left his apartment. Cut off his phone, the whole bit. As I said, it might be nothing. But you never know."

"Okay. Thanks for that. I'll let you know if he shows up. Anything else?"

LaPierre turned his cup around in circles on its saucer.

"André, you called this meeting. I don't think you've told me what you came here to say."

LaPierre granted the point. "Listen, Émile. We've been colleagues a long time. We'll be colleagues again. I'm going to beat this rap. I won't sit here and try to convince you I'm an altar boy. I went to that garage to have my old junk heaps fixed for free more than once. I took advantage for personal reasons. But me, I took advantage for professional reasons also. I can prove it, too."

"How?"

"You took a tap out of Kaplonski's office. You get a report back on that?"

"I did."

"It was old issue." The pale man seemed tired now, as though he was running low on fuel.

"How do you know?"

"Because it's mine. One of my trips for a repair job, I put it there. Slipped it under the table with contact glue. The paperwork on that tap is buried, but it goes back sixteen years. The person who requisitioned that tap was me. As far as the books are concerned, it's working a felon's house. Except the guy's been dead ten years."

Cinq-Mars sucked air and seemed to expand on his side of the booth, straightening up to look LaPierre squarely in the eye. "That's your tap? If that's your tap, I want the tapes."

"I thought you'd say that." He tried on a weary smile.

"Don't mess with me, André. I want the tapes." Cinq-Mars sucked rapid breaths.

"What are you, a homicide detective these days?"

"Hand them over."

"I'm keeping them—"

"The hell you are!" Although he kept his voice low, the fury of his tone was apparent, and Cinq-Mars lightly pounded the table. He attracted the attention of the waitress, who retrieved the coffeepot and moved their way. LaPierre waited for her to pour and move off before resuming.

"First of all, they're illegal, so I'm not going to flash them around right now. Any evidence on those tapes gets squashed. I'd rather let the information lead me, and nobody will know where the trail got started."

"That's a crock. That's *not* what we're talking about here."

"Second, I might need the originals to get myself off. They prove I was working. The department will only reinstate me if they can pitch it to the press. The tapes help me with that. Finally, it's my tap, Émile. I don't give a damn, it's my tap and therefore they're my tapes. I'm not turning them over to you."

"Are you so afraid I'll make an arrest? What's on the tapes, André?"

"I'm reviewing them."

"You're on suspension! You have nothing else to do! How long can it take?"

LaPierre smiled, seemingly enjoying himself. "You know how it is. You go over things in the background, the meanings of conversations, shit like that. It takes time, Émile."

"What the hell are you up to?"

LaPierre smirked. "Maybe that's the question of the hour. Some of us've been asking it about you."

"What's that supposed to mean?"

"You turned me over to the papers. I know it. I can't trust you with the tapes when they're all I got left."

"What's on them?"

"Not much. I don't have some big operation. A few guys go over to Garage Sampson, and I happen to follow them there. Hit the record button. Sometimes I swing by for the hell of it. Turn on and see what comes up. Mostly I get nothing. It's not like I recorded twenty-four hours a day."

"Mostly?"

"Oh, I got something, Émile. I got something good." From the inner breast pocket of his overcoat, André LaPierre teased Cinq-Mars by slowly pulling out an audiotape.

"You bastard."

"You don't have many friends left, Émile. If I knew what you were up to, maybe I could trust you with everything. Until that day comes, the original tape stays with me."

Cinq-Mars was adamant. He stuck a forefinger in front of him. "Give me one good reason. One. So far you've given me cause to advocate for your suspension."

LaPierre slid the copy across to Cinq-Mars. He made a move to leave the table. "Maybe there's some little thing on the whole tape that might incriminate me, Émile. Who knows? You don't seem to under-stand how real cops work. You've forgotten. You've been high and mighty for so long you're afraid to muddy your knees. Me, I've been down on my knees so long I've forgotten how to walk. I got scabs. My knees prove I'm a cop. Besides—*ha!*—who trusts who anymore, Émile?"

"What are you giving me?"

"A couple of days before Christmas Eve. I wasn't feeling so hot. I was home so I turned on my bugs. Most were quiet. I got conversa-tion on one, so I hit the button and went to bed. I was sick, Émile. The flu was coming on but I didn't know it yet. Just felt weak. A few days later I find out my murder victim works for Garage Sampson. Then I think, wasn't that the place I tapped?"

Cinq-Mars put his hands to his head in genuine astonishment. He was not sure whether he was elated or furious. "You kept it to your-self until now?"

"My gold mine, Émile. You got your own. This one's mine. Listen up, I'm going to beat my suspension. I'm coming back. I'm studying the tape. If I get more than this—and don't kid yourself, this is hot—maybe we can trade."

"Withholding evidence, André," Cinq-Mars warned him.

"Ill-gotten, Émile. Which means it's not evidence at all."

"André— Come on, man, this isn't about trading."

"You don't think so?" He stood and adjusted his coat and scarf. "I want my career back. Help me out with that. I'm giving you Kaplonski. I didn't go after him in interrogation because he's not Number One. The tape will tell you that. I played Kaplonski soft because that's my strategy. He's the only guy we've got who can lead us to Number One. Listen to the tape. It'll give you Kaplonski for conspiracy to commit and accessory to. That should be good for you. All I'm asking is that you don't block me off. Help me back in, then maybe you'll get to hear the whole tape."

"So there is something on the rest of it."

"Good night, Émile. Have a safe drive home. Sometime, you'll have to tell me why you live so far out in the country. I'm surprised you even come to town these days, everything must be so snowy white and pristine out there."

Cinq-Mars remained in his seat, watching LaPierre go. The tape in hand, the existence of more—the rendezvous had been worthwhile. He would have to wait a bit to hear what was on the tape, but it sounded as though LaPierre was giving him Kaplonski. Perhaps he had already heard about his charade with Kaplonski that morning. In any case, he had to wonder what had prompted this change of heart. As well, a clue that he thought he'd culled from the meeting made him despair. He would have to check it out.

The time had come to drive home and listen to the tape along the way. Cinq-Mars hesitated. LaPierre's gift might break the case, although he sensed that it could be as much a trap as a revelation. He was deeply suspicious of André LaPierre, and if he was right, his colleague was mired in trouble more deeply than penny graft. He was grateful, though, for one thing. Anxious to hear the tape, he didn't have time for a mountainous slice of cheesecake. For this and for the present, he'd have to remember to thank LaPierre later.

10

Cinq-Mars woke his partner after midnight, calling to let him know
that he was on his way. Halfway home, having listened to the tape
for the first time, he popped a pulse light on the dash, U-turned at a
risky crossing, and headed back to the city and Mathers's apartment,
foot to the floorboards.

With tea and scones, the men huddled around the tapedeck in
Mathers's living room. The furnishings were a combination of new
things bought on sale and older pieces handed down from parents or
culled from a flea market. Mathers was using bricks and boards for
his bookshelves, but his stereo equipment was first-rate. The television
rested on a crate, but it was a good TV. Cinq-Mars suspected that
the sofa and chairs represented input from Mathers's wife, Donna.
They'd splurged a little, and he hadn't attributed a taste in vibrant
colors to his partner.

"Why are you working at this hour?" Mathers asked.

"LaPierre called. He set up a meeting." Cinq-Mars was less brittle
with Mathers in his home. The younger man suddenly seemed
strange to him. Perhaps the casual clothes he wore, jeans and no tie,
accounted for the difference. He tried sitting in a chair but found that
he was more comfortable joining his host on the floor.

Mathers snapped the tape into the player.

The voices were audible and surprisingly distinct given the poor quality of the sound. The policemen easily distinguished Kaplonski's gruff
baritone. The second voice was unknown to them, foreign, an accent

embedded in most, but not all, of the speaker's words. Cinq-Mars wanted to pin the voice on the Russian captain, but he was doubtful.

The tape began with the sound of someone pacing. Heavy breathing occupied the aural space close to the mike, and little peripheral
noise was detected above the audio's gentle static. Cinq-Mars concluded that the conversation had taken place at night, or on a weekend, after the staff had vacated the premises. The first word uttered
on the tape belonged to the stranger. He'd said, *"Artinian."*

"That is correct, sir," Kaplonski was saying. *"Hagop Artinian."* He was
close to the microphone. Agitation caused his breath to be audible.
"Sorry about this crap."

*"No. That is good. Knowing problem is better than not knowing. We must find
a way that is good,"* the unknown voice replied.

"The voice, Russian?" Cinq-Mars asked. He stopped the tape a
second.

"Definitely," Mathers attested. "Remember when you were grilling
Captain Yakushev and you chided him for his change of accent in
the middle of the conversation—?"

"So?"

"When this guy said the boy's name the first time—Artinian—the
accent slipped. It sounded almost British."

"Who goes around talking in fake accents?"

"Somebody who'd be tough to bust on a witness stand if all you
had was an audiotape."

Cinq-Mars clicked the play button again.

Kaplonski was agreeing with the other man, although it became
apparent that he didn't realize what the stranger had in mind.

"Hear that?" Cinq-Mars provided opinion throughout. "Kaplonski goes along with this guy no matter what he says. Never once
does he contradict him. The man has authority. Kaplonski's scared
shitless of him."

"We must find out one thing—the boy, he speaks to who?"

"Yes," Kaplonski concurs.

They heard the stranger suggest bringing the boy down to the ship.
"We talk to him private. There he say to us what he has say to us."

Kaplonski raised the issue of security down at the docks.

"That is one problem. We have one more, yes? You say boy is maybe to be suspicious?"

"He's looking worried to me."

"I am thinking about this."

A scheme is hatched that's complex, intricate. The boy will be informed that he is needed to move drugs. He will be given a time and place to meet with Kaplonski and others designated by the man with the Russian voice. From there, they'll travel down to the ship. Everything will appear routine. Once on the boat, things will change for the boy. He'll be outfitted in a Santa costume and taken to a cabin where an electric wire will be clipped to his genitals. In that room, in the dark, he will surrender the name of his contact. *"This not difficult."*

"Yes," Kaplonski agrees. He sounds glum.

"We eliminate Artinian," the man says. *"This not difficult. We do this soon."* Carried off the ship, the dead boy will be deposited in the car.

"Hear that? The accent changed," Mathers noted.

"Security at the entrance to the docks," Kaplonski points out, *"might check the trunk. They do that, the creeps. More'n half the time when I leave they check my trunk."* He lacks the courage to speak against the enterprise, instead he sorts through obstacles, trying to change things. Inadvertently, he assists the operation.

The stranger explains that the boy will be wearing the Santa Claus outfit and sitting up in the backseat. *"He eliminated no blood bleeding."*

"No guns or knives," Cinq-Mars interpreted the phrase to mean. "Strangulation. Notice, the meat hook isn't mentioned."

"No one will be suspicious of Santa on Christmas Eve," Mathers noted.

"In car need big bag, empty boxes inside. In car we hide boy behind big bag. You need that later."

"Me?" Kaplonski asks.

The dead boy will be moved to his apartment. Well before his death he'll be told that the drug rendezvous will take place there. But he'll be told that it will happen at a time much later than the hour he actually returned to the apartment as a corpse.

"I don't know how you get him upstairs with nobody seeing," Kaplonski says, still trying to abort the plan with logic.

"That is right. You don't know how."

"He doesn't mention cleaning the place out," Cinq-Mars said.

"You, Kaplonski, you go inside. Dress also, you, like Santa Claus. Go to room where is dead punk, his place, where he lives. We take keys from him. You leave by back way. Maybe police question to you, you say them nothing. Prove yourself to me this way. If need it, we get to you good lawyer. Not to worry, Mr. Kaplonski, my good friend, police have nothing on you, nothing."

"No, only that the dead Santa worked for the man leaving his place—by the back way—in a similar Santa suit and without his presents," Cinq-Mars scoffed. "Explain that one, Dogface."

"They wanted Kaplonski busted?"

"They didn't figure only two of us would show. They thought I'd follow procedures. They put Kaplonski at the scene of the crime with his dead employee. There's more about that later, and the guy's halfway convincing. But they definitely didn't care if Kaplonski walked or not."

"Why I have to be there? I don't understand. I will do it, don't get me wrong, but this is not my usual line of work. Why I have to go there? Just phone the cops."

"Good question," Mathers noted.

"Listen to the answer," Cinq-Mars pointed out. "It's better."

"You had you a spy in your house. You give to him job, you made to him friend, yes? You give to him information, identity. To spy you give a way in to see the work of our brothers. Contact, you gave him. You responsible are, Mr. Kaplonski. Now, today, you expose to me him. This is good but much damage is done. Friend, you do what we ask you. We want to know, are you man of goodwill? We want to be knowing this. Are you man of goodwill, Mr. Kaplonski?"

"Yes, I am a man of goodwill."

Cinq-Mars chortled. "You idiot," he berated the tapedeck. "You don't even know when you're being sucked in."

"You go to apartment where is dead boy. We want for his contact to follow you, boy tells to him come. This way, for sure we know contact is good. This way, contact reveals himself. They wait for Santa Claus. We give them Santa Claus living, alive, outside house. Inside Santa Claus is dead. They will know why is dead. We say to them we found your spy. We deal with spies this way. This is show, Mr. Kaplonski. This is trial and judgment to them for to see."

"Listen to this, Bill. The first sign of gumption on Kaplonski's part."

"I don't know what it's like where you come from. Here the cops are different. Over here they don't like threats."

"That's telling him."

A fist, or perhaps a book, thuds heavily upon a table. *"They learn! If do not fear my threats, they fear my acts!"*

"Yes, sir," Kaplonski says, retreating fast.

"He's never called anybody 'sir' before in his life," Cinq-Mars sneered. "He's calling this killer 'sir'!"

The portion of tape that André LaPierre had chosen to surrender had reached its conclusion. Bill Mathers and Émile Cinq-Mars sat hunched over on the floor in the late night gloom of the apartment, thinking things through.

"LaPierre gave you this?" Mathers marveled. "I suppose I'm not surprised. I picked him for a cop who'd fudge the law."

"I'm in a quandary. The boy was killed, and the people who did it were willing to give us Kaplonski. That's what it sounds like to me. Trouble is, we didn't pick up Kaplonski that night because we weren't guarding the back door."

"When we did pick him up, he had a Mafia lawyer in tow."

Cinq-Mars conceded that point reluctantly. "The thing is, we never arrested him for murder. What bothers me is—are they giving us Kaplonski now? Have they found a way to do it?"

Mathers ran his hands together and fidgeted. "You're saying that if LaPierre is dirty, the Mafia or the Hell's Angels are giving us Kaplonski. They meant to do it the night Artinian got whacked, but we screwed up their plans. So they're doing it now."

"It's a possibility. What's wrong with that idea, Bill? What doesn't fit?"

The policeman took his time in answering. "We don't know what Kaplonski knows—the identity of the man on the tape. I'd like that information. If the Mafia, or the Hell's Angels, are giving us Kaplonski, they're also giving us the only man we know who also knows that guy's identity—his face, probably his name. Why do that?"

Cinq-Mars had to hoist himself into a chair or his body would seize up. He lumbered up, stretched, and coiled back down onto the sofa. "I've asked myself the question. I keep coming up with one possibility.

How and why would they risk giving us Kaplonski when he knows things about them? The only answer I get comes out the same way every time. If they give us Kaplonski for the crime, and keep their lawyer close to him so he stays content and mute, they're in a position to take Kaplonski away from us."

Mathers blew out a slight whistle of air as he caught up to his partner's thinking. "How would they take him away?"

In a single sweeping motion Émile Cinq-Mars brought his hands together, raised them, and separated them outward again. "Boom," he said quietly. "We think we have our killer. Next, we lose him in a blast. Technically, the file might remain open, but we both know it'd be a dead issue. No pun intended."

"Kill a man. Give us a likely suspect. Kill the suspect. I appreciate the logic. But bikers, they don't usually go to that much trouble, do they?"

"Different situation. The dead boy was an informant. Killing him is a lot like doing a cop. For all they know he was a cop. They'd guess we'd take a special interest. So they're covering their tracks. On top of that, it helps them out with their other problem, the one about Kaplonski and what he knows. They have more than one reason to do Kaplonski, what they're looking for is the most bang for their buck. Maybe they think they can use him to shake us off their shoes. Another thing, it's not the locals running the show. It could be this guy on the tape. We already know from the boy's death that we're dealing with a different mind, a trained mind. I think I know what to call him. Last September, the Angels put on a show. They were probably trying to impress someone who could do them some good. The Wolverines had a name for the man they were entertaining—the Czar. I bet you that's the guy."

On his knees, Mathers started rewinding the tape. "Do you think the boy gave up his contact?"

For the first time on this visit, Cinq-Mars smiled. "He was a smart boy, Bill. Tough kid. Either that or he was coached. When tortured into giving up a name, he gave them mine."

"That's why they hung the sign. *Merry Xmas, M-Five.*"

"They were so damn proud of themselves. Hagop gave them a

believable name, probably in a believable way. It made sense to them. I'm the guy with the secret contacts, everybody knows that. They probably shit their pants when they heard my name. Hagop put an end to the torture, he saved himself more suffering. I wish I'd known him. He had courage. I'm laying odds that he kept the name of his real contact to himself."

Mathers stopped the tape and hit play, listening, then continued to rewind. He went a little further back and adjusted the volume lower. "So you're convinced LaPierre's dirty?"

"He might be filthy. Bill, when you helped Jim Coates cover himself, you did a good job, right? LaPierre's out looking for him. So far he can't locate him."

"Émile," Mathers interjected. Crouching close to the machine, he seemed quite animated. "Listen to this." He played a bit of tape and turned the volume way up until his wife, thinking of their sleeping child, slipped her head through the swinging kitchen door with a finger to her lips. Mathers rummaged for twin sets of headphones. As Cinq-Mars donned a pair, Mathers quelled a laugh—his superior looked like a being from another planet, totally out of his element. He played the section of tape again.

They removed their headsets. "That static. Sounds like a sweeping motion."

"My thought."

"Jim Coates?"

"Possibly."

"LaPierre wouldn't pick it up. He's not that good a detective."

Mathers hesitated a moment to allow the compliment to register. "He has more tape. From it he could've found out that Coates was there, that he knows the stranger. Or, if LaPierre's dirty, he could've been told that Coates knows."

Cinq-Mars stood and stretched high. "LaPierre bothers me. I know I'm capable of misjudging a man."

"Then judge the evidence. Nothing else."

"It works either way. He could be holding on to more tape to protect himself. He could have kept this tape secret to promote himself, to make a dramatic arrest. He could be giving us Kaplonski because that's the right thing to do. He could be going after Jim Coates because Coates is the one who knows the identity of the killer. All that is perfectly plausible."

"But you don't buy it?"

Cinq-Mars looked at Mathers. "I haven't made up my mind. He could be keeping the tapes secret because they incriminate his friends. But why did he record them in that case? He could be revealing this tape now because the Angels are using him to give us Kaplonski. If he's a dirty cop, he could be after Jim Coates to get rid of him for what he knows. If he's just being a lousy self-interested cop, he could be after Jim Coates to find out what he knows and use that information to solve the case himself."

Mathers stretched out on his side on the floor, propped up on one elbow. "There's two things in André's favor. He made the tape. Maybe that's an assumption, but it's reasonable. I don't see why he would do that if he was one of them. And the tape gives us the voice of the killer. It's a changing voice, but we wouldn't know he existed otherwise."

"There could be a reason for the tape we don't know about," Cinq-Mars suggested. "Like the Angels were checking up on Kaplonski and LaPierre does their audio work."

"A stretch," Mathers said.

"Granted. The Czar, if he's the killer, could be long gone by now. He might be back in Russia for all we know. They could be sending us on a helluva wild goose chase."

"So where do we go from here?" Reaching behind himself, Mathers punched a button and rewound the tape entirely while Cinq-Mars paced the small room, stepping around children's toys.

"With respect to LaPierre, we watch and wait. With respect to Jim Coates, we find him, we talk. With respect to Walter Kaplonski, we arrest him."

"Now?"

"Something tells me the sooner the better. I'm not betting heavily on his life expectancy. Now I wish I hadn't shaken him down."

"How come?"

"If somebody hits him, I won't know if it's because Déguire thought we talked a deal in the car and he reported back to André, or because André gave him up to fit their scam. Maybe they're giving him up just because I nearly brought him in. I won't be a single step ahead."

Mathers snapped the tape out of the deck and struggled to his feet. He handed it over to his partner, then helped him on with his overcoat. "Let's hope the bad guys weren't thinking that way, too. If letting us have the tape was a way to give us different options, we're up against some pretty smart cookies."

Cinq-Mars shook his head. "This feels murky. Like we won't find bottom. I hate to think what's down there, how deep it goes."

Mathers tried to kid him out of the blues. "This from the detective who doesn't believe in conspiracies? You disappoint me, Émile. You sound like you're ready to change horses."

He was surprised by the look Cinq-Mars gave him. The depth of the man's weariness struck him. He seemed older, more frail in this light than he had previously noticed. "You're a good detective, partner. I'm surprised you haven't figured that one out by now."

"Maybe I have," Mathers confessed.

"Yes? What's your thought?"

Mathers breathed deeply before he began. He did feel nervous about this. "I think your public disdain for conspiracies is a deception, a strategy. I think you're after conspirators, organized crime. I think you only pretend otherwise."

Cinq-Mars conveyed in his weary gaze a measure of respect. "That's part of it, Bill. I'm impressed. Truth is, I'm terrified by the alliances being cobbled together these days."

Mathers gathered that he was being admitted more deeply into his partner's thinking than had previously been allowed. "Émile, can I meet you downstairs? Give me a sec to change and speak to Donna."

"No need to explain. Take your time. I've been there."

After midnight, along the street known as the Main, Julia Murdick entered four bars, hunting around in each. The street was officially called Boulevard St. Laurent (St. Lawrence, in English, after the river) and was the demarcation zone for the east and west sides of the city. From here, addresses on the crossing streets started at number one, ascending in either direction. All streets that crossed the Main had to be designated as being either east or west. The eastern side of Montreal was predominantly French, the western side largely English, while the Main itself attracted a coalition of ethnic communities. Historically a crime center, rough and ready, the Main was a spawning ground for petty crooks, turf where criminal gangs had to cut their teeth before extending territories. It continued to attract prostitutes and deadbeats, addicts and artists, beggars and thieves, ambitious losers of every description, and the in crowd piled in behind them. At night its bars and eateries pulsed with the rhythms of a new generation.

In the fourth bar she entered Julia caught Norris's eye, took a turn around the space, and checked the bathrooms to confirm that she didn't know anybody there. She joined Norris at his table. Although it was nearly one in the morning the place was packed. Montreal was a nightlife city, the Main a nightlife street.

"Hey, Snoop, how're you doing?"

"It's good to get out."

"Like old times."

"Old times, Sel? Old times ended ten days ago. That doesn't constitute *old* times. Ten days ago is *recent* times."

He raised a bottle of wine to fill her glass. "Seems like a dog's age to me."

"Tell me about it."

Norris laughed. "I have a better idea. *You* tell *me* about it."

She ran her right hand through her hair. "Another working session? No time to relax? You invited me out under false pretenses, Sel."

"Give me a break, Jul. Doesn't this beat E-mail?"

"Oh, throw me a bone, Selwyn! Ask me to roll over, sit up, and beg."

He laughed at her consternation. "Talk to me. Go ahead. What interests you, Jul?"

The bastard had a point. The world had changed. Smiling, she conceded. "You go first. How's the state of the world, Selwyn? Are presidents calling for your advice?"

"Just the one." She didn't know how to interpret that grin.

"What's your—" She hesitated, trying to frame a simple question in such a way that he might answer. He had resisted, gently at times, and categorically on other occasions, any attempt to prick his guise. "What do you do, Selwyn? Besides what you do. I mean, publicly. If somebody came to your door and said, 'We're the government, what do you do for a living, sir?' How would you respond?"

"I wouldn't."

"But they're insisting."

"I'd ask to see my lawyer."

"Seriously."

"Seriously? I'd shut the door in the government's face."

"Come on, you know what I'm trying to say. What do you tell the world you do? There must be times when you have to say something."

"Depends who's asking. Hey, do you want a bite? Take a break from student fare." The waitress had come by to take their food order. Julia did a quick scan and chose the Waldorf, Norris opted for a *croque monsieur*.

"Selwyn?" she asked after the waitress departed.

"Different people receive various responses. Which can be problematic, of course. Officially, I'm affiliated with the Public Affairs Section of the Consulate-General here in Montreal."

"The consulate-general?"

"That's right."

"Of what country?"

"Good, Snoop. Never let anyone answer in a vague way. Stay on him until he owns up."

"Bugger off, Selwyn. Answer the question."

"The United States of America."

"Ah."

Norris laughed more heartily than he had intended, enjoying the exchange. He relished the company of this attractive, cerebral young woman. "What do you mean by that?"

"By what?"

"By your *ah*."

"I'm not telling."

"You're not?"

"I'm the inquisitor here and you, Mr. Norris, the inquisitee."

"Is there such a word? Tell you what, I'll make a sportsman's bet with you. By the end of the night, I'll get more information out of you about yourself than you'll worm out of me about myself, even though you're asking the questions."

"You're on! You're getting nothing out of me! Nothing!" she taunted brightly. She was already hooked on the release of tension, the joy of being out, the pleasure of food that came from sitting down with a companion to enjoy it, the sensation that for tonight, at least, she was part of a crowd. "So. Selwyn Norris, Public Affairs. Where's that at? Sounds like a crock to me. Sounds like a handy cover-up for covert operations. Bells are going off, Mister Buddy. *Ding! Ding! Ding!* What do you really do in public affairs?"

His eyes teared as he laughed and Julia was pleased. She could not say a word, it seemed, that did not delight him. "Julia, you ask the right questions. As soon as we've concluded our current enterprise, once you've finished your education, let's think long and hard about the best prospects for your career."

"In what?"

"What would you prefer?"

"No dice, Selwyn. Answer my question and quit trying to change the subject. Who do you think you're playing with here, some amateur?"

"Salut!" Norris said, raising his glass to her. He sipped, gazed at her, turned away to study the room a moment, noticed a problem, and told Julia, "Don't look now, you've been spotted. *Don't—look.*"

All her discipline was necessary not to spin her head around.

"Who? A Hell's Angel? Is this a diversion? It won't work, pal. Not on me."

"He's coming over. Be cool, Julia. We can slide through this."

"Hello there," said a voice, not one she recognized. Julia raised her head slowly and identified the newspaper reporter, Okinder Boyle. "Heather, isn't it? Heather Bantry?"

"Yes! Mr. Boyle. Ah, hi!"

"Hi." He waved a hand in a nervous gesture, taking quick glances at both Julia and her tablemate. "I was just, you know, out, and saw you, I thought I recognized you—back then I was so sick I wasn't sure—and yeah, so, here you are. I was surprised you never called back. How's your father doing?"

"Dad! Great. Thanks. We got him out of the tunnel."

"Oh yeah?"

"He's in a much better situation now."

Selwyn Norris returned Boyle's glances with a slight smile but made no effort to introduce himself. If his student handled this properly she'd tolerate the mild awkwardness and leave the social graces up to him.

"That's good to hear. Maybe I should do a follow-up. That story aroused a lot of interest. Tell you what, give me your number, and I'll see what I can do."

Julia was aware that she was under scrutiny, that this was the first time Norris had seen her in the line of fire. "Sure. That would be great. Oh!" She ground her forehead into the heel of her palm. "What's my new number again? I never call myself." She looked at Norris. At that moment he could deny knowledge of her phone number, make one up, or deliver the correct number to the reporter. His call. She had cleverly moved the responsibility along to the more experienced partner, and her mentor was duly impressed.

"Do you have a pen?" Norris asked.

"Right here." The columnist took out a small pad and pen and waited, poised, for Norris to speak again. Seated, Norris looked across at Julia, then reached over and took her hand in his, affectionately, possessively, grinning at her consternation. He told Boyle her number and Julia noted that it was accurate.

"Okay. Thanks. Listen, I'll leave you two alone. It was great seeing you again, Heather. I'll give you a call."

"Please do. Thanks for the piece on my dad. It was great."

"Thanks. So long."

He melded into the crowd. "Interesting," Norris assayed.

"How'd I do?"

"Terrific. No wonder this operation is going well. But I knew that—you can think on your feet. Jul, you went through other bars before coming in here?"

"Yup. I did five deceptions before reaching the street. Good ones."

"He spotted you in one of the bars. Then followed you. He can't afford this place."

"It's not *that* expensive. He could have been here already."

"Boyle gets by on a frugal budget. You've seen his room."

"What do I do when he calls? Why did you give him my real number?"

Their food arrived, and Julia suddenly realized she was famished. She'd eaten at seven, but six hours had passed since then. Eating late was part of the Montreal style.

"He's up to something," Norris mused. "He wanted your phone number, that's why he came over. The thought didn't occur to him on the fly, as he tried to make out. What does he want? You? A date? A story? Something else? If he's going to nose around Carl Bantry, it's better if we control things."

"All wise and good, Selwyn, but I still want to know what you do in public affairs."

Norris laughed. "Nothing dramatic. I'm a political analyst. I'm here to study the possibilities of Quebec's secession from Canada, what the repercussions would be for the United States."

"Okay," she said quietly. "That's very convincing. Now tell me, is that what you really do and this thing with me is a sideline? Or is what we do together your main concern, and the political analysis thing your cover?"

Norris bobbed his head from side to side. "Is there a third option?"

"Is there?"

Norris leaned in closer across the table. "Listen, Jul. There's something you need to know. Commit this name to memory. Émile Cinq-Mars."

"Émile Cinq-Mars," Julia repeated aloud.

"Sergeant-Detective Émile Cinq-Mars."

She said the name back to him again.

"If anyone is onto you, for whatever reason, and they want to know your contact, and you have no choice, give them that name."

"Why him?"

"He's a famous detective. They'll believe you. He's safe because he's such an important person. The Angels can't afford to go after a cop with his profile. Already the Wolverines have been set loose, after that poor kid was blown up. Imagine what would happen if they killed a cop. Step over that line and the gloves really come off. Give up the name—Sergeant-Detective Émile Cinq-Mars—and watch your enemies leave you alone. They won't go after him."

"Or you," Julia added.

"Mentioning his name will give you instant leverage. Giving them mine won't do a thing."

"Don't be a martyr in other words."

"Don't," Norris agreed, raising the stakes of their work together, because he had never before acknowledged this level of danger, "be a martyr."

Can I trust you, Selwyn? Julia wondered as she poked a fork through her salad. *Who're you looking out for here? Me or you? Can I trust you?*

"Something's been on my mind," Norris began.

"Shoot."

"I didn't want to suggest it before. I never want to compromise your decisions. It's important that everything you do be voluntary."

"Allez vite, Sel." Like most Montrealers, she'd fallen into the habit of using phrases from one language to create an emphasis in the other. "What's up?"

"Your place is bugged, probably you're tired of always being on guard."

Julia laughed in her chaotic fashion. "Makes masturbation difficult! No way will I give those goons a performance. And, *no!* Don't you dare tell me that my propriety is suspicious! I will not masturbate for their listening devices. When I'm really horny I run the tub."

"Stop, stop, Julia, you're ranting. I can't talk about these things with the ease of your generation."

"You're squirming!"

"I was wondering, would you consider coming home with me tonight?"

She had picked up a chunk of walnut between her fingers. "Ah— and sleep on the sofa?"

"Not what I had in mind."

She nibbled on the nut. "You mean— But. You mean it? You know about my steeplechase arch thingee and— Do you want to?"

"I want to. Very much. Forget about the arch. There's plenty of other ways for two people to enjoy each other."

"Teach them to me," she blurted out.

They were quiet a moment, looking at each other.

"Finish your salad, Jul," Norris suggested. "And your wine."

"Do I have to? Can't we just go now?"

Squad cars, fire trucks, and ambulances had preceded the detectives to Walter Kaplonski's door, lights flashing off the brick and glass of sedate neighborhood homes. A police barricade had cordoned off Kaplonski's block, and Bill Mathers displayed his badge to be admitted, although they could not travel far through the battalion of emergency vehicles. Émile Cinq-Mars parked, and the two men strolled down the rest of the way.

What they expected to find they found.

The roof of a Lincoln Town Car had been peeled back by the explosion, both the trunk and hood had lifted and crumpled, the driver's side door blown off. The remains of the car were charred and had been doused with water. Ice coated the vehicle now. From his vantage point Cinq-Mars noticed that the steering wheel was absent, either sheared off in the blast or sawed away to extricate the driver. The only question about fatalities would be the number.

"They take no prisoners" was all that Cinq-Mars said.

Mathers considered his partner's words. "Émile, they sent you a message, slung it around Hagop's neck. Doesn't that bother you?" He wrung his gloved hands, his breath billowing in the cold air. "I know it takes guts to be a cop, but sometimes, at night, when I'm looking at my kid asleep? I think about how much I want to see her grow up. I want her to have a father. These guys, like you said—man, they don't mess around."

Cinq-Mars had been watching his partner as he spoke, traveling with the words back to their origin. He recognized that bravado was a necessary component in a police officer's personality, but he had never admired the trait. He appreciated more this reasoned response

211

to danger. To be a policeman and also a father or a mother were never compatible duties. "Personally," Cinq-Mars remarked, "if they're going to blow me up, I'd rather they overdo it than not do it enough."

Mathers managed a tight smile in the cold. "How sanguine of you, Émile."

"We're practically immune, Bill, don't you know that?"

"Come again?"

They were making their way over spaghetti coils of fire hose and around clumps of neighbors who either lived nearby and had been jolted out of their beds or had penetrated the police perimeter by scaling backyard fences. Cinq-Mars appeared to be in no particular hurry to investigate the crime, and perhaps, Mathers surmised, he wished not be to seen by more than a few of his colleagues.

"The gangs only go so far. Step over a line and the wrath of the Wolverines falls upon them. Somebody killed that young boy, Daniel. A biker gang, obviously. Since then the Wolverines have been smoking them out. They've got the manpower now, they've got the budget, they're getting legislation through which will allow them to seize assets, including bunkers and clubhouses. They keep on the bikers' case day and night, they hassle their friends. But, it's all remained civilized. Pretty much. Now. Add a campaign of cop killing, or kill a celebrity cop like me, and the rules will change. The Wolverines, and us, too, we'll all become wild men for a while. Some cases will be lost in court because the evidence was wrongfully acquired, but some cases will be won, and more important, gang operations will be disrupted, sympathizers exposed. Some of the bad guys will be dead. Maybe some of us, too, but that's not the point. Before the Wolverines can get really tough like that, the bikers have to cross that line. Let the Wolverines go on a rampage for six months or so, they'll raise havoc with biker operations. Cop killing, now that's a big line crosser. But you know, if they really want to make life miserable for themselves, they'd kill a cop like me, a celebrity cop, a local hero. I have immunity, Bill. So do you, now that you're my partner. I'm not saying don't be careful. Your name is on your mailbox. I think you should take it off as soon as you get home. Start doing more of the little things to protect yourself. But this won't happen to us. You should know that."

Mathers nodded. He had not expected the response. He wanted to contradict his superior, point out that one biker gang or the other had killed a child. That was a big line crosser, too, but he understood. To combat the enemy, you always had to show that you had greater force to prevail against them, and that the only thing restraining that force was an understanding that certain things would not occur. The biker gangs were feeling the heat from killing a child. Go any further, and they'd feel a lot more.

Mathers stopped and looked up to see who Cinq-Mars was waving over, and out of the crush of people Detective Alain Déguire emerged. Cinq-Mars had assumed a position on the snowy knoll of a neighbor's lawn from where he had a good overview.

"Sergeant," Déguire greeted him. He was wearing his usual grim look, as though everything was a riddle to him, as though whatever had caused that gouge in his forehead had left him permanently confused.

"Alain, you're working long days. Who's the investigating?"

"I am."

Cinq-Mars gave him a second look, and the younger man shrugged to suggest that it was no big deal.

"We're strapped. With LaPierre suspended I had to fill in. You don't need a crystal ball to say this is a biker hit, the Wolverines will take it over. I'm just here because it's late. By morning they'll be in charge."

Cinq-Mars appreciated the man's modesty. "I need to know something from you, Alain. It's important."

"Yes, sir?"

"Did you tell anybody about my meeting with Kaplonski this morning?"

"No, sir."

"You answered very quickly," Cinq-Mars cautioned him. "I want you to think about this. It doesn't matter to me if you did or if you didn't, I just need to know the absolute truth. Did you discuss this morning with anyone?"

"I don't need to think about it," Déguire said testily. "Look, the way

213

things have been lately, I'm not talking to anybody about anything."

"Not even LaPierre?"

"What do you want from me, Sergeant?"

"The truth. Why is that such a difficult commodity these days?"

Déguire joined Cinq-Mars in surveying the confusion of flashing lights and flurry of official procedure. A bombing employed an impressive array of people.

"Me and LaPierre, we talk every day," Déguire admitted. "I talked to him this afternoon. He's my partner. I didn't give him any details. Didn't have any. I told him you picked up Kaplonski then released him."

"That's what you told him?"

"Yes, sir. When you asked if I talked to anyone, I didn't include my partner in that. Of course I talk to my partner."

"You told LaPierre we picked up Kaplonski and—what? twelve hours?—no, sixteen hours later Kaplonski is dead and you're the IO."

Déguire kicked some snow around with his boot. All three men stood with their hands in their pockets and their breath was visible in the night air.

"I'm a good cop," Déguire said quietly. "You want to come after me for some reason, go ahead. I'm a good cop."

Cinq-Mars looked at both junior detectives and shook his head, as though it was hard to ever decide. "If you want to know what I think, Alain, you're on the right track. You're on my mind. Any time a cop goes down, it's inevitable—everybody wonders about the partner."

"There's no proof against him."

"So he believes. But I'm not a judge. Tell me, you work the day shift, isn't that right? I always see you around in the day."

"I'm supposed to be days. We're strapped right now." A morgue van was trying to make its way in, led by a cop car with its cherries flashing, the lights cutting across the faces of the detectives talking on the knoll.

"So you keep telling me. Who set it up for you to work this case tonight?"

"My duty officer."

"Who is?"

"Gilles Beaubien."

"Excuse me? He's suspended."

"That was revoked this evening. The flu's taking so many guys down, he's filling in with the task list." Déguire was nodding, jutting his chin out, defensive in all his remarks.

"Really? Now what do you think about that, Bill? Did you hear? Beaubien's back, and nobody told me the good news. Alain, if you work days, how did you happen to be working the night shift on Christmas Eve, when the Artinian boy was killed?"

"Are you investigating me?" Déguire wanted to know. He looked from Cinq-Mars to Mathers and back again.

"I'm asking you a question," Cinq-Mars told him.

"I don't have to answer," the officer replied.

"No, you don't."

Déguire thought back. He worked his toe around in the snow again. His facial muscles were pulled tight with growing rage. "That was a different story," he recalled. "Me and André, we booked off. We had the best days off. Christmas Eve, Christmas Day, New Year's Eve and Day both. First time I ever had all those days. What André gets, I get, we're a team. He has the seniority."

"That's usually how it goes," Cinq-Mars noted. "How'd you get booked on?"

Déguire rocked his head a few times, then rubbed his chin on the shoulder of his coat, as though he was trying to buy time to think the question over. "That's a mystery. André called me late in the afternoon, said he'd booked us on standby, for later. I was pissed off. You got Christmas Eve off, then just like that, you don't. Probably somebody did a favor for André, that's what I figured, so he traded shifts."

Mathers was staring at his colleague wide-eyed as if he was going to pop a rib. Cinq-Mars nudged his elbow, and he shifted demeanor, as if disinterested.

"In other words, André LaPierre has the flu, but instead of staying home with the day off and taking care of himself, he books on."

Déguire considered the scenario and nodded to indicate that that was how things had been. He offered no explanation.

"Alain, if you're a good cop, you will not speak about this conversation to André LaPierre. I don't care if he is your partner. Don't give him anything from your investigation tonight except what he'll read in the morning papers. If you're not a good cop, if you're a dirty cop, then go ahead, tell him anything you want. But in that case, when you're talking to him, say hello from me."

Alain Déguire walked away ten feet and then came back. He was fuming, and when he talked his lower jaw didn't move. With his anger mounting he looked like a ram anxious to batter something. "It's you old guys, you know, who always talk about standing up for your partner."

"I'm aware of that," Cinq-Mars answered.

"I'm loyal to the guy, he's my partner. But it's you old guys who think it's a fucking marriage. I'm not fucking married to him, you know."

"All right. I'll take that under advisement."

"Fuck you."

"I'd watch your tongue there, Alain. I'd think about controlling my temper if I were you."

Déguire gave his body a shake and then his head to relieve the worst of his wrath. He aimed his index finger in the senior detective's face. "I could have been your partner and Bill could've been LaPierre's. Then you'd be busting his balls tonight and not mine."

"That's possible," Cinq-Mars conceded.

"I don't see why I have to be taking shit for that asshole."

Cinq-Mars waited for that remark to clear the air before he asked him about it. "Are you calling my good friend LaPierre an asshole, Alain? What happened to your sense of loyalty?"

This time Déguire stepped right up to Cinq-Mars, and although he was two inches shorter, the uneven snow underfoot made them level. He put his eyes inches from the senior detective's and glared at him with his full fury. Cinq-Mars was reminding himself that at all costs he had to avoid butting heads with this guy, because he'd come out hearing bells after that collision. "I am loyal as a partner," he declared, with defiance and with something else that Cinq-Mars noticed, bitterness. "I have said nothing that would hurt him. That doesn't mean that I don't think he's the biggest asshole this side of the moon."

"I'll take that under advisement as well," Cinq-Mars noted.

Déguire twisted his shoulders around and spun on his heels and twisted his shoulders again, not knowing how best to combat his fury. He shook a finger at Bill Mathers, then aimed it again at Cinq-Mars. "I don't understand," he said, and his confusion was inherent by the way he trembled. "You're a hero to us guys, you know. How come you get a squarehead for a partner? It's not right that an English guy should get what you pass on."

"We're both cops," Mathers reminded him quietly, startled that he was hearing this point of view so directly.

"You don't get it," Déguire thrust.

Sarcastically, Mathers said, "I guess not."

"I don't care that you're a squarehead," Déguire claimed.

"Not much you don't. Anyway, I'd watch who you call a square-head, Alain. Have you looked in a mirror lately?"

Déguire stood there a moment, looking off in another direction, breathing heavily. He was trying to calm down before he put his foot in his mouth again. When he finally pulled himself together, he addressed Mathers directly. "He's a hero to us French guys. That's all I'm saying. You get him as partner. You're English but you get him. Meanwhile, I draw André LaPierre for the past six months and the guy's shit, you know? He lives like shit." He shook his head a little more. "I'm sorry," he said, glancing quickly at Cinq-Mars. "Forget it, all right?" He felt sorry for himself now, knowing that he had behaved badly. He turned to leave.

"Alain," Cinq-Mars said, and he nodded with his chin at Mathers, "he's a squarehead, but you know what? I don't see any big chip on his shoulder. Maybe you should think about that." He wasn't looking at him, just saying what he wanted to say and letting his words ride.

With that, Déguire turned slowly on his heels and stomped down the knoll, back to his duties, his walk infused with renegade fury. "Alain!" Cinq-Mars called after him. He knew that the pressure could get to some guys. "How many?" He indicated the burnt-out Lincoln.

The young man had to stop and think, work to displace his fury for a few seconds. "Two," he managed to answer, and his voice was sounding civil again. "Kaplonski and his wife, we figure. Both unrecognizable. The baby-sitter says they went out together. They arrived home on time. Started backing up, then *boom*."

"Find out where they went. That's where the bomb was planted."

"Yes, sir."

Bill Mathers and Émile Cinq-Mars returned to their car. Reporters were arriving in droves now and television crews setting up. Cinq-Mars had to wave off the journalists who recognized him.

"Does this confirm LaPierre?" Mathers asked. LaPierre knew that they'd picked up Kaplonski, and now the poor devil was history. LaPierre had booked himself on for Christmas Eve when he didn't have to. Circumstantial evidence might not hold up in court, but it mattered a great deal to any smart cop. Mathers was distressed. That a policeman could act as a pawn for the Hell's Angels shook his confidence in the scheme of things. He showed surprise when Cinq-Mars said no. "How come? Sounds to me like he arranged to be the IO for no good reason. You're thinking he had some other excuse to put himself on the case? It's suspicious to me."

"Reasonable doubt, Bill. I've got one tucked in my pocket."

"Show me." They talked across the roof of the car.

"It might have to do with why André won't share the tapes with us. He might have recorded Kaplonski and the Czar like he said. But he didn't listen to the tape the day after the murder or whenever he got over his flu. He listened to it beforehand, when he was home sick."

"Beforehand? You're not saying—?"

"Either way, clean or dirty, he knew that boy was going to be bumped."

"Then how's he clean? He did nothing to stop it!"

"It's only a theory. Consider this. Kaplonski was supposed to get arrested that night and LaPierre wanted that to happen. He figured he knew how to find the Czar, if that's who the Russian is—straight through Kaplonski. After Mr. K lawyered up, with a biker lawyer, things got complicated. LaPierre lost his nerve. Like you, he gets nervous around people who blow up their enemies. Which doesn't make him a good cop. It makes him a shit cop. But it's possible he let that boy die so he could have the glory of solving the case. Now I'm ready to hoist him on a pole for that, and there's no stick sharp enough, but

218

I'm not willing to say right now, categorically, that he signed on for a shift that night so he could get this case and manipulate the evidence to keep suspicion away from the Angels. Since when do they care? I'm still diddling that one."

They climbed into the car, and Cinq-Mars had to blare his horn to bully journalists' vehicles out of the way. A couple of uniforms came by and directed traffic. He skirted the worst jam by driving on the sidewalk, got stuck in a snowbank, and uniforms had to shove him out. Finally they were free of the whole circus, riding down empty streets in their nocturnal quiet.

"Where to?" Mathers asked. He was hoping.

"Home," Cinq-Mars confirmed. "Where we should have been all along."

"There's still one person who might know the identity of the Czar, who heard him set up Artinian's murder with Kaplonski. Jim Coates."

"LaPierre might think so, too. He's looking for him. You know where he lives, partner—only you. Let's keep it that way. Let the Coates boy sleep for now. Catch a bit of that ourselves. Finding him tonight won't make him any safer. When you go, take precautions. Be paranoid. Personally, I'd wait until you come for work on Monday. If you see him, warn him to lie low. Tell him to lie so low the ground looks high. If he talks to you, fine. If he doesn't, don't scare him off. Build trust. Under no circumstances do you bring him down to Headquarters."

They drove in silence awhile, hitting every red light along the way. Cinq-Mars avoided the expressways, and the city appeared weary, restful, asleep. Oblivious to bikers' bombs.

"You know," Mathers mentioned as they waited at an intersection, "it's a funny thing. When I became your partner I was excited to be involved with downtown felony crime. A day later I'm involved with a homicide investigation. Before I know it, I've elbowed in on the work of the Wolverines. Now lately, especially today, I feel like I'm doing Internal Affairs' job. Tell me something, are we taking on the entire Police Department as well as every criminal in the city?"

Cinq-Mars chuckled as the light turned green.

"What's so funny?"

"Just think, Bill. All that, and we've only just begun."

Shy about her body, worried that some day she might balloon up like her mother, not knowing what to expect because of the steeplechase arch, Julia Murdick undressed and snuck under the covers of Selwyn Norris's bed while he dallied in the bathroom. She had been sexually precocious, active since thirteen, ready for teenage adventures, but she had never been held in the arms of an older man. Driving to his place, Norris had continued to be restrained, quiet, attentive. Unaccustomed to such patience, she was reconciled to the possibility that he might actually be a really lousy lover, but she needed to find that out for herself, once and for all.

She waited.

Listened to the toothbrush, the taps, the toilet. Boys weren't like this. She supposed that adult sex might be terribly boring.

From the en suite he entered the dim light of the bedroom and Julia turned on her side, supporting her head with one hand. She loved the luxury of the room, the size of the bed, the clean sheets. She had never made love on such a big bed in such a huge bedroom in such a vast apartment with quiet jazz on the stereo and the lights of downtown perfectly reflected in the window.

Norris pulled the curtains closed.

"There's my girl," he said.

Julia replied, *"Nooooo!"* She punched the mattress.

"What?"

"Girl is so so so politically incorrect, especially, I would say, in younger woman-older man relationships."

He leaned over and through the duvet squeezed her left big toe until she kicked him off.

"What do you call that?" she complained. "Foreplay?"

"At least you're back on the right subject."

The bedside lamp stayed on as he undressed. She admired the full, well-formed chest, the trim waist. He was not particularly muscular, but he had good tone, and she found the gentle aging of his pecs endearing. Just a light fluff of white chest hair. His penis was rising, and Julia enjoyed the view and yelped when he submarined under the covers from the foot of the bed, pulling her calves, then her thighs and hips under him. She wanted to be coy, but the novelty, the urgency, the long wait had her making yipping noises that embarrassed her, and when he surfaced she didn't know what to do so she walloped him.

"*Ow!* Julia! You're so— You're so—"

"What?"

"Physical."

"Yeah?"

"Beautiful, too."

"Oh, here we go. Man seduces woman with compliments."

He shut her up by kissing her then, the moment a surprise. His lips were nice. Soft. Interesting. She worried that hers were chapped. His tongue played along the edges of her mouth. She heard herself sigh, and Julia let herself feel this. It had been so long, her last boyfriend had not traveled with her to Montreal, and never had it been this slow, this . . . methodical. She moved to hold him, and in the action her body wrapped his and now she was willing to be hungry for this, the attention, the company, the sex, the return of desire, and it was stronger than she had expected or had been willing to count on. In wrapping her legs around him and cradling him, she felt safe again, she was made secure again. The madness of the world and the audacity of their work together and the risk of their enterprise contrived to excite her and all the dangerous moments and tense hours converged and her body swayed against his and everything they did together finally made some kind of wacky nutty crazy ludicrous sense.

She reached for him, and touched him, gave him an earnest, medical, squeeze. She felt awkward and silly and not so experienced after all as he moved to love her in ways her body would allow. Julia heard herself sigh again, utter involuntary sounds as though to keep contact with herself, quick jabs of pleasure, and she spoke to him, her words wanton, making him laugh with her language, but her whole attention was desirous of him now, she was needy in ways she hadn't realized, desperate in ways she hadn't anticipated, and Julia was grateful just for the flash of emotions and pleasure.

He knew not to enter her but placed himself over her, his body upon hers.

Finding his rhythm, Julia moved with Norris in the still night and simultaneously felt so extraordinarily safe amid the heightened danger of her life that that confluence of sensations bolted her ahead of herself, she gasped and felt torn apart. With cries and a great shudder of her limbs she was fierce now in his arms and joyful, and everything—she knew—the whole business was worth it, especially the danger, especially the anxiety, she gave herself up to this tempest and this calm and if she stayed so close to Norris that she could not determine whose skin was hers or his she'd know then that everything would be all right, everything would be just fine.

He soothed her, and brought her down gently, and she moved above him to pleasure him. "Okay, old man," she whispered. "You're in for it now. You have no idea how much I needed this. I was getting nervous out there, Sel. I was getting doubtful about myself, you. I've been worrying. Did you know that? Is that why I'm here? Some nights I want to scream in my sleep."

"Poor baby."

"I feel their bugs in my house as if they're nattering at me. Some nights I want to talk. Babble. I want them to come over and get me. I have dreams about being tortured by Hell's Angels and they really are devils, they really are hideous. Don't give me that look. I'm okay. I'm *okay*. But for the *stress* that you have put me through you will now suffer the consequences."

"Then I win," she heard him mention under his breath.

"What'd you say?" she whispered back.

"I win. We had a bet. I'd get more information out of you tonight than you would extract from me even though you were the one asking the questions. You have confided in me down to your heels, girl. I win."

He was good, she had to admit that. But that was all right. Her life depended on him being good at what he did.

She nuzzled his chest, moved her hands over him. "Enjoy your victory, Champ," she conceded. "Because now you're going to pay. Big time."

11

In order to be themselves, the Banker and Julia needed to overcome their own fastidious training. A walk through Mount Royal Park and up the mountain on a cold, sunny, breezeless afternoon was proving to be fraught with difficulty. For a few hours they wanted to forget about being the bikers' banker and his caregiver, but it wasn't easy.

They had set aside the afternoon to play hooky from their covert lives. Julia had been having qualms about their mutual dependency. While she'd enjoyed a portion of time to get to know Selwyn Norris, growing familiar with him, learning to trust him, she'd been paired with Arthur Davidson—alias Carl Bantry—alias the Banker—knowing little of the man. That lack of knowledge irritated her. For Arthur had become a symbol of her folly, the person who most perfectly represented her willingness to endanger her life without logical rationale. What did he have to offer in a time of crisis? Right in her presence, as if she was invisible, the Banker had speculated on how she might hold up under pressure—but what about him? Why did he and Norris worry about the woman while clearly displaying confidence in the man? Why doubt the young one and not the old? During their initial tests he'd performed well, as had she, but could she trust her life to him if things went wrong? She decided to take him for a walk on the mountain where Norris had first introduced himself to her, where they could view the treacherous city and discover whatever there was to be revealed.

Strolling into the sun they tried to strip away the veneer of their fake personas to speak as friends, as cohorts. Anyone watching would

223

not mistake them for lovers, for they'd promptly separate if accidentally they touched. When listening to him, Julia would stretch her
neck high and back, analyzing his remarks rather than taking them
into her care and nurture as a lover might do. Arthur walked most
of the time with his hands in his pockets, an insular man uncomfortable with company, protective of himself and his secrets. His smile
was winsome, though, and anyone could tell that he cared about his
companion, a care that was friendly, possibly fatherly in nature.

Not that anyone looking carefully would judge them to be a father
and daughter out for a walk. Their body types were notably opposite.
Julia was tall, square at the shoulders, and inclined to put on weight if
she didn't watch herself. She had an hourglass figure. Arthur was a full
head shorter. His posture was sloped, his shoulders rounded, and he
was moderately thin for his age. His form was pear-shaped, rather
womanly. He had to take quicker short strides to match her long ones.
His baldness accentuated a rake to his forehead severely different from
her flat brow, which actually broadened near the top. Her nose lifted
and her nostrils flared where his nose dipped, the nostrils hardly visible. Her skin was a fine feature, drawing the utmost benefit from her
age and sex. His showed thirty-year-old acne scars along the jawline,
and in bright light capillaries were visible. Unlike Julia's fine lines,
Arthur's large eyebrows over his smallish eyes were his only startling
natural feature, except for his decidedly unnatural, precise, square scar.

"What happened to your cheek?" Julia blurted out. She'd been
rehearsing a roster of questions, and one slipped loose, spoken before
she could censor herself. From the time they had first met, the patch
below his right eye had intrigued her as a badge of experience or,
possibly, of error.

"I got shot," he stated bluntly. The words settled in the clear air
to crystallize upon the snow. Below them tobogganers hooted and
slid, and the two selected a downward path bleeding away from the
broad clearing into the trees.

"In the face?" Julia asked. She implied her dismay, her disquiet.

The Banker declined to mock her for stating the obvious. "Point-
blank range. Small-caliber weapon, fortunately, or I wouldn't be here
now."

"Fortunately," Julia said, the irony of the word apparent.

"It could have been worse."

"Could it have been better? I mean, what happened?"

A path through the trees to the summit remained open in winter, packed down by snowshoers and hikers. A measure of agility would be required on the steeper, icier sections. They forged on and after a dip commenced the incline, and Arthur offered Julia a hand up.

"Julia—" the Banker began, then stopped. "It's hard for me to call you that. Do you mind if I stick to Heather? I get nervous. I'd rather not slide into bad habits."

"I know what you mean. I feel dumb when I say Arthur. You'll always be Carl to me. *Dad*. Let's stick to those names."

They walked on. "I've come to my post as the Banker legitimately, Heather. Once when I was a branch manager my bank was robbed. Over my career as a teller, loans officer, and manager, my branches were robbed four times."

"That's when you were shot?"

"I wasn't working for Sel, if that's worrying you. The contrary—he rescued me. Selwyn gave me back my life. After being robbed three times, I was a trifle blasé about the whole rigmarole—a mistake I won't make again. On the day in question a robber barged into my office to keep me from touching off alarms. His buddies riffled the tills, waved guns around, shouted threats. You can't help but be scared when someone's waving a pistol in your face, but I was reasonably calm. I checked the guy in front of me, made mental notes on the details that help with identification later. With each robbery I'd improved my recall. That time, a scuffle broke out with a teller. She was attractive, and one of the punks touched her in a lewd way. She screamed, she was instantly hysterical—who could blame her? She began flailing at him. The robber panicked and shot her. Whether it was deliberate or whether the gun went off accidentally I don't know. I do know that he never gave her a warning. He never gave her a chance."

"My God."

Arthur took a deep breath. She could see that he still had to deal with the emotions from that day. "By that time the bank was full of people screaming and robbers were shouting crazily. I jumped up. I didn't do anything, it was involuntary, I just jumped up from my chair. The guy in my office knew he had more on his head now than armed robbery. The moment was heightened. We were both petrified. He knew I'd checked him out. He raised his pistol from his side, slowly. I tried to argue, make him see sense. He swore at me, quietly, I'll never forget that, like this was all my fault, then the son of a bitch shot me in the face."

They reached a cut in the rock formation of the mountain that required careful handholds and patient steps, and Julia climbed across and offered a hand to her partner. Arthur chose a slightly different route to span the gap which momentarily left him spread-eagled, his balance dependent on her hand, before he was able to transfer weight from one foot to the other and spring across. After that they climbed side by side along a widening portion of the trail, their boots digging into crusted snow. Below, cars whizzed up and down Park Avenue, oblivious to their adventure.

"Did the teller die?"

Arthur wet his lips in the dry cold. "She's a paraplegic."

"That's terrible." She did not know what to say and felt oddly contrite. "What about the robbers?"

He shook his head. "The man who shot me was killed in a holdup four months later. I ID'd his mug shot down at the morgue. Which was a pleasure. The other shooter will get his someday. I'll never have the satisfaction of knowing it, because I don't have a clue what he looked like. But losers like him don't make it through without getting hurt."

"That poor girl."

Arthur strode on with his head downcast. "All she was doing was working at a bank to earn a modest living. All she did was get scared when molested by a man with a gun. For that she'll never walk again."

The anger in his voice impressed Julia. She had not recorded this passion in her partner before. He'd been so easygoing—forceful, at times, and committed, but his demeanor had come across as even and uncomplicated. "So, *Dad*, is that when you chose to become a crime fighter?"

He smiled quickly, slightly, as they took alternate routes around a boulder. The divergent trails came together again, and the man took the young woman by the elbow and walked alongside her that way.

"I might as well tell you, I was a mess for a time. Seeing a young teller gunned down, seeing a pistol pointing in my face, believing at that moment I was a dead man, getting shot myself, learning later that my teller was crippled for life—I never wholly recovered. I was a nervous wreck. I was fiercely, illogically angry." He was staring straight ahead now, as though revisiting that wrath. "To make a long story short, I had a nervous breakdown, went through a lifestyle change, divorced, became a drunk, the whole shebang."

"Different, but not totally dissimilar from the real Carl Bantry," Julia noted.

"No coincidence, of course," the Banker determined. "Selwyn chooses us wisely." Every bone in her body yearned to pursue that one question. How *had* she been chosen? What did Arthur know about it? "I remember when Hagop was scrutinizing you."

"Hagop?"

"Santa Claus. The boy murdered on Christmas Eve."

"*He* found me?"

"Sel gave him the coordinates. That's the word he uses when he wants someone in his sights. You had to be smart. Attractive, but Hagop was not to get carried away. That's not a slight, by the way, but you know what I mean."

"Do I?" Julia responded. "Just what were the physical requirements?"

"He didn't want someone who'd distract a room. You had to be noticed, to be appreciated, but you shouldn't be the center of attention."

Julia decided that she could accept the restricted attributes as being complimentary. "What else?" she pushed him.

"You had to be bright. A reader. Bilingual, French and English."

"What else?"

"Bit of a loner. Superior to your peers in both intellect and self-absorption."

"What!"

"You had to be foreign to the city, not living at home, ideally on your own. Romantically unattached."

"Holy. Anything else? Height? Hair color? Ethnic origin? SAT results?"

"I didn't get all the details." Arthur chuckled. "It was Hagop's gig."

"So—like me—you were conscripted. Selwyn Norris wined and dined you, brought you along slowly?"

"The day I met him I was drinking in a bar along the Main. Selwyn came in the door and walked directly over to my table. Guess what he said."

"I have no idea."

" 'Drink up, Arthur Davidson. It'll be your last shot for a while. You've been through the dark, had your butt reamed. The time has come to stand in the light.' "

"You knee him in the testicles?" Julia wondered. "I would've."

"Too pissed. But he had my attention. I was drunk as a skunk, and he was dramatic enough that I took him to be my guardian angel. That was my first thought. But what I said was, 'Who're you, Dickhead?' "

"Funny. I said something similar the first time we met. How'd he respond?"

" 'Those bastards who shot you down like a dog and put your teller in a chair for life were working for someone. I'm after the men responsible, but I need your help, Arthur Davidson. Sober up now so you'll be man enough later.' "

The two walked up to the ridge of the mountain where the stone lookout stood guard from a precipice. A *calèche* moved off with winter tourists kissing in the cold on that high trail above the city, the sled skidding on the snow, the breath of the horse vaporizing in great billows. The driver gently clucked his tongue and slapped the reins to keep his beast going. In the frigid air the breath of the two hikers proved they were panting from their ascent.

"Why do you do this, Dad?"

"Why? Everything I do now is revenge for my teller. The work makes sense. Shuffling papers no longer makes sense. Signing loan applications no longer makes sense. I do it because this simple, sad little banker is a fighter at heart. I do it because, like you, I'm hooked."

They surveyed the city below them, chimneys smoking in their winter slumber like so many drowsy old men puffing away, huddled in a private club. The city seemed a peaceful, contented place, the altitude and sunlight on the winter snows contributing admirably to the illusion. Perhaps it was the easy white breath of the chimneys across the winterscape that reminded Julia she stood upon a dead volcano, that the elevation of her view had been created by molten rock spewed from the bowels of the earth. She stomped her feet to keep them warm, as though striking a compact with the frozen ground.

"Heather?"

"Hmmm?"

"Why are *you* doing this?"

With that simple question she understood that his intentions for this day mirrored her own. She had come to figure him out, to get down to his core, to discover if she could trust him with her life. He wanted to know if she'd seize up when times got bad, or come through for him. Would she, like the teller who panicked and got shot, freak out at the wrong moment? Or, when the chips were down, would she be brilliant, would she shine?

Julia had no corresponding tale to tell. She had no anecdotes to pinpoint the moment when she had turned toward this work. Nor could she move to any pat answer, for had she really thought this through? Was she not merely a puppet on Selwyn's strings, happy to be manipulated, to go along for the ride? How could she convince him of her commitment? Now that she was asking the pertinent questions, how could she convince herself?

Sensing her dilemma, Arthur coaxed her along. "To do this, you're risking your year at university, your career, your future, your—"

"Life?" she asked back. "Yeah, well, my life I care about, those other things—" She let it drop.

"What about those other things?"

Julia thought awhile. The city was so huge below her. When Selwyn had driven her up here to skate, he'd stopped at this lookout to explain the ways of the world to her. She'd responded to that, she'd reveled in that, although she'd tried to keep Selwyn from knowing that much about her. But he had known. He had had her pegged.

There was the matter of the steeplechase arch. She used to think that the pain she experienced during sex would go away, or be corrected. Then she'd found out that she'd have to live with it. Selwyn

had shown her that she could still take a lover, as long as they adapt-
ed to certain compromises, so it didn't seem as important now as it
had a week ago, or even a night ago. To be unable to have children
the way other women did was part of it, too, that verdict still slumped
inside her as chronic bad news, but that wasn't the whole deal either.

"My parents were children of the sixties," she began. "They're
divorced, of course. My mom raised me. I've had between four and
six stepfathers. How many depends on which ones I'm supposed to
count and which ones were, in my mom's words, 'merely itinerant.' "

After a moment of silence, Arthur suggested, "So Selwyn is a father
figure to you, something like that?"

"Oh, fuck off."

She had a way of uttering profanities that made men smile. Selwyn
did, and now Arthur was beaming as well.

"My parents bought a farm, back when they were still together.
They'd had some hippie-commune idea about living off the land that
never got off the ground. No pun intended. Good thing for them it
didn't, they would've starved. Anyway, we still own the farm but we
use it as a retreat. What was supposed to have been a veggie patch
is a parking space for German cars. You can swim laps in the stables.
You get the picture. Buildings were added and others expanded, we
had to keep growing to keep pace with the divorce rate, to accommodate the new kids from this marriage and the old ones from that
one. I have no brothers and no sisters, but *half* brothers, *half* sisters?
Who can count?"

Julia sighed, not knowing if this was making sense to him, frus-
trated by her inability to declare what drove her. "What scares me,"
she said, "what scares me isn't the Hell's Angels. What scares me is
growing up against yourself, in opposition to yourself. What scares me
is setting out in life with a catalog of ideals and one by one by one
by one ripping them into shreds. Defiling everything you stood for.
That scares me more. Giving up what you believe in and totally,
insanely, abusing what you believe in for the rest of your natural-born
days. That scares me more."

She looked at Arthur. The force of her glare made him stop and
look back at her. "I will not do that. I will not live that way. I will

230

stand up for what I believe, and if that means taking action that backs me into a corner—from which I can never retreat—fine, that's great, that's what I want. I don't want a way out. I've seen what a way out can do to a person. I know what it's done to the people I love, to my mother and my father and even to my stepfathers. They're good people, but what are they *doing*? I don't want a way out, Arthur. What I want is a way to live that makes sense for me. For me. And this makes sense."

She let him hug her. Anyone watching would not know what to make of the unusual couple wrapped in each other's embrace on the mountaintop above the frozen city.

That evening, Bill Mathers was pleased, upon entering the stable, to discern a draft of warmish air, although once his eyes had accustomed themselves to the sallow light, a dampness crept under his skin. He smelled the dust and straw, recalled a childhood memory of visiting the country, and listened to the animals breathing. The hanging bare lightbulbs that lit the stables, fifteen feet apart, created shifting shadows as they swayed on their cords. Horses shuffled gently in their stalls. Ambling by them, Cinq-Mars proffered soothing words for each animal. He swung a gate open and picked a leather-and-steel halter off a hook upon entering the stall. He fitted it on a small gray mare and led her out, hitching the animal to crossties.

"Knell's Bells," Cinq-Mars said, introducing her. "She's come up a little stiff in her old age, haven't you, girl?" He knelt before the animal and rubbed liniment into her calves. He worked with firm, gentle hands, the horse receptive to his ministrations.

"Who's your other guest, Émile?" Mathers asked pointedly. He remained one stall away, keeping the horse in front of him and leaning with an arm against a support beam.

"Raymond Rieser, an old friend."

"I know. You introduced us, remember? Why's he here?"

Cinq-Mars worked his hands upon the leg. "Raymond may have something to offer. That's part of it. It's also a test."

"Testing who?" Mathers wondered aloud.

"Let's tuck you in for the night," Cinq-Mars said to the mare, ignoring his partner's question. He unhitched Knell's Bells and led her into the stall, turning her forward. "One job done." He came out and closed the broad door and hung the halter on its hook. "Ah," he noted as the outer entry opened, "Raymond."

The man who joined them was large, barrel-chested, with a florid complexion and an extravagant gray mustache. His shoulder-length hair was tamed in a ponytail. As he spoke he doffed his unlit pipe. "You're a monster, Big Guy, inviting friends for dinner then making us shovel manure before we eat. You're an ogre, Cinq-Mars." The man's normal speaking voice veered close to a shout.

"Working up your appetite, Ray. I wouldn't want a morsel of Sandra's fine meal to go wanting."

"Fat chance. So, Detective," the brusque man was saying while he tugged at his suspenders and sucked his pipe, turning to include Mathers, "you are partner to the inimitable Cinq-Mars. How are you surviving that?"

Mathers struggled to grin. "Getting by, thanks. It's been an experience."

The two men stood aside as Cinq-Mars led another horse from its stall. They watched as he hid tablets in the core of a split apple and fed the animal its medication.

"See that?" Rieser asked. "He's a devious sort. Full of tricks."

"Are you a horseman, Raymond?" Mathers asked him.

"In my day. Thankfully, that time has passed."

"Ray was a Mountie," Cinq-Mars stated. "Intelligence." Formerly, the Mounties were responsible both for police work and for intelligence on the national level, as if they were the FBI and the CIA rolled into one. In more recent times, the intelligence role had been passed along to a new civilian branch, emulating the CIA, which put old spies who had also been Mounties out to pasture. "Gentlemen," Cinq-Mars announced as he put down the hoof and led the horse back to its stall, "a quick discussion before we return to the company of our fine women and drink to their good health."

Only at that moment did Bill Mathers realize that Émile Cinq-Mars had been drinking to the good health of fine women for a while, for he had previously attributed his host's expansive manner to a reflex of hospitality. He noticed him stumble slightly as he seated himself upon a stool, waving for his companions to settle around him.

"We have, Raymond, a situation."

Rieser passed up a side bench and overturned a large wood bucket to use as a chair. He nodded to indicate that Cinq-Mars should proceed, inscribing a signal in the air with his pipe. Scrunching down, Mathers balanced on the balls of his feet and picked up a length of straw from the stable floor that he played between his fingers.

"As you've heard, I'm privy to information from sources unknown. The suggestion's been made in recent days that no less than the CIA has sponsored my success. I put it to you, Raymond, why would an agent of the CIA be interested in the work of the Montreal Urban Community Police Department? Domestic crime in a foreign jurisdiction—unless you enlighten me otherwise, it makes no sense."

Rieser furrowed his brow, then shook his head. "What does the young guy say?" he asked.

Mathers confessed, "I'm fresh out of theories."

The man palmed his pipe and reflected further. "Truth be told, Émile, it's not possible. Plausible? Not in the least. The CIA, catching what? Burglars? Petty drug pushers? Car thieves? The notion is ludicrous."

Cinq-Mars vigorously scratched behind one ear. "And yet?"

"That's it, you see, I have to put a knot in my own shorts. Let's begin from the other direction. Assume the CIA is involved. Then the questions become how and why? How? In my experience, there are three possibilities. One, a rogue, an individual agent, working for his own reasons. Tough one to decipher, but file it to the back of your mind. In the second scenario, the CIA has an operation that involves you for reasons unknown. In the third case, the CIA has no overt operation but has sanctioned an agent to behave as a rogue, and to get a certain job done by whatever means necessary."

The policemen waited in the drafty barn, where the horses snorted gently and moved around in their stalls. The former Mountie had to think things through.

"The world's changing. There's less demand for espionage. Enemies have become friends and friends competitors. Consequently, we have agents with time on their hands, looking to stir up trouble in order to make themselves useful. Now, that's *how* the CIA could be involved. The question that remains is why?"

A horse touched a hoof lightly, rhythmically to its stall, starting other animals to whinny. Four hung their heads outside their stalls as though listening to this conversation among men, grappling with its meaning.

"Why be involved in our domestic crime? Because domestic crime increasingly includes international crime and the CIA sees itself as better able than the FBI to root it out. They're positioned to operate behind enemy lines, step around the law. It's been reported that a number of ex-KGB officers have moved into the rackets in Moscow. The CIA might see a role for itself defending the country against the same old people, only this time wearing capitalist pajamas. Also, there's been disturbing news. The old KGB has been re-formed, and expanded, under a new name, the FSB. It's possible that the FSB is looking to be self-financing. They may have formed a fund-raising branch. Which means the FSB could evolve as both an intelligence agency *and* a criminal gang, a scary thought."

Rieser paused to reflect and draw on his pipe, and Mathers took advantage of the lull to pose a question. "Raymond, why here? Canada. Why not Moscow, or New York City?"

The visitor's nod underscored the worth of the question. "That could be the easy part, Bill, at least in theory. Inside the USA, the Company would be trespassing on FBI turf. What constitutes a covert operation on foreign soil becomes a violation of constitutional rights on home ground. I'm not so naive as to think the CIA does not operate on home ground, but they have more freedom, more scope, more capacity to function effectively when operating on foreign soil. On alien ground, the rule of law is nothing more than a weather forecast." He paused to tap his pipe. "Another point. Consider that the Russian gangs—from something you said earlier, Émile, I gather they're involved—consider that they might be happier operating an American base out of Canada, away from the scrutiny of the FBI. Their presence alone could induce the CIA onto the scene. They don't respect borders any more than the gangs do."

The three men considered these affairs in the quiet gloom. Stretching his stiff limbs, Cinq-Mars hoisted himself to his feet. "Interesting. Anything else you'd like to ask, Bill, before we head back to the house?"

Mathers considered Rieser's comments. "You said there'd be three ways for an agent to be involved. Care to prioritize them?"

"Prioritize! Now there's a fine bureaucratic word. Do you mean, what's my hunch? Okay. I'll say this—if the CIA is *not* here in pursuit of Russian gangs, you're dealing with a rogue. If they *are* involved with gang activity, the agent is working independently. This is not a project within the Company's mandate, which means it would be a covert operation even among the spies. Likely, higher-ups know. But only a few. Which makes your agent a man of experience and expertise, worthy of being trusted with the mission." Rieser stood as well.

Cinq-Mars kicked dirt around a moment. He retrieved a broom and swept a patch of floor. "Any other gems, Ray, before we go back inside?"

The former Mountie knocked his pipe in his palm, as though sifting through clues left behind in the ashes. "Only this. If the CIA is involved, they'll be serious about their operations. They're not likely to brook any upset by two gentlemen cops such as yourselves. They have power. They have ways and means. You might be in this against the bad guys, but if you step on their toes, you could find yourself on the wrong side of the good guys, too. You're brave men. That might not be enough. This may be a time for extreme caution. Don't be careful, be damned careful."

Cinq-Mars heavily sighed. "All right, listen up. We're heading back to the house. There will be no further talk of this matter. Both of you are charged with providing us all with an entertaining evening. Now, let's leave the company of horses and join our own kind, shall we?"

Ray Rieser was first out the door, and Bill Mathers took advantage to touch his partner's elbow. "Did he pass his test?" he whispered.

Cinq-Mars's voice was cold, cutting. "The bastard—my very old friend—he sold me out."

12

Cautious to a fault when protecting a source, Sergeant-Detective Émile Cinq-Mars arranged to meet Okinder Boyle in a small café along rue St. Paul in Old Montreal. Close enough to Headquarters to be accessible, the venue was sufficiently distant to diminish the risk of being spotted by cops trolling for a morning fix of caffeine. Cinq-Mars occupied a booth in the rear, his eyes keen on the door, drinking a pot of coffee while waiting for the journalist to show.

The detective gave *Le Journal de Montréal* a quick read to ascertain that nothing reported on the Kaplonski bombing was news to him. Splattered across the front page was another grisly photograph of the garroted Lincoln. Satisfied, he returned to the comfort of his cup, consciously resisting glazed cherry Danishes aglitter on the countertop.

Cinq-Mars enjoyed being in the city, loved the traffic of office workers piling in for coffee and croissants, the buzz of conversation, the ritual greetings and daily commiseration. The habits of others gave him pleasure, a sense of constancy, just as Sandra's rituals in the barn established a rhythm that evoked life's continuity. He was not enamored with routine himself. As much as he loved horses, he was not inclined to their day-in, day-out care, a shortcoming he'd unearthed one summer as a student in animal husbandry. In those days, when he was young, strong, and energetic, hard farm labor was of no consequence to him. What he learned was that he possessed a wandering mind, that repetitive tasks soon had him talking to himself, off on a discourse unrelated to the moment. Cinq-Mars had hoped to elevate his studies in animal husbandry to pursue a career as a veterinarian, but few spaces were available at the two universities where he applied, and at the time his English had proved inadequate for one, his science marks less than sufficient for either.

What he loved about working with cows and horses in close proximity to vets was attempting to solve the riddles of animal illness. In one case, Cinq-Mars had discovered the contamination of well water that served a particular barn after becoming sick himself with similar symptoms. Aware that the young man had been thwarted in his first choice of career, the vet on duty had suggested that he become a detective. Spoken half in jest, the comment would weigh on the youth. He did not want to muck out barns all his life. A limited number of graduates were being hired into government bureaucracies dedicated to animal welfare, and in any case those positions had seemed tearfully boring to him. On the other hand, he did enjoy investigating things. Exploration kept his attention. He preferred work that was patently *interesting*. If a job could intrigue him for a good chunk of time, he was willing to endure whatever bouts of boredom came attached. The young Cinq-Mars suffered little ambition to accumulate wealth. He got a kick from figuring people out yet was himself aloof. Why not be a policeman? In due time, a detective? With the avidity of youth, Émile Cinq-Mars supposed that he might actually be good at the job.

Within days of the initial suggestion, he began to think of police work as his profession, his vocation. He dispensed with any notion of being a small-town cop, although the countryside and its villages constituted his heritage. In such circumstances he'd be recognized and scrutinized, the goldfish in a bowl, made to wear a uniform throughout his career, a situation antithetical to being a crack investigator. He read Sherlock Holmes mysteries. Montreal was renowned, indeed legendary, for crime—that was where he would go. To a place he had never been. The city would become his London. He'd be a big-city cop, a Montreal cop, promoted one day to the rank of detective. He drove into the big city in a borrowed pickup and marveled as the humpback mountain, with the Oratory shimmering in the bright sunlight like a crown doffed to one side, then the sparkle of skyscrapers rose into view above the broad glacier plain. He crossed the Champlain Bridge and observed below the overpass the scoff of poor communities like a beckoning nod of destiny. In his blood and bones he felt his future here. Within minutes of first speaking to a recruitment officer, young Cinq-Mars impressed upon the man that he was not about to be denied.

And he was not.

What confounded Cinq-Mars, what wore him down at times, was the lack of professional pride exhibited by so many of his fellow officers. He kept up with professional training, attended conferences and symposia, making contact with officers from various jurisdictions, cities, and countries, on the off chance that one day he might want to call upon their services or expertise—as he had done during the past weekend with Raymond Rieser. Along the way he had attended innumerable lectures, and one stuck in his craw. An academic studying the behavior and makeup of policemen in several cities concluded that cops and crooks were more alike than first thought. Both were moths attracted to the flame of crime. They reveled in the excitement, the rush of danger. Both were seduced by the need to be at the center of things, to be in the know. They hated to be on the outside looking in. Both groups had difficulty with routine. Both were aggressive. Both liked guns. Both were righteous. Both saw themselves as living outside society. As did crooks, cops viewed themselves as social misfits. Both groups were tribal and attracted to codes and rituals. The lecturer had suggested that criminals and policemen lived on flip sides of the same mattress. Policemen, by upbringing or fluke or circumstance, were more inclined to conform to the law than to break it, that was all. Some cops would probably have become crooks if they hadn't been hired to enforce the rules. He went on to make the case that policemen must be wary of policemen. In a fellow officer lay the seeds for criminal behavior. Cinq-Mars was left with the impression that the lecturer considered criminals the more courageous of the two tribes, while the weaker band, lacking the guts to commit crime and more fearful of prison, wore the badge.

Following the talk—which enraged him—Cinq-Mars appreciated that he had come to police work through different weather than his fellow officers. He was not the man described in the lecture, he was not an opposite mask. He hated routine and liked to be in the know, nevertheless his choices in life had never been between robbing a bank and catching the thieves who did. He became aware that police-men often emerged from the same streets and circumstances as the crooks they chased down. From locker-room chats he gathered that a solid percentage of his cohorts had flirted with crime as kids. They'd been caught, or frightened, or turned around by a strong family con-nection. The ones who'd been hockey players unable to make the pros were more likely to relate memories of their fights on the ice than goals scored. Cinq-Mars considered that some cops were effec-tive because they thought like crooks, and his rage was gradually replaced by worry that he might fail at his profession because he did not suffer that requisite tarnish to his nature.

He'd gotten over the momentary loss of confidence, emerging with a heightened sense of his place within the department. He learned that he could teach himself to think like crooks by empathizing with them and, more important, by allowing the Roman Catholic in him to come to the fore. If he was a creature of God, and a man with a God-driven destiny, then surely what was intrinsic to him had specif-ic, if undetermined, value. In time Émile Cinq-Mars grew to believe that, through maintaining what he saw as purity of purpose, his role was to be the conscience of the Police Department, to remind his fel-low officers of the thin line they walked between civility and abuse, between discipline and disorder and, significantly, between justice and vengeance. Similarly, he reminded cops that crooks were the bad guys, in need of repair or incarceration, that cops were not supposed to be their own worst enemies. Overall, he ceded any pretense to being one of the boys in blue, and set himself apart.

As Cinq-Mars sipped his coffee, ruminating, Okinder Boyle fairly bounced through the door, offering up a morning eagerness that amused the older man. The journalist ordered a *chocolatine*, a croissant filled with a rich dark chocolate heated to dripping. Cinq-Mars feared the temptation about to be placed across from him.

"How've you been?"

"Good, Émile, thanks. How's the world treating you?"

"Can't complain."

"No kidding. At your age, that's hard to imagine."

"Bear in mind, Okinder, who's carrying a gun."

"I forgot. Truth is, I hope I'm as well preserved as you are when I'm ninety-five—whoops, sorry, don't shoot—fifty-five."

"Fifty-six, but who's counting?"

Boyle's *chocolatine* arrived, and the young reporter bit into it lasciviously. He closed his eyes, chewed, and returned the pastry to the plate. Cinq-Mars observed an infinitesimal amount of chocolate dribble out from between his lips. "Detective, long story. Bear with me, all right? I've had a helluva weekend."

"I'm all ears," Cinq-Mars vowed, eyes on the chocolate.

Boyle reminded him of his Christmas Eve visit to the tunnel and his talk with the Banker. He discussed the visit from Carl Bantry's daughter, Heather, who'd been bent on assuring that the tale about her father was printed.

"And then a few days ago I received a visit from another young woman, also claiming to be Heather Bantry, who directs me to *her* father, who is the *real* Carl Bantry who is living in a nursing home on the south shore, thank you kindly, not inside any damn tunnel."

"Hold on. There are two Carls and two Heathers?"

"Exactly. Except that one father-daughter combination is real and the other one's a CIA plant."

"We are definitely jumping to conclusions here, Okinder. You're not saying you have proof of that?"

Boyle was dusting the crumbs off his fingers and smiling mischievously. "Okay. Sheer speculation. But face facts. A group of men is planted in a tunnel to direct me to someone called the Banker, only he really isn't that person and those men usually aren't there. I've checked. The Railway Police go through the tunnel nightly. Nobody can make fires and live there. It just so happens that the Railway Police get a few days off around Christmas. So these *actors* took over the tunnel *after* a seed had been sown in my head. They were very convincing. Anybody would've been taken in by them." Boyle first wet his lips, then took a gulp of mud. "Now I find out there's a real Heather and a real Carl Bantry. So I visit Carl on the south shore, where he's minding his own business in a nursing home for dodo birds. He's pretty sound. He tells me, and his daughter confirms, that his bills get paid by his former employer, by the bank."

"And *is* the bank paying?"

"I inquired at the bank when I first did my story. They didn't know his whereabouts. Their financial support is minimal. Their insurance company sends checks, which apparently get siphoned off by his wife. That part of the original story bears out. I checked back with the bank over the weekend. They weren't overjoyed to hear from me, but there you go. As far as two executives are concerned, they are not supporting Carl Bantry in a nursing home. Why deny it? The information would only make them look good. I called back the nursing home. They don't know who's paying the bills. They receive direct deposits monthly."

"Interesting."

"Isn't it?"

"You haven't leapfrogged into the lap of the CIA, not yet."

"I visit Carl Bantry in the nursing home Saturday morning. Same day—that evening, Saturday night—I get a visit from the original Heather, the fake one, trying to find out what I'd been doing there, how much I know, what I plan to write. *The fake Heather knows I visited the real Carl.* She has to admit that she's not Heather Bantry, she has no choice, but she won't tell me her real name. If I publish, she warns me, she'll probably die, her death will be on my head, and— get this—the people who do her will be the same gentle folks who broke Hagop Artinian's neck."

"Whoosh," Cinq-Mars exclaimed.

"Then she gets to play her final card. If I don't believe her, she says, I can call up the famous Detective Émile Cinq-Mars, and he'll convince me not to publish."

"She said that?" He shook his head. "Still no CIA connection."

"Hey, it's come up before. I don't find it such a stretch. The chick was trying to make me think she's a cop. She wasn't saying so flat out, but she's letting the insinuation ride. She has to give herself some kind of connection, doesn't she? She can't exactly let on that she's being run by the CIA. More news, Émile—I've seen the guy."

"What guy?"

"The CIA guy."

"What CIA guy? Who—when?—where?—how do you know?" Cinq-Mars didn't know what he needed to hear first.

"Friday night, before my caper to the nursing home, *after* I've learned about the second Heather, I met Heather One, the fake, in a bar. Actually, I saw her walk through the bar I was in and look around. I followed. She did the same thing in another bar. After that she went into a third and met this older guy. Well-dressed dude. They held hands, talked up close, looked into each other's eyes, that sort of thing. So I went over and said hello."

"You didn't."

"I'm not shy. I asked the fake Heather—when she's over at my place the next night—who was the guy? She tries to pass him off as her stepfather. I call her on that. Since when do college girls hold hands across the table with their stepdads and look dewy-eyed at them? She admits it's a story. Again, she offers no explanation. He's the guy, Émile. He's the one."

"What can you tell me about him?"

"Midforties. Well-dressed. The threads jump out at you. Good-looking for a suit. What can I tell you?"

"How about the make of his car? How about the fake Heather Bantry's phone number? No! You have a phone number?"

The reporter had a hit of java. "Tried it this morning. The chick answered. I hung up. Friday night after I talked to them, I followed them out from the bar. They walked through a building where I lost them, so I just headed back to the club scene to do what I planned to do all along. Drink and meet girls. What do I see? The two of them coming out of some *other* building. I mean, who walks through a bunch of different buildings for no reason except people who don't want to be followed and who think they might be? They got into a car and were out of sight before I could catch up. All I saw was that the car was green."

"Too bad."

"But Saturday night, after the chick left my place, I slipped downstairs and caught a glimpse. Again, no plate number. It was dark, and the light over the plate was out. But the car was an Infiniti Q Forty-five. There aren't many of those in town."

Cinq-Mars was beaming. "Okinder Boyle. Good work!"

"Just call me Steeplechase B. Here's the phone number."

The reporter ripped off a small sheet from his pocket notepad and passed it across the table to Sergeant-Detective Émile Cinq-Mars, who, as if it had been written in invisible ink and might momentarily vanish, committed the number to memory before stuffing it away. Speechless awhile, he finally managed to say, "Thanks, Okinder." He cleared his throat. "Saturday night, probably just after the young woman was at your place, I received a call from the man in the Q Forty-five. He pulled me away from a dinner party I had on. I don't know who he is. We've had contact, but I don't know him. He prevailed upon me to beg you not to publish."

"I'll consider myself persuaded. It's the big story I'm after here."

"Someday you'll have it." Cinq-Mars put his elbows on the table and rubbed his hands. "How were the pastries?"

Boyle laughed. "Come on, Émile. Splurge. Live a little for a change."

"Maybe I will," the detective intimated. "I may have something to celebrate." He and his new friend grinned.

Detective Bill Mathers made his way along narrow, congested streets to the mechanic's last known address. Spotting a mailman on his way up the walk, he decided against ringing the kid's bell and waited as the man selected the appropriate key and entered. The postal worker held open the door for the loiterer, and the cop followed him to the cubbyhole of mailboxes. The man slung down his sack and started sorting.

"Anything for Jim Coates?" Mathers asked after a bit.

"Regulations, sir. You have to use your key. I can't hand over mail if I don't recognize the face."

Mathers displayed his badge.

"Same difference," the mailman told him.

"I don't want his mail necessarily. I want to know if he received any."

The man checked the box. "There's a postcard and a letter."

"Who from?"

The man took the mail out. "The postcard's from Brazil."

"Who from?" Mathers asked.

"How should I know? I can't read the signature. Look, I'm not supposed to do this."

"Every mailman alive reads postcards. In the history of the postal service no mailman has made it through his career without reading postcards."

The man was older than Mathers, in his forties, made fit by his profession. Under his winter cap gray hair showed at the temples. He took another glance at the card. "It's nothing. You read it," he said.

Somebody was traveling in Brazil wishing Jim Coates was there. At first Mathers deciphered the signature as reading, "Me," but by comparing the letters to others on the page he discerned that the scribble could be deciphered as "Mom."

"What about the letter? Who's it from?"

"No return address."

"Postmark?"

The man checked. "Local."

"Thanks. I appreciate your help."

He climbed the stairs to the third floor and knocked on Jim Coates's door. Footsteps approached, and the youth opened the door, the chainlock in place, peering sleepily through the narrow gap.

"Hi there, Jim. How're you doing?"

"It's you." He unlatched the chain and let him in.

"Glad to see me?" Clearly, the kid had just clambered out of bed. He was wearing jeans which he hadn't zipped and the black T-shirt he'd probably slept in. He shrugged, yawned, and fastened his pants. "You should be," the policeman admonished him.

"How come?"

"You don't know?"

The youth shrugged again. "I heard about Kaplonski," he admitted.

Mathers strode deeper into the apartment, sizing things up. "That's right—Kaplonski. Blown to smithereens. Not much left of him. Imagine that, eh? You go to park your car. Put it in reverse—*kaboom!* Off to kingdom come. All of a sudden you're ringing the bell at the pearly gates wondering why nobody's answering."

The youth was smoothing down his wild hair a bit, rubbing sleep from his eyes.

"That was some garage you worked at, Jim. One of your co-workers gets his neck snapped, a meat hook through the heart, your former boss gets a keg of dynamite under his ass. Makes you wonder who's next." Mathers ceased his examination of the apartment, nondescript except for the lack of a telephone, and confronted the youth again.

"Good thing I'm out of there."

"I'd call that an understatement, Jim. Do you have any coffee?"

The request surprised the young man. He had to defog before answering. "Yeah, maybe, I think there's some left."

"Could I trouble you? I've been running on empty and we've got a few things to sort out. Looks to me like you could use a cup yourself. I need you wide awake."

Mathers followed him into the kitchenette and checked things in there. No phone, a sink full of dishes, and as the young man opened the refrigerator door to take out the cream, he saw that he had food.

"You working, Jim?"

"I got a job, yeah."

"Great! Mechanic?"

"Naw, tire place. I repair flats, install new tires, stuff like that. It's good. It's around cars. I get training and the pay's okay, it's all right."

"I'm happy for you. You should be reasonably well hidden in a garage like that."

Coates looked at him as he measured out the coffee. "Nobody's looking for me," the boy postulated.

"No? You got a phone yet?"

"No, but, there's no point being stupid about it."

"I'm glad you're keeping your head down, Jim. That's important. I don't want to scare you, but word on the street is, somebody might be wondering where you are."

Coates appeared to be waking up by the minute. "Why? I don't know nothing."

Mathers performed an extensive grimace and sucked air between his teeth. "That's the thing, Jim. That's the point of view that doesn't wash clean anymore. Truth is, if you knew nothing, then nobody would care about your existence. But people care. Maybe the same people who did what they did to poor Hagop. Old Man Kaplonski didn't stand in their way either, did he? He probably considered himself a friend of the family. So I'm thinking, either you know something and know what it is but you're not telling us, or you know something and you haven't figured out what it could be. Either way, you know something, Jim. The evidence points in that direction."

Pouring water into the back of the coffee machine, the young man did not seem up to issuing further denials. He was looking a trifle pale.

"I got a call last night from my partner. Wanted me in early. So I've been going all morning. Sure could use that coffee. Remember him, Jim? My partner? He gave you a rough ride down at the garage. He had me in early to talk about you. He's concerned about a few things. Your safety, for starters. He's also bothered by something else, Jim."

"What's that?" Coates was washing out cups.

"We know that Hagop Artinian was up to something. My partner asked the question 'How did Kaplonski find out?' I told him I didn't have a clue. Then he says to me, 'We know Artinian told somebody else about what he was doing.' That's true, he did that. My partner—do you remember him, Jim?"

"Sure, yeah, Cinq-Mars. I got his card. He's a famous guy I found out."

"That's right, he is. He's a great cop. Anyhow, my partner is asking these tough questions, you know? Brutal, that early. He had a point though. If Hagop told somebody about what he was doing once, maybe he did it twice. Could've been a chronic problem with him, a pattern, talking too much. So my partner was wondering, how come Jim Coates got friendly with Kaplonski all of a sudden?"

"I didn't," the youth objected.

"Cinq-Mars, my partner, he's saying things to me like, 'That boy was put in charge of the garage, all by himself, Christmas week. That's a lot of responsibility when it's a hot garage. How come he was trusted? And if he wasn't trusted, why didn't they waste him back then?' Those are good questions, and I didn't have the answers. Seems like you were in Kaplonski's good graces."

The young man just stared back at him.

Detective Bill Mathers returned the look. "If he wasn't trusting you, maybe he was testing you. What do you think about that? Leaving you alone in that garage to face the cops—was it a test? Or maybe he was tying your leg to the can."

"I don't get it," Coates said. "What're you saying?"

"Another thing. You didn't give Kaplonski much notice, did you? None, in fact. You just left. Tell me, Jim, what's your mother doing in Brazil?"

"What do you care? She's on her honeymoon."

"That's good. I mean, it's good she's out of the country. Nice guy?"

"He's good for her, I think. He got me my job."

"We'll have to talk to her when she gets back."

"What do you mean? *Why?*" The timbre of his voice broached hysteria.

"I'll go with you if you like. We have to explain that people might come around looking for you, that she can't let anybody know where you live or work."

The youth was panicking now. "Who's coming after me? I mean— *why?* What did I do? I don't know nothing."

"Jim, listen to me. We have to get serious about your protection. You know what that means. You can lie low awhile, but down the road, a new identity maybe, a safe house. Expenses, Jim. For expenses I need authorization. To get that, I want the information at my fingertips, so I can make a case for you with the brass."

"I don't know nothing!" Coates burst out. Simultaneously, the coffeemaker gurgled, followed by a hissing noise, and the pot was ready to be poured.

"Nobody's judging you. Maybe in your shoes, at your age, I would've done something similar. Hagop Artinian gets all the credit, the best jobs, the free time off. He's tight with the boss. Then you find out—because he tells you—that he's doing this other stuff and—"

"I didn't give him up—"

"Sure you did, Jim, of course you did, that's not so hard to figure. You told Kaplonski that his golden boy was really a spy—"

"Oh shit!"

"You're in it above your shoe tops, aren't you, Jim? I think that coffee's ready now."

"Fuck!"

"I know. Just pour the coffee. Start with that. Keep it together. Then we'll go in the other room and you can tell me about it."

"I don't know nothing."

"That's what we call denial, Jim. That's what we call wishful thinking. You *wish* you didn't know anything, but you know the identity of that Russian, don't you? We call him the Czar. Did you know he killed Hagop? He did. With his bare hands."

"Oh, fuck."

"Easy, Jim. Relax. We'll take care of this. Tell me about him. He must be a powerful man. I mean physically. Is he a big guy, Jim?"

"He's a freaking giant."

"That figures, the way he broke Hagop's neck. You know, between the Hell's Angels, who blew up Kaplonski, and the freaking Russian giant and his gang, and the Mafia who are probably in on this, too, you sure as hell went out and made yourself the wrong bunch of friends. How old is he, Jim, the man we call the Czar, about?"

His shrug seemed to stem from the incomprehension of youth, equating all persons above a certain age as old. "Forty. Fifty."

"Sixty?" Mathers asked.

"No. He has a lot of hair, it's dark."

"Not bald. Not gray. Height?"

"Six-four, or better."

"Thin, fat, medium?"

"There's no stomach on him, he's in shape. Always wears a suit. Outside he wears a cape."

The Czar. This was confirmation. In September, when Cinq-Mars had been with the surveillance team from the Wolverines, even in the heat the man had worn a cape. "Handsome, ugly?"

Another shrug. Mathers finally received his coffee, and he waved off sugar and cream. "Hard-looking, you know. Scary in a way. He looks like a Russian, like one of those hockey players. Like he's never smiled in his lifetime."

"Any marks, scars?"

"Yeah. Big one. From behind his ear," Coates said, and he drew the line under his own jaw, "to the front of his chin."

"That could be surgical," Mathers theorized. "That's the kind of scar they cut for a bypass to open up the main artery."

"This guy doesn't look like he'd have a heart problem."

"You never know. There's nothing like a coronary bypass to get a man into shape. Did he smoke? Eat greasy foods?"

"I don't remember him smoking. *No, that's right!* He came in one time and told Kaplonski to butt his cigar."

"There you go, you see? The man's a health fanatic because he's had a coronary bypass. You see what you can find out when you put your mind to it? Now, Jim, you have to tell me this. Did you give up Hagop to Kaplonski?"

Coates was quiet, staring into his cup.

"We have to have something, Jim, to protect you. If things go bad, we want to be on your side. If Hagop told you something, then you have to tell us. Tell us what you told Kaplonski."

He seemed disinclined to talk.

"I won't kid you. Talking to Kaplonski about Hagop was not a good thing. I can see how it happened though, I'm not judging you. Tell me what Hagop said, that'll put it right."

"How can anything put it right?" Coates demanded bitterly. He took a sip, and his hand shook and his lower lip trembled. "Hagop's dead."

Cinq-Mars had warned his partner to keep the boy on his side, no matter what. Break him down, but no matter what, befriend him.

"You didn't do it, Jim," Mathers reminded him in a soft voice. "We both know that. We can't bring Hagop back, but we can put away his killers."

Tears welled. His head hung down. When Coates spoke he hesitated, grasping his words, forcing them from his lips. "I told Kaplonski—Hagop was a snitch."

Mathers was patient. He coaxed him along. "How did you know that, Jim?"

"He told me. Like you said. He confided in me. I said something to him one time about him being a brownnoser. We were working late. He said he wasn't no brownnoser. Said he was spying on Kaplonski."

The youth wiped his eyes with the back of one hand and tried to sip his coffee, lips aquiver.

"Who for, Jim?"

"For the cops. A bigshot cop, he said."

Mathers stepped down from the stool and stood close to the young man. "He said that?"

"Yeah."

"He didn't mention anyone else?"

"Not that time."

"But another time?"

"He said he had the whole CIA in back of him. I didn't believe that bullshit."

Mathers took a couple of deeper breaths. "You tell Kaplonski about that?"

"About the CIA? No. I'd sound like an idiot. About the rest, yeah."

"When does your mother get back, Jim?"

The young man wiped his nose and eyes on his wrist. "Thursday."

"Okay, listen to me. We'll have that talk with her. We'll work something out so we don't embarrass you. But start packing. People know where you live. You've been receiving mail. We have to stop that. No more mail, Jim. No more letting the world know your where-abouts. All right? You've done the right thing, Jim. Don't talk to your landlord or anything dumb like that. Let me take care of that part. Don't tell anybody you're on the go. Just pack."

"He has a tattoo," the boy said out of the blue.

"What?"

"I never saw it. He always wore suits. Hagop told me. He said he had a tattoo on his chest in the shape of a star. Hagop said it meant he was one of the godfathers of the Russian federation of gangs, some bullshit. He had all these stories. The CIA. Russian gangs. I thought he was nuts, man. I didn't believe it."

"Now you do?"

The boy shrugged. "He talked too much and he's dead. That's serious truth."

Mathers gulped the last of his coffee and gave the young man another pat on the back, then headed out. Cinq-Mars was right.

Coates had betrayed Hagop Artinian. That was why he'd run, because of his complicity in murder. That had scared him as much as any idle fear for his own life. Even now he didn't have a clue about the real danger he had created for himself, all he had was the barest inkling.

The Lexus pulled up to the curb, and Julia Murdick climbed off her stool in the coffee shop, dropped coins across her bill, and stepped outside. She climbed into the plush front seat.

"Everything in shape?" Gitteridge wanted to know.

"Dad thinks so."

"That cash get moved?"

"Child's play. Dad's grumpy. He wants a real challenge."

Gitteridge stared at her.

"What?" Julia asked.

"Let's make a withdrawal," he commanded. "See if it works."

"The money works," she insisted. "It'll buy things."

"Let's go see."

"All right," she agreed. "Let's."

The car peeled away from the curb.

With the meeting called for eleven sharp, Sergeant-Detective Émile Cinq-Mars made it in the nick of time. Rémi Tremblay had cleared his desk, his secretary was holding calls, and the moment Cinq-Mars entered she shut the door behind him with a sense of finality, as though only one man would emerge from the room alive.

"Good morning, Émile."

"What's this I hear about Beaubien?" stormed Cinq-Mars. His chin was clenched and there was no mistaking the flame in his eyes.

"He's been cleared."

"That's a crock."

"Would you like to rephrase?"

"His name's on that damn list!" In his mind, two officers, Gilles Beaubien and André LaPierre, were possible informants. He preferred both suspended. If one came back, it definitely should not be the superior officer, who carried the greater potential to do damage.

"Émile, the boss studied the case personally." The only man whom

Tremblay called boss was Police Director Gervais. "He's accepted Beaubien's explanation that a uniform was assigned to get his car repaired. The uniform was offering, he's a brownnoser. He got it fixed, told him he did it himself. No charge. Beaubien's had his wrists slapped. You don't ask a uniform to do your personal business. But that's it. That's all."

Cinq-Mars put a hand behind his neck and gently shook his head. Things never worked out the way they should. "You know I respect Gervais."

"He has enormous respect for you, too, Émile. He's in your corner. He takes personal pride in you. Unfortunately, even the boss is not a saint."

"What's that supposed to mean?"

Stiff and formal behind his desk, Tremblay lent his tone an air of authority, an inflection of experience, as though initiating Cinq-Mars into the back-room politics of the department. "Director Gervais is a bit miffed to have a captain in trouble with the law. Is that a surprise? He wants the issue to vanish, so he's helped the process along. The matter has been investigated, Beaubien has been chastised, the issue has gone away, like magic."

"This is outrageous," Cinq-Mars declared, his voice calm, deliberate.

"Really? What're you planning to do about it, investigate the boss for collaboration with the Hell's Angels?" Seldom inclined to sarcasm, Tremblay used it to good effect now. "Émile, can you not see your way clear to accept that his job is largely one of public relations, essentially one of image, that his primary objective here has to do with public confidence and department morale?"

"Funny, I thought his primary objective was to create an outstanding police force."

"Émile," Tremblay explained, "it is. When he fails to achieve your lofty standard—his own high standard—the compromise objective turns on public confidence. Nothing we do will work without public confidence."

"A regular increase in the budget, you mean."

Tremblay conceded the point with a gesture of his hands. "We live in a time of restraint. The Police Department must be spared cutbacks. Support for the force begins with public confidence. Surely you can understand that much."

"So in order to keep the money flowing, an incompetent boob, an idiot, a corrupt administrator with known links to Kaplonski and possibly to others, an officer who is potentially a traitorous informant, is put back on the job. Tell me—is he still directing our case?"

"He's not."

"Why not? He's been reconstituted. Who took him off our case?"

"Director Gervais," Tremblay admitted.

"On what grounds?" Cinq-Mars pressed, curious now.

Tremblay hesitated, taking time to form his words in the most politic way possible and yet, as Cinq-Mars divined, convey the weight behind the official course of action. "Captain Gilles Beaubien has been relieved of responsibility with respect to any ongoing investigation that involves organized crime on the grounds that there may be potential for conflict of interest. He's been delegated other assignments."

"What assignments?"

"The duty roster, vacation rotation, statistical analysis."

The two men, old friends, colleagues who had been through the wars together, who had entered the combat of the streets as young men, survived and flourished and progressed, locked eyes. Tremblay's gaze conveyed to Cinq-Mars that he should ask no further question, cause no further trouble in this regard. His look disclosed that any further query would be met by stony silence, or by official rebuke. Cinq-Mars did not speak, while in his own eyes he indicated thanks to a friend from whom he'd been distant for too long. As if answering a covert cue, the men stood together. In shaking hands they confirmed their intention to enlist in the battle ahead, without words, trusting no one, but together, engaged.

Beaubien had been restored but not vindicated.

Permission, Cinq-Mars knew as he stepped out of his colleague's office, for him to proceed, without sanction, but more important, without impediment, had been granted.

Julia Murdick had been a passenger in fine cars in recent weeks—Norris's Infiniti, once in a Cadillac that belonged to the biker in the beige suit, now the Lexus Gitteridge leased. "Only fools buy," he said.

She closed her eyes and rested her head on the warm leather. Her tush had been toasted on so many car seats during the winter she wondered if she could accept being driven in a lesser vehicle again. They drove on, and the traffic was light. Reaching their destination, Gitteridge took his time finding a worthy parking spot, one with ample room for other vehicles to maneuver. They finally clambered out two blocks from the bank's front door, and twice Gitteridge stopped to gaze back at his car, as though he expected to see hub-caps being heisted.

"You're a walking advertisement. You should go on TV."

"You don't understand." She had to agree, she didn't. He shot another glance over his shoulder, but they had turned a corner. "Today's going to be all right for us, isn't it, Heather?"

"Something's got you spooked," she told him.

"You're a college girl. What do you know about the real world?"

"I'm a quick study."

"I'm counting on that. Know something? You walk funny."

She was bounding along beside him, her head bobbing up and down. Quickly she reined herself in, realizing that her walk was par-ticularly exaggerated due to anxiety, fear. She thought things with Gitteridge were going fairly well, but the goof over the weekend was still nagging her. The real Heather Bantry had showed up, and she had had to go to Okinder Boyle's house and bail them out of that jam. She was mad at Norris for the oversight, but when he explained that the real Heather lived in Seattle now, she could see how her showing up had been a surprise. Nobody had guessed that McGill would put on a national debating festival, or that that would matter, that Heather Bantry would be on a team. Still. Mistakes were so damned dangerous. "There's a term for it," she told him. "Not my walk exactly, what causes my walk."

"What's the term?"

She stopped to explain herself, bending over and looking down at her legs. "See, my shinbones don't appear to travel straight, they swerve, or so it looks, but they're not the problem. The problem starts with my feet, what's called the pronation, they roll inward toward each other, which causes the knees to point inward also. I'm knock-kneed, if you must know. I have emu kneecaps. The patella sit in a recess, but because of the pronation and the attendant problems, the outer quad muscles of my thighs get overworked compared to the inner muscles, consequently they develop more, and because of that they have a tendency to pull the kneecap out of alignment. That puts the whole knee apparatus out of wonk and ligaments overcompensate and the knee tries to rearrange the whole works and so I develop, sub-consciously, this whole other work-sharing ethic thing to help my leg bones and joints and muscles get along. Nothing cooperates. Overall I'm a pathetic mess. A chiropractor's wet dream."

Gitteridge could not confirm anything Julia said because she was wearing pants. She looked up, suddenly aware that she'd been bab-bling, aware also that at that moment she was frightened half to death. "What's the name for it, the term?" Gitteridge probed, his voice cold, and he was watching her with a skeptical gaze.

"Never mind. Is something wrong? Is everything okay, Mr. Gitteridge? You looked scared. You look like somebody just stole your Lexus."

"It's in our best interest that everything works as planned."

"Then come on," Julia urged. "Let's get on with it."

Gitteridge talked as he walked. "It's been a tough year. Turf wars. One biker blows up another. Nobody knows who gets hit next. In September, the bikers' banker was blown into pudding. Since then the boys haven't had much luck with their financial management. Until your dad. They have to show some people they can handle money, move it around, demonstrate they're on top of things. Your dad's in the right place at the right time. Funny how that worked out. You should understand, Heather. Don't rub these guys the wrong way, but you have a certain limited leverage. They have to answer to a high-er authority. As long as they're cozying up to their new partners, you'll be safe. Your dad'll be taken care of, too."

Julia walked and she was screaming to herself, *New partners! New partners! He must mean Russians! Like Selwyn said!* "Thanks for the advice, Mr. Gitteridge. I can use it. Some days I don't know what I got myself into."

"Handle this, Heather. Don't bail out. That's important, to you, to your old man, to me. You don't want to know what happens if you bail out."

Julia was fittingly subdued. "I'm not bailing," she vowed.

"Tell me something," he asked.

"What?"

"What's the term for what's wrong with your legs?"

"Why do you want to know?"

"I'm curious."

"I'm not saying. It's too humiliating. I don't tell anybody that." They wound up on Peel Street in a snarl of traffic, waiting for the light to change. After crossing, they walked into a branch of the Canadian Imperial Bank of Commerce.

"What do you want to get done?" she asked him.

"Verify the account balance and make a test withdrawal. I don't want to be the one who lands in jail. I'll stand behind you and watch."

"This is one of seven accounts."

"Do you have something better to do today? Did you have other plans?"

She shook her head. She wished he'd lighten up. "Do I get lunch out of this, at least?"

"McDonald's."

"No way. We're eating upscale or I'm not participating."

Gitteridge gripped her wrist and squeezed hard. "When do you get to understand that you never tell me what to do?"

"Fine." She shook him off, and he let her, not wanting a scene in the bank. "Go back to the Angels or whoever," she whispered hotly, "and tell them you couldn't get the money back because you'd rather rough me up in a bank than do their bidding." She arched an eyebrow. "Do you think they'll be understanding?"

"Very funny. What do we have to do here?" he demanded.

"We can ask for a printout of our company statement. See if any transfers have come in from Eastern Europe. We show our ID. Make a withdrawal. This one's in both our names."

The teller, a pleasant, brightly attired woman in her fifties, heavily made up, easily accommodated their requests and counted out two thousand dollars to cash the check Julia wrote against the account. They returned to the street.

"Are you telling me that that's not enough for lunch?"

Finally, Gitteridge grinned. "It's not our money. Don't forget that."

"I ain't that dumb."

His cellular phone warbled. "Hang on." He found a nook in the building out of the wind and chatted for a while. He waved her over when he was finished. Gitteridge clutched her wrist as he had done before and this time twisted.

"You're hurting!" She looked around, frantic. Pedestrians paid her no mind.

He tightened his grip.

She believed her wrist might snap, the skin tear. "Please. Stop!"

"Tell me," he demanded.

"What? What? Please! Mr. Gitteridge!"

"Tell me the term for your legs. Now. Tell me or I won't let go. I'll hurt you."

She was in the grip of a crazy man, her own fear rampant now. She had not anticipated Gitteridge freaking out. "What is this obsession with you? It's called malicious malalignment, all right? Please, don't repeat it."

"Malicious malalignment."

He let go.

Julia rubbed her scorched wrist.

"You're in luck," he informed her calmly. "We've been invited to lunch, and it's not McDonald's."

"Where?"

"The harbor. We're lunching aboard ship. Smile, sweetheart. You're the guest of honor."

They walked back to the Lexus. She could hardly see for the tears in her eyes as he held the door for her. She crawled in. Her wrist was hurting. Gitteridge got in behind the wheel and started up. "You're very good, Heather," he told her. "You and your father have passed our tests with flying colors."

"Why'd you squeeze my wrist so hard?"

Gitteridge chuckled lightly. "There was something you weren't telling me." He was checking his side mirror for a break in traffic. "There must never be anything you don't tell me. Nothing is private. Do you understand that now?"

"Yes, sir," she said in a wisp of a voice.

He was looking across at her again, shaking his head.

"What?"

"You're very convincing."

Convincing?

He moved the car into traffic, and they drove down to the water-front.

The leader of the Hell's Angels, on a rare visit to the city, ordered another beer and cut a patch from his steak. When he talked he waved his fork in front of him. When he wasn't talking he was eating or drinking. Wee Willie had a jag on for food, and his companions kept clear.

Wee Willie was wearing his usual attire, sports shirts that hung loosely over permanent-press slacks. He had learned to wear the clothes in Vegas, and now he hardly ever put on his biker uniform. He only did so to make someone fearful, or to demonstrate that he was just another boy with a wild heart looking to party.

He burped with fervor, laughed at himself, and nodded for his bodyguard to move so he could claw his way out of the booth. Two bikers accompanied him to the bathroom. One checked the room first, then both stood guard at the door. The restaurant had steadily emptied since the arrival of the bikers—despite their conservative dress they possessed an attitude, an air, that scared people—and only the patrons at a couple of tables had persevered to the natural end of their meals. No one went near the bathroom while Wee Willie was there.

His timing was impeccable. While he was pissing, a Jeep Cherokee came hurtling through the restaurant's handsome glass window, plowing chairs and tables and sending civilians for cover. The driver of the vehicle had jumped before impact and now was on the run.

"What the fuck!" Wee Willie bellowed, and he leapt out of the toilet, unzipped.

"A truck!" yelled one of the bodyguards, who had run back down the hall. "Smashed through the window!"

"Get in here!" Wee Willie commanded.

The three men locked themselves in the men's room. Their other companions at lunch did the same in the women's. Later the police knocked on the door.

"Is it gonna blow?" Wee Willie wanted to know before he opened up.

"Naw," the uniform told him, "something happened with the crash. They couldn't detonate."

Wee Willie and his friends emerged from the toilets then. They surveyed the shambles of the restaurant. Photographers snapped pictures, and a journalist dared to ask Wee Willie for a comment. "Fuckups," he told them. "They gotta be careful. They might've hurt somebody."

"Wasn't that the general idea?" the reporter inquired.

Wee Willie took exception to his tone. He reached out and closed his fist on the man's topcoat, pulling him into range of his beery breath. "Fuckup," he told him. "They might've killed a citizen is what I meant."

A few witnesses took the remark to be gallant, as if he was some kind of modern Robin Hood. They didn't understand that he was looking out for his own best interests. Killing citizens was bad for biker business. It aroused the Wolverines—that lesson they had already learned.

Run ragged, Bill Mathers interviewed the Korean manager of a gas station that had been ransacked and robbed of cigarettes and soft drinks overnight, while it had been closed. The man called the burglars cowards, shaking his head and repeating the word until Mathers consented to utter it also. That cordial agreement satisfied him. They rehearsed it together as a mantra, *cowards*, the Korean grinning broadly. "Yes," he persisted, "cowards, cowards," bowing forward. Mathers was saved by his beeper. Calling the department switchboard, he learned that a message had come through from Estelle Myers, Hagop Artinian's ex-girlfriend, whom he had interviewed earlier.

Finished with the burglary report, Mathers headed straight for the young woman's place in the student ghetto and rang her bell. He was quickly buzzed up.

"Hey, Detective! Long time!"

"Estelle. Nice to see you again."

He shut the door behind him. When he turned she had bounded onto the bed, bouncing there. Estelle was wearing old jeans and a loose-fitting top and she looked delectable to him. He felt an ample cross section of his heart spring from his body and leap beside her.

She had tucked her ankles under herself, rocking only slightly now. "You know what?"

"What?"

"In an uptight sort of way, you're kinda cute for a cop."

"Gee, thanks, Estelle. I'll take that to the grave. Now what's up?"

"I have some friends who have a teensy-weensy problemo that maybe you can help them with?" She bounced again and did a quick pivot, so that she was kneeling on the bed now, clapping her hands in an odd way, the fingers splayed out so that only her palms made contact one with the other. "*Plus!* I have information you're gonna wanna hear, Mr. Policeman!" When she stopped her imitation of a small child clapping, she put her hands on her hips, and the pose was scarcely resistible, all breasts and pelvis to his eyes.

"Are you trading information? If you know something, Estelle—"

She swung her legs around so that she was sitting on the bed again with her bare toes just touching the floor. He was beginning to wonder if she was high on something.

"Estelle—you owe it to Hagop's memory to say what you know."

Mentioning the reason for the investigation subdued her nubile exhibition. She twisted her torso, trying to wiggle free from obligations. "I'll tell you. I will, I will. I'm not trading. But I have these friends, and if I can help you out then it doesn't seem so unreasonable to me that you can give my friends a break. I don't see what you're so fired up about. Isn't that fairish?"

Mathers was willing to bend. In rhythm to the young woman's movements, the upright trunk of his ethics swayed as a tender sapling in a gale. "What did your friends do?"

"Okay, they were having a party," Estelle told him. "Nothing drastic. Normal student stuff, and yes that means a bit too loud. That's really their only crime. So! Neighbors complained. The cops came to the door, blah blah blah—some guys made a few remarks that maybe they shouldn't've, and all of a sudden they're busted for dope. Mere possession. I mean, bop my bottom with a banana—marijuana and hashish? Nobody's been arrested for smoking that stuff since the *Mayflower*, or the flower children, or whatever."

"Are you on some of it right now?"

"Nnnnoooo, I'm just happy to see you that's all."

He really could not resist being charmed by her and didn't know why he bothered. What would it cost him to have a fling with a girl like this? The warring angels scolded him as he knew they would. Weird. He might successfully conceal his guilt around Donna, although that was questionable, but he'd never manage to look Cinq-Mars in the eye again. No dice. Not this time. Probably never—a realization that saddened him.

He was a choirboy. Mathers had to admit that. He liked being mischievous, that was his big secret. Flirting was mischief. Anything more than that, he reverted to being a choirboy again, that was his way of being, why he was a cop.

"Estelle. What's up?"

"Can you help my friends?"

"Sure, why not? Now tell me what's up."

"Really! You can? You mean it!" This time she bounded on the bed once off her bottom onto her knees, then onto her feet with her head scraping the ceiling. Landing back onto her bottom again, she bounced repeatedly.

"What are you on?"

"Nothing! I'm just happy! Can't a girl be happy?"

"Do you have something for me?"

A part of him hoped that she would slander that question and propose an offer too indecent to resist.

"Last Friday night!" she said, and for the first time he grasped why she was giddy. She was high on knowledge, on information, she was high on the news she bore. "I was walking down the street—my street. I was coming up to a car that'd left its motor running. No biggee, but you know, I'm a woman, and women get raped in the ghetto, so, you know, I keep an eye out. There's one guy in the car, but everything's cool, but as I get close to the car I notice this name tag thingee on its tail end."

"Yeah? So?"

"Q Forty-five! The car was an Infiniti Q Forty-five! That's when I remembered!"

Mathers was immediately attentive. "What did you remember?"

"You asked me to call with anything that might seem important. Maybe if I remembered something peculiar, or out of place."

"That's right. I did."

She bounced again. "One time, I saw Hagop, across the street from where I was standing, talking to a slick-dressed man. The man got into a green Infiniti Q Forty-five and drove away. A little while after that, somebody asked him who was the guy with the fancy car. Hagop told him it was his uncle. He didn't know I was listening in. Why did he lie? Hagop never lies. I know Hagop's only uncle, and he wasn't that guy, and he doesn't drive that kind of car."

Mathers was taking in every word. "And this Q Forty-five that you saw the other night—"

"Was green! It was green green green! So what do I do? I see the plate and memorize it, and I keep on walking and repeat it to myself until I've got it and, Detective, here—it—is."

She plucked a slip of paper from the tight front pocket of her jeans.

Bill Mathers was dumbfounded. "Estelle. God. Thank you."

"You'll want to know the names of my friends."

After Mathers duly noted the information, Estelle held the door for him, and on his way out she stretched up on her tiptoes and gave him a kiss on the cheek, slightly to the left of his mouth. He hesitated. She pecked him again and smiled. "You are cute," she said.

"Yeah, and you're trouble."

"Only in your mind, Detective."

He nodded, offered a slight wave good-bye, again thanked her, and headed down the stairs. Going out the door felt as close to an escape as anything he had experienced. Bill Mathers believed that he had survived by the slimmest, the most fragile, of margins. His heart beat at a runner's pace. He had something to show for his turmoil—he might have the license plate number for Émile Cinq-Mars's mysterious source in hand. Rather than present him with it, Mathers decided that first he would run it down himself.

In the intimate cabin on the Russian freighter Julia Murdick was on pins and needles throughout lunch. Fear circled underneath her skin. Gitteridge had introduced her to a tall, dark, well-groomed, well-dressed Russian, who had flinty eyes and spoke with a mangled accent. The man talked a great deal about the cleverness of Carl Bantry and studied her with a smile perpetually curling at the side of his mouth. He had wide, sensual lips. During lunch a seaman entered the cabin and whispered in the Russian's ear. He waved him out, then explained to his guests, "A policeman. A nuisance. A flea. We will dispose of this irritation. We do this, us." He continued to wave his hand in the air, as though brushing dust from a mantelpiece.

She and Gitteridge exchanged a glance.

The Russian stretched across the table and caressed her cheek with his thumb. "Perhaps you like for to see ship, Heather," he suggested. "Is interest for you?"

She consented, choosing to err on the side of politeness, of compliance.

"Come."

Gitteridge was to remain behind.

The Russian showed her the bridge, where she met the diminutive captain, a sullen, uncommunicative fellow, then brought her down into the hold, where the volume was impressive, the space cold and forbidding. The walls, ceilings, and floors were steel, the paint chipped and faded. The Russian, who had not proffered a name for himself, led her through the massive machine works and up into the ship's complicated plumbing and hydraulics.

Down below two Hell's Angels in full biker colors intercepted their tour. They grabbed her arms and the Russian said, "Come, this way," leading her toward a darker area. They shoved her through a door he held open. Inside, she turned. The men came in, and then the steel door slammed shut and the echo reverberated harshly in her brain. She couldn't breathe. She felt claustrophobic. The room was tiny, filled with pipes and valves. The bikers were huge and they regarded her with disdain and the big Russian was smiling.

She returned his look, fearing rape. Worse. Discovery.

"The police, they call me Czar. I have accepted this name. It is good, yes? You may call me by this name."

He took her hands in one of his. She gasped. A biker put a hand on one breast, squeezing. She cried out and resisted. The Czar ran his free hand along a cluster of smaller pipes, choosing a cool one. He held her wrists down on the pipe and told her to keep them there, and she obeyed. The stray hand was off her now. The Russian had turned his back.

"Now, Heather Bantry," he said, "we see. About you we see."

"What's wrong? What'd I do?"

"You not talk."

A handcuff snapped over one wrist. He pulled her other hand under the pipe and held it in place and snapped on the other cuff, binding her to the pipe. He flicked off the overhead light.

She was alone in the dark with the three men.

"Now we see about you," he declared, and she readied herself to scream.

She could hear them breathing.

The Russian stood behind her, breathing, lightly running his fingers up and down her spine. He moved closer. Slowly he ran the backs of his fingernails down one side of her face and throat, and his touch was like a blade. A biker reached up and pulled on her hair. She cried out. The three men laughed lightly. "This is nothing," the Czar scolded her. "This only to begin for you." Then he opened the door, there was that flash of light, and they left her alone in the dark.

Her legs lost strength. She bumped her head. She hung from the pipe, unable to stand, already begging that she would not soon die a horrible death. She believed she would. Who could save her now? *Selwyn? Selwyn!*

13

Yawning mightily, Sergeant-Detective Émile Cinq-Mars leaned back in his swivel chair and stretched his arms and shoulders before rubbing the tiredness from his eyes. Long past being weary, he still had to hang around the station before risking the long drive home. That morning he had arrived before seven—it was now past midnight—and he allowed himself the extravagance of leaning forward, dropping his head into the crook of his elbow on his desk, and closing his eyes. *Oh, blessed sleep.*

By his own evaluation, they were making progress on several fronts. He had a number for the fake Heather Bantry, from which an address had been gleaned. The woman hadn't been home all day, which was worrisome. He hoped she hadn't been spooked by the cop staking out her place. He'd chosen not to disturb the premises without first attempting to discern her circumstances. Hagop Artinian's apartment had been bugged, he believed, so hers might be as well. An intrusion by cops could compromise a precariously fragile situation.

Bill Mathers had come up with a license plate for the Q45, but it did not match any computer record. It was bogus. The computer printed out a false name and a non-existent address. The CIA theory was sounding less fantastic by the hour. Given the leaks in department security, Cinq-Mars had rejected the idea of issuing an APB for the car, fearing that his source might hear the bulletin before any uniform. He'd rather his source burrow no deeper. Cinq-Mars would have to settle for marshaling a few good cops to keep their eyes peeled.

He had torn a strip off Mathers, which was too bad. The poor boy was delighted to report that he had the plate number in hand, and Cinq-Mars had been excited to receive it. Procuring the number had been real police work. But then Mathers had screwed up. He'd had the number run down through regular channels, and worse, over the police band. He just didn't get it—regular channels were not secure. A grand opportunity might have been blown.

And yet, his head down on the desk, the squad room empty, the detective sensed that they were closing in on his source.

As for other matters, they had distance to cover. Jim Coates's Russian—this so-called Czar—was unknown, he could be anywhere on the planet. André LaPierre had been feeling the pressure of his suspension. Gilles Beaubien was suffering from reduced responsibilities and increased department scrutiny. Women in the secretarial pool were under the eye of Tremblay's investigation. A net was being cast—at sea, and in the dark, but a net.

He had greater freedom. That had to count for something.

The wait was proving to be interminable. Max Gitteridge had called. Gunfire in a bar had pulled him away from the care of his nightclub to the nurture of a client in lockup. The lawyer wanted to talk to Cinq-Mars about that shooting, but there was no reason why he should and Cinq-Mars assumed that Gitteridge was inventing an excuse to speak to him privately. But why? He was stuck waiting for the lawyer to show.

More coffee. He shouldn't. His nerve endings were frayed, tingling. Then again, he had a long drive home ahead of him and the highway would be quiet. He should probably fill his thermos, keep himself primed for the trip. Sleep later on in a caffeine spin, perhaps, but sleep alive.

Cinq-Mars made the walk to the coffeemaker and remembered only when he arrived that he'd finished the dregs on his last trip. He fixed a fresh pot and returned to his cubicle and finally heard the man's steps crossing the squad room floor. He had little use for Max Gitteridge. The system demanded that an accused have the right to counsel and a rigorous defense, but he was under no obligation to admire the defenders. Some trial attorneys were shysters, he understood that. But a few defense lawyers trod in dung up to their eyebrows. Confederates in crime with their clients, they rankled Cinq-Mars. Likely, they'd never be prosecuted. On the other hand, in Montreal, a number of lawyers who defended the bad guys had been discovering their life expectancy in sharp decline. One had been car-bombed, another shot in his office, another vanished with no known trace. In its own roundabout way, with an occasional sense of discrimination, frontier justice was being meted out.

Cinq-Mars knew Gitteridge by the sharp staccato of the taps on his heels. He stood up and watched him make his way around the squad desks to the cubicle, unaware that Cinq-Mars was peering over the divider. His head kept bobbing around, checking things out. What was curious to Cinq-Mars was that he looked less like a man interested in discovering information than a man worrying about who might have him in his sights.

"Evening, Max," Cinq-Mars said boldly, and the little guy jumped a foot.

"Good evening, Émile," Gitteridge said, his fright and testiness evident. "I bet you like to jump out at old ladies when they're walking down the street." He stood at the entrance to the policeman's space, between the cubicle dividers. Most of the skeleton crew of detectives working nights were out on the streets. One lone typewriter clicked away.

"Mr. Gitteridge, my sympathies."

"For what?"

"Losing a client."

Gitteridge scratched his chin. "Kaplonski. That was a shame."

"He'd have been better off incarcerated."

"Hindsight is a great source of wisdom, Émile."

Cinq-Mars offered a conciliatory smile. "It's not like I didn't warn him."

"Did you?"

"I told him he might have it coming. What can I do for you, Counselor?"

Gitteridge stepped further into the room and deposited his briefcase along with his cashmere coat on a chair. He moved over to the window, loosened his tie, plunged his hands deep into his pockets. The lights of the squad room reflected back upon him. "I've got a client in lockup. A shooting."

"Murder?" Cinq-Mars asked, wondering, *What does this have to do with me?*

"One victim's too high to know he's been shot. The other one's hanging by a thread. I'm unhappy with the investigation, Émile. I'd like you to hear my client's story. Judge for yourself." Gitteridge looked at him then. He stared at him so hard that Cinq-Mars was compelled to meet his eyes. "You have a reputation for integrity, Detective. That can come in handy. Come upstairs to the lockup with me."

Cinq-Mars analyzed the situation. The case had nothing to do with him. His integrity as an officer would be irrelevant to Gitteridge. The best that he could deduce was that the lawyer wanted to talk to him but not where they were standing.

The lawyer retrieved his belongings, and Cinq-Mars followed him out. They made their way down broad, high corridors painted an institutional two-tone—beige and what his wife called puke green. Each man was silent. They took the stairs the two flights to lockup. Near the top of their ascent their pace slowed, both panted, and Gitteridge indicated a bathroom. He held the door open. In the quiet of a latrine, in the nocturnal stillness, they'd converse.

The tiled room, recently mopped, stank of urine and cleansers. Gitteridge entered a stall and hung his briefcase on the hook and his winter coat over it and came out again, hands in his pockets, a grayness to the pallor of his skin. The overhead bulbs were bare, their light uncompromising. He strolled across to the frosted glass window and leaned down to breathe fresh air. Without a separate thermostat, the room became unbearably hot in winter, and the window was left open a notch even in arctic conditions. "Miserable fucking weather," he mentioned.

"Might as well be Moscow," Cinq-Mars agreed, enjoying the innuendo.

Gitteridge straightened up, his back to Cinq-Mars. "More like Siberia," he concluded. Moving over to the sinks, he turned on a tap and watched the water flow, then leaned down and splashed his face.

He kept the tap running as he dried himself on paper towels from a dispenser.

"You can turn that off," Cinq-Mars advised.

"You never know," Gitteridge warned.

"You've chosen well. You can turn it off."

Gitteridge shut the tap. He remained standing with his hand on the faucet, leaned forward slightly, his head offset to one side.

"What I said at your desk is true." The lawyer spoke in a hushed voice now, as though compensating for the echo in this chamber. "You're a righteous cop. That can be useful in certain circumstances."

"How so?" Cinq-Mars rested his weight against a sink.

Gitteridge straightened up. "Maybe a few things can be said to a righteous cop without the words traveling back to their origin. It might be possible for me to say a few things that will stay put. No other cop will hear about it. Not one."

"That's probably true," Cinq-Mars agreed. "Some things don't need to be repeated."

"Has she told you yet?" the lawyer asked.

Cinq-Mars was sufficiently adept at both interrogation and negotiation that he was not about to be fazed by a ruse. "Has who told me what?" he asked back, without blinking.

Gitteridge smiled thinly.

If the lawyer wanted to tell him something, Cinq-Mars was listening. He was intrigued by the man's motivation. He guessed that fear had inspired Gitteridge more than anything else.

"I don't know if she got word out to you. Maybe she hasn't had the chance. If she did she might have included my name. I'm here to tell you that this has nothing to do with me, Émile. I heard the information for the first time the same moment she did, and I'm here to tell you myself, in person, so you know that I'm not attached to this."

Cinq-Mars waited. Then he said, "Let's assume, for the benefit of this conversation, that when you refer to 'she' I don't know who you're talking about. Can we start there?"

"Naturally. But I'll tell you how I know, so we're free of bullshit. She contradicted her cover."

If Gitteridge was studying him for a reaction, Cinq-Mars had none to provide. He waited.

"Malicious malalignment."

"Excuse me?"

"That's the term for the problem with her legs. Trouble for you is, I did a background check on her. Put a gumshoe on it. Even read her high school yearbook. That gave me a picture, but you know, faces change. Hairstyles, hair colors, looks change. Heather Bantry, the real one, the real girl, was a sprinter. The real one never had this malicious malalignment thing."

The young woman's identity had been compromised. Cinq-Mars understood her life was now in peril. "Why tell me any of this, Counselor? What's in it for you? Don't you have interested parties to inform?"

Gitteridge rubbed his fingers across his jaw, then played with the ends of his loosened tie. He swallowed a couple of times. Gone was his usual smarmy cockiness, and it seemed as though he spoke more elegantly when he was scared than when he was trying to be threatening. "As you know, Émile, I have worked around ruthless men on occasion. That's no secret. It's my job. But it seems the world is changing. In the old days, there was a culture, an understanding. A person was allowed a life, a certain segregation between his personal and professional hours. These days, there's a new way of doing things, it's not so easy for some of us to adapt."

This was getting too oblique for the detective's liking. *A new culture? Was he referring to Russians again?*

The lawyer sighed heavily, then said, "Hagop Artinian."

"Yes?" Cinq-Mars unconsciously held his breath.

"They found out he was one of yours. That's why they suckered you into chasing down a false Santa Claus then hung the sign on the boy. They wanted you warned off."

"I figured."

"Artinian made some penetration, nothing too serious, but closer than anyone appreciated. You know what happened to him. You also know what happened to the person who, inadvertently, helped him get inside."

Kaplonski.

"So?"

"Don't play coy with me, Émile."

"Mr. Gitteridge, we are playing coy with one another. That's our theme song for the evening."

The lawyer broke off looking at him and bent down and fussed with his tie again. He looked like a man trying to rearrange his life. "This girl, she's made good penetration. Now I find out she was never a sprinter, that she could never have been a sprinter, that she has a bone deformity in her legs called malicious malalignment. She penetrated through me. She came into the organization through me. If I sell her out now, I'll be given a pat on the back and turned into the next cherry pie. It's the new way of doing things. It's taking care of business in the new world order."

Cinq-Mars let that settle. This was good news, extraordinary news. A mole had penetrated the network of the Hell's Angels through their own lawyer, and now their lawyer was running scared. "What do you have to tell me?" he pressed.

Gitteridge drifted to another place as he idly fingered a button under his tie. Probably he had never crossed this line before, and once crossed he knew that nothing would be familiar on the other side. He snapped back, and reported at last, "There's going to be a bump."

"Who's the target?" Cinq-Mars whispered.

"A cop. That's all I heard. I don't think your mole has picked up more than that, but you can ask her."

They looked at each other and the radiator pipes rattled and the wind blew through the gap in the window. "Me?" Cinq-Mars asked quietly.

The lawyer shrugged.

"It won't do you any good telling me if I'm the one who gets whacked."

"Good point, Émile. If I had to guess, and I do, I'd say they won't whack you. We both know why. The Wolverines have a big push on, a good budget. Knock you off, they'll be on a rampage with public blessing and full powers and double the financing—for years. But I can't say categorically that it's *not* you either, or if it's a good cop or

271

a cop who works for them. Maybe they've found a way to manage it. Could be arbitrary. I don't know. I do not know. If I did, probably I'd tell you. But there's something else at play here."

"What's that?"

"The girl inside has heard about it. They'll be watching. This could be nothing more than a test to find out if she snitches. If they see measures taken, Émile, or pick up a nuance within the department—something they're good at—your girl goes *boom*. Protecting yourself, protecting anyone you think is a target, puts her in jeopardy."

"They'll follow through, test or no test?"

"I'd bet that way. It's a different culture, Émile. I can't say it won't be you."

"Date?"

"They tend not to rush things."

"Location?"

"To be determined."

"Most likely a bomb?"

"They prefer noise."

"What else can you tell me?"

"Nothing. Émile, your girl has marked me down as an accessory. I'm not implicated here. I was present for the same conversation she overheard. I've come straight to you with what I know. They only want us to know a little, not a lot. Under the new system, everyone who works for them must prove he's dirty."

"Everyone?"

"No exceptions. I've told you what I've got. Émile, if the fact that you know gets into the wind, then it's her or me who did the talking. If it's her, I go down too, because I'm the one who carried her into the system. If it's me, then she goes down with me, obvious reasons. Is your snitch aware of the consequences? I don't think so. Walk slow, Émile."

Gitteridge could be spreading manure to see if he'd stoop to sniff. He could be tilling the landscape to find out what weeds grew. Cinq-Mars had to step softly. "I don't know about any girl," he reiterated quietly.

The lawyer did not bother to reply.

"Your concerns in this matter have been duly noted, Mr. Gitteridge.

I will do what's in my power, should it come to that, to exonerate you of complicity in this affair. But now, you must do one more thing."

"What's that?"

"Give me the Russian."

Arching an eyebrow, Gitteridge shook his head. "Do you want to hear something that's truly astonishing? I do believe I would if I could. Why? Because he's the one who's upset the applecart. He's the one changing the rules. In the old days it was understood that a lawyer was a lawyer, everyone agreed the lawyer should not be impli-cated, that he stayed above the fray, that's how the system worked. These days, there's only one interest that needs to be satisfied. And I can tell you that it's not mine."

"Give me something," Cinq-Mars insisted.

"What can I say? His name is Sergei. He likes to call himself the Czar, because he heard that's what the Wolverines call him. He's tall, a big-shouldered guy, dark-haired, he's got a scar under his chin—here—that follows the jawline."

"I know all that," Cinq-Mars told him.

Gitteridge eyed him sharply then. "How many points in a star?"

Clueless, Cinq-Mars returned his stern look. "How many?"

"You haven't done your homework, Émile. You're not up to speed. All right. I'll give you this one. The answer is eight. Look for an eight-pointed star."

"The tattoo," Cinq-Mars said. He could tell that Gitteridge was impressed that he knew even that much. He silently thanked God for Jim Coates.

Gitteridge entered the stall again and retrieved his briefcase and overcoat. When he emerged, Cinq-Mars was slouching by the door.

"You go one way, Émile, I'll go the other."

"That's how it's always been, Counselor."

"Good luck."

"I could use a dose."

Cinq-Mars gave Gitteridge time to clear the building, then returned to his cubicle. The station clock said one-ten. He put on his coat and jiggled keys in a palm. Starting his car promised to be an adventure. In these days of threats and bombs, he might be better off checking out a cruiser to take home. First, fill the thermos.

In the basement garage, Sergeant-Detective Émile Cinq-Mars stepped up to his blue Taurus wagon, put his key into the door lock. For the sake of that young woman, he couldn't change his pattern. He had to remain consistent. He wondered if Steeplechase Arch would be in touch anytime soon. The man might discern that the plot to kill a cop was indeed a test, that the best way to pass it was to keep the information mute. Let someone die to preserve the integrity of the operation. It wasn't as though the bastard hadn't done that before, it wasn't as though he hadn't sacrificed one of his own. What would be the loss of a cop?

Would Arch call? If he learned that the target was Cinq-Mars himself, would he risk informing him? *"Thank God for Gitteridge,"* the detective murmured as he inserted his key into the ignition. He was hardly able to believe that he had uttered those words.

THREE

———

THE EIGHT-
POINTED STAR

14

2:12 A.M. The locksmith had dozed off in the backseat of Cinq-Mars's cruiser. Now the ground fairly trembled. The machines' cantankerous roaring drew closer. Before long, an armored division of snow removers crossed the Main, then St.-Urbain and Clark Streets, and Émile Cinq-Mars prepared to move.

He'd tucked the car high on l'Esplanade, a distance up from Mount Royal Avenue with a clear view across the park to the apartment. The fake Heather Bantry had yet to return home. Cinq-Mars raised his hand, circled a finger in the air to signal the young couple in the car behind him. The pair stepped out and strolled down to Mount Royal, romantic in the snow.

"Young love." Mathers sniffed.

"What's eating you?"

"They don't even know each other."

"They're under orders," Cinq-Mars pointed out.

"Looks like he's feeling her up."

"I suppose you want the duty?"

The couple dodged the monster blowers, gaily leapfrogged a snow-bank plowed by graders, and strolled arm in arm to the apartment block. Mathers awakened the locksmith, and the three of them climbed out of the car and headed down also.

The pair ascended the steps to the apartment building, kissed on the stoop. Way too passionately for Mathers's liking. Their initial under-cover job and they were having sex. Arm in arm, the two entered the building and Mathers ambled down to the rear door. He waited, and checked his watch. The junior cops opened the door from inside.

"You kids having fun?"

Both seemed flushed.

"There's no need to get carried away."

"We were told to make it look good," the woman said.

"You're officers of the law," Mathers reminded them. He didn't know why he said that, or what it meant. After that he held his tongue.

Minutes later the locksmith knocked—a mistake—and came in. Cinq-Mars entered last.

"Wait." Cinq-Mars held the door open a crack. Snowblowers and graders were active, their diesels roaring, and a long line of trucks waited in single file to be loaded with snow, the idling motors cacophonous. Small sidewalk plows scooted ahead of the graders, and pulsing amber lights flashed off the buildings. Tow trucks cruising the side streets emitted annoying wee-waw sirens to jolt residents from their slumber to move parked cars. In the corridor, the building quavered and windows rattled. Cinq-Mars seemed satisfied. "Let's go."

They ascended to the fourth floor. The two rookies guarded the stairs at either end of the hall to warn of intruders. The locksmith kneeled down by a door and faced the lock. He'd already classified the job as a snap, but he required a patch of time.

Cinq-Mars tapped him on the shoulder. Put a finger to his lips.

The locksmith waited through a lull outside and started up again as the bedlam resumed. He was a small man, lithe, his fingers dexterous. He opened the door while the machines were especially vocal.

Leaving their boots and shoes in the hall, Cinq-Mars and Mathers pulled on foam slippers over their socks. They entered the apartment and soundlessly shut the door behind them.

This was illicit, everyone knew. This was illegal entry.

Penlights shone the way. Cinq-Mars had brought along a DC fluorescent lantern to be used if conditions allowed—the swarm of revolving lights made it viable. The two men stood silently side by side in the lamp's glow, feeling as though they'd been here before, alone in a barren apartment.

The rooms were empty.

Speech was prohibited. In response to his partner's nod Mathers moved to investigate the closets. He feared the moment, feared he'd find another dead kid. Each vacant closet allowed him to breathe again, then the next clutched at his heart. No body was found on the premises. The apartment was truly empty.

Swept clean.

Cinq-Mars bent down to study the electrical outlets, and Mathers aimed the light. At first, the older man touched nothing. He appeared to be studying dust along the baseboards. He gestured for a screwdriver, which Mathers went out on tiptoe to fetch from the locksmith. Cinq-Mars removed the wall plate with extraordinary care, certain to make not the slightest sound. Mathers leaned in. His senior eased him back a bit. He didn't want him breathing too close. Mathers saw it then—a wee silver transmitter wedged under the socket.

Silently, Cinq-Mars restored the wall plate.

He remained on his knees. The convoy of equipment outside was moving along, creating less racket, although the building continued to tremble. He had to act quickly. The detective moved down the wall to a small phone box, which jutted out from the baseboard bereft of active lines. Jacks were available in various spots around the apartment, but this box struck him as promising. Cinq-Mars removed the cover. Inside was the usual jumble of wires, and he deployed his penlight to show Mathers what was out of the ordinary.

A small receiver, wired to the phone line.

The first bug picked up conversations around the room, benefiting from the holes in the socket, transmitted the sound ten feet down the wall to an amplified receiver, which dispatched the news across the telephone network to an unknown destination.

Cinq-Mars returned the cover to the box and signaled to evacuate the room.

In the corridor he put his footwear back on and walked over to the cop watching the main stairs. He whispered that he wanted his topcoat. He returned and, after the locksmith had secured the door again, used the coat to mop up their winter melt. Cinq-Mars returned the coat to a grumpy-looking cop, and everybody headed down.

Once again, the young lovers made a spectacle of themselves on the front stoop, this time to attract attention while the officers slipped out the rear. The pair headed off, the locksmith crossed to his unmarked van, and Cinq-Mars and Mathers, choosing alternate routes, reconnected at their squad car, where Cinq-Mars drummed his fingers across the wheel.

His partner waited.

"At issue," the older man began, "is whether the bug was dropped before the apartment was emptied out—or after. I'd say after. It's a recent implant. The dust on the wall plate doesn't coincide with the dust on the quarter round or the baseboards, or with the dust on the other plates. The plate was disturbed. The same thing happened in Hagop Artinian's apartment."

"What does that give us?" Mathers pondered.

"Whoever removed her stuff wants to know if she's been missed." Cinq-Mars spoke slowly, quietly, as though directed by the late hour to be discreet. "If they've pulled her from view, they'll want to know who gets nervous. They think about her being connected. But they don't know. So they run a test. Or, if they happen to figure she's connected, they might want to know to whom. That's scary. In that scenario, they suspect somebody besides us."

"Your source."

"Whoever he is."

They waited in the stillness of the car. In his rearview mirror, Cinq-Mars saw the young police officers coming the long way around to pick up their vehicle. They remained in character.

"At Hagop's place, I'd bet money they took their bug out. Here, they put it in."

Mathers broached the one question he'd rather not have mentioned. "Do you think she's alive, Émile?"

Cinq-Mars shook his head with an instinctive determination. "Bill, until we find her hanging in a closet with a meat hook in her hide, we proceed on the basis that she is. I don't want to lose this one. No way. No more dead kids."

Mathers struggled with the implications. "If we treat her as alive, that means she's being tested."

"Which means we never indicate that we know about her existence. As of now, pull all surveillance off the apartment. As far as we're concerned, she does not exist. We mention her to nobody."

Mathers took a deep breath and released an arduous sigh. "Now what?"

"Take the morning off, Bill. Catch up on your sleep. Pay your caseload a little attention tomorrow afternoon. Or is that today already? Whatever. If I can swing it, I'm not coming in until tomorrow night."

"To do what?"

Cinq-Mars bobbed his head from side to side, as though that remained to be decided. "The device was sophisticated. The installation professional, top-notch. We've heard mention of KGB, FSB, there's talk about CIA. I bet those groups can recognize one another's handiwork. The best chance that woman has is if the Angels never think CIA, and if they have an ex-KGB officer among them, they might. If they're testing her, we want her to pass. If she's being initiated, we want her to get through. Otherwise, the SQ will find her in a ditch somewhere, chain-sawed into cordwood."

"Tomorrow night?" Mathers reminded him after a pause.

"I'm curious. How far does LaPierre go with his gadgets? Maybe I'll pay him a visit."

Cinq-Mars started up the car. He figured the officers in his mirror were kissing just to get Mathers's goat, but he was too tired to play along.

"I learned stuff tonight," Mathers let on. "Émile, at your place—in the barn. Why did you tell me that your friend betrayed you?"

"Ray knows too much. His caution was too deliberate. When he warned me about a rogue, he had somebody specific in mind. I could feel it. Hell, the damn horses could feel it. You know what? You put me on to him."

"Me? How?"

"You said my source probably knew me, if not directly then through someone close to me. For a while I was even careful what I said around Sandra, just because she's American. But then I figured, if I was CIA, coming across the border, how would I find out who to contact in the department? Chances are, I'd check with Canadian Intelligence, call in a favor, see what that did for me. Ray pointed Steeplechase Arch to my door."

Mathers considered the news a moment. He was falling asleep. "Is that selling you out? Your career prospered, Émile."

"Aiding an organization to manipulate a friend is betrayal. Keep that in mind in case you're tempted. Do you want a lift home, or back to HQ?"

"HQ," Mathers stipulated. His car was there. He had no intention of taking the morning off as Cinq-Mars had suggested. He'd need his car, if not at the crack then fairly early in the day.

As a premonition of spring, a tickler, a boost to civic morale, the winter thaw arrived in the early morning hours, taking the form of a torrential downpour. Sometime after dawn, blue skies became prevalent.

An immaculate day.

Émile Cinq-Mars and Sandra Lowndes released their horses to the three paddocks abutting their stables, and the animals kicked up their hooves in the melting snow. Heavy with foals, mares slouched and rubbed themselves along the fences, content enough. Given to a spell of enchantment, the couple observed the animals, assured that winter would end, that the rituals of spring and summer would again pertain. The countryside would bloom. While they were immersed in the frigid dark of winter, for either of them to have imagined the prospect had seemed attributable to fuzzy-headedness.

The couple stood in their boots leaning on the corral fence. Both grinned as though a jubilant breeze had passed through them.

"I guess I've been a problem boy," Cinq-Mars lamented.

Sandra stood with her chin on her hands, elbows and forearms resting along a fence rail. "You've been distant," she acknowledged, deliberately being gentle with him.

He moved closer to her and brushed her cheek with a finger, shifting a strand of straw-colored hair away from her eyes. Sandra turned and lowered her head, meditatively touching her lips with both thumbs. Her husband crossed his arms and hung them on the top rail, a foot up on the lowest rung.

"We are why we are," he stated.

Sandra observed him intently. She knew when he desired his words to settle, when he expected their import to be esteemed, their weight affirmed. At times his riddles were too arcane for her sensibility. "Which means what exactly?"

Cinq-Mars did not become agitated by this direct rebuttal to his mood, in itself promising. "The phrase meant a lot to me when I was younger. Back then it carried the weight of revelation. Now it means nearly as much, but in a different light. We are why we are. Think about it."

"Give me a hint."

The movement of his chin, she noticed, even the rhythm of his words, closely matched the gait of a dressage horse crossing the paddock, its neck nicely rounded as though responding to the aids of a phantom rider.

"The world puts up its pet phrases—'You are what you eat,' 'Be all that you can be,' 'I think therefore I am,' 'Things go better with Coke.' One morning, I woke up with a line in my head, 'We are why we are.' It stuck."

"What does it mean to you?"

He shrugged, as though that was less important now. "That we're here for a purpose. That that purpose dictates who we are, what becomes of us. We're on the earth for a reason, and when we know the reason, we get a glimpse of who we are. I got it into my head that my purpose in life was to care for animals. I wanted to be a vet. That wasn't possible, so I became a cop, an altogether different sort of zookeeper. I rationalized that I'd gotten my destiny mixed up at first."

Two polo ponies ran off at a gallop until they hit the deeper snow, which flew up alongside them and caused them to disappear momentarily behind a blizzard of their own creation.

"I took the phrase personally—*we are why we are*—and grafted my own ambition onto it. 'I'm a cop because that's why I'm here, to be a cop,' that sort of thing. Either I'm older and wiser or simply less concerned about how my career affects the universe, but I now apply the phrase generally. We are who we are because of why we are."

He was allowing his words to settle again. Sandra asked, "Then why are we, Émile?"

He repeated his shrug and allowed the cathedral vault of his eyebrows to rise, indicating that the answer did not reside with him, that the best he could offer was speculation. "Perhaps we've been put here to care for animals. In a sense, our communal purpose *is* to be vets."

"You're losing me, Émile," she warned him.

He smiled, and she was glad to see that brightness illuminate his face for a change. Just as spring lurked behind the cover of winter, she believed that the man she'd married remained underneath the worry and burden of his occupation. Perhaps it was the sunlight on his face again, the unbuttoned jacket, or being out-of-doors, finally, without a hat. He was looking years younger. Strange, because she knew that he hadn't slept much, that he had tossed all night.

"Cats and dogs live in our homes because they know how to control their bowels. If horses and pigs and goats and lizards and elephants and hippos could handle their personal hygiene, we'd have domesticated them aeons ago. Giraffes in the living room, rhinos in the kitchen. Gazelles in our backyards if we could afford the real estate."

"Think so?"

"Absolutely!" He raised a hand to emphasize his point. "One of the earliest myths of our culture is of Noah saving animals from mass extinction. I consider the myth to be embedded in our genetic code, because that's why we *are*."

"Exactly what vitamins are you taking these days, Émile? I want a complete breakdown of your prescription list." Feeling happy again herself, she was delighted that it was so easy to arouse a smile from his usually dour, priestly visage.

"I've been thinking, Sandra, about the history of life. On earth it's been marked by catastrophe. The mind of nature has a long memory. Nature has never forgotten the Permian period, for instance—a mass extinction that came on fast. We nearly lost the planet. Ninety percent of ocean species, gone. Seventy percent of reptile and amphibian families, thirty percent of insect species, vanished. I think nature said, 'Holy cow, that was a close one!' "

"Nature didn't have cows back then."

Cinq-Mars had to check himself before he took her meaning, and there it was again, an unmistakable upturning around the edges of his mouth.

"All right, so nature said, 'Jumping leaping lizards!' Do you want me to go on?"

"Don't stop."

He nodded, thinking, finding his place in the scheme of things, working his way back through the musings that had interfered with last night's rest. "Okay, so nature sees itself come close to being anni-hilated, and it thinks, 'What we need are robust creatures for land. Let's create dinosaurs. To support complete domination by the dinosaurs, we'll create plant life and animal life for their consumption. Let's hope they're tough enough to endure whatever comes next.' They weren't, as things turned out. So after the dinosaurs journeyed off into that good night, nature made another choice. This time it banked on brainpower. But brains had to be placed within a tough species, a competitive, aggressive, strong-willed species, because the earth is no place for wimps. So humankind evolved, developed with the express purpose of endlessly enhancing its mental capacity so that the species could care for the planet, so that we could anticipate nat-ural and interstellar catastrophes. We are who we are because of why we are. We have lived with dogs in our dwellings since the Stone Age. We ride horses. We have deified the cat. Meanwhile, Hell's Angels exist because down through the ages we required and acquired their traits—the barbarian interest in expansion, the aggression. Ultimately, they may still be with us because they're an archaic remnant of our-selves we haven't wholly solved. That's why we create so many trou-bles for ourselves, why we war, to develop our sense of survival, to enhance our ability to solve problems, to heighten our belief in what is right and what is wrong, to propel our technology forward, to make us capable of crisis management for what must surely lie ahead."

Sandra stared at him awhile before she coughed with apparent sig-nificance. "Excuse me, sir. But it sounds as though you're making excuses for the excesses and horrors of the species. Humankind has delivered the world to the brink of destruction—men, especially, I might add—not cats and dogs."

"To the brink but not over the brink, that's my point. We are who we are because of why we are. It's our role to learn to manage anni-hilations and extinctions. We're here so that nature can have a mind

285

with which to keep itself company—an organism with which it communicates. We're here as crisis managers to preserve not merely our own species—which was the problem with dinosaurs, their inability to manage the environment—but our companion species also. Everything we do trains us for that calling. Whether it's engineering or theology, war making or economics, literature or crop dusting, everything we do and have done ultimately revolves around learning to lovingly manage the world and avoid catastrophe. We're babes in the woods, in terms of our time on earth, we're in kindergarten. We've got a long way to go. Together we're just one complex Noah building an ark."

"Which means what, Émile? Will you honor the Hell's Angels for being ruthless? Will you refuse to arrest them?"

Cinq-Mars moved over slightly and dropped an arm around her shoulders, tugged her closer to him. "No," he conceded, again with a smile, acknowledging that she had not been as serious as he might have preferred. "But they started me thinking. I was wondering why people bother to romanticize them. It's been a long time since they were postwar rebels, a bunch of bomber pilots looking to revive past glories. Now they're drug runners and murderers on wheels who wear sports shirts and pressed pants, unless they're putting on a show specifically calculated to induce fear. Even people who fear them also tend to think they're cool."

Sandra's sudden burst of laughter startled them both.

"What?"

"Cool. I've never heard you use a word like cool before."

"I know the lingo."

"Yeah, like maybe twenty years behind the times, but that's okay. It's a surprise, that's all." She returned his affection by circling both arms around his waist and squeezing. "Go on."

"Like it or not, we're not surprised by their presence, or by their behavior. Bikers have been chronic throughout the ages. They're leftovers. They're representative of our past, and it can be romantic to think about sloughing off our responsibilities and returning to a different time. There's a Hell's Angel who plays in the Quebec Symphony, so we think, 'Hey, maybe these guys aren't so bad, maybe they're just misunderstood.' "

"The romantic, sensitive rebel," Sandra put in.

"If we forget that a bomb is a bomb," Cinq-Mars marched on, "that murder is murder. No misunderstanding there. But I was wondering, why are they invading Montreal again? We drove them out, years ago. We cracked the back of the Mafia as well, they've never returned to full force. Now the Angels live in the countryside and small towns and do well, their lives are comfortable, they're unbelievably rich—filthy rich—they do good business and have smooth country roads to ride their Harleys on and the SQ pretty much leaves them alone. They wear fine clothes and are planning to open a chain of fast-food restaurants. Why do they want back into Montreal, where they're forced to battle the Rock Machine with bombs and be hassled by cops? Then it hit me."

"What did, Émile?" She encouraged him with another hug.

"A reporter, jokingly, asked the Angels where they stood on the matter of Quebec independence. They replied, everyone thought in jest, that the Angels preferred to see Canada stay together. But I tried to figure out why they would say that, why on earth would they think that way? They'd have the SQ in their pockets, the Mounties would be out of their hair. Then I caught it. They're going national. They control the east coast already. Their puppet gangs rule the west. Their next move is to take back Montreal, then annihilate the Outlaws in Ontario."

Sandra nodded. "They're expansionists. Nothing new among criminals."

"Except that they had retreated. What's their motivation for the new moves? The Russians. They're the ones saying to them, Take Canada, make a move on America, we've got Russia, the European Hell's Angels are getting stronger, between us we'll run crime through half the world. After that we'll make treaties with the Asian gangs. The Angels want to be part of the bigger deal, because if they declined, if they said, Sorry, we're content to be country squires for now, thanks very much, we like the quiet life, we're thinking of planting apple trees and seeing if more of us can't play in the symphony, they'd've been driven out, and the Russians would have helped with the big push. It's crisis management, Sandra, it's expand or be smashed."

A gray gelding nuzzled each of them in a quest for attention before skipping off again.

"How bad is it, Émile?" Sandra asked her husband, her voice hushed.

He had wrestled with the matter throughout the night, listening to the rains storm, beat on the windows, the roof, feeling the warm air of the thaw on his skin. Achieving resolution had restored a sense of freedom, liberated him from his timidity, his restraints. If he was going to lose his wife, he would do so because he had chosen to include her in his life, not exclude her. If he was going to wreck his marriage, he would do so on his terms, rather than be governed by fear and apprehension. If he was going to die, he would put right what needed to be put right. Overcoming fear was integral to his mission from here on in, and that process had to begin at home, or not begin at all.

"Until now, I was afraid to let you know what was going on in my life because the news isn't good."

"Right. I know how you go around sparing me bad news. You buy me a shotgun and enough shells to hold down the fort until the cavalry arrives. You ask me if I can shoot straight. That really convinces me that everything is peachy." She had moved away from him, pacing. "What about now, Émile? Have you made an arrest? What's changed?"

"No arrest."

"What's changed?"

He sighed. He gazed back on the horses, as though they inspired courage. He turned to her. "Sandra, it's bad. I can't hide it from you anymore. Also, I'm not sure that I can go it alone anymore. I'm not entirely self-contained. I'm too old for this. I need you. I need to confide in you. I can't tell you everything that's going on without scaring both of us half to death, but I need to talk to somebody. I hope it'll be you, Sandra. If you want to leave, I can't blame you. I'll understand. I'll make it easy. But I hope you stay."

Sandra Lowndes studied her husband's face before she also turned as though to consult the horses. She observed their grace and pleasure, their friskiness out on such a day in the middle of the most confining of winters. When she turned to face him again, she tucked her head into the small hollow just under the front of his shoulder. She loved that spot. How she loved that quiet spot.

Before noon Mathers was traveling into the quiet residential community of Notre-Dame-de-Grâce west of downtown, driving up Mariette Avenue to Police Station 15. This was a nice suburb. Mathers could see himself living here in a year or two. The houses were duplexes in the Montreal style, the landlord living on the bottom floor, a tenant above. The homes were a good size, red brick, built in the thirties, when craftsmanship still meant something. Good mahogany in those homes. Stained glass on doors and front windows. Small yards, front and back, were covered in melting snow now, but Mathers imagined that his wife could putter in a flower garden in the summertime without it being too much work.

The rains had come. The swift January thaw melted snowbanks into ponds.

The parking lot to Station 15 had history. An unarmed black youth had been shot dead by a policeman there, a bad killing. Either it was a murder or the cop was too dumb to have been allowed to carry a weapon. He said it went off accidentally. Since the black kid was running away, that theory hadn't impressed anyone.

Even quiet neighborhoods had their troubles.

The killing had shaken the city. Black immigration to Montreal from the Caribbean had been growing at a terrific rate, and there were those who resented the new arrivals. Many French considered themselves to be the oppressed people here. They were trying to create a society for themselves. The rallying cry of the independence-seeking government of the day and their avid supporters was *Québec aux Québecois!* Quebec for Quebeckers. They got away with it because the slogan was originally intended to mean no English, an attack against the powerful. But to many immigrants, who were the disadvantaged, the powerless, the chant seemed to be aimed squarely at them. For some, the death of the black youth had been a trial of the community. Who was the victim? The dead boy, or the French police officer who had lost his job? Mathers knew that the question should never have been put forward, but in some quarters, and around watercoolers in the department, it had been raised. That's when he felt his separateness, that at a certain point he would always be defined by his colleagues as being English, for his opinion on such a matter was neither welcomed nor considered, he was one of *les autres,* the others, the English, he wouldn't be able to understand, and worse than that he was probably out to get them, to make them look bad, he couldn't be trusted.

Mathers checked things out. There was something to be said for living in an English neighborhood. Among your own. He thought that he might like to try it sometime. If that's how the cultures remained separate, then so be it. He knew the language, he worked among the French, he loved Montreal. But if he couldn't be trusted, the hell with it, he'd live among the English. He couldn't batter his head against a wall forever.

At the entrance off the rear parking lot, Mathers flipped open his coat to flash his hip shield and asked to see Constable Normand Lajeunesse. Directed to a second-floor office, he found the uniform lazily filing reports. Mathers knew that he was working for a task force on auto theft.

He put the cop in his midtwenties. Watched him grudgingly move around the room, as if his assigned tasks could give him cancer. The story on Lajeunesse was that he had risen quickly in the force before tumbling with greater speed.

"I'm not here about a car," he told him when the man finally came over.

"That's what I do, cars." He was thin, six-two, a strong-boned, intelligent face, and he was hostile.

"I want to discuss Sergeant-Detective Émile Cinq-Mars." His partner had suggested this himself, a while back. The meeting was overdue, and Mathers sensed that it had become necessary.

Lajeunesse looked at him as if warning lights blinked inside his head and sirens were rampant. "Sorry, who'd you say you were? Internal or—"

"Bill Mathers. I'm partner to Émile these days."

The young officer was genuinely curious. "What do you want with me?"

"Can we talk someplace? Take ten, Normand."

Lajeunesse led him to a small kitchen nook where they were alone. Mathers missed these suburban comforts at HQ, where he never put a sandwich down for fear cockroach guerrillas would whisk it away.

"What's up?" Lajeunesse asked him.

"How did you find the experience?"

"What experience?"

"Being partner to Cinq-Mars."

The young man stretched his fingers taut, then relaxed them, as though releasing tension. He repeated the exercise twice more. "I don't understand. What're you investigating, Detective? Or should I ask, who?"

They were seated in small plastic chairs at a flimsy white table, and Mathers was too tense, too anxious, for the environment. He stood and paced, a bear in a pen. He came back. "Things are going on," he said. "I can't tell you what. I see you here, doing paperwork, in uniform—it makes me wonder. You wore gold on your hip like me, you were partnered to the most celebrated cop in town, like me. Maybe I don't want my next job to be filing clerk."

Thinking it over, Lajeunesse deduced, "You're the one with the gold shield. If you don't know what went down, I'm not filling you in."

"Cinq-Mars said you spied on him."

That level of information truncated the young man's rebellion, and he let himself snap back in his chair. He looked like a smoker. In this modern building he'd probably have to take himself outside.

"I was *told* to spy on him. It was my job."

"For the department?"

"You'd turn it down? Got me my shield. I was told Cinq-Mars was a bad cop, what did I know? Nobody liked him, I knew that much. They said if I helped put him away, my career would be in high spin. They promised nobody would know but me. So I was stupid. Shoot me—I believed them."

Mathers nodded. "This was Internal Affairs?"

Lajeunesse blew that thought off and shook his head. "I wouldn't sell out my worst enemy to Internal Affairs. Those guys can't squat for shitting."

"Who then?"

"Brass."

"High up?"

He shook his head slowly. "Pipeline. No names, no ranks. Emissaries."

"How'd you know you were on a pipeline?"

"Got me my shield, didn't they?"

"So what happened? Cinq-Mars finds you out, he can't bust you down to the filing room."

Lajeunesse stretched out in his chair, his long legs traveling under the table and emerging out the other side, his arms stretched upward behind him. His body seemed tightly strung with a perpetual strain, and Mathers guessed that that had not always been the case.

The lanky young man smiled a little. "Émile wouldn't work that way even if he had the stripes. He found me out. Don't ask me how. How does Émile know anything? He just knows. Probably he suspected all along. I flunked one of his tests maybe, so he laid a trap for me and I stepped in it. Émile told me, and I told the pipeline, we were busting a warehouse for cocaine. Cinq-Mars was going in without a warrant because he distrusted the courts, he was going in without backup because he distrusted cops. So the brass had him. Not for anything corrupt, like they told me he was, but they had enough of him to rein him in, take the shine off his badge."

Nodding, Mathers agreed, "He's not airtight with procedures."

"When he wants to be, he is. Don't assume otherwise," Lajeunesse warned.

"So what happened?" Mathers did his best to be comfortable in the sterile environment. Everything was white—the walls, the table, the cabinets, the chairs—as if they'd been hospitalized and the next item on the agenda was a lobotomy. He put his feet up on a chair.

"Him and me, we bust the warehouse. I'm expecting more cops, to nail us for procedure. What we get is high-caliber semiautomatic rifle fire. My vest took a hit, the one Cinq-Mars forced me to wear. Knocked me on my ass. We're pinned down and I figure we've bought it, that's it over for both of us. There's more fire. We're toast. I'm shitting my pants and I mean for real. This is a war zone."

"How'd you get out alive?"

"The new fire? Turns out it's from our side. Cinq-Mars had half a dozen off-duty cops show up—city cops, SQ, Mounties—good old boys who just happened to be in the neighborhood, off duty but armed to the teeth. Figure that one. Their weapons just happened to include cruiser shotguns. We're pinned on the floor and Cinq-Mars is saying to me, 'East of Aldgate, Normand. East of it, baby.' "

"Do you know what that means?"

"Nope. You?"

Mathers did his best to think this through, but he was having trouble. "You walked into an ambush that Cinq-Mars had pegged ahead of time?"

"Better get up to speed in a hurry, Detective," Lajeunesse advised. "You never know what's coming your way."

"I need help here."

Lajeunesse leaned into him. "I don't know what you're after, Detective. I don't know who you're asking for, if anybody. Maybe brass. Maybe yourself. Maybe you got your own pipeline, who knows? Whatever your situation, I suggest you get this and get it good."

Mathers put his feet back on the floor as a sign of his devotion to whatever the man might proffer. "I'm listening."

"Cinq-Mars—smart guy, right? Let me tell you how smart. Not only does he figure out that I'm leaking information upstairs, he also figures out that what I say goes no higher up the ladder. He figures out it doesn't go anywhere on the ladder. There is no ladder. He figures out that my information goes from me, to my pipeline, to Mafia, to Hell's Angels. Tic, tac, toe."

Mathers was breathing lightly now, as though a deeper breath might interrupt the flow of knowledge. "A trap," he concluded. "To bump off you and Cinq-Mars."

Lajeunesse was staring into the detective's eyes now and shaking his head, slowly. "They wouldn't kill Cinq-Mars," he said. "Who'd dare? Hell would bust loose. Back then, they don't want Wolverines up their ass, although they have them now anyway."

Mathers listened, and wondered about a quiet voice murmuring inside him now, clamoring, wanting out.

"You?" Mathers asked quietly.

"Figure it out, Detective. I die, Cinq-Mars gets a message and my link to the brass dies with me. Cinq-Mars finds himself in deep shit for being in that warehouse with no warrant and no backup, a dead cop on his hands. It turns out he had a warrant in his hip pocket, of course, he had backup, too, but my pipeline didn't know, I didn't know, and the shooter sure as hell was unaware. There's no investigation to talk about. The shooter got off fourteen rounds—that tells you he's no innocent. He took one back at him in the eye. I had a bullet in my chest pocket. Cinq-Mars had his secret warrant, and the backup cops were an accident of fate. The whole thing went away. Except I got busted down to the rank of pencil, on suspicion of leaking news. I never deserved the rank of detective, now they're saying, in the first place."

The detective took a moment to absorb the news, then stood to leave. "Did you tell Cinq-Mars who?" he asked.

Lajeunesse just looked at him, sneering a little.

"Tips," Mathers prompted him. "Maybe not names, if you don't have them, but leads. He could figure it out if you gave him leads. Cinq-Mars can carry a clue a long way."

"I never told him squat."

"Why not?"

"That bullethole in my pocket was enough of a message for me. Didn't faze Émile all that much, did it? But they weren't shooting at him."

Mathers nodded, as though he sympathized. He knew that Cinq-Mars, with his quietly fierce nature, would not go along with this logic. "And now? You've been stuck in this hole for some time. You're staying quiet?"

Lajeunesse uttered a sour little laugh, rising as well. "Either you're too naive for your own good, Detective, which I doubt somehow, or you're here to find out how solid I am. If you're representing the shits who lined me up, the deal holds. I told the emissaries, I die, I lose my job, letters get sent, the information, every detail I know, gets distributed. In the meantime, I'm solid."

Mathers shrugged. "So that's how it is."

"That's how it is."

"You know, I can see where you can't tell me. You can't trust me.

But you could tell Cinq-Mars. Give him your leads. Ask him to keep quiet. At least he'll know who he's after. At least he can figure out who to watch out for."

Bill Mathers was tired from his late night, and he hadn't been paying attention, but in the brief silence that ensued a thought raced up his spine and cranked his head higher. He only glanced at Lajeunesse. He required no further confirmation. Of course. That's what this cop had done. He had told Cinq-Mars what he knew, and Cinq-Mars had resolutely and astutely protected him in order to spare the man his life. Having letters to send if he died or got fired was probably a notion hatched by Cinq-Mars himself, to keep him alive. Mathers recognized that if he gave any indication that he had figured this out Lajeunesse might panic. *Cinq-Mars knows! Or he's got good clues. He probably knows which cops he's gunning for and who's been gunning for him.*

Mathers moved quickly to change the subject. "Listen. There's a car I've been trying to run down. I've got the make, no VIN, and the plate number. But we enter this into our computer system, we draw a false record. I'll give you the plate number. Maybe you can work on it, on the side. Get down to Motor Vehicle Records, snoop around. You don't have to. I'll never mention it again unless you do. Report back to Cinq-Mars if you want, you know he's not dirty. If you can help us, that'd be great. If not, I understand."

Mathers wrote out the information, tore off the sheet from his notepad, and passed it across to Lajeunesse. The man regarded the number.

"At least it's police work," Mathers told him.

Lajeunesse concurred. "Thanks," he said.

Outside, Mathers sidestepped puddles getting back to his car. He had work to do that afternoon. Police work. He had bad guys to chase down, perps to apprehend, victims to interview. He'd go through the motions, although his heart wouldn't be in it. Today, the work he loved had been eclipsed. Forces were at play that scared the Jockeys off him. Now he knew why Cinq-Mars was always so damn secretive, so infernally cautious. Cinq-Mars knew that the enemy was everywhere.

The enemy thrived on the outside and, as he had been trying to get his new partner to appreciate, the enemy dwelled within.

15

Thursday, January 20, after midnight

As night descended upon his pastures of melting snow, Émile Cinq-Mars was consumed by an itchiness, a readiness. He remained calm, napped intermittently, and visited the horses. When Sandra went up to bed, he kissed her good night and sliced off a piece of pumpkin pie for the road. He needed to drive city streets by night. How could he chase down nocturnal prey by daylight? Getting up before the crack was a questionable virtue when criminals were hitting the sack at that hour. The time had come to move when they moved, to be awake and in the vicinity whenever they broke loose.

He needed, now, to be a cop like André LaPierre.

Water was everywhere, in puddles and pools. Intersections were lakes. The wipers were hard-pressed to keep up with the spray from other vehicles. Cinq-Mars drove on, preoccupied, intent.

In the city, he drove through downtown, neon lights reflecting off the wet black streets, and he turned up Jeanne Mance, then onto Park Avenue as it crossed the eastern slope of the mountain. On his left, facing east, the lighted cross hung above the city as if suspended in the darkness in midair. Cinq-Mars ascended the mountain and parked in the high lot on the eastern ridge, a man alone among lovers swarming over one another in their bucket seats.

From here one could ascend a path to the cross, not a pleasant walk in this rain or on the slippery footing precipitated by the thaw. In any case the cross was best viewed from a distance, when it was not seen as a disgruntled mesh of steel and lightbulbs. The mountain had always

296

claimed the spiritual heart of the city, and the active spiritual forces of each era always claimed the mountain. The early Iroquois farmed the southern flank. When the leader of the first European settlement—who was aptly named de Maisonneuve, *of the new house*—prayed for the retreat of floodwaters, he prophesied that the community would be spared if a cross was erected upon the highest point of the mountain. De Maisonneuve shouldered a cross upon his back and lugged it up the hill, no easy task through the thick woods, and the waters obligingly receded. He did hold a strange notion of what constituted the highest peak, choosing instead a mere promontory, but vows made in crisis were usually compromised, even Cinq-Mars knew that.

Neither did the modern cross rest upon the highest mark, standing instead upon ground that provided the best sight lines to the eastern, and Catholic, district of Montreal. The cross sloughed off the business whirl of downtown, and the English suburbs to the west, the light-bulbs shining instead upon those who, for a time, had professed reverence for the Church.

The mountain attracted and divided, magnetized and sequestered. On one side, huddled against a sharp slope, the English-speaking university of McGill. On its opposite, gentler haunch, Université de Montréal, French-speaking. Off its satellite hill was the wealthy, largely English city of Westmount, while on the *other* flank lay Outremont, equally affluent but French. The mountain provided a sprawl of cemeteries, English and French and Jewish, as though the height shortened the journey upward to heaven and brought those who visited nearer the realm of their departed.

Émile Cinq-Mars felt, at that moment, nearer the realm of the departed. A squall went through, and the windshield wipers thrashed time. He deeply wished he still smoked, would have crumbled at that moment if a cigarette had been offered. Before him the vast eastern stretch of the city glittered, winter white, all the way out to the oil refineries and the tip of the island. He felt the city's thrum, the rain's insistent throttle, the relentless rhythm of time. The mountain on which he stood was ancient, although what remained was merely the hole in the volcano, enduring for aeons, becoming the landmark that drew people to its slope, a city born. High up, quiet in his car, Cinq-Mars drew nurture from the beloved mountain, which had been his first view of the city. He was like the mountain himself. He was the plug. The section that did not wear down. The rock that remained after the lava shell was torn away. He would be the last, the very last, to erode. He remained.

Before him lay the glacial city and the night.

He started his engine again, and headed downhill. Cinq-Mars turned his thoughts to André LaPierre as he drove east, and soon he began to circle his colleague's apartment, each time narrowing the diameter of the ring. He possessed insufficient knowledge. To overcome that deficiency he would seed a few lies, broker a few threats, to determine whom he could agitate the most.

Ready, Cinq-Mars parked his Taurus wagon and walked up a block in the South Central section of the city near the magnificent arching spans of the Jacques Cartier Bridge. He rang a doorbell and checked his watch. 1:02 A.M. He rang the bell again, at length.

If LaPierre was crooked, he wasn't living in the lap of luxury as a result. If he was a clean cop, he had to be given marks for dedication. He dwelled among the working poor, where he could hang out with the rough boys. South Central was a back-door community. A working con out on weekend parole could rap on a window and fence what he'd swiped in Westmount, cross the alley to purchase what he needed to get high, choosing his poison, then sally up to the corner to arrange a sleep over. The danger here was in crossing the wrong path, for this was the heart of Rock Machine turf.

As in most of the island city, where land was scarce, homes were crammed tightly together here. The back alleys teemed with life in the summer. In the winter it seemed that everyone disappeared. Flats were small. The quality of construction of newer buildings was haphazard, the old buildings tumbledown. In summer, you could hear your neighbors snore, or listen to late night movies on their TVs. Winter was a time of hunkering down and of trying not to go crazy in the enclosed spaces. Balconies were mounded with snow. Streets here sloped down to the waterfront, and the air at all hours was boisterous with the sounds of traffic, of cars speeding on the bridge across the St. Lawrence.

The return buzzer finally sounded, and he went in.

Cinq-Mars climbed the inside stairs, his rubber overshoes quiet on the wood. LaPierre was waiting in his underwear. He didn't appear particularly surprised that he was being disturbed in the middle of the night, only by whom.

"Émile?" The taller man's hair was tousled, his eyes disturbed by the faint light of the foyer. "What the hell?"

"We need to talk, André."

LaPierre let him in, and Cinq-Mars walked down a short hall to the living room where a young woman padded through in her bare feet and loose gown on her way to the refrigerator. Cinq-Mars offered his colleague a look of measured disapproval.

"Saint Émile, don't lecture me."

He was right. The woman was none of his business, although she could pass as a hooker. Probably LaPierre wasn't paying, just enjoying another perk of his profession, like getting a car fixed by auto thieves and protesting that that was his job, that he had to hang out with the desperate and what he called the brokenhearted, because that's what they were whenever he busted them. He had to take advantage of his opportunities, which was why the hooker in his house was seventeen. If he hadn't been on suspension maybe she'd've been twelve.

"Can I turn on a light at least?"

"Let me," LaPierre told him. "I don't want it bright."

The floor lamp emitted a low beam. Even so, the young woman returning with a beer in one hand shielded her eyes. As her hand came up, the sash on her robe unwound, exposing small breasts and the patch of pubis. Young and worn, Cinq-Mars assessed. He had an urge to check her arm for marks.

"You on the clock, Émile? Like a beer?"

Cinq-Mars wasn't sure if he was working officially or not but decided it was irrelevant. "Thanks."

LaPierre uncapped a couple of St. Ambroises, brought the bottles in from the kitchenette, and sat across from Cinq-Mars. "Sorry, Émile—you want a glass?"

"The bottle's fine, André."

"What's up?"

"I've been going over your situation."

"Yeah? It's a fox-trot, Émile."

"There's something you could help us with. It wouldn't look bad if I get to report that you gave us a hand up, even with your ass in a sling." He wished the guy would put his pants on, not sit there in his briefs. He was strictly lowlife.

LaPierre spread his arms wide to welcome any positive suggestion. "That's all I'm asking for, Émile. A fair shake."

"Around four months ago, André, you covered a hit. A Hell's Angels' banker got blown in a 4Runner. Remember that one?"

"Turgeon? No. An English guy."

"Turner."

"That's it."

"You were the IO."

LaPierre shrugged, took a swig of beer. "Biker hit, Émile. The Wolverines snatched it up."

"They always do. They were on the scene and I happened to be with them. But you were the IO until they took it over."

"My privilege to supervise the mess. Shit River. Body parts every which way. We scraped him off buildings. Scraped, Émile. With putty knives. Those damn Wolverines'll do anything for a clue."

"The way the body blew—was that so unique?"

LaPierre shrugged again. "Somebody gets blown, he gets blown. But, yeah, I can't say I've seen a body shoot like that before. The blast came up under him."

"Interesting," Cinq-Mars mused.

"How so?"

"The Wolverines reached the obvious conclusion. The Rock Machine blew up a guy working for the Hell's Angels."

"They're not dumb, Émile."

"I made the same assumption. But something's come up. It's possible the hit was only made to look like a biker hit. It's possible a third party got involved and copied the Rock Machine MO."

"This is news, Émile."

"I can't say much. What I want is access to your memory. Go over

300

the bump. Write down any discrepancy between a regular Rock hit and that one. Begin with the body parts."

"Émile, this is prime stuff. Who're you thinking for this?"

"I'm close but I'm not there yet. I'll think about cutting you in later."

"Come on, Émile, I'm dying here."

"I'm not there yet. Sweep the floor for me now, I'll mop it for you later. I'm not forgetting that so far you haven't played much tape for me."

"I don't believe I'm impeding."

"It's a discourtesy." Cinq-Mars stood, walked to the window at LaPierre's back, looked down upon the dormant street below. "It also doesn't help your case much."

"Everything is timing. I want to see how things fall."

"You know some boys down at SQ, don't you? You've doubled up on enough cases with Wolverines by now."

"We get along." He took a swig from his beer.

"I bet you could go down there and ask for the Turner file. If a pretty girl knows you're suspended, talk her through it. Chances are, the SQ doesn't give a hoot about that anyway. Take a look at the file. See what that brings you."

"Now you're starting to ask a lot, Émile."

"I'm worried sick about your retirement, André. Keeps me awake at night. Why should a new muffler sink you for life? It was partly business, like you said. Some cops get to live in the muck. That's a verity. Hey! Since I'm here, how about showing me your tape room, André? I'd be keen to see that."

"Are you asking or telling?"

"Are you offering or refusing?"

"That's why you're really here, isn't it?"

LaPierre looked like a beaten fighter on his corner stool, humiliated, dejected, dazed, too weary to pull up his shorts, too whipped to stand.

"Don't think that way. I'm dead serious about the Turner investigation. Now, come on. I bet you showed that hooker your gadgets."

"I don't pay for it, Émile."

"Watch it, André. Be careful. Don't put your pride as a man

301

before your pride as a cop. That won't work in front of any panel I can think of."

LaPierre hung his head, then managed to stand. In an apartment with low ceilings he looked particularly tall. Cinq-Mars followed him into the bedroom, where the girl lay naked swigging beer, leafing through a fashion magazine. The apartment was subtropical. Her robe was bunched up around her feet, and she did nothing to cover herself, but looked up, wondering if something was about to unfold that would involve her and would she have a choice.

"In here," LaPierre directed. He kept his gear in a large walk-in closet. Stepping inside, Cinq-Mars pulled the cord on the overhead. One end of the closet was reserved for clothing—suits, trousers, shirts on hangers, laundry in a corner lump on the floor—the other had been developed as a miniature workshop. LaPierre did his own repairs. The gutted remains of old mobile units sat wrecked upon a shelf, gleaned for their parts. He'd stored tape recorders and headphones and a series of old microphones along the shelves. For Cinq-Mars it brought to mind the old days, when they'd felt free to tap anybody anytime anywhere. He stayed in the closet awhile, drinking his beer.

"So?" the giraffelike man in his underwear asked him when he came out.

"Relax, André. I wanted to know if you were state-of-the-art. If you were state-of-the-art I'd want to know the name of your bankroll."

"I'm primitive, Émile. It's a hobby, all right? Nothing more. A hobby that gives me an edge."

"You rebuild them?"

"I rework the relics to use those new watch batteries."

"You're a genius. I didn't know. Keep in touch about the Turner case."

"Will do."

"Take it easy now."

"All right. Hey, that Coates boy show up?"

"Hide nor hair. Does that worry you?"

LaPierre made a face. "Maybe he got in deeper than love. I hope he shows up someday."

"That would be good."

"Thanks for this, Émile. I think."

"Hey, buddy, you don't have to worry about me. I might stuff another cop in the can, but I won't flush."

With that final bit of stroking, Émile Cinq-Mars left and walked back to his car, confident that he had put serious matters into motion. It had stopped raining. No plan made sense unless it accomplished a variety of functions. That way, it never looked like a plan, it didn't take on the appearance of a ploy. In providing LaPierre with intriguing information, he was increasing the man's worth to the Hell's Angels—if he was their cop. They'd want to know what the eminent Cinq-Mars was doing, where the thread might lead, what mysterious third party had attacked pretending to be the Rock Machine. If LaPierre was a conduit for that sort of news—and was the cop designated for a hit—the turn might keep him alive. Cinq-Mars also hoped that the news traveling into the core of the Hell's Angels might keep himself alive if he was their intended target. The Angels might prefer to keep him breathing once they learned that he was scoping something out for them.

News of an unknown, murderous third party would excite the wolf pack. They'd never figure a college girl—or the CIA—as involved, so the lie could relieve pressure there. With luck, the word traveling back through the skin of the Angels to his source might exhort that individual to establish a more equitable dialogue. That man—especially if he was CIA—would want to know what Cinq-Mars had up his sleeve. Or, that person might use a contact—Ray Rieser, perhaps—to investigate.

If the information did travel through the Hell's Angels, get picked up by the conduit that Steeplechase Arch was running inside the gang, then return to him through Arch, that would pretty much confirm LaPierre as dirty, since he was giving this news only to him. Cinq-Mars dearly hoped this leak would resolve the matter.

He climbed into his car, held his breath, and started the engine. He breathed out. No bomb. He sat behind the wheel, nagged by suspicions and doubts. He had to mull through conversations with André in the past, cross-reference those with what he'd gleaned in the man's communications room. André had told him one time that his equipment was mobile, which Cinq-Mars had confirmed in the closet. No long-range equipment, no antennae on the roof or in the house, no cables leading outside, no phone jacks in the cupboard. But hadn't André also told him that he had recorded Garage Sampson from his home, while he was busy getting ill with the flu? He did not appear to have that capability, and in any case that contradicted his previous mention of being strictly mobile. At the time, Cinq-Mars had picked up on the contradiction and considered it significant. He loved contradictions, they were the cracks in concrete through which his mind traveled. At the time he could not process the information, he hadn't known enough, his suspicions had not matured. Times were changing now. He had one more jig in the saw of the puzzle, and he had to wonder exactly where it fit.

He put his car in gear. No bomb. Pulled out onto the street. No blast. If he could help it at all, he would never shift into reverse again. That sort of behavior was just asking for trouble.

Cinq-Mars headed downtown. He wished he knew a uniform on the night watch he could trust. Someone who wouldn't mind waiting outside for a young woman to emerge from an apartment, who wouldn't mind following that hooker home and discovering where she lived. Someone who wouldn't feel a crimp because he was also spying on another cop. Thinking that way, he began to wonder what Okinder Boyle was up to, how he'd take to cop spying. Would he like to make the acquaintance of that girl, gain her trust, maybe write her story? It wouldn't be the first time civilians had been brought onto the case.

This'll get dark, Sergeant-Detective Émile Cinq-Mars warned himself. He grimaced, waiting for a light to turn green. *This could go dim.*

As he drove again, he could not discern the black rim of the mountain, but the clouded, soft glow of the cross positioned it for him, giving him his bearings, reminding him again that he, Cinq-Mars, was near the center, and that this was up to him.

They arrived in the middle of the night. They did not bring food. Eight Hell's Angels filed into the one-room apartment to stand in twin rows on opposite sides of the bed, and Julia Murdick sat up and shielded her eyes from the overhead light. They did not speak. They stood around the bed, a mute Greek chorus ancient and decrepit and willfully subhuman, and she was afraid and hungry and alone and finally defeated. They weren't wearing snappy dress slacks and sports shirts, like Selwyn had said they would. They were showing their true colors, their biker colors.

"Please," she whimpered, her voice scarcely audible. "Don't."

She hadn't eaten since lunch on the ship.

They'd left her alone in the dark for hours. Faint light leaked in where the pipes came through the bulkheads and across the ceiling. Enough for her to see the rat walk and sniff her. She remained there through the night, unable to sit, and in the morning the captain of the ship visited and she was weeping and she asked him, "Are they going to kill me?" and he waved his forefinger at her as if this was her fault, and he promised, "Not kill you on my ship," and she did not know if this was good news or a death sentence. The captain seemed angry about it all. He led her to the latrine, but they came back afterward and he handcuffed her again.

That night the captain had her moved to a stateroom, where she was locked in but not shackled, she could drink water, and the next day she promised not to make a scene and was driven from the docks in a BMW, through the security gate, and down the highway to a Hell's Angels' compound and fortress deep in the countryside known as the Eastern Townships.

They gave her an apartment of her own.

But they did not feed her that day either, and it was now the middle of the night.

The man she knew as Jean-Guy walked in and stood off to one side, apart from the others, as though he had some ceremony, a ritual, to perform there. He wasn't wearing biker colors like the others. He never did. He was always a snappy dresser. He wore a beige suit and a salmon shirt. She glanced at the others, and they observed her without expression and their bellies hung out and their chains made noise when they shifted their weight and a few carried knives. They wore rings and medallions and tattoos and pieces of bone in their vests. Their hair was long and shaggy, their beards a mess. The men looked at her with drippy eyes as if stoned and they reeked of gin and armpit stink and Jean-Guy crossed his hands like a funeral parlor director, in beige, and stood off to one side. He seemed to be waiting.

Under her breath, Julia implored, "Please, no."

He came in then, the Czar. Impeccably attired, as if he used the same tailor Jean-Guy did, except that he wasn't wearing a jacket. He had on a crisp white shirt and his trousers were pressed, she noticed that. He wore a black tie loosened at the collar. As when she'd first met him on the ship, before he'd handcuffed her to a pipe, Julia was struck by the hardness to his eyes, by the fullness of his lips. This time she also noticed how sharp were his cheekbones, and in this light his ears appeared to droop lower than normal. Perhaps it was the ears that made his whole head seem out of trim, odd. She figured he was in his mid- to late forties. The Czar picked up a chair from the modest dining set, and Julia feared he'd smash it over her head. She was flinching, edging down in the bed. Turning the chair around, the man sat in it backwards at the foot of the bed, resting his forearms and elbows on the ladder back.

She wanted to get a look at his eyes. She wanted to find a measure of humanity there.

"We call you the banker's daughter. There must be joke about that."

She edged up slightly under the covers, trying to get her body beneath her. She was fully clothed. "She was only a banker's daughter." Her voice trembled. She heard smelly fat men breathing as though standing upright was a strain for a few of them. "But all the men took a loan."

"They told to me you had sense of humor."

"Who noticed? Nobody I met—" She was trying to be brave here.

"Shut up. We are not this time having conversation."

Julia froze on the bed, her heart erratic in her chest. She fought the impulse to beg. The tall man looked like he could crack her in two by thinking about it.

The Czar said, "You did good to us, Heather Bantry. Money your father moved is good money. Is most beautiful money, yes? Clean money. You impress me. Police no have power to move money like this."

She covered her mouth with her hands and breathed heavily.

"The last days are hard on you. We need to know this thing. Is she soft like marshmallow? Or is she hard enough? What we do to you is not so bad. But we do to you worse than police do, worse than woman's prison. You survive us. That's good. That shows to me you are not marshmallow. How did you get so strong, Heather Bantry?"

She hardly had a voice. "I'm not so strong," she protested. Selwyn had taught that she couldn't be. Strength was suspicious.

"Do you know who is in room, Heather Bantry?" the Czar asked from his chair. "You are here with famous men called Filthy Few. You know why they called that?"

She shook her head no.

"These famous men, they go on television news. You should know them. They can to you be friends. Everyone he made his name killing some bastard for our business. What you think, Heather Bantry?"

She could not find her voice, her breath, a thought.

"I was told to me you got a mouth on you, yes? I want to hear what you say. Do you feel yourself honored, banker's daughter, to be with famous men?"

Julia managed a squeak. She tried again. "Yes."

"You should not sleep with clothes on. Take clothes off to me."

Fear overwhelmed any notion of modesty. She undressed and felt dizzy and hardly realized what she was doing, out of touch with herself, each button a challenge.

"I like woman who strip slow," the man in the chair said, and the others in the room laughed.

The Angels were enjoying this part.

"But I tell to you, I don't have all night," the man said.

"Please," Julia pleaded.

"Shut up," the Czar said. "Come. Hurry. We have seen before bodies."

She undressed more quickly then, as though her fear had been grafted onto the task at hand. She was awkward on the bed and felt dizzy and the terror had entered her in a way that spared her panic, put her apart from herself, distant from anything that might transpire.

When her clothes were off she pulled them back over herself to cover her nakedness and hid behind her knees.

A biker ripped her clothes away.

He felt through her garments, checking again for a wire that was not there.

The man stood and gazed upon her. He seemed remarkably tall as she looked up at him, fit and muscular, a welcome change from the big bellies in the room, and from this perspective she had a clear view of the scar that ran under his jaw. He lifted his chair again and this time moved it farther away from the bed and turned it around to face her. All his moves, she thought, were deft, controlled. "You to us have done good service. We wish to you be rewarded, Heather Bantry. Is that good news to you?"

She had to concentrate to nod. Her pulse beat at a ferocious pace.

"We use your father for us, yes? He is man with talent. Now it look like," the man said with a shrug, "you must remain yourself attached to your father. I talked to him. He is hopeless case. Always around and around in a circle in his head. Who can keep him straight? You, it seem like. So, banker's daughter, you have talent too. That is good. We like this. You make your father like normal person."

Just like Selwyn said. "It's no problem. I'll work for you. It's not a problem."

"Yes, no," the man said. "We demand somebody working for us to live to high standard, yes? You understand?"

Julia nodded.

"We ask to you initiation, Heather Bantry. This way, we are knowing you are one with us."

She nodded again but did not comprehend.

"Good. What should I do to you? I could give you to Filthy Few."

Julia whimpered, she couldn't help herself.

"I agree. That hard on you. You might not survive. These men not gentle men. We want you in the end alive. We want to you be happy to us. We want also you to fear us, this be sure. You are afraid, banker's daughter?"

"Yes."

"Good. But not enough. I have your attention?"

accent had vanished. He spoke perfect English. "We have our brother organizations around the world. This is the Eight-Pointed Star, Heather, symbol of the Russian Brotherhood, of our power and unity, and of the coming together of our Families and Brotherhoods. You will wear a tattoo like this. Without all the detail—you're only a hangaround—but the Star will protect you. No Hell's Angel will hurt you while you wear this Star. Half the world will fear you. You will wear this star upon your breast, Heather Bantry. I'll arrange for the tattoo tonight. Do you understand?"

"Yes."

"Do you accept?"

Selwyn? "Yes."

"That is first part of your tribute to us. The second part is this. Anyone who comes into our organization now, who gets close to us, must do one thing no cop would ever do. You will do what we ask?"

She moved her eyes around the room. And nodded yes.

"You accept your initiation?"

She nodded.

"Good. A cop's been causing us trouble. He's to be dismissed. Jean-Guy is working on a present for this cop. He's a master. He'll train you how to plant the device, show you how to push the button. That can't be so hard. This cop will be dismissed, and you'll do the kill. Understand?"

She nodded.

"Accept?"

She nodded.

"Say it!"

"Yes," Julia Murdick said.

"Will you kill the cop to us?" He reverted to his fake accent again.

"Yes."

"Say it!"

"Yes," she answered more loudly.

"Tell to me what you do, banker's daughter. Tell to me!"

Her voice was faint, the room quiet to accommodate the sound.

"I will kill a cop for you," she said.

"You bomb him? You explode him to bits?"

"I will bomb him. I will explode him to bits."

"You'll blow up his ass?"

"I'll blow up his ass."

"This is good. I want you to be one of us, Heather," the man said. "I'm not from this country, but I respect the customs of every land. Where I live, where I come from, where I was trained, we do not blow people up just to kill them. But here it's a custom of the Angels. We respect their customs, yes?"

"Yes."

With a nod of his head he signaled the others out.

"Close door!" he shouted to the last man leaving, who was Jean-Guy.

"Oh no, oh no," she whimpered.

"What are you afraid of, Heather? You can't be a virgin."

"It hurts me. I can't. There's something wrong with me. I can't have sex. I don't want to get pregnant. I can't have babies. My body's not normal, please, you'll rip me apart, please, I mean it. I'll do anything else you want. Not that."

Her own words terrified her. She had told this dangerous man that she would do whatever he wanted. She felt defeated, completely overcome. Lost.

The man came over to the bed and leaned across her. He kissed her. She met his kiss with corresponding mechanical fluctuations of her own lips. He moved his mouth above her ear. "Kiss Star," he whispered. "It's your hope. Kiss the Eight-Pointed Star, Heather." He parted his shirt to expose his chest again, and she brought her lips to the center of the Star and kissed. "Use tongue, Heather." She did so. "This is good." He unzipped himself and pulled himself out and stroked himself and made himself large. He put his hand on the back of her head and he said, "Start me," and Julia fellated him and he put his hands on her ears and pumped her face so hard she thought he'd rip her ears off and he spurted inside her and she swallowed and believed that a plague had infected her, believed a poison had contaminated her bloodstream and was spreading inside her and she would be consumed by infection. The man tucked himself away and buttoned his shirt over the Star and headed for the door. He put the chair back against the wall and retrieved his tie. "I like you, banker's daughter. That's good for you. It's either me or them. Take your pick." As he departed he smiled, briefly, then turned off the lights and shut the door.

Julia lay in the dark, flat on her back with one knee up, immobile with shock.

The door opened and she gasped again, recoiled again, feared death, then craved it, quickly.

The light was switched on.

A man wheeled in a tray of food.

An array of sandwiches and a choice of juices in small packets on a dainty silver cart.

He left.

She stared at the food.

She was free to eat.

But she did not, could not, comprehend food.

Her breast was to be tattooed. Mutilated. Then she'd kill a man, a cop.

Why did I do that, suck him, what did I do?

She had something worse to do. She had said it. She had repeated it.

He's going to make me kill somebody. Oh God. God.

Émile Cinq-Mars waited in his car for Okinder Boyle, closing his eyes to give them a rest. He had phoned the columnist by cellular, saying he wanted to meet him in half an hour. At the other end the silence was momentary. "Sooner, if you want," Boyle had responded.

"Make it ten minutes. On the street. Your place."

That time was up. Cinq-Mars was hoping the boy would not arrive until the conclusion of the piano concerto on the radio, a wish rudely interrupted by a sharp rap on his window. He snapped the music off, and the journalist went around to jump in the other side.

"Pulling the night shift, Émile?" Boyle asked him.

"I suppose this is the middle of the day for you."

"Nearly bedtime. I'm glad you called. What's up?"

"What's your position on forgoing sleep?"

Boyle was ready for anything. "No problem. What do you need?"

"I need someone who isn't a cop to spy on a cop."

"Guess what? I'm volunteering."

"I appreciate that, Okinder. He has a girl staying with him right now—I want you to make contact with her. Be exceedingly careful. I don't know if she loves him or despises every breath he takes. Find that out. Maybe you can approach her from the point of view of a journalist, but don't give away who you are. You've already sewn this guy's ass to the can—"

"What guy?"

"Sergeant-Detective André LaPierre."

"Ah."

"Be wary."

"'Nuff said. I'll be careful. Émile, I need to talk to you about Garo Boghossian."

"Hagop's uncle. Your boss. What about him?"

A gentle rain hit the windshield, a brief sprinkle.

"I've been keeping him apprised. He wants to know what's going on with the investigation. I've kept him informed about things, but he's been less than forthcoming about his own activities."

"Which are?"

"He just called. Apparently he spends most evenings and a lot of his nights driving around the streets of Montreal."

The detective's sympathy was waning with the late hour. "Is he having a breakdown?"

"No way. Apparently he's been hunting down green Infiniti Q Forty-fives."

Cinq-Mars tapped the steering wheel a couple of times. "I can't stand this. Too many civilians are involved here, beginning with the fake Heather Bantry."

"Including me, when it comes to that. I haven't been a liability, have I?"

Cinq-Mars conceded the point. He was accustomed to losing debates to this young man.

"He's found one, Émile."

"A Q Forty-five? Okinder, they're out there."

314

"He knows that. He's been following Q Forty-fives in his free time. He tails drivers from the workplace to their homes, or from their favorite bars home, whatever. He checks the people out, decides they're benign, and moves on. But tonight, he came across one that sounds interesting. We should go see him. He lives close by."

Cinq-Mars considered the news, choosing in the end to relent. "Better take two cars. Then you can leave Uncle Garo's for LaPierre's place."

"I don't have a car," Boyle told him.

Cinq-Mars gave him an irate look.

"I can't afford one," he defended.

"Can you drive, at least? All right, use mine. After Uncle Garo's you can drive me back to HQ. I'll check out a squad car. We'll go see him first."

"Lend me your phone, I'll let him know."

They arrived in four minutes, made contact over the intercom, and ascended in the elevator to the fifteenth floor of a downtown high-rise. They were met in the hall by a wild-haired, animated man. "Come in come in come in," he insisted, and the two men entered the apartment.

"You're Cinq-Mars. I'm glad you're on my nephew's case."

"I'm not. Officially." In surveying the apartment, the detective liked what he saw, the plethora of books, the patina of study. Electronic gadgetry was kept to a minimum and, while the apartment was comfortable, he got no sense of excessive material possession. The bachelor's home served as a retreat for thought and inquisitiveness, which Cinq-Mars appreciated, although he also wished that men of intellect would not aspire to being men of action. "I understand you've been tailing luxury automobiles."

"All over town, Detective. South shore, west island, as far as Hudson. Up north. Wild goose chases, every one. But I've stuck with it."

"And tonight?"

"Tonight—can I get you something? Coffee?"

An eye-opener would not be unwelcome. "Thanks. I could use a cup. Okinder, too."

"I'm going undercover," Boyle remarked proudly.

"Okinder," objected Cinq-Mars, "the first rule about being under-cover is that you don't tell anybody you're undercover."

Boghossian shook his head in agreement. "I have to kick his butt myself."

"You old farts," Boyle summed up.

They had drifted toward the kitchen, which was visually connect-ed to the main living and dining area by a pass-through in one wall. Boghossian went through and put the coffee on, then came out again.

"Tonight I followed a green Q from downtown to the east end."

"Did you get a plate number?"

"Yup." The editor rummaged through his billfold. He pulled out a slip of newsprint and handed it across to Cinq-Mars.

"This isn't the number we've been looking for," he stated.

"You *know* his license plate?" The tremor of his dismay caused a row of wineglasses to tinkle slightly.

"We've known for some time. It's untraceable. Our prey has the capability of providing his own license under fictitious identification."

The editor ruminated on this a moment. "So it's possible that he changes his license from time to time?"

Cinq-Mars tapped the hard bone behind his ear. "It's possible," he said, meaning that it was highly unlikely. "What sparked your inter-est in the car?"

"One, the car went into the east end. I'm sorry, but a vehicle like that hardly ever shows up in those neighborhoods. Two, the driver parked on the street—so did I, farther down the road. That's a risk, to park a car like that there. Three, I followed the guy on foot."

"A man."

"One man. Well dressed. Got no closer than that."

"Go on."

"He walked *five* blocks. Five. He went into a building and I waited outside. I was hoping to see a light go on, so I could find out what apartment he was in. No light came on."

Garo Boghossian seemed quite enamored by his report. He looked from one of his guests to the other, his arms crossed, beaming.

"That's it?" Cinq-Mars asked him.

His face fell. Boghossian realized then that in his excitement he had left out the most important development. "That's not it. I went back to my car to come home. I walked right past the spot where he'd parked—and his car was gone. The Infiniti was gone! I'm sorry, but how does that happen? Who parks five blocks away from his destination, goes into a building by the front door but never comes out that door, turns on no lights whatsoever in any apartment, and somehow gets back to his car *by a different route* and drives away? Who does that? Any normal person you can think of?"

The story did carry the validation of intrigue.

"We don't have the car," Cinq-Mars reminded him. "All we have is a license plate that may or may not be real."

"You can run down the plate or whatever policemen do. If he turns out to be a married accountant visiting his mistress who mistook me for an angry husband, then fine, there's nothing to this. But that's not all we've got, Detective."

"What else?"

"I told you I followed him from downtown. I spotted the car as it emerged from an underground garage on Mountain. Not a public garage, you understand, the Q Forty-five came out of an apartment building on Mountain Street. I know which one. Either the guy lives there or he has friends there. Odds are, he'll be back."

Taking note of the avid faces of the civilians before him, Cinq-Mars had to smile. "Mr. Boghossian—"

"Please, call me Garo."

"Garo. You may call me Émile. Tell me about the license plate. It's wet out. It's hard to see at night when the roads are shiny and water splashes your windshield. Was it an easy thing for you to read the plate? Could you have made a mistake? Did you get a good look?" Cinq-Mars was gunning for a particular clue.

"It was hard to see, sure. I didn't want to get too close. You're right about the sheen of water."

"I think what Émile is asking—" Boyle was about to postulate.

"No, Okinder. Please, don't prompt him."

The reporter was dutifully silent.

"Listen," Boghossian said testily, fearful that he was being cited as an unreliable witness, "at one point I had no choice. We both got the

317

same red light on Sherbrooke. I had to drive right up behind him. I double-checked the plate then."

"Did you write it down then?"

"Yes, I did."

"That's when he made you."

"Pardon me?"

"That's when he knew he was being followed. A man like that is aware of the driver behind him. That's why he did the walk, to shake you off his tail."

"Jesus Murphy."

"So you saw the license, no problem."

"Square in my headlights. Which was important because he didn't have a light over the plate."

Cinq-Mars snatched a glance at Boyle, already knowing he'd find the young man beaming. They both knew that green Q45s were rare in the city, that the car had not caught on. How many of those vehicles had their license plate lamps burned out or intentionally extinguished? Possibly just the one. When Boyle had failed to catch the number of the car parked on his street, he'd given the lack of a light above the plate as his excuse.

"All right," Cinq-Mars decided. "Garo, I'm going to ask you to watch the Mountain Street building until I send a replacement. What're you driving?"

"A blue speckled Subaru wagon."

"Speckled?"

"Rust spots."

"Okay. You'll be relieved in a couple of hours. I'll let my man sleep a bit. Meanwhile, I'm running Okinder over to another site. I want him in position before dawn. After that I'll come back and arrange your replacement. Do you have a cell phone?"

"Yup."

"Let's exchange numbers. I don't care if the car's in the apartment now. What I want you to do is report if it arrives, try to follow if it leaves. Either way, call me on the cellular. I'm sorry about your nephew, Garo. I'm profoundly sorry about the suffering your family's endured. Usually I'm not too happy about civilians playing cops and robbers, but in this case you've done your nephew's memory a service. You've honored him."

"Thank you, sir."

"Let's roll," Boyle chipped in.

"No no no no *no*! Let's not *roll*. Let's keep our heads up and do our assigned tasks properly. Garo, what are the chances of having that coffee in a thermos?"

"Damn good, if you ask me."

"I'm asking."

Cinq-Mars established Garo Boghossian farther up the steep hill from the apartment they were putting under surveillance, instructing him to sit in the backseat opposite the driver's side. In this way the car would appear to be empty if scanned from an upper window. Spotted from ground level, the editor would look like a passenger awaiting the return of friends.

At Headquarters, Cinq-Mars switched to an unmarked squad car, and Boyle followed him out in the Taurus. He chose a parking spot on the same side of the street as LaPierre's apartment. The gentle incline provided good sight lines. Cinq-Mars sat with him a moment and told him what he hoped to collect from the girlfriend. He said he'd understand if he wanted to back out now. Boyle sat glumly, chewing on the news. With reluctance, the young man consented to proceed.

"How do you know she'll come out?" he asked him.

"I went into his bedroom closet. Never mind why or how. The girl had no clothes in there. She keeps a robe at his place, probably a toothbrush, but she has to have a place of her own where she keeps her stuff."

"You should think about becoming a detective when you grow up, Émile."

Cinq-Mars left him the thermos. "There's a lane at the top of the street. Duck in there if you need to take a leak."

"The voice of experience," Boyle mocked.

For a moment Cinq-Mars attached meaning to his words, and regretted that it had to be so.

16

Thursday, January 20, before dawn

Émile Cinq-Mars drove back downtown at a fair clip and along the way awakened his partner over the cell phone. "Up and at 'em, Bill. Saddle your horse. We got stuff going down."

"What time is it?" the sleepy voice asked. He must have looked across at his bedside table. "It's not five yet."

"Are you awake?"

"More or less."

"Call Alain Déguire. Meet me at Ben's, the two of you. Smoked meat for breakfast, Bill. It'll put hair on your chest and sludge in your arteries."

"When, exactly?"

"ASAP. Sooner. Time is of the essence."

Cinq-Mars snapped off his cellular as though to emphasize the point and sped down streets that were relatively quiet, racing the cabbies answering radio calls. Ben's was an all-night deli downtown. As always, the fifties-era venue was brightly lit, and Cinq-Mars chose the Poet's Corner. All around the room, which was vast, hung the photographs of stars who had traveled through town. Lemmon and Matthau. Cole Porter and Sophia Loren. Movie stars, singers, comedians, from the vaudeville era to the present, a rogues' gallery of the famous with their signatures and pat messages to the owners of Ben's. Frank Sinatra. Bob Hope. In one alcove, the poets of the city had been granted space, so among the Hollywood stars hung the mugs of local scribblers. From here Cinq-Mars had a good view of the street through a wall of windows. He ordered eggs and sausage, toast and orange juice. He'd been running on caffeine and pumpkin pie for too long.

Detective Mathers landed, looking as though he'd been roped with a cowboy's lariat and dragged through the streets. He bumbled into the bright room, squinting, puzzled. Cinq-Mars feared that a waiter might escort the miscreant out when Alain Déguire bumped into his fellow officer from behind. He was unbuttoning his coat and doing up his shirt at the same time, and together the two dazed young men found Cinq-Mars and staggered over.

"Sit," Cinq-Mars advised. "Eat. This could be an interesting day."

Déguire seemed relieved that he could eat and drink before dashing off, while Mathers remained miffed about his interrupted sleep. They packed away a good breakfast, and Cinq-Mars plied himself with coffee and watched.

"Alain," he began, "you were the IO on the Kaplonski blowup."

"For a while. The Wolverines took it over."

"Before they did, you were involved. Did you find out who Kaplonski was visiting that evening?"

"He was down at the University Club, near McGill."

"Since when is Kaplonski an academic? Was the bomb planted inside or outside the car?"

"Inside. That seems to be the new biker style."

"Both gangs?"

"Ah, no," Déguire corrected himself. "The bomb inside the car makes it a Hell's Angels' blowup."

Mathers roused himself enough to ask a question. "What's going on, Émile?"

His senior ignored him. "Who was he visiting at the University Club? Or are you telling me Kaplonski had a degree?"

"He and his wife had dinner with his lawyer."

"Gitteridge?"

"That's right."

"Who checked the club?"

"I went down myself," Déguire said, "while I was still the investigating, before the Wolverines tossed me out."

321

"Good man. Do you know what's significant for us about the University Club?" Cinq-Mars asked.

"No. What?"

"No indoor parking. None for blocks. You have to park on the street or in a small lot that's usually full. The bad guys would've known that. Did Gitteridge and Kaplonski leave together?"

"The staff said they didn't. The doorman saw Gitteridge shake Kaplonski's hand and kiss Mrs. Kaplonski on the cheek. He left later, five minutes or ten, nobody's sure."

"What's this about, Émile?" Mathers asked.

Cinq-Mars raised both mighty eyebrows to remind his partner that he should know better than to ask direct questions when other people were present. "Alain," Cinq-Mars decreed, "I'm going to give you an assignment. This is important, so I think you should take it as a sign that I like your face. Besides, you never would've told us about Christmas Eve if you'd known what was going down that night."

"What'd I tell you?" the confused officer asked.

"You said LaPierre booked back on after booking off."

"What's the big deal?"

"The fact that you don't know is in your favor, Alain. You're in the clear with me. I want you to understand that."

Déguire nodded. "I appreciate it, sir."

"On Mountain Street, up the hill, down from Penfield, a wild-haired man is sitting in the back of a blue Subaru wagon. He's keeping his eyes peeled on an underground parking garage. He'll show you which one. I want you to relieve him. He's a civilian, Alain, so don't go getting cop-chatty with him."

With a grave earnestness, Déguire accepted his instructions. "What're we looking for?"

Cinq-Mars looked first at Mathers, to convey the warning that he had better keep his mouth shut this time if he knew what was good for him. "We're waiting on a green Infiniti Q Forty-five. We don't know if it's in the garage and will be coming out, or if it's already out and will be going back in. Either way, I want to know when it's spotted. The guy in the Subaru will give you the plate number. If you see the car, call me on the cellular. No police communications. Understood?"

"Yes, sir. If he leaves?"

"Follow him. He's smart, he's accustomed to slipping a tail. When you follow, call me immediately, then keep me apprised. I'll be driving to find you."

"Yes, sir. Anything else?"

"Just this. Don't be lax. You're up against a professional. Everything you do, do smart. I'll understand if this guy beats you, but don't beat yourself, all right?"

"Okay. Sir? What do we want him for?"

"I'm not saying. I'm trusting you, Alain. I expect that trust to be reciprocal."

"No problem, sir."

Alain Déguire was off. Through the windows, Cinq-Mars and Mathers saw him cross to his personal vehicle, a Jimmy.

"You've found your source?" Mathers asked, marveling.

"Looks like. Bill, until now you've been the only one who deals with Jim Coates. That just changed. Take me to him."

"My car or yours?"

"I'm driving an issue. Let's burn city gas."

On the drive, Bill Mathers was briefed on his partner's meeting with Garo Boghossian and the news about the Q45. He was not brought up to speed on what Cinq-Mars intended to cover in the meeting with Jim Coates. "Play it by ear" was the best the senior detective would allow. A false dawn illuminated the east in the rearview mirror, shepherding a cold front that crossed the island and transformed water-covered roadways into skating rinks.

"You been to bed at all?" Mathers asked Cinq-Mars.

"Not lately."

"Things not going so well at home?"

"Things are fine at home, not that it's any concern of yours. Some cops just do what it takes to get the job done, and I happen to be one of them."

"Some cops take a whole day off to contemplate the breeze" was Mathers's riposte, thinking of yesterday and trying to get his partner to crack a smile. He guided him through the tough municipality of

Verdun, and they followed a canal out to Lachine. The city was named for the rapids nearby, for an early explorer believed that if he shot them successfully he would land in *la Chine,* French for China. "Next corner, left, then park."

Stepping out of the car, both men were astounded by how swiftly the temperature had dropped. They had to watch their footing as they crossed the glare ice to Jim Coates's new apartment building.

"Good location, Bill," Cinq-Mars praised him. "A boy like Jim fits into a neighborhood like this."

Mathers rang the buzzer according to a code the two of them had worked out. They were getting Coates up and had to wait for his response. He was on the fifth floor this time, and they went up in the elevator and found the boy standing in his doorway in his underwear wondering if his world was about to end.

"Put your pants on, son," Cinq-Mars told him as he barged into the apartment, thinking that he should have told LaPierre the same thing. "We want to talk to you."

While the boy dressed, Cinq-Mars went around the apartment turning on lights. He grabbed a straight-back chair, plunked it down in the center of the bare living room, and indicated for Coates to sit in it when he emerged. In a twinkling, he had transformed the apartment into an interrogation chamber.

Having no idea what was going on, Mathers made himself comfortable on the sofa at the boy's back while Cinq-Mars paced in front of him. He seemed to be fuming, building up steam. Finally, he put his hands on his knees and leaned down into the boy's face.

"Are you telling me it was jealousy?"

"What?"

"Don't say *what,* Jimmy. Say, *pardon me?* Or let me know that you don't understand the question."

"I don't."

"Are you telling me, Jimmy boy, that you were jealous of Hagop Artinian and that's why you turned him over to Kaplonski? Now you think about how you answer me, son, because I'm going to think about your reply."

Jim Coates squirmed on the hard chair. He was still half asleep.

"Yeah. I mean, yeah. You know, Hagop had everything. He got time off, the easy assignments, he went to lunch with the boss. On top of that, I mean, he was a university guy. He was getting an education. Always I had to do the shitwork and get yelled at, and what did I have to look forward to? Hagop had it all."

"So you were jealous of him?"

"I guess so. Sort of."

"Did you know he had plenty of girlfriends? Girls loved him, Jimmy, what do you think about that?"

"Nothing. I'm not surprised."

"Does it make you jealous?"

Coates didn't know if he should say. "Hagop's dead," he whispered.

"You can't be jealous of a dead man, is that it?"

He nodded to indicate that that was true.

"Tell me something, Jimmy. How did it feel to be jealous of Hagop Artinian? Did it rot your socks? Did you think about him half your waking hours? Was it like being in love, Jimmy, like you didn't have a brain of your own, all you could do was think about the other person? I really want to know."

The boy had to consider his response, and Cinq-Mars gave him time. "I used to think about him. Not all the time. Not so much. Once in a while."

"During these moments, Jimmy, would you get into a rage? Think evil things? Would you dream about punching him out, something like that?"

"No. I mean, I don't know. Nothing serious," the boy said.

"You ever dream about killing him?"

"I didn't kill Hagop!" Coates objected. *"Jesus!"*

Cinq-Mars stared at him intently, motionless. "We'll take it one question at a time, son. Did you ever dream about killing him?"

Coates squirmed and uttered stressful sighs and twisted his body around to shake things loose. Mathers was equally focused on Cinq-Mars himself. He could not clearly discern whether his partner was possessed or whether the ferocity of his determination was an act, put on for the boy's sake. He could not figure out where this line of inquiry might lead, why he was tilling soil that had been plowed before.

"Yeah, okay, so I used to wish maybe something bad would happen to him. Not all the time. Just once in a while if I was pissed off or something like that. What's the big deal? He'd be working under a car and I'd wish maybe the car would fall on him. Okay? So what?"

"Jimmy, so what? The boy's dead! You wished him dead and now he's dead. Now, Jimmy, you can't live your life unless you confess. You know that's true. You can't live with this thing on your shoulders. You knew, when you squealed to Kaplonski, that something bad would happen to Hagop. You knew you weren't dealing with Boy Scouts. Talk had gone around the garage. Your own eyes were open. Nobody's ever called you blind. Jimmy, you knew that Kaplonski and his pals were people nobody crossed. You had that on your mind. Talking to Kaplonski was no different than having a car fall on Hagop's head, isn't that right? You knew that."

The boy's chest cracked. "I didn't—think—they'd *kill* him."

"Maybe not so clearly. But, Jimmy, you knew you were running the risk, didn't you?" Cinq-Mars was speaking softly now, coaxing the confession out of him. "You imagined they'd beat him to a pulp. Maybe he'd survive that, maybe not. You were willing to take the risk. In your imagination you knew it was possible that somebody might get teed off enough to shoot him. These were people like that. You knew who you were working for, didn't you, Jimmy? Be brave. You have to be brave here. Look at me."

The boy sat with his body shaking and his head slung low, and Mathers, behind him, knew those eyes would be flooded with tears, that the boy was veering close to his core.

"You knew, didn't you? After you got the information from Hagop, all you could think about was being a snitch. You didn't want to do it because you're a good kid, but it was on your mind, gnawing at you, eating you up inside. You were so damn jealous you didn't care what it meant to poor Hagop. You didn't think about that. You just thought from your rage, from your savage envy, from your conviction it wasn't fair that someone should have so much when everything was so hard for you. Isn't that right?"

From his back, Mathers could see the boy nodding, giving in. "I guess so," he whispered.

"You don't want to be jealous anymore, do you, Jimmy? You want to put it behind you. You want to get on with your life, be a proper man, someone people respect. That's the kind of man you want to be, isn't it, Jimmy? To do that you have to get rid of the jealousy part, and then the guilt for what you did. That's your enemy. Take what life gives you and earn the rest. Right, Jimmy? There's no point being envious of someone else, it'll only destroy you. You know that now."

The boy had slumped forward, the ache inside bending him double. Cinq-Mars rested a peaceful hand upon his shoulder and let him weep. After a minute he pulled the boy's shoulders back so that he was sitting upright again.

"Listen, Jim. You told us about the Russian, and that's good. But I want you to think back to that night. Clean yourself up inside, you have nothing left to hide. Cast your mind back to the night the Russian was in the garage. This was after you told Kaplonski. You were sweeping up, weren't you?"

"Yeah."

"You were trying to hear what was said. You had to be. You'd squealed and now Hagop was going to be punished and you wanted to know exactly what they'd do to him."

"I couldn't hear much."

"You wanted to hear, though. You left the door open a crack. I know that because we can hear your broom on a tape. You were doing your best to listen in. It's okay if you didn't hear it all, we've got that conversation taped. But we need your eyes, Jimmy, to confirm a few things. Through the glass that separates the drive bays from the office area you could see the Russian, am I right?"

"Yeah."

"Was he alone?"

"Kaplonski was there."

"Nobody else?"

"No."

"Did he drive a car inside?"

Coates shook his head.

"Pay attention. Think back. It was cold weather. The snow was piled up against the curb, parking space was at a premium, especially on a night like that when everybody was staying home. Did the Russian drive a car inside?"

"No. He didn't."

"Did you hear a car outside with the motor running?"

The boy thought hard. "He had a car outside. I don't remember the motor running."

"Good. Now. How do you know he had a car outside? Maybe he took a cab."

"Just before he left, he told me to tell his driver to bring the car up. I had to go outside and wave at him."

"You did that? Did you see the driver, Jim?"

"No."

"No?"

"It was dark. He didn't come in. All I did was wave and he started the car."

"What can you tell me about him?"

"Nothing. He didn't get out. The car was ordinary."

"What does that mean?"

He shrugged again. "An American car. Big. GM or Ford."

"Come over to the window, Jim."

Mathers got up and accompanied the other two. More dawn light was showing, and the streetlamps provided adequate illumination in this neighborhood. Just then, Cinq-Mars's cellular started ringing.

"Yeah?" he asked. He listened a moment. Then he said, "Hold on, will you? Just hold on."

He held the phone in his hand by his side, and with his other hand he grasped Jim Coates by the elbow. "Look at the cars parked outside, Jim. Tell me which one most closely resembles the car you saw that night."

The boy surveyed the block. "That one there," he said, and pointed.

Coates had chosen the unmarked police cruiser in which Cinq-Mars and Mathers had arrived.

"Know your enemy, Jim," Cinq-Mars said quietly. "Your particular enemy was jealousy and now it's guilt, and like everyone else your enemy is yourself. Know your enemy and kick its butt. You can do that now, son. You've met yourself tonight. You didn't give up Hagop just because you wanted to be the apple of Kaplonski's bloodshot eye. You gave him up because you wanted a car to fall on your friend's head. You knew exactly what you were doing. You've seen that now. Now you know yourself. That's your one chance to set yourself free. Take it."

The boy turned back away from the window and moved to an armchair, where he collapsed in exhaustion and misery.

"Yeah?" Cinq-Mars said into the phone again. He listened awhile. "What?" he shouted. Then yelled louder, "What?" He listened another moment and hollered the loudest yet, "*What?* All right. Give me that address." Cinq-Mars extracted a notebook and pen and wrote a number while cradling the phone between his shoulder and ear. "All right. You stay put. I'll be there as soon as I can."

"Déguire?" Mathers asked after his partner had put away the phone.

"Civilian. We've got to run, Jimmy. Will you be all right?"

The boy nodded.

"Good lad. Just so you know, I'm betting on you. Let's go, Bill."

When they reached the hall they heard the elevator in use. Cinq-Mars had no patience to wait. "The stairs!" he exclaimed, and started off at a run. Jogging behind him, Mathers was already fearing the slippery streets ahead with this gung ho maniac behind the wheel.

17

Thursday, January 20, after dawn

The city's mechanical wizardry combated successive blizzards of snow and prevailed every time. Ice proved to be a more competitive adversary. As traffic increased, the streets jammed with immobile cars, expressways resembled parking lots, and the hilly streets downtown became impassable. Salt trucks sat motionless in the gridlock as the temperature sank and sirens wailed across the graying dawn. The system had broken down. The only responsible weapons were prudence and patience, and on this morning Sergeant-Detective Émile Cinq-Mars possessed neither in adequate measure, pushing his unmarked car hard while the headlights flashed in alternate sequence and a blue beacon pulsed from the rooftop. He leaned on the horn, resorted to the siren once, and fought his way downtown.

They drove on, and he climbed Guy Street, where cars had failed to manage the steep slope in either direction and city buses ascended or descended by increments. Pedestrians emerging from their highrises hung on to lampposts or fell. At the top of the hill, where the massive Montreal General Hospital stood like a castle overlooking the city, ambulances wove through stalled traffic. Lights flashing, Cinq-Mars wheeled across both sides of the road to pick his way through the checkerboard of vehicles and made a hard right on Wilder Penfield. Here the high-rises took advantage of being on a mountainside and were especially tall, overlooking downtown. Access was via steep streets only, and few cars had made it through, giving Cinq-Mars clear passage. He sped quickly. At Mountain Street he stopped abruptly and told Mathers to jump out, join Detective Déguire halfway down the hill.

"Excuse me?"

"What part of that didn't you understand?"

"Where're you going?"

"Tick, tock, Bill. No time for chitchat. Relieve Déguire. Let him take a whiz. Keep a close watch. I don't want this guy slipping through our fingers."

"Émile, come on, nobody drives a Q Forty-five on a day like today. It's asking to get pranged. If he has someplace to go he'll either walk or cab it."

"Watch anyway. We're not dealing with just anybody. If he leaves, tail him."

"Émile—"

"In case you're wondering, that's an order."

Reluctantly, Mathers stepped out of the car and promptly fell on his derriere. He shimmied into a snowbank.

"You all right?" Cinq-Mars called to him. The side door remained open.

Mathers thought about it. He had been awakened prematurely, commanded to be downtown. He'd witnessed an interrogation which demonstrated that his own had not been sufficiently vigorous. He was now being delegated to wait in a car with an officer he didn't much like on a mission that looked like a huge waste of time, and in the meantime he was sitting with his ass on ice. Both wrists ached, his tailbone felt bruised, but he was not about to seek his partner's sympathy. "I'm fine," Mathers grumbled. Struggling to his feet, he slammed the door shut.

"Same to you," Cinq-Mars said to no one in particular as he bolted back onto Penfield. Where the one-way avenue curved upward around McGill University, a bus had slid sideways into an old Beetle. Uniforms were on the scene, and Cinq-Mars employed his siren to clear spectators out of his way. Once through, he had to contend only with ice, as his was the lone car on the road all the way up to Pine and down to Park.

He drove with reckless intent.

East of downtown, he was working against the main flow of traffic, which provided him with roads less traveled and, consequently, better salted. He drove fast and turned off his emergency lights only as he neared his destination. Working people had left, leaving a selection of parking spots, and Cinq-Mars checked the address he'd gotten over the phone while in Jim Coates's apartment. He exercised more caution getting out of the car than he had driving it and skated on ice to the door. He rang the bell.

Okinder Boyle came down the inside stairs to let him in.

The place was run-down, smelly. The stench of old meals hung in the stairwell. Plaster had been gouged from the walls as if tenants periodically pulled tantrums, and a quick glimpse confirmed that the spray paint of graffiti offered nothing of interest—the usual sexual and racial slurs and inept rage.

"She's here?"

"Upstairs," Boyle told him.

"She understands? She's willing?"

"LaPierre's not her favorite guy. Which helps a lot. She seems willing, Émile, but she doesn't want to make trouble for herself."

"She's already got trouble."

"I gave her my word. I'm trusting you. Don't let her down."

"Let's head up."

Boyle opened the door for Cinq-Mars on the second landing as though he'd been living there a fortnight, guiding him into an unkempt, filthy, dark apartment. They stepped around clumps of unwashed clothes. Alone on a lumpy sofa in the living room, the girl wore jeans and a green shirt now, unlike at their first meeting.

"I'm Sergeant-Detective Émile Cinq-Mars." He flashed his hip badge. "Do you remember me?"

"You were at André's last night. You had a peek, I remember that. Then you went snooping in his closet."

"You're not going to mention that again, are you?" he asked sternly.

She reached across to the arm of the sofa and retrieved a pack of smokes and her lighter, selected one, and lit up, studying him through the smoke. "That you was in his closet or gave my muff an eyeball?"

"That I was there at all."

The girl had hard eyes and a determined slant to her chin. She'd known a measure of depravity through her teenage years, although her youth showed through the crust. Part of her persona was an act, the larger portion was composed of a bitterness that could not be faked and was impossible to conceal. She shrugged. "I got no need."

"What's your name?"

"Lise," she said.

"Lise Sauvé," Boyle added quietly.

"Are you using, Lise?"

"He said it didn't matter." She indicated the journalist with her chin.

"I'm just asking the question. I need to determine what sort of witness you'll make."

"I won't be no witness."

"No?" Cinq-Mars asked.

"I'll whore for me, I ain't gonna whore for no law."

She sounded as though she was quoting someone. "Trouble is, that's what we're asking you to do, isn't it?" he suggested gently.

The girl thought about that a moment. "You want me to spread my cheeks for medical science, I'll spread my cheeks. But I ain't gonna open my yap on no witness stand. For sure, not for the law."

That didn't sound like a quote, but like her own truth, her own definition of limits.

Cinq-Mars was weary enough that he would not have minded a seat. Disinclined to touch anything on the premises, he remained standing. "This young man has told me that you're willing to make a donation to our cause. That you have something I can use. You're willing to give it up voluntarily, and write down that you did so voluntarily. Is that right, Lise?"

"A donation?" She almost cracked a smile. "Now that's a word for it. Yeah, I'm willing to donate. Ain't good for nothing else, is it? Not where it's hanging out. A donation. I like that. I don't want no trouble out of this, that's all."

"You won't get any from me, Lise. How long's it been?"

She shrugged. Boyle answered, "Less than two hours now."

"I wasn't asking you," Cinq-Mars told him.

The girl shrugged again and asked, "What's it matter?"

"I want to ascertain that it's one hundred percent pure. I don't want a mixture, if you know what I mean."

"I got a fresh batch," she told him, smiling now, trying not to, poking her tongue into the side of her mouth.

"All right. You want to get your stuff on, we'll go. When's your next fix?"

"I can make it to eleven, twelve if I got to."

"You holding?"

"André took care of that."

"André's your pal."

"Oh yeah. He's my guardian angel. He's a charmer."

Downstairs they helped one another across the ice on the sidewalk and made it over to the police issue. "Want me to drive your car back?" Boyle asked him.

"On ice? I don't think so. You can come with us."

The girl slid in the back alone, and Boyle clambered into the front. She noticed the absence of window and door handles. "Crack-up, I'm stuck here."

"I got skates on my tires, Lise. I was born driving on ice."

Cinq-Mars alone spoke on the journey downtown, talking into a cell phone to Dr. Marc Wynett, a pathologist at the Royal Victoria. He told him what he wanted, and Boyle shook his head as though he could not believe the indignities that some people suffered to stay alive. He shook his head again when Cinq-Mars typed up a document at the hospital and passed it across for Lise to sign. Boyle read it first. He leaned over her shoulder and had a little trouble with the French but deduced both the gist and the implications.

"You've got it wrong," Cinq-Mars whispered to him. "This keeps her alive."

"But if she dies, you've got that contingency covered."

"That's my job," the detective reminded him.

"It's not mine," Boyle said, and he walked away while Cinq-Mars read his copy aloud to Lise Sauvé. She signed without protest and a minute later was called in to see the pathologist.

"It's a grim world," Cinq-Mars told the journalist.

"Is that some kind of justification?"

"The girl wants to do it."

"Just because that's true doesn't make it right."

"It has to be done."

The journalist went over to the water fountain for a drink. He came back and sat on the bench beside the policeman, whose arms were folded on his chest.

"There are times," Boyle said, "when you want to be on the side of those who get kicked around in life. Sometimes you kick them around a little yourself, and you think you're doing them a favor, that you got to kick them around to keep them in line, that the line is good for them. In my book, Émile, just because something is necessary doesn't make it right."

The detective nodded. "I think that's true, Okinder. Keep thinking that way. You've got a job to do and it's not mine. I've got a job to do and it's not yours."

"Someday, when it's safe, maybe I'll do a story on her. I'll mention today. You won't come out of it smelling like a sweet petunia."

"Neither will you," Cinq-Mars mused.

"I'm complicit. I don't deny that."

Cinq-Mars looked sideways at him. He respected this young man a lot.

They waited in the dreary alcove, and Wynett was the first to emerge. Sticking his head through the swinging door, he chirped, "Prime sample," and disappeared again, as though he'd rather not be party to the procedure either. When Lise Sauvé eventually returned, she seemed surprised to find them still there. She was accustomed to being dropped off at hospitals and found it novel that someone would actually wait around.

"Now what? You gonna arrest me for something?"

"I'm driving you home."

"At least if a cop car cracks up we got a radio."

"I'll walk home," Boyle announced.

"So do I get to sit in front?" Lise wanted to know.

"Will you keep your hands off the siren?" Cinq-Mars asked her.

335

"Sure."

The solemn eagerness of her response made him smile. "What about the radio?"

"No problem."

"The shotgun?"

"I hate guns."

"Fine. You'll sit up front."

"All right," Lise declared. She seemed really pleased. "All right."

She was seventeen they'd found out, exactly the age Cinq-Mars had guessed, but he was thinking that, in the quiet of her heart, in the depths of that cubbyhole, she was stuck at around seven.

Detective Bill Mathers enjoyed a special fondness for meticulous police work, asking questions, piecing together bits of evidence, working down a chain of witnesses to find the crook holding the bag and wearing a scared, half-crazed gape induced by crack and fear. Grown tired of arresting juveniles for adult crimes, he had wanted out of the suburbs. He'd rather arrest crooks than brats. You could have a conversation with a crook. What he liked about police work was asking the right questions, what he didn't like was sitting in a cramped car exchanging asides with a man with whom he had nothing in common and who didn't want to be there either, who had also been awakened prematurely.

"Got much cash on you, Alain?"

Detective Déguire fished out his wallet and counted forty bucks in tens and fives.

"I've got fifteen," Mathers told him. "Put in thirty-five of yours to my fifteen, we're up to an even fifty. Sounds like a fair-sized bribe to me."

"Hey, Bill, I don't want any trouble with your partner."

Mathers held out his hand, flicking the fingers into his palm. "Come on," he said. "Fork it over."

"Who're you bribing?"

"I'm going in."

Déguire looked across at the building. He was no less bored with this detail than Mathers. "As far as I'm concerned it's your money, your action. You're doing this over my objections."

"Cough up."

Pockets flush, Mathers climbed out of the car and sidestepped his way down the slippery slope to the apartment building, finding good traction only as he crossed the recently salted street. He had his eye on the doorman in the heavy woolen overcoat with the gold braid epaulets and the peaked cap who greeted visitors with a smile and sent residents on their way with a cheerful word of caution about the footing. Doormen were bribable, weren't they?

As he got close, he got lucky. The subterranean garage door opened, and he waited to see who was coming out. Rather than a vehicle, the janitor and an assistant emerged with buckets of salt they spread across the incline by hand. Mathers strolled down that hill, not bothering with the front door. He believed he was home free, striding past the janitor and the assistant, who said hello, making it to the door, when a loud baritone interrupted his progress. He looked up at the doorman gazing down upon his wretched trespassing soul.

"Excuse me, sir?" the man said. The god of this dominion, a defender. "May I help you?" Politeness was inherent to the man's position. The tone and words conveyed a more explicit thrust—*who are you and what do you want, scumbag?*

Mathers knew that if he blew this one Cinq-Mars would have his hide tacked to a barn door in a countryside where real wolverines prowled. Reaching inside his coat, he unclipped and flashed his hip shield. "Police," Mathers stated with some force of his own. "We're investigating a hit-and-run, checking garages in the downtown area." *Beats a bribe*, he thought, which had potential to backfire besides being difficult to afford. "Shouldn't be too long," he added.

"What kind of car?" the doorman demanded, choosing to exercise authority.

Mathers considered the premises. "An Audi," he said.

The doorman nodded. "We have a couple. But none of our tenants would ever leave the scene of an accident."

"You know that? We figure the driver was inebriated. I suppose your tenants don't drink either."

Most toddled home tipsy. The man acknowledged as much with a slight nod. In moving away he neither granted nor denied access, and

337

inside Mathers moved quickly to meld with the gloom of the garage.

The first thing that struck him was that all parking spaces were assigned apartment numbers. Stall 2301 was home to a green Infiniti Q45. He copied the plate number and knew he should get back outside and report. But he headed for the elevators. Mathers continued to be bothered by the Coates interview. Cinq-Mars had pushed the boy deeper and farther than he had done, and he was the one who was supposed to be adept with young people. He had blown it. Cinq-Mars had had the advantage of knowing what he was after, yet the fact remained that Mathers had failed to get everything out of him. What upset him more was that Cinq-Mars was obviously on to something and was shutting him out of the spree. Didn't the old man trust him? Okay, if Cinq-Mars wanted to keep him outside of things that was his privilege. For his part, he'd also act on his own. Mathers ascended to the twenty-third floor and stepped off the lift.

This was an affluent zone. Mathers was dumbfounded to discover that no corridor existed, only a small landing fronting twin doors. These apartments would be immense. He listened at the door of 2301 and heard no sound, and nothing at the opposite address either. The carpet was thick, the doors heavy. An illuminated buzzer was beside each door. Mathers was tempted beyond his better judgment. He pressed one, setting off a musical chime. *Cinq-Mars will kill me.* He swung around and pressed the button beside the opposite apartment as well.

Then waited for someone to answer.

Footsteps approached 2301.

Bill Mathers kept his back to that door.

It opened behind him. He turned, threw up his hands, and apologized. "I'm sorry, sir. I goofed. Rang the wrong bell by mistake."

The gentleman was neatly attired for the hour. Graying, with a high, narrow forehead, prominent cheekbones, and a sharp nose. His eyes were unwavering, at once reproachful and intrigued. The eyebrows were thin.

"Who'd you want to see?" he asked.

Mathers gestured with his finger, turning. "Twenty-three oh-two," he said.

"Who," the man asked, "in twenty-three oh-two?"

His hand still upraised, Mathers did a quick inventory of his options. He offered a conciliatory smile. "I'm toast, aren't I?"

The man did not reply and chose to cross his hands in front of him, tilting his head as though to more acutely observe him.

"I don't know who's in twenty-three oh-two," Mathers admitted.

"That's not surprising, given that the apartment is unoccupied."

With a laugh, Mathers brought his hands apart, then back together again. "It's you I've come to see."

"Think so? Who do you think I am?"

Mathers scratched his forehead. "Beats me." He sighed. "I don't know who you are, sir, but I think—I'm pretty sure—I'm willing to lay even money—that Sergeant-Detective Émile Cinq-Mars would like to talk to you."

The man had good eyes, Mathers noticed. They didn't flinch, they didn't break the connection.

"You are?" the man asked.

"Mathers, sir."

The man tugged an earlobe. "I've heard good things about you, Mathers."

"Thank you, sir."

They stood in the quiet of the foyer, the elevator's gentle whir the only attendant sound. "If the illustrious detective Émile Cinq-Mars would like to speak to me, Detective Mathers, I suggest that he drop by. Since you now know where I live, he's welcome to do so. You can tell him I said so."

The man moved to close the door on their conversation.

"Ah, sir?" Mathers asked.

The man paused to listen.

"If I lose you, sir, if you were to vanish, Émile would have my scalp. Would you mind if I made the call from inside?"

The question was considered in silence a moment. "Detective, I do. As to your quandary, it's yours, not mine. Rest assured, I'm not about to run like off some petty criminal on the lam. If Cinq-Mars wants to talk to me, he knows where to find me. As far as your anxiety goes, I couldn't care less." He shut the door.

339

Mathers hit the elevator button. A building like this had to have a fire exit, and a man like him would only live in a place he could escape. *A service elevator! Yes!* Straight up from the basement for groceries and tradesmen and movers. The elevator door opened, and he pressed the button for the garage.

Mathers bounced lightly on the floor as though to speed the car's fall.

He was running the instant the door opened. Mathers spotted the doorman spy him and hurry along behind. Going past the dumbwaiter, he heard it before he saw it. The gizmo was in motion. He put his arm straight out with his badge in the doorman's face. "Go," he said. "Leave."

"Sir! I am sorry. What is your business here?"

He brought his hand to his side, switched the badge for his pistol, and pointed that at the doorman. "East of Aldgate," he told him, inexplicably. This time the man backed off in a rush.

The dumbwaiter stopped, rocking under a load. The doors were shut, but he saw the latch being turned from the inside. Some exit. Mathers stood aside. The two hinged doors swung open from the middle. Mathers stepped back in front. Before him, curled in a serpentine pattern, was the gentleman from the twenty-third floor. His spine was steeply curved, his head between his knees to fit himself into the cramped quarters. He was sitting on his coat.

"Undignified," Mathers suggested to him. "Completely without class."

"Hell, it was worth a try," the man said.

"You have more to hide than I know about."

"Help me out of here, Detective. Be a sport."

"This could work as a holding pen."

"It's the only trick I had. Okay, so it didn't work, but it's not your place to rub it in."

Mathers needed him on his feet and mobile. He frisked him where he sat cramped in a ball. No weapon. "Crawl out of there on your own," he ordered. "Give me the slightest provocation and I'll shoot."

"What's happening?" the doorman fretted. "Is that you, Mr. Norris? May I be of some assistance?"

"You're asking the wrong person," Mathers warned him. "Go outside. Look up the hill. Put your hands over your head and wave them like a maniac. Either do that or I'll stuff you in this hole and send you up to the penthouse."

The man was not easily dissuaded from his sense of duty.

"Do as he says, Hamilton," the man called Norris advised him. "I'll be fine."

As the doorman ran off, the gentleman unraveled himself and emerged by degrees. He dusted himself off, stretched his spine, straightened up, and gazed upon his captor. "Something I've been meaning to tell you, Mathers," he said.

"Yeah? What's that?"

"Your timing stinks. This is not convenient."

"Tough," Bill Mathers answered, unable to diminish his smile.

Receiving the call from his partner over his cell phone while ensconced in his cubicle, Émile Cinq-Mars responded with blind fury. He was utterly enraged that Mathers had taken their prey into custody. He had not issued that command. More important, he hadn't determined what he intended to do with his source once caught. A serious negotiation lay ahead, and the first rule of horse trading was to know more about the animal than did his counterpart. He wasn't there yet. Cinq-Mars resorted to English to properly insult Bill Mathers.

As soon as he had taken down the particulars, he cut off their connection and headed out.

On the way down in the elevator at HQ, Cinq-Mars confronted what really irritated him. He'd wanted to apprehend the man himself. He desired the privilege of being first on the scene and had visualized poking his big nose into the unknown countenance of the man familiar to him only as a telephone voice.

He set off in an unmarked car across the city of ice.

A second rule of horse trading was to turn every disadvantage into a benefit. He had wanted to capture the man himself. That a junior detective had done so could be worked to his own favor. Don't let the culprit believe that he was the center of the universe, or the focus of an investigation. He had merited nothing more than the attention of a junior officer. Make him believe, or suspect, or worry, that he was an inconvenient cog in machinations that traveled beyond his understanding. Sabotage his control, dispel the man's natural savvy, diminish his import. Make him sweat.

Driving, he received another call, this one from André LaPierre.

"I'm surprised you're awake," Cinq-Mars told him, a lie. He had assumed that their conversation would stir his colleague to prompt action.

"Émile! I told you I'd get on the case. Talk to me. What's going on?"

"You tell me, André."

"That hit—the gang's moneyman, George Turner, the English guy—definite discrepancies. Looked like the work of the Rock Machine, but a few wrinkles were added that nobody's seen since."

"Such as?" To hear enthusiasm in LaPierre's voice again was heartening, although Cinq-Mars wondered what had put him on edge.

"Okay, the Hell's Angels plant their bombs *inside* the vehicle. This was on the outside, wired on, like the Rock Machine does."

"No problem there."

"Except the Machine arranges dynamite in a different hill. I just found that out this morning."

"What's that mean?"

"I hope you appreciate this, Émile—this is pure powder from the Wolverines. They've got the cutest filing clerks, by the way, you should've joined them. Okay, Angels load the casing with their blow sticks in a pyramid. Each stick fits in the grooves formed by the two underneath it. Consequently, each layer is not as wide as the one below."

"The Machine?"

"Straight up. They put the bomb case up on its narrower end and pile rows that way, so when they lay the bomb flat again, each row sits directly on top of the one below. Not in the grooves, but right on top."

"And in that blast?"

"Outside the car, like a Rock Machine hit, but the hill was like the

342

Angels do. Two more things. The casing was unique. But here's the big one. Both the Angels and the Machine either use remote control to detonate or they hot-wire to a timer. This one was a combination of both. It could only blow on timer ignition, but it also carried an on-off receiver. The bomber could decide to make the timer hot, or make it go cold if he suddenly chose not to ignite."

"What do the Wolverines make of that?" Cinq-Mars was driving with one hand on the wheel and managing a road surface that had improved considerably now that salt and sand were down. Crumpled cars from the morning nightmare abounded, waiting their turn for tows.

"They worked a theory that makes sense. The last Rock Machine member to die prior to that particular blast was their own bomber. The Wolverines think they hired from outside for the blast until their own personnel got up to speed."

"Has the theory held up? The Machine's bombed since."

"That's what's so interesting. It looks like they went back to the old bombing practices without changes. That tells me they always had somebody trained to take over. Émile, come on, is there a third player? What do you have? If that bomb wasn't a biker hit, I can take back the portfolio. This should be my investigation!"

"You're on suspension, André."

"You know what I mean, Émile. When I'm off suspension."

"I can't say anything right now, André—"

"Émile! Come on. Give me something. I'm giving you prime stuff. Is there a third gang?"

Who do you tell if I tell you? "The Angels could've bumped off one of their own, made it look like a Rock Machine hit, but hired people outside," Cinq-Mars proposed. If André knew better he wouldn't like the suggestion.

"Why bother, Émile?"

Cinq-Mars was stopped at a red light. He preferred to do his thinking in motion. LaPierre had to be handled with care.

"They don't want gang members knowing they're bumping off their own. It's a messy world, André."

LaPierre offered him dead air, mulling it over. The light turned, and the cars, nervous about ice, started moving slowly. Cinq-Mars, impatient, drove on, looking for a way to get past them.

"That's possible," LaPierre allowed. "But is there a third player, Émile?"

Did he detect a note of desperation in that voice? Did LaPierre depend upon a third player to validate himself in the Police Department, so he could take over the case, or to validate himself within the Hell's Angels? LaPierre was anxious for a way out, Cinq-Mars believed, and whatever reason might be motivating him, he was willing to toss him a bone. "André, I think there could be a third player."

"Who, Émile?" His voice sounded breathless. A blip in the quality of the cellular service, or was LaPierre hungry and dependent upon a response?

"Could be their old Mafia pals aren't as chummy with the Angels as they think. I've got my reasons to say that. Another possibility, well, I hate to say it, André."

"Tell me."

"Not over the phone. Meet me back at HQ. Say, two hours?"

"You got it."

"See you then."

They signed off, and Émile Cinq-Mars turned up Mountain Street to meet the man who had been directing his life for so long.

Cinq-Mars parked across the street from Detective Déguire's Jimmy and shut the engine. For a few moments he followed procedure left over from his days as a uniform whenever he yanked someone over to make an arrest. He remained perfectly still. He waited. The ploy gave the other person time to get nervous or make a break for it or start shooting. This time, he ended the brief delay by doing something he had not done before. In the Jimmy sat the man who had manipulated his existence, to their mutual benefit, for so long. He was also the agent whose activities had caused the death of one young man, possibly others, and was probably the man behind blowing up George Turner. In the car sat an emissary of a powerful, covert organization. Cinq-Mars had nothing on him. Everything from here on would be negotiation. Skill. Ploy. Tactics. He rolled down his window. Rather than go over to the man that Bill Mathers had captured, identify himself and display his shield, and commence a formal discussion, the detective merely put out his hand, crooked one finger, and signaled the rogue over to him.

Cinq-Mars wanted to watch him cross the street. He wanted to observe his expression, his body language from the comfort of his own car. He did not want to give this professional that opportunity himself. Lives were at stake. He had to embark upon an exchange, a session of horse trading, that would summon the depths of his abilities. Given that the other guy possessed the bulk of information, there was no advantage too slight, no hedge too insignificant, no psychological link too weak not to be deployed.

The captive waited for a line of cars coming down the hill to pass. He gazed up the incline, as though he was thinking too, and stepped back from the salt splash the vehicles were bound to create. The gesture drew the detective's attention to the man's clothes. Fine threads. He drove a distinctive car. He had family money to call upon. Did this work not for the paycheck but for the charge. Cinq-Mars held up his cellular to make sure that Mathers had his turned on. He called him. Their prey had crossed the street halfway, where he waited for a truck ascending.

"Bill, you said you caught him in the foyer. Did he have his coat on?"

"Sitting on it."

"He didn't return to the apartment?"

"No, sir."

"Good work." He hung up and put the phone away.

The man jogged to cross behind the truck and ahead of a speeding taxi. He came around to the side of the policeman's car, and for the first time, before he got in, their eyes met. Cinq-Mars noted the gentle smile, a certain smugness, a conceit of superiority his source could not suppress for trying. He opened the side door and bundled himself into the front seat, arranged his coat, and removed a glove before extending his right hand.

"Émile Cinq-Mars," he said. "It's an honor."

"An overdue meeting," Cinq-Mars told him. He tugged at the fingers of his driving glove, peeled it off, and gave the man's hand a firm, brief shake. His source had been the first to offer his hand, and Cinq-Mars was the first to withdraw.

"Everything in its own time, Émile. The timing for this meet leaves a lot to be desired. From my perspective, it's premature."

"What's your name?" Cinq-Mars recognized that the man was seeking to control the conversation. He wasn't going to let him.

"You know how it goes, Émile."

"Sir, what name do you commonly use?"

"Selwyn Emerson Norris, to my friends and colleagues."

"Who do you work for?"

Cinq-Mars treated his captive as he might a minor felon. He glanced at him, took in a lot, but most of the time he checked the street and his mirrors as though this entire process was routine and something of a nuisance. His attitude differed greatly from their telephone conversations. He was severe, critical, impatient, and remarkably indifferent, whereas previously he had hidden his emotional state.

"I am a public relations officer with the American consulate."

"No, sir, who do you work for? You're CIA, or there's a remote chance you're FBI. Which?"

To Cinq-Mars, it seemed that Norris was doing his best to swallow a smirk. "I'm not at liberty to discuss it."

"CIA, then. Exposure won't sit well with either of our governments."

"Émile, get serious. You've got nothing of substance. Don't stick your neck out. Too many bureaucracies and jurisdictions are only too willing to chop it off. Including mine, if push comes to shove."

Cinq-Mars shifted his weight behind the steering wheel to confront Selwyn Norris more squarely. He had offered a feeble threat and been roundly snubbed. He deserved that loss. But in horse trading, he was often willing to stumble early and cause his competitor to feel more secure, thereby weakening his defense.

"Here's the deal, Mr. Norris."

"Please, Émile, call me Selwyn."

Cinq-Mars burned his glare into him, tilting his head back to present the austere slope of his nose to full advantage. "Mr. Norris, we are not friends, and you shall not refer to me as Émile again."

"I can assure you, there's no need—"

"The only assurance I need from you is that you understand, fully, what must be done here. This is the deal—I want the young woman out."

In the face of the policeman's righteous ire, Norris took a deep breath, letting the air expire slowly. He faced forward now, studying the street that Cinq-Mars had abandoned, no longer quite able to stare him down. "I'm afraid, Sergeant-Detective, that that will not be possible."

"Wrong answer," Cinq-Mars warned him.

"You have to understand the situation," Norris told him.

"Explain it to me," Cinq-Mars said with a voice like a drill bit.

Norris rubbed his chin. "I don't know how much you've cobbled together, how much you have discerned, or how much you've speculated upon—"

"No, you don't," Cinq-Mars confirmed.

"But I do know that this is bigger than you can imagine. What we've done is infiltrate the world's most notorious gang right at the moment when it's making a move to a larger stage. We are working at the gang's core, where the money is. How it's moved and buried and spent and invested will be known to us. Are you telling me that that's not important news? Are you telling me, as a police officer, that such information is negligible? Do you think it can be traded away in a simple barter between you and me?" He met his glance again, his eyes going back and forth as though looking into the eyes of Cinq-Mars one at a time.

"What I'm telling you," the detective persisted, "is that the young woman comes out."

"You're making this unnecessarily difficult. You have nothing on me, Sergeant-Detective. I'm under no obligation to speak to you."

"If you don't, I'll arrest you."

"For what?"

"For driving with a burned-out bulb above your license plate."

Norris laughed. "You haven't lost your sense of humor."

"Too slight a charge?"

"Somewhat," a bemused Norris agreed.

"I could arrest you for driving a vehicle with illegal plates, and for tampering with police computers. In a pinch, I could arrest you on suspicion of murder."

Norris continued to chuckle. "Are you absolutely certain that I cannot call you by your given name? I'd prefer if we were friends."

"You don't think murder is a serious charge?"

"I don't think you're serious about concocting the charge."

"Don't be so sure," Cinq-Mars warned him.

"Whose murder?" Norris asked.

"George Turner, the original Hell's Angels' banker."

There, a nick. The response had not been expected, and his captive underwent a turn before recovering. The evidence was slight, but the minute waver behind the eyes, the quiet swallow, the failure to immediately indicate incomprehension, were revealing. He had touched him, Cinq-Mars was certain.

"Who?" Norris asked.

"Too late," the policeman scoffed. "Don't bother."

The agent shook his head. "What are you up to, Émile?"

"Sure, go ahead, call me Émile. Don't think I won't hang you out to dry."

"We've been through a lot. We've worked together to put perps away."

"None of which was any of your business."

"You didn't raise an objection at the time."

"I want the woman out, sir. I don't want to find her as I found Hagop Artinian."

His nod came from a serious place this time. "Allow me to explain."

"Go ahead."

He seemed to be looking into himself, as though he knew that he had to appeal to the highest instincts of this detective. Cinq-Mars was known for his ethics. To entertain him with falsehood held no promise. What Norris had to do, what Cinq-Mars expected him to do, was to explain his position from a moral core.

"The Hell's Angels, as you know, are making a move on Montreal against the Rock Machine. Through their puppet gangs, they've already secured most of the country. Quebec's a battleground, and once the dust settles, Ontario becomes the next war zone. The result is predictable. The Angels will control crime from coast to coast. That makes them your nemesis, not mine. So what does that have to do with me or other Americans? We've got our own troubles. Well, I'll tell you. Relationships are forming that involve us."

The car was not warm, but Selwyn Norris paused for effect and to undo the top buttons of his overcoat.

"A new organization has been created in Russia that combines former and current members of the KGB—which is now called the FSB—with traditional Soviet gangsters. They used to be enemies. Politics put them in bed together, and I have to tell you, as someone with knowledge of these matters, they will provide a formidable enemy. What's going on in the former Soviet Union has allowed gangsters to prosper as never before in world history. The speed of their rise, the virulence of their methods, the value of their enterprises— Émile, it's something to behold."

"I'm aware of the challenge, Mr. Norris. But the young woman comes out."

"Émile, this is not a question of jurisdiction. It involves domestic crime, yes—but national and international crime as well. We happen to know that a Russian has gained influence over the upper-level leadership of the Hell's Angels."

"Give me a break—"

"Wait! Hear me out. Okay, the Angels would never allow an outsider to be in charge. You're right there. But in terms of strategy, in terms of how they're going to operate and with whom—that's been usurped. They've been seduced. They've been shown the promised land, and they can't believe the riches in store. How many Angels are in Quebec? A hundred and eighty?"

That was not a guess. It was accurate. Cinq-Mars nodded.

"The hierarchy will know wealth beyond belief."

"It's not your fight, Mr. Norris."

"No? We have intercepted certain exchanges. It's not only the

Hell's Angels and the Mafia and the Russians who are lining up together, aiding and abetting, consorting. Overtures have been made. They've been mulled over and key matters agreed upon. The Russian KGB/FSB agents have made contact with militia groups in the American Midwest, and in the Dixie States. The plan is that the militia will undertake to bomb government buildings, bring down airplanes, burn black churches, assassinate politicians, disrupt commerce and the social peace, instigate race riots and skirmishes—in short, do their thing, live out their maniacal, racist fantasies, and have their campaign well financed with safe havens provided in other countries for anyone forced to flee the law. The idea behind this assault is that within a climate of civil unrest, when the FBI and civic police are strapped to the limit dealing with terrorism, the Russian federation, the Hell's Angels, and the remnants of a resurgent Mafia will rise in that fire, dominate not only criminal activity but legitimate activities as well. Their dominance, their role, will hardly be noticed, so focused will the authorities be on internal terrorism. That's what we're up against, Émile. The rending of my nation in order to drag it down closer to the level of the former Soviet Union, so that criminals have a free hand, so that violence prospers, unabated, so that civil peace disintegrates, so that the races are violently pitted against one another, and every man, woman, and child walks the streets in fear and trepidation. That's what we're up against—and you want me to cease the battle, to give up what chance we have of terminating the organization behind that vision of the next century, just to spare one young woman? One young woman, who, I might add, is perfectly secure within the organization she's infiltrated."

"Is she?"

"She is, Émile. You have my word on that."

"Then consider, Mr. Norris, that I know about her."

Norris's chin went back a notch, as though reacting to a well-timed and well-executed punch. He needed a moment to recover.

"From the outset, Émile," Norris said, "I knew you were a man to be trusted with covert information. It's one of your attributes, a reason why you were chosen."

Cinq-Mars smiled. The gall of this man, to think that he could be recruited also, just like the kids. On the other hand, he thought again, had he not been?

The agent had seized the initiative in this discussion, the momentum was on his side. He had fought for and acquired the high ground, leaving Émile Cinq-Mars without a moral stance, defending a merely personal, merely domestic point of view. Now that he had received the best that this man could deliver, it was time to unleash his own arsenal, one volley followed by another.

"You're missing an essential element here, Mr. Norris."

"Am I?"

"Your agent, this young woman, has been compromised inside the Angels. The damage has been contained for the moment, but that can't go on indefinitely. The woman must come out because her usefulness to you is about over. If she doesn't come out, her chances of survival are minimal."

Norris listened, perhaps respectfully, and gazed upon the detective for a few prolonged moments. Cinq-Mars guessed that he was getting up to speed with what he had not said as much as with what had been voiced. Cinq-Mars had intimated to him that he also had informants inside the Hell's Angels, for how else had he drawn information out? By saying that the damage had been contained, he was suggesting that he had successfully quashed information set loose inside the gang. In the end, Norris shook his head, "Sorry, Émile. You have to do better than that."

"How so?"

He gestured with a hand. "I haven't seen any cracks in her security."

Perfect. Norris was fishing, trying to hook whatever Cinq-Mars knew and reel it to the surface, but in doing so he had admitted to a position. Now Cinq-Mars could assume an alternate perspective that diminished his adversary's viewpoint. "Are you familiar with the phrase malicious malalignment?"

Pressing his lips together quizzically, Norris shook his head.

"Ask your agent about it. Then remind yourself that the real Heather Bantry had been a sprinter. Then think—fast, because we don't have much time—about getting her out. She's no good to you in there."

As he had intended, Cinq-Mars had given Selwyn Norris several matters to ponder simultaneously. He had revealed, as though accidentally, that he knew the pseudonym of his agent, and had knowledge about her Norris lacked. He had also disclosed that he knew about the real Heather in significant detail.

"Malicious malalignment?" his source repeated.

"The key phrase. It has to do with a misalignment of the bones in her calves leading to her knees. She can't run properly. She was never a sprinter. If I were you I'd get on this quickly. Keep in touch. We don't have much time."

That abruptly, Norris had been dismissed.

Sergeant-Detective Cinq-Mars watched his adversary ascend the steps to his apartment building, to be admitted with a timid salute by the doorman. He did not appear to speak as he passed the guardian, as though his mood had been considerably upset despite the sudden release. Cinq-Mars started his car, checked the street, and drove to the opposite side, facing what was now only a flutter of oncoming traffic. The detective rolled down his window while Déguire did the same on his Jimmy. Mathers leaned forward to listen as well.

"Follow me," Cinq-Mars instructed, and he touched the gas pedal, careening uphill, arousing a blare from an angry motorist.

18

Pacing the limits of his cubicle—what he called his cage—Émile Cinq-Mars waited for the phone to ring, wondering who'd call first. After leaving Selwyn Norris in a funk on his doorstep, he'd taken the junior detectives to the University Club, where Walter Kaplonski had enjoyed his last meal. The three cops traipsed through the establishment, concentrating on the men's room. As Alain Déguire had told them, patrons to the club, upon entering and being greeted by a porter, retired to the downstairs bathroom to remove their outerwear and freshen up. Then they ascended to the bars and dining rooms aloft. The bathroom was elegant with marble walls and floors, and the junior officers were impressed that everyone scrubbing up received an individual towel. Communal brushes and combs were also available.

"Get a degree, take out a membership," Cinq-Mars instructed them. "You can come in here and wash your hands all day."

"And never run out of towels," Mathers added, still amazed.

Outside in the cold, Cinq-Mars had instructed the young men to pick up the lawyer Gitteridge.

"What if he's in court?" Mathers asked.

"What if he won't come in?" Déguire tacked on.

"He'll come along if you've made him bleed. He's that kind of guy."

Something was on the burner, the two young cops could smell the smoke. They exchanged a glance—they had no more arguments—and headed off to track down Gitteridge.

The telephone rang at long last, jolting Cinq-Mars from his rumination. He answered brusquely. "What?"

The front desk said a man by the name of Raymond Rieser had arrived to see him.

"Send him up unescorted. He knows the way." Cinq-Mars severed the call, then flung the instrument against a partition. The portable wall bent under the impact, and the telephone clattered against a filing cabinet before bouncing onto the floor. A couple of officers poked their heads in, but the sight of Cinq-Mars alone and fuming inspired them to move along. Calming himself, the detective gathered up the phone again and slammed it back down on his desk.

He paced, waiting.

Rieser loomed large in the doorway, his grin boisterous beneath the cartoon mustache. "Émile! You old sod!"

"Hey, Ray, what brings you to town?" Cinq-Mars took the man's elbow in his free hand as they shook.

"Chores, a little shopping. Finally finishing the basement. Thought I'd hunt down a few power tools I covet."

Cinq-Mars happened to know that Ottawa was a better city for buying tools than Montreal, but he didn't say so. He suspected that Rieser had flown, that he had caught a flight with seconds to spare. "What're you wearing?"

Under his overcoat he had on a kind of jumpsuit, as though he planned to either skydive or toboggan. The colors were startlingly neon, red with yellow and orange trim. "You like?" He did a turn around the cubicle, modeling.

"You're a bizarre man, Ray."

"Keep the world off balance, Émile, so nobody pins you down."

"What brings you to town?" Cinq-Mars pestered him.

"Told you, chores. Nothing much. Thought I'd drop by. So tell me, how're you getting along with that case we discussed?"

Sitting, Cinq-Mars leaned back in his swivel chair and placed his hands over his lap. "I've met the guy."

Rieser's jaw dropped. "You met him?" He sat down himself. "No way! Tell me."

"We had a chat. He's CIA."

"No guff? CIA?"

"Yup. He thinks the world's in danger, that it can't get along unless he interferes with my job. Glad you dropped by, Ray. I was meaning to say thanks again for your help. Your analysis made a whole lot of sense to me."

"Glad to be of use. Congrats on making the contact, Émile. Good police work, that. How'd you do it?"

The phone rang just then, and Cinq-Mars picked up to Dr. Wynett, calling from his lab. Wynett cautioned that the lab work could not be rushed, but he had made good progress on the other matter they'd discussed. "Tell me."

Cinq-Mars scratched down the information. Wynett explained that he had struck gold on his third call. He had a concise history for him, with a name, place, and dates, and he withheld his best news to the bitter end—he could predict the future, the time and place for an upcoming appointment.

"Thanks, Doc," Cinq-Mars acknowledged. He had to contain his euphoria with Rieser in the room. "I'll get back to you. Someone's with me right now." Rieser made overtures to step outside, but Cinq-Mars waved him into his seat. "I'll be in touch soon. Really appreciate what you've done. Bye, now."

"Sorry, Émile, I don't mean to be in the way," Rieser fussed.

"Not at all. I needed an excuse not to spend half the day with that guy."

"Glad to be of service."

Cinq-Mars smiled, looked down, then returned his gaze to Rieser. "Would you like to be of further service, Ray?"

"Why sure. Absolutely, man. Anything you ask."

"All right." Leaning forward, Cinq-Mars crossed his hands on his desk. "Ray, you're busted. I want you to hurry back to Selwyn Norris, tell him I've made you." Rieser scarcely reacted, but his head did flinch, imperceptibly. "Tell Norris if he wants to find out how I got to you, and how I got to him, he'll need another mole. If he wants to know how deep I go inside the Angels, he won't get the info from you. Tell your CIA contact for me, Ray, that I go so deep into the Angels that any time I move they get an irresistible urge to scratch."

"Émile. Émile—" The voice was faint, obsequious, pathetic.

"Spare me, Ray. I trusted you. You sold me out. You put work ahead of our friendship."

"That's not it, Émile. There's serious shit around. Desperate measures—"

"Yeah?" He stared at him, not allowing the man's eyes a moment's reprieve. "How desperate do you want to get, Ray?"

"Émile—"

"Your CIA agent sanctioned a whack. He took out a Hell's Angels' banker to create opportunity for himself. Murder, Ray. Were you in on that, too?"

Rieser put up his hands. "I know nothing about it."

"You're his lackey. Why should you?"

"There's not fair, Émile. Come on now—"

"You come on."

"Émile, there's stuff going down that would stand your hair on end!"

"There's always reason to betray a friend, eh, Ray?"

"I have my duty. This wasn't easy for me. That's all I've done here—duty."

Somehow, pleading his case in a neon jumpsuit diminished Rieser's credibility. "I thought you retired from duty, Ray. Well, you just keep it up. Go back to Norris. Tell him we've got a cop on the Angels' hit parade. There will be a bomb, and we've identified the next victim. I'm disappointed he didn't let me know. Tell him if they play that tune—and I survive—I'm holding him accountable. Go on, Ray. You don't want to stick around to see me get mad."

The telephone was ringing again, and Cinq-Mars let it while his old friend made himself upright, adjusted his bearing, and headed out.

Cinq-Mars picked up the receiver. "Yes?" he demanded.

Mathers advised, "Bringing in you-know-who. ETA the garage in five."

"Do it in private. In the garage, tell him to cover his head with his coat like he's worried about photographers. Use the prisoner elevator, express him to the ninth floor. When you're up, have him walk behind you, like you're not together. It's for his own protection. Tell him that and he'll believe you. Upstairs, put him in an interrogation room and lock him in. Make sure nobody knows he's there. Stay with him, both of you."

"Got it, sir."

"Over out."

Émile Cinq-Mars sat back in his chair and inhaled a deep breath, released it slowly, and checked his watch. Just enough time to make the officers' lounge and snitch a sandwich before hustling back for the meeting with LaPierre. A man like Max Gitteridge, who operated clubs by night and by day led the hectic life of a litigant, could probably use a little quiet time to himself. Come in from the cold. Simmer on low heat. Cinq-Mars resolved to let him stew.

Inside Arthur Davidson's bedroom, Julia Murdick opened her blouse and peeled back the edge of her bra to display a portion of the Eight-Pointed-Star tattoo. Then the tears flowed. She wept for her abused body. Arthur had become as much her surrogate father as her real dad or any of her stepdads. He wrapped her in his arms and issued cooing sounds in her ear. "There there," he said. Under his guidance, she slowly sputtered to a stop.

"Daddy?" Julia whispered.

"Yes, dear?" he whispered back. They resorted to the routine of speaking directly into each other's ears.

"I'm supposed to kill a man today. They expect me to plant a bomb."

"When, Heather, where, who?"

"I don't have details. Soon. They canceled a reconnaissance because we don't have time. Does Sel know what's going on? Did he know I was missing?"

"He's in constant touch," the Banker whispered. "We worried about you, girl."

"I'm holding up. They don't know me. But I have to do this murder, it's my initiation. Daddy, I can't kill anybody!"

"I'll E-mail Sel. He'll think of something. Just play along."

"He won't make me do it, will he?"

"Faith, Heather. He'll find a way, but we need to know who and where."

They turned to a stern rapping on the door. Jean-Guy reminded her, "We need to get started, sister. Go through procedures."

"In a second!" she called back in French.

Julia and Arthur held hands, looking into each other's eyes, wanting to say, *We've made it through until now, we'll bust through this, too.*

Julia broke off first. "I got to go."

Her surrogate father beckoned her into his embrace again. They both held on tight.

Julia returned to the living room, where Jean-Guy had little to add to his straightforward instructions. The car they wanted to smack would be parked by a jockey at a ritzy club. Cars there were jammed together, the keys left inside. Julia would enter from the side rear of the lot, which meant hopping a low stone wall. Given the pileup of snow it shouldn't be a problem, but she had to wait until the jockeys weren't watching. If one spotted her, she had to be a "pretty girl for him, explain your old man forgot his briefcase."

Sure. Let one more person identify me. I'll be in hiding forever.

They reviewed how she was to slip the bomb into the car. The street was a busy one, the intersection nearby more hectic still. Wait for the noise of traffic to muffle the car's open-door chime. Put the bomb on the seat. Remove the key from the ignition to stop the chime. Place the bomb under the driver's seat. Lift the side lever on the case so that it would dig into the seat above it and prevent the bomb moving around. Replace the keys, and shut the door soundlessly.

Terrific. Leave my fingerprints on the bomb casing, the keys, the door handle. Why don't I just leave a business card behind with a number where I can be reached? She guessed that she was not supposed to think about such things, that that was not how her mind was supposed to work.

"Now," Jean-Guy instructed, "practice."

"Get off it."

"Do what I tell you. The chair's the car. On this little table I put the keys. Pretend they're in the ignition. Now go."

She ran through the scenario three times with neither interest nor difficulty, sliding the bomb across the carpet under the chair.

"Good," he said. "Excellent."

"What's the name of this club, Jean-Guy? What street's it on?"

"Never mind."

"You mean you don't know?"

"I'm waiting for a call."

"Can I have something to munch on?" The Angels had occupied the apartment in her absence, making Arthur a prisoner. They'd moved in their own food and refreshments.

The main room was open to the dining room, where Arthur kept the bulk of his equipment. The Banker was busy at his keyboard, running through figures. Julia went over and pulled up a chair beside him. She gave him a peck on the cheek and looked over his shoulder at what he was doing. When the coast was clear she leaned into him and whispered in his ear. "Message. Some club. Near a busy street and busier intersection. High-class neighborhood. Crowded parking lot for members. Send it."

Arthur nodded. "Command," he said, communicating what had come in while she'd been with Jean-Guy. "Provide details on malicious malalignment." She felt herself toppling. Arthur's hand on her knee kept her in the chair. She fought against keeling over and breathed deeply, listening to her partner's advice—"Easy. Steady. Steady on." Footsteps were drawing closer down the hall. "Answer, Heather."

"Message. My legs," she said. "A deformity. Gitteridge knows. Send it."

Arthur again nodded. His fingers were nimble upon the keys. Julia looked at the screen. Nothing he typed appeared. The screen was a mask.

"Neat," she said. "Daddy, be aware. Malicious malalignment—it might mean we've been discovered."

He nodded before breaking off their mutual gaze.

Julia arose to receive the coffee and sandwich being offered by Jean-Guy.

Intent on a cafeteria bologna sandwich despite the thinness of the meat and the tasteless bread, Émile Cinq-Mars had his break interrupted in

359

the officers' lounge by Captain Gilles Beaubien. "Émile, a word, please, my office."

"Sir, I'm swamped, really."

"A word, Émile." The man was always willing to pull rank over pragmatic concerns. He was already walking away, and the irritated detective wolfed down his lunch while he tagged along.

He followed the captain past a fleet of secretarial desks made vacant by the lunch hour, into his sumptuous office. Cinq-Mars sat in one of two chairs facing the broad, mahogany desk while Beaubien elected to stand, hands tucked in his trouser pockets, his jacket open, stomach humped over his belt as he gazed upon the city. "I'm in a pickle," he confided. Half the time Beaubien spoke in that silly manner.

"What's on your mind?" Cinq-Mars had never been summoned to a meeting with Beaubien from which he did not retreat with more unnecessary work upon his shoulders and a reduced will to tackle it.

The man played with the coins in his pocket. The gravity of his present mood was rare, perhaps unprecedented, and Cinq-Mars grew interested. "They come at you when you don't expect them, Émile, when you're not looking. They're standing in front of you and you can't recognize their faces."

Cinq-Mars classified the man's words as a preamble to confession. First, the excuse for the sin is bequeathed, chewed upon, presented. Then the inviolability of the sin is addressed, its magnitude, the ruthless stalking of a vulnerable victim. Finally, the confession itself is released to the light of day.

"Things seem simple enough at first," Beaubien soldiered on. "One morning, you change a tire on the freeway coming into work. You grumble about it over coffee. Somebody asks if you want the old tire repaired. You give the man a look. He shrugs. It's no big deal. A tire. I'm a policeman, I need good tires, I often wear down my tires in the service of the city. What can it hurt?"

Beaubien gave his sergeant-detective a quick glance, to see how he was taking this. Cinq-Mars offered neither loathing nor sympathy. Like a psychiatrist solemn in his chair, he waited to hear more. Like a priest mute in his confessional, he anticipated the deeper fabric of repentance.

"Your car comes back. The blowout ruptured a sidewall, there's no hope for repair. One tire can't be replaced by itself, it's dangerous to drive with unequal tread. Consequently, you have two new tires. You ask, how much? The guy gives you a shrug, a smile. It's no big deal. There's no bill and nobody cares."

The man was nodding now, as though the murky had at last cleared. "Nothing comes of it. One day you need a repair in a tight month, there're other expenses, and this is the difference—this time you seek the guy out yourself. Your car gets repaired. There's no bill. What's the harm? What damage has been done? None, really, except this time they want a small favor in return. An infinitesimal favor. It's nothing. How can you refuse someone who's shown you kindness? A felon looking at thirty days, max, gets off because his prints were wiped from a stolen VCR. So many perps, who cares about a B & E?"

He could no longer stand, the burdens were intensifying. Gilles Beaubien sat down, folded his hands, and stared at a space on his desk between them.

"They do more favors for you. Help with your career. Provide information that gives you an edge. You, Émile, especially you, you have contacts. Everybody knows that. You accept information. Not only you, not just me—every detective has contacts, every cop is willing to receive information on consignment. You mention in passing that you are up for promotion but so-and-so will get the nod. Two days later, so-and-so has a black mark printed against his record, a reprimand in his file. Little is asked of you. So much is granted.

"You learn one day that your credit card limit has been increased, that the limit will be paid on your behalf every six months, no questions asked. But you ask questions anyway. You protest. You say, I don't want this, I didn't ask for this, I don't accept money. No one's listening. Every six months five thousand dollars is paid into your credit card account whether you have a debit or not. You do not give it back, there's no one to give the money back to. No one calls. No one makes a request of you. Finally, you just accept. Money is paid. It doesn't matter. No big deal. You are not the first cop with a blemish and you won't be the last. Besides, you've done nothing to help the other side, nothing of significance. Your own side has no use for you. Fellow officers laugh at you. What do you owe them? Loyalty?

Ethics? No one respects you. You owe the department bugger all."

Cinq-Mars folded his arms across his chest, wondered if he hadn't gone through a similar experience. Was the only difference between himself and Gilles Beaubien the accident that he, Cinq-Mars, had responded to the overtures of the CIA, and allowed himself to be sucked in, while Beaubien had been victimized by the Hell's Angels? He didn't think so on first perusal, but the argument could be made.

"Then one day, a day you knew would come, you're invited to a meeting. You're asked to supersede the Promotions Committee. You have the power to do that under special circumstances, and you don't have to explain yourself. A young man is given his shield, the rank of detective, and assigned to be Émile Cinq-Mars's partner. You're thinking that now you know how Émile does it, that he takes favors from the bad guys, that he must be a dirty cop himself to make all those busts, that someday you'll expose him as the dirtiest cop of all."

Cinq-Mars could not keep his silence here. "Was Normand Lajeunesse dirty, or just being used?"

Beaubien squirmed around on his rear as though bound to his chair by invisible restraints. Cinq-Mars guessed that he didn't have to go through the theatrics to come up with a reply. That he knew the answer.

First, the excuse is proffered. "I didn't know, Émile, what they intended." Then the inevitability of the action is recorded, as though all errors of judgment and deficiencies of character had been ordained by fate itself. "The wheels were in motion, I was only a pawn." Finally, the sin itself is broached. "Normand didn't know you were bringing your buddies along on that play. His job was to let you take him into the warehouse where he'd shoot you dead. This I found out later. He couldn't, not with your arsenal backing you up. He always makes it sound like he didn't know your friends were along, but he detected them, Émile, before he went in. He was calling it off. What he didn't know was that the other side had a sniper in the rafters to take him out if he turned color. They were probably going to burn him anyway. A cop killing a cop takes the edge off the killing, keeps the bikers out of it, keeps the Wolverines at bay."

Cinq-Mars had other matters to discuss, queries, ploys, but first he needed to know where Beaubien intended to go with this. The captain hadn't finished his speech.

"Now you know that you're in deep. Everything got botched, a cop was shot. A bulletproof vest protected him—you tell yourself, he was a dirty cop anyway—but a cop was shot. You tell your voices you want out. You tell them you've done more than they ever should've asked. They issue threats, say they'll reveal you, ruin you, so you back off the hard talk. You strike a deal. You make them promise they'll never ask such a terrible thing of you again. They promise. With evil men, now, you are making pacts."

Neither prodding nor discouraging him, Cinq-Mars merely waited. The man had gotten himself into what he called a pickle, he was damn well on his own. He had acquitted himself with an excuse, now he was prepared to embark upon the eminence of his crime, not to revile the crime but to glorify it, to declare that the combined forces of the world could not have stood ground against the tyranny.

"Émile, what can I do? I say no, I will not accept your gifts, and they describe my daughters to me. They tell me about the schools they attend, the names of their teachers, the color of the car their ballet instructor drives, how their best friends wear their hair. They tell me the names of my daughters' hamsters and goldfish. They will kill my daughters, Émile. They snip the buttons off my wife's blouse while she's taking a nap in the afternoon, in our own house, and they send them to me in a small black box meant to look like a coffin. They are everywhere, they know everything, they are ruthless, they are not human, they mock the idea of mercy. Émile, they say to me, *from your lips to our ears.* Then I know that I am alone. I can't talk to anybody. Who will save me? If I bring up the matter in the department, my children don't make it home from school. My wife goes shopping and the car blows up."

"You should have spoken to the boss."

"I did. At last. I told him that if he kept me on suspension the chance of my children surviving to their next birthday was negligible."

"Ah," Cinq-Mars said.

"Émile, now I'm speaking to you. I need you to save me. Director Gervais can give me back my job, or what looks like my job, but he cannot remove the enemies from my house. Émile. Please. Help me."

Cinq-Mars shook his head. "No," he said.

"Émile! Please! You want me to beg you?"

The detective leaned forward, his forearms resting comfortably on his knees. "Tell me why you are talking to me now, Gilles. Without that, I will not help you." He swiftly raised a finger to interrupt whatever his senior was about to say. "The truth, Gilles. No stories."

The large man sighed. "I have nothing to give you, Émile. I've been told that soon I will have more room to maneuver."

"What does that mean?"

"I always complain to them that my hands are tied. They have decided to undo the knots. I don't know, Émile—I don't know—but I believe they intend to remove one or more police officers. I have the impression that they are prepared to kill us again, like they were when Lajeunesse was assigned the job. This time, I don't think they'll miss. I can't be sure, but I think you're the target. They botched it the first time, of course they're going to try again. These people don't give up. Émile, Émile, my heart's weak. I can't take this anymore. I can't sleep. I can't be calm. I need your help. I'm not so dirty, Émile, I'm not that dirty! But I'm in this situation, I'm having this trouble, I can only talk to you. Anyone else, it's from my mouth to their ears."

Cinq-Mars nodded solemnly. Eventually he stood, moved toward the door. Turning back, he said, "I'm not going to my grave worrying about you. Remember that if I die, you're on your own. Until then, you will cooperate with those in contact with you. Play along. You will also inform me of everything that passes between you and them. Leave nothing out. If you are tempted to leave something out, the lives of your daughters are on your head. For now, that's your only hope, Gilles. You might also want to pray that I remain alive. If I don't, you won't, that seems likely to me."

Abruptly, he left the captain to his woes and headed down to his cubicle to find LaPierre, their appointment overdue. Things were happening, the air was rich.

André LaPierre looked and smelled as though he'd already enjoyed a liquid lunch, which, Cinq-Mars suspected, had been both more nourishing and more satisfying than his bite of bologna. A radiance seemed to shine from the man's eyes, born of an intensity, the swift rejuvenation of vigor. "Émile! You got to tell me now. What's going on? This could save me, man, this could bring me back in."

"How do you figure?"

"Are you dense? If that killing isn't biker-related, the Wolverines are off the case and I'm back on."

"Only if you're reinstated."

"We've been through this. Let me help out, Émile, any way I can. Put in the good word. I need my job back, buddy."

Cinq-Mars nodded with the fullness of a sympathetic colleague. "André, keep your voice down, all right? This is hush-hush."

The man put a finger to his lips.

Cinq-Mars leaned into him and whispered. "This is big. Look, I've got the kids, Mathers and Déguire, upstairs with a perp. Have to look in on them. Do you mind? Come upstairs, we'll take a room next door, we can chat, no one will disturb us. I may need your expertise on this one, André."

"Lead the way, partner."

Throwing his coat over his sleeve, LaPierre consented to be escorted out of the squad room and to the elevators. He exchanged courtesies with other cops encouraged by his buoyant mood. The word had gone around that he'd been severely depressed of late, and his friends were glad to see him back in form. A few wished him good luck.

Mathers and Déguire had marked their names on the chalkboard outside Interrogation Room 9, so Cinq-Mars brought the other officer along to Room 8. "I'll check how things are going," he said, leaving LaPierre stranded.

In the stark light of Room 9, Max Gitteridge was beside himself, stressed out by the delay. "What the hell do you want, Émile? I'm a busy man."

"Sorry, sir. Brass held me up. You guys all right?"

Déguire and Mathers indicated they were fine, and Cinq-Mars told them he had to go next door and would be back soon.

"Where're you going?" Gitteridge demanded.

Cinq-Mars told him to hang on awhile longer. "All will be

explained in due course. I promise, sir, you will not consider this a wasted day. Are you hungry, Mr. Gitteridge? Would you like a coffee? Some juice? Déguire, stay here. Don't let anybody in. Mathers, buy this guy lunch." Neither officer appeared pleased with his assigned task, but Gitteridge responded with a shopping list. "Tell you what," Cinq-Mars suggested. "You get his coffee from the squad room," he told Déguire, "and you fetch his lunch," he told Mathers. "That'll be quicker. You don't mind if we lock you in for a few minutes, sir? I don't want someone walking in on you. Being here is not something you'd want to explain."

Gitteridge was only too willing to have his privacy defended.

The moment the three officers departed the room, Cinq-Mars told his glum colleagues, "Forget lunch, I'm not feeding that shyster. Follow me." The younger men fell into step behind him, thoroughly confused. They entered the observation chamber off Room 8 and did a double take spotting LaPierre on the other side of the one-way glass. "Listen in. Run a tape," Cinq-Mars instructed them, and he promptly returned to the room with his suspended colleague, removing his jacket and rolling up his sleeves as though this could be a long haul. LaPierre, they saw, seemed perturbed by the gesture.

"Émile, what's up? You look like you're ready to shake me down."

"Why do you think that?"

"Did you bring me here under false pretenses? Don't mess with me, partner. I want to know. Is there somebody on the other side of that glass?"

Cinq-Mars laughed. "Who would I trust on the other side?"

LaPierre chuckled along with him. He had had his confidence nicked, he was wary but anxious to believe that everything was okay here, that Cinq-Mars had come around. "Okay, André, this is how it's going to play out. I have to clear some things up, then I'll tell you what's on the burner. It's big stuff. It'll change your situation. But you haven't had a clean nose lately, so I have to check that out."

"Go ahead. I've got nothing to hide that you don't know about."

"Let's start with the Jim Coates tape," Cinq-Mars suggested. He stood, leaning forward, with one foot up on a chair, his fist pressed down on the tabletop.

"I knew it." LaPierre laughed. "It's in your craw. Maybe I'll release the tape soon, if I can get leverage, you know? I'm backed into a corner here."

"So I guess in your mind you associate that tape with Jim Coates, just like I do?" Cinq-Mars asked him.

The tall man swallowed hard. "What?" He knew that he'd been nailed.

"Where'd you make the tape, André?"

"Where?"

"We've been in this room before, me and you. You know how I hate to repeat myself."

"Émile—" LaPierre tried to plead him off.

"Answer the fucking question!" Cinq-Mars raised his fist up and brought the side of it down hard on the tabletop. LaPierre flinched.

"Easy, Émile. What do you think I am, some punk you can scare?"

"Don't tell me to take it easy, André! Do you want to know what I found out? Do you want to know what I know? Normand Lajeunesse was a hit man for the Mafia. He was hired to take me out except he had a belly flop, so a backup sniper took him down. He told the bad guys that he'd spotted my buddies, that's why he didn't shoot, but I'll tell you something you don't know—he never spotted my buddies. He suffered a serious belly flop and that's that. Couldn't pull the trigger. The only reason he's alive today is because my buddies came in behind us. Bright boy, he turned them into his excuse. Otherwise, the Angels would've taken a hacksaw to his balls by now. I'm not in a good mood, André. Cops are killing cops and I seem to be a target. Now, tell me, *damn it*! Where did you make that tape?"

"In my house."

"Bullshit! You don't have the capability. You don't have a remote receiver. Where did you make the tape, André? You're losing ground fast with me."

"You motherfucker," LaPierre muttered.

"Answer the question."

"So I drifted by, what's the big deal?"

"You tell me. What's the big deal, André?"

LaPierre's body was bobbing now. He put his elbows on the table, then took them off, shifted from one side of the chair to the other, looked down, up at Cinq-Mars, away from him. He was fuming, but no incriminating word escaped his lips.

"You need time to think about that one?"

"It's not something I want to admit, that's all."

"Worse things than admitting to a frailty," Cinq-Mars coached him.

He sighed heavily, shook his head. "All right. I did a random drift. In my line of work it's something I do. Unlike you, I don't have it easy. I don't pick up the phone and listen to a goddamn golden voice at the other end. I work for my busts."

"Yeah, so?"

"I saw lights on at the garage." He sheltered his face in his hands, then shook himself, as though forcing himself awake. "So I listened in. I heard what was going down. This was my break, you know?"

"Then what happened?"

"He left. The guy with the accent. I followed him. I have friends in the Wolverines. They're looking for a guy they call the Czar. I figured this guy was him. Down the road I skidded into a snowbank. I lost him. I had him, I lost him. Like some rookie. A kid ended up dead. I didn't want to admit I was on it before it went down. Then, you know how it is, I wanted this bust for myself. Is that such a fucking crime?"

Cinq-Mars shook his head with his evident disappointment and straightened himself up. "Did you see the guy? Get a description?"

LaPierre indicated not. "Too dark," he said. "He was wearing this big, black, capelike coat with the collar up. He had on a hat, you know? Then I skidded out. It could've happened to anyone. I mean, I was off duty. I'd had a few. The road was slick. I missed the turn, *poof*, he's gone."

Cinq-Mars nodded. "What car was he driving?"

"I don't know. Bimmer, I think."

"And he was driving?"

"Yeah. Sure. Who else?"

"Hang on here, André. Sorry to put you through this, but you know how it goes."

"No sweat."

"Let me check on the kids' perp. Give me a couple of minutes."

"Take your time." He nodded emphatically.

In the corridor outside, Mathers opened the door from the observation room. Cinq-Mars was heading into a meeting with Gitteridge and wanted to go alone. "Watch his ass," he instructed. "If he moves, show yourself. Tell him to get back inside. If he needs to piss, bring him a cup."

Cinq-Mars inserted the master key to Room 9 and went inside. He locked the door behind him. "Mr. Gitteridge," he said.

"No food?" the lawyer asked, apprehension apparent in his voice.

"It's crap here anyway. If those boys don't show they're doing you a favor."

"I want to call my secretary. You have to let me."

"What're you going to tell her? That you're incarcerated? That you've decided to sing to the police?"

Gitteridge uttered a dismissive little laugh, a contemptuous flutter of his lips. "In your dreams, Émile. I told you what I have to say. Consider yourself lucky getting that much."

"Should I get down on my knees and kiss your shoes for that? Maybe you'd like to bend over so I can plant a wet one on your ass?"

He cocked his head to one side. "If that's your inclination, Cinq-Mars, suit yourself."

"Mind who you're talking to, Counselor."

"You, too."

Cinq-Mars began to pace, making several passes on his side of the table before gripping the back of a chair with both hands and staring down the escarpment of his nose upon the diminutive Gitteridge. "I visited the University Club this morning. You're a member?"

The lawyer scratched his upper teeth across his lower lip before answering. "I presume you know that or you wouldn't be asking."

"Kaplonski ate his last meal with you. It's a shame about the wife, isn't it? She was an innocent party."

"I don't have all day, Émile," Gitteridge pointed out.

"During dinner you went down to the cloakroom. Don't bother with denial, it's been confirmed. From the cloakroom you went out to your car, to your Lexus."

"I wanted to make a call in private."

"Since when is a cell phone private?"

"That's not what I meant."

Cinq-Mars was shaking his head aggressively. "You never made that call, did you, Counselor? That'll be confirmed by your phone records. Instead you opened your Lexus and removed a bomb. You took the bomb across the street to Kaplonski's Lincoln Town Car. You had his keys, which you'd taken out of his coat in the cloakroom, where every member and guest has a private stall, and you put the bomb under the front seat as you'd been instructed and trained to do." Cinq-Mars took a moment to view how his captive was taking the news. He looked catatonic, motionless, transfixed. "You set the bomb. You returned to the club, put Kaplonski's keys back in his pocket, went back upstairs for dessert and coffee and a nightcap. How'm I doing so far?"

He stirred, squiggling in his chair. "You're exhibiting a spectacular imagination, Detective. You actually earn your living at this?"

"There're no bills at your club that pass across the table, just a monthly tally. Which means you picked up the tab, so we can safely say that you bought him his last meal. Nice touch. Your idea? You think that eating with him in public gets you off? You stayed behind when Kaplonski and his wife went home, but not for long. You followed him home. You waited for an opportune moment, Max, but you were running out of time. Push the button, Counselor. Come on, just push the button and Kaplonski goes boom. Just push the damn button! Couldn't do it, could you, you yellow-bellied sap-sucking shyster?"

His lips fluttered. "What's that supposed to do? Get my dander up? I'm supposed to confess now to prove my manhood? How'd you get your reputation?"

"You creep. You couldn't do it even when you knew you'd be next otherwise. So you followed him all the way home. Because of your yellow-bellied cowardice you waited until the last second, just when he was backing up. You finally pushed the damn button. Because of your yellow belly you had to blow up Kaplonski and his wife in front of the house where their children were sleeping. Those kids probably can't sleep there anymore—or anywhere. You couldn't spare them that?

You had to wait until the last damn second? You had to wake them up to their sound of their mother and father being blown apart?"

"I'm a lawyer, Detective. If you want to charge me with something, go ahead. Otherwise, spring me."

"You came in on your own reconnaissance, Counselor."

"Right."

"Your fingerprints were on the bomb. Is this what you mean by the new culture? Even lawyers have to get their hands dirty—really dirty?"

"When did you get a sample of my prints?" Gitteridge asked quietly.

"For starters, they're all over this table. I haven't run them yet, Gitt, but you know what I'll find. We already know the bomb casing is covered in prints, and I mean covered. I guess they were watching when you toted that bomb from one car to the other. No gloves allowed. You couldn't rub your prints off. I guess you were watched as you followed Kaplonski home. It was him or you. Not such a tough choice, really, huh?"

"Don't you"—Gitteridge was exhibiting signs of defiance—"mock me."

"Question—why were prints left on the bomb? Answer—to implicate the bomber. You're traveling with a tough bunch these days, Counselor. Not only do you have to kill people, but you have to be traceable, you have to be cornered. If ever you become a Crown witness, you're easily discredited. They've got the goods on you. That's why they insisted that you dine with Kaplonski in a public place. That's why they forced you to handle the bomb without gloves. You blew up your own client, Counselor, then sat your shyster ass down and sent his estate a bill for your services."

Gitteridge was not admitting to anything. "Are you charging me, Sergeant-Detective?"

"What's the good of that? You'd never make it to trial date."

He looked at him then.

Cinq-Mars returned his gaze.

Gitteridge needed a moment to think. "What do you want?" he asked quietly.

"A name. Who killed Hagop Artinian?"

He shook his head slowly. "I don't know. I wasn't around."

"Am I looking at a pattern?"

He looked him in the eye again. "Could be," he said.

"Give me the name. You know I've got you. We can check your phone records, you didn't make a call. You know you didn't go into the cloakroom to get a cell phone because you've got one in the car anyway. All of which is academic, because if we charge you, if you're out on bail, you'll be blown sky-high. Know what occurs to me? You won't give me the name because you're under the false impression that the person you name will turn around and name you. As a lawyer, you can defend against circumstantial evidence, but it's a tough slog against a witness. But I'm saying, it's a matter of priority. Who do I want more, Kaplonski's killer or Hagop Artinian's? If it's the Russian, just give me the Russian. If it's not the Russian, not technically, give me who it is technically. Don't think of him as a witness, because you won't make it to trial. Think of it is as your only chance to escape this."

Gitteridge fidgeted. "You don't want to know," he said.

"Don't patronize me. You're in no position."

Gitteridge thought about it, but he shook his head. "Cops look after each other," he said. "Give me something else I can do for you."

"Wait here. Not that you have a choice. I'm locking you in again."

Émile Cinq-Mars marched the few steps down the corridor to where André LaPierre sat waiting. He barged into the room and slammed the door behind him.

"André!" he shouted. "The reason you cut the tape off is because your name is on it. You get mentioned. The Russian, Kaplonski, both, they said your name. They mentioned you as you drove up to give the Czar a lift back to his ship. Am I right or am I right?"

LaPierre put his hands apart and uttered fragmentary, quick breaths. "What're you saying?"

"You want to know what bothered me, André? You want to know what made me take a look at you?"

"Émile, what're you saying?" This attack, after Cinq-Mars had departed on cordial terms, had him searching for composure.

"That day we drove to Garage Sampson, the day of the bust, remember?"

"Yeah. Sure."

"You still had the flu, you had symptoms. You blew your nose, André."

"So?"

"Folded phlegm neatly into your handkerchief. I said to myself, why's he doing that? What's he up to? André has always been an oaf. It's more like you to ball up your Kleenex and toss it on the floor. Or on the street. Or you'd blow your nose on your sleeve. Since when do you fold your snot into neat little sections?"

LaPierre fought for words by gesturing with his hands. "What's with you? Who cares how I fold my handkerchief?"

"You know how I am, André. I don't solve crimes, I figure out crooks. I figure out people. Now I've got this oaf in my car who's folding his handkerchief. You've had colds before, you've never done that. So I file it away, partner. I put it to one side, where I can see it, you know? Why is André LaPierre behaving as though he has discovered the merits of sophistication, of courtesy, of hygiene? Is there a new woman in his life, what?"

"I'm leaving. You've fallen out of your tree, Cinq-Mars."

"Then I meet you in that restaurant, and you've got these little shaving cuts. Remember? You always have shaving cuts. I don't know why you never went electric. Too modern for you. You'd rather hack yourself to death when you're down with a hangover. This time, you have cute little Band-Aids covering the cuts. Now why is that? You always came to work rough, specks of blood on your skin, like you're a real man. The brass could make you wear a suit, make you cut your hair, shave and shine your shoes, they could write all that down in the regulations, but they couldn't make you wear your clothes properly, or cut your hair properly, or shave properly, eh, André? You'd look too much like a cop then."

"Do you have a point?"

"André, you read the pathologist's report. Is that when you found out about the skin and blood under Hagop Artinian's fingernails? What happened, André? In the fury of the moment, you didn't realize

Artinian had scratched you? Or did the people you work for now insist that the blood under his fingernails stay put, just in case you ever got weak in the knees. You're a homicide detective. Suddenly you're cautious about your bodily fluids. I asked Wynett if DNA could be taken from a phlegm sample. Were you wondering about that yourself? It can't be, not usually, unless there's blood in it, which happens, but I bet that worried you enough. Blood though, and blood around me—now you were anxious to protect yourself. Would you like to donate a sample of your blood, André, so that we can do a DNA test? What better way to prove your innocence?"

LaPierre tried to stand but stumbled over his chair and finally kicked it out of his way, sending it careening across the room. "Wiseass. Tests can be shifted. You're not getting any damn sample out of me." He pointed at the one-way mirror. "Whoever's behind that glass, I'm not saying I can't pass the test, I'm saying I don't trust the department not to frame me up."

"You can lead us through what precautions should be taken. You're a pro."

LaPierre leaned over the table. He sneered. "Shove your test ass-backwards up your dick. I will not submit to the humiliation."

"Gee. We've heard that a few times in our day, haven't we, André?"

"Up yours, you damn priest."

Cinq-Mars smiled, looking away. His beeper went off just then, and he fumbled to find the button to punch. "Fortunately, André, we won't be needing a sample from you. We already received a donation on your behalf."

LaPierre gazed at him. "What're you talking about? You can't take a sample off me without my authorization, and I'm not giving it."

"Not everything is up to you. You have a little friend. Lise. Seventeen years old. This morning you had anal sex with her, do you recall? You gave her your spermatozoa for safekeeping, a gift. What was yours became hers. Of her own free will she has donated your sperm to our study. You know these things take time, André. You also know the match will be made."

Sergeant-Detective LaPierre rocked as though absorbing a couple of direct shots to the gullet. When he spoke, his words broke forth as an incantation, as though his grievances had evolved into a chant, as though he had rehearsed this litany frequently. "You worm, Cinq-Mars. I'm a real cop. I work in the real world."

"Were you coerced, André, or did you volunteer?"

"I get down with the slime and the dipshits, I hang out with the fuck-ups and the slugs, I don't sit around on my farm brushing horses."

They stared each other down now. "I bet you volunteered. You knew it was coming anyway. The Russian hot-wired his testicles—"

"He did, and that boy screamed."

"When he hollered out my name, you couldn't stand it anymore. Once again I was in there ahead of you."

"Sending little boys to do a man's job."

"You went to his throat, you wanted to rip his head off, you tried."

"You think I'm a dirty cop? I got inside. I got inside the Hell's Angels. I got inside the Russian gangs. I was moving closer. More time and I could have busted the assholes from here to Moscow, from New York to Minsk—"

"Except you found out that I already had a plant in there ahead of you."

"You're damn right I choked the little fucker." LaPierre turned to face the mirror. "I choked the little fucker's neck."

"Just because you were jealous of me. We were supposed to be on the same side."

LaPierre raised his palm high and slapped it down hard on the tabletop. "I choked the little fucker's neck to put him out of his misery! That's why I killed him, you shit! High and mighty Cinq-Mars! Never gets his hands dirty! Well some of us have to do things."

"Kill?"

"Some of us have to get down in the sewer and muck shit. They had that boy wired up. They were torturing him. He was screaming his head off. He was pleading for death."

"So you did him a favor?"

"He was crying for his mummy. He gave you up, Cinq-Mars. That was enough. He didn't deserve no more. They were going to keep it up, these are not humans, Cinq-Mars. They were enjoying themselves.

I stepped up and put my hands on his throat and I took the life right out of him. I saved him more pain. I helped that boy the only way I could."

"Yeah?"

"Not that you know about these things. You don't know how bad it gets. You don't get dirty like real cops do."

"Think not? I get dirty enough to scrap a young girl's behind to preserve your DNA sample. I get dirty enough, André. But if a boy is screaming under some kind of inhuman torture, I don't wring his neck."

"Yeah, tough guy, what would you do?"

"I'd take out my badge and my gun and I'd start making arrests!" Cinq-Mars roared. "And if some sonofabitch didn't like it, I'd shoot the bastard!"

The blood pulsing in his neck, his breath rapid, LaPierre hesitated before responding.

"But no," Cinq-Mars pressed him from the other side of the table, "you couldn't do that, could you, André? Why not? Why not? Because you were getting inside the Hell's Angels. You were getting close to the Russian gangs. You were going to bust them wide open one day. You just had to get through your initiation. You had to prove to them that you were a bad guy, a mean killer, there was nothing you wouldn't do for them—"

"You got to go the distance. They don't mess around. You got to show you will do what you have to do and—*listen to me, Cinq-Mars!* They're strong and getting stronger. There's no room anymore for candy-assed cops! You got to be just as tough, just as vicious, as bad as them or they'll win, damn it! They'll win!"

Cinq-Mars shook his head. "You don't get it, do you?" he asked softly.

The man was breathing heavily now, the pressure of his life pumping his chest. "Get what?"

"You killed that boy to go inside the gangs, to pass your initiation. You killed him prematurely, André. They'd already told you you were going to do it. You just jumped the gun, that's all. You agreed, ahead of time, to kill that boy because you wanted to make bigger arrests than the usual, you wanted to be on the front page. But the reason you killed that boy on the spot with your hands was because you thought he was my informant. You thought I was in there ahead of you. That enraged you. That's when your killer blood took over. That's when you became manic enough to do it. That's when you ceased to be a cop in any way, shape, or form, that's when you became a jealous murdering asshole. You killed Hagop Artinian because you were envious of me! You could've saved him, you could've pulled your gun and started shooting, except you were too damn jealous to do it. Know how I know? You hung that sign around his neck to make the point. This was your big case and you were scared shitless I was going to beat you on it. Well, you know something? You were right. I am going to beat you on this case."

The beeper went off once more, and Cinq-Mars again punched it quiet.

He pulled up a chair and sat across from LaPierre. "You became them, André. You became the enemy."

"I was going inside them. I was doing my fucking job!"

"The thing is, André—" The beeper sounded again, and Cinq-Mars cursed, *"Taberhuit!"*—a sacrilege for him—aiming a furious glance at the mirror, punching off the device. "The thing is, I didn't direct that boy. He gave me some stuff, but I didn't run him inside the Angels. Until he died, I didn't know his name. He gave me up because he was trained to give me up, in order to spare himself further pain."

"What do you mean?" LaPierre asked, and his voice was vacant, parched, as though the last lick of his fury had been discharged. "Who?"

"I told you, didn't I, that I'd reveal who else has been involved? I bet you were hoping to deliver the news back to the Angels. Raise your standing in the community. I'm afraid we can't allow that. Hagop Artinian worked for the CIA. So you see, André, from the beginning, you were way, way, way over your head."

The detective looked at Cinq-Mars and appeared to wobble in his chair.

"André LaPierre," Cinq-Mars said, raising his voice, and the other man straightened as though to receive the news while erect, "you are under arrest for the murder of Hagop Artinian."

The door to the room burst open then. Mathers was hanging on to the knob, seemingly out of breath.

"Yes?" Cinq-Mars asked calmly.

"Message for you, sir. Urgent."

"Go ahead," Cinq-Mars decreed. "Report. We're all officers here."

"Steeplechase Arch, sir. He says time is of the essence."

"Déguire!" Cinq-Mars shouted, still staring at LaPierre.

In a moment the other detective showed. "Yes, sir?"

"He's your former partner."

"Yes, sir."

"Will you execute the arrest?"

"Yes, sir. I will."

"Cinq-Mars," LaPierre interrupted, speaking quietly, firmly, with a forced dignity. "I'm inside the Angels. Right inside. Use me, man. Let me walk this off. I'll work inside the Angels for you, inside the Russian gang. This is too good an opportunity for you, Émile."

Cinq-Mars looked across at his former colleague, who was playing his last chit, the final move in his game. LaPierre was at his most vulnerable, and consequently at his most malleable. He could be manipulated, moved, run. Questioned now, he would respond.

"Why was Artinian in a hutch with that hook in him?"

LaPierre shrugged. "The boy died early, because of what I did. I interfered with their torture. The Czar wanted more information. He wanted the boy's apartment swept clean because we'd all been there and he didn't want old socks lying around. He wanted the place checked for bugs, notes, whatever. At the same time, we had a problem, we had to get the dead boy up the stairs. So the Czar had all his stuff moved out, even the hutch, then we put the boy in the hutch in the moving van and tried to move him back upstairs. But he kept falling out of it before we could get him off the truck. His weight would shift and the musclemen, the guys from the ship, they'd lose their balance. The Russian did it. The hook was in the truck. He rammed the hook through his back and hung him from the bar in

378

the cabinet. That kept him from falling out and they moved him back upstairs again. In all the commotion nobody who might've been watching noticed that one piece of furniture was going the wrong way. In, not out."

Cinq-Mars nodded. "The table was too big to take down the narrow stairs?"

"They didn't have the tools to take it apart. Everything else fit okay. So we just wiped the table clean of prints."

"Tell me something, André," Cinq-Mars pressed. He had him now. He had him believing that there might be a way out for him. As long as that thread dangled LaPierre was going to talk, he was going to sing the blues. "Why did you spend so much time in the crapper on the night of the investigation? It wasn't just flu."

LaPierre rolled his head around, trying to think that one through. "It'd been a day, Émile. My nerves were shot. I had to get myself together. I knew you were out there. I didn't want to face you, all right? I was scared you'd buzz through me. I needed time to myself, Émile."

"That's touching," Cinq-Mars told him. "The murderous heart goes gummy. You should've been in the room, André. Hanging that sign on him was a big mistake. You could've cleared me right off this case. Maybe you were looking to get picked."

LaPierre needed a moment to digest the news. "How about it, Émile? Let me walk this off. Run me inside the Angels. You can't say no to that."

"There's a problem with that scenario," Cinq-Mars informed him. At his back, Mathers and Déguire waited quietly, respectful, in awe.

"What's that?"

"Hagop Artinian is dead. Does his killer go unpunished? Not in my book."

"Goddamn, Saint Émile," LaPierre seethed.

"Want a lawyer, André? You're going to need a good one."

"You bastard."

"You got any suggestions?"

The man knit his fingers together and stretched his lengthy neck. "I'm not impressed with the lawyers for the Policeman's Brotherhood," he determined.

"Who then?"

This was crucial. Choices were being made. LaPierre looked up. "Get me Gitteridge," he said.

Cinq-Mars nodded. "That's the side you're on."

"Once you're in, you can't be out," LaPierre explained.

"Mathers!" Cinq-Mars shouted, as though the man was not five feet away.

"Yes, sir?"

"Did he leave a number?"

"Yes, sir."

"Then come with me. Déguire, what do you think of your partner now?"

"Not much," the young man stated.

"Do the arrest. That'll keep your head above it around the department."

"Thank you, sir."

Cinq-Mars strode away at a rapid clip and stopped first at Room 9, and went in alone. "This is the deal," he told Gitteridge.

"I'm listening."

"I'm the only one who knows you did Kaplonski. I just arrested LaPierre for the Artinian murder. I'm running a DNA test. He doesn't have a prayer."

Gitteridge patted the tabletop, taking the information in, computing what it meant to him, and wondering what was coming next.

"I'm going to forget about Kaplonski for now. LaPierre has asked for you to be his lawyer." The man looked up. "I guess he wants everybody to know what side he's on. He's also going to tell you that the CIA's been involved in bombing bikers. He'll want to use that information to bargain for support inside the Angels. I don't care what you tell him, but you're not passing that information along to anybody. What he says stays strictly confidential between lawyer and client. Got that?"

Gitteridge was staring at him intently now. "Is that it?" he asked quietly.

"Are you kidding? That is definitely not it. That's just it for now."

Gitteridge nodded, knowing that he could have expected no less, and no better.

"Déguire's booking him. You can see him in a few minutes."

In the corridor, Émile Cinq-Mars grabbed his partner's elbow and steered him toward the elevators. "Let's roll."

19

Émile Cinq-Mars and Bill Mathers merged into traffic on the Villa Maria Expressway and headed for the west side of downtown. "I overheard a touch of gossip, Bill," the senior detective intimated.

The young man's head was still busily churning the repercussions of LaPierre's arrest. He hadn't felt much of a kick collaring Hagop Artinian's killer when he wasn't anyone he wanted him to be. He knew that the consequences would be dire. Once again cops would have their noses rubbed in doo. "So give it up."

"You had a talk with my former partner."

Mathers immediately felt uncomfortable. "You suggested it."

"At the time I didn't know he was a hit man for the Mafia."

Mathers shot him a look to confirm that he wasn't kidding. "Lajeunesse is dirty?" he asked. Immediately, he was fearful. If that was true, he may have compromised their situation by having had Lajeunesse run down the Infiniti.

"Not exactly," Cinq-Mars said.

Mathers waited for him to cut between two trucks before prompting him once more. "Are you planning to explain that or do I have to shoot you in the hip?"

"Lajeunesse is a hit man for the Mafia. A Hell's Angel without the tattoos. He's not a dirty cop because he never was a cop. He was always Mafia-Angel shit. They sneaked him onto the force, promoted him inside the department. Then they found him something to do."

"Which was?"

"Bump me off. Too bad for him, he'd hung around cops too long. Softened up. Gotten friendly. The boy lost his nerve."

"So now he shuffles papers."

"You don't think he's useful at that? No wonder they move hot cars around so well."

Mathers pushed a hand through his hair. Bringing it down, he punched the dash. *"Taberhuit,"* he swore.

"What's wrong?"

"I had him run down the Q Forty-five for us."

In anger, Cinq-Mars sped ahead to their exit, jamming his car into the ramp's single file. "Can't you get this, Bill? The bad guys live inside us. We cannot be trusted."

"I've got it now, Émile. Once and for all."

Cinq-Mars cut up Guy Street and stopped on a red.

"Knowing we're looking for a car, what does that do?" Mathers asked apologetically. "Does it break us?"

"Hard to tell. The Angels don't know what we want with the Infiniti. If it was just them, I wouldn't worry. They wouldn't know what to do with the information. But this KGB thing bugs me." Cinq-Mars rapped a knuckle on the wheel. "If they know too much, if they know we're looking for the CIA, then Selwyn Norris is in danger, and his mole's been marked."

He made an illegal left on Sherbrooke, where they spotted the Infiniti Q45 fifty yards west of St. Mathieu outside the gates of an old, imposing, dreary seminary. Cinq-Mars parked behind it and struggled out. "You better drive," he shouted to Mathers, "before I get mad and hit somebody." The younger man stepped out as well to switch sides. Cinq-Mars opened the passenger door to the Infiniti and plunked his derriere onto the leather seat. He banged his boots together to knock salt off before swinging them around onto the plush pile carpet. He pulled the door shut.

"I'm glad you called, Mr. Norris. Fill me in." The luxury of the automobile had the detective feeling unkempt after his sleepless night and the day's rank diet.

"You understand my situation," Norris stated.

"And you, mine. I want the young woman out."

"As I told you earlier, I can't save one agent and wreck the entire operation. This is too important. You're the horse trader, Émile, what do you suggest?"

Cinq-Mars had anticipated that it would come down to this and wondered if the woman knew that her mentor would barter for her life, sparing her only if the payoff was worth the price. "Let's deal."

"You want the woman out. I want a contact working inside the Hell's Angels and the Russian gangs."

"Mmmm," Cinq-Mars demurred. "You want more than that, I'd say. You want the top guy in North America for the Russian crime federation, his head on a platter. And I suspect you wouldn't mind being relieved of criminal charges that pertain to the murder of the original Angels' banker."

Norris's right hand squeezed the car's gearshift with each of the policeman's points. "So I'm greedy." He smiled. "You are too, I bet. You want the Russian headman yourself, for the murder of Hagop Artinian."

"Nope, don't," Cinq-Mars interrupted. "I've got Artinian's killer in lockup."

The agent looked at him more intently then, the smirk suddenly gone from his lips. "Not the Russian?"

"You don't know as much as you'd like about the Angels."

Norris chewed on his lips then, a mild concession. This was not a trade that he necessarily had to win, but he had to come away with particular benefits. Cinq-Mars had not mentioned his rival's most critical need, choosing to wait for a more advantageous moment. Similarly, Norris had not mentioned the policeman's most critical need. A horse trade, they were both saving what really counted to the end.

"I'm impressed, Émile. You've worked a link inside the Angels. I could make good use of that resource. Perhaps we ought to consider an exchange suitable to both sides."

"The woman comes out," Cinq-Mars reiterated, "with her so-called father. I don't want any more bright-eyed civilians in there."

"All right," Norris considered, "let's say we take this person out. Keeping her safe on the outside won't be easy, but let's pretend it can be arranged. The father has to come out with her, of course. But I need something back. This isn't tiddlywinks. The social fabric of my country is affected. Lives are on the line. This coalition of gangs can't be allowed to gain the foothold they're after. What do I receive in return, Émile?"

Cinq-Mars rubbed his chin, as if mulling the decision for the first time. He reminded himself of his own rules. Never allow the competing party to believe that what is placed on the table was easily relinquished. "Mr. Norris, I'm willing to introduce you to someone currently inside the organization."

Norris rocked his head from side to side to indicate that the proposal was of moderate interest. "I checked, Émile. My protégé spoke about malicious malalignment to one person, one person only. That gives me the name of your contact. I'm impressed. The Hell's Angels-Mafia lawyer, now that's good work. Maybe you should be on my side of the fence. Trouble is, now that I know him, I don't need you to give him to me, do I?"

Cinq-Mars raised his right hand, gently shook his forefinger in the air, a gesture intended to demonstrate that Norris's posture came as no surprise. He had anticipated the response, deliberately led Norris down this road. Cinq-Mars had not counted on Gitteridge being enough—the man had flaws. "You need me to work the introduction, Mr. Norris. You're not dealing with a concerned citizen. He's halfway as sociopathic as the rest of them, except that, for him, fear's a motivation. He's rabbit-hearted. I have leverage, you don't. I've got him dead-to-rights for the murder of Walter Kaplonski, so if you work around me I'll reel him in for Kaplonski, leaving you with nothing. You need me here, Mr. Norris, you need my hands-on contact."

Seated in the car, Norris had little room to maneuver, few places to look where he could guard his eyes. He gazed momentarily out his side window until he noticed that Cinq-Mars had leaned forward to observe his reflection. Glancing in the rearview mirror, he caught the eyes of Bill Mathers in the car behind.

"Problem is, Émile, Gitteridge brought my agent into the Angels. Sponsored her, so to speak. When Hagop was found out, when he was killed, Kaplonski was next on the list for being the guy who brought him in. I hate to say it, but Gitteridge may become a target. I might be trading live bait for dead."

Cinq-Mars started to rock in his seat with the rhythm of his words. He spoke with force. "They wiped out Kaplonski because he'd become a risk, a weak link. We had his garage, we connected his business to the Russian freighter—he was of no further use. Worse than that, he'd become a liability. We had his nuts in a vise. They took Kaplonski out because they couldn't trust him. Did he screw up, bringing in Artinian, or did he bring him in knowing he was undercover? The Angels couldn't be sure. They also didn't know how he'd hold up if we booked him a bunk in prison. Kaplonski lived too well to appreciate the benefits of hard time. They could make an example of him, he wasn't much more use than that. Now Gitteridge— he's passed his initiation, he's done a bump off, it's categorical that he's not in my pocket. Besides, a lawyer at that level is not so easy to replace as a dumb car thief."

Norris shifted around to observe Cinq-Mars squarely. "Let's say I accept Gitteridge. If you're letting him off for blowing up Kaplonski, then you're obliged to let me off on the banker. You can't pin it on me, we both know that, but I don't relish being hassled by the eminent Cinq-Mars."

"That one I can let go," Cinq-Mars acknowledged, although he was not about to make the offer without receiving something further in return. "But you will keep me informed of your addresses at all times that you're in this country. Never mind city—country. If you're not under my nose, I'll be looking you up to see what's cooking. If you're found here without having reported in, you will fall under my scrutiny."

"That brings up another issue." The man checked his watch for the fourth time since they'd been in the car together. Cinq-Mars was counting.

"What's that?"

"This operation remains covert. No rumors. No press. No suggestion around the station house of Company involvement." What Norris required most—dead air, raw silence—had been broached as if it was trivial.

"I'm no miracle worker. I'll do what I can manage. Mr. Norris, do we have a deal?"

Selwyn Norris knew better than to rush into a handshake with this man. "Not yet," he hedged. "I still have a problem with Gitteridge. What you said is conjecture. Chances are, the moment the woman inside is taken away from the Angels, Gitteridge becomes a target, no matter what you say. Not everything they do is logical. The Czar is here to establish a regime in which anyone who compromises their situation dies. No mercy. He's laying the groundwork. I don't see where he'd think otherwise with Gitteridge. The contrary. Gitteridge can do major damage. He's less likely to be lenient with him."

Cinq-Mars hit a fist into an open palm and raised his voice a notch. Norris knew the moniker for the Russian, the Czar. Which meant that his nerve center had picked up on stuff inside the Wolverines. "If nothing else, understand this. Your young woman is not safe. The malicious malalignment error compromised her position. You are not trading from strength, sir."

"She's being initiated as we speak. If she passes that test, she's in. I presume your snitch on the inside won't turn her out."

The threat that she was undertaking her initiation alerted Cinq-Mars. He wavered. Even in the most deliberate and artful negotiation, circumstances might arise where desperate measures became appropriate. "Mr. Norris, are you waiting to hear my fallback position? We have a senior cop who's traded off. If Gitteridge blows up, I'll give you the cop. Run him as a double agent. He'll have no choice. He has to do what he's told no matter who does the telling."

"LaPierre doesn't interest me, Émile," Norris told him. "He's a wild man. He's a lost soul."

Norris knew about André. From Artinian? "Higher up. Petrified wood. Fully diluted and compromised."

The mention enhanced the light in Norris's eye. "In that case, we almost have a deal. Change the fine print."

"How so?"

"I want the higher-up included with Gitteridge or, if it comes to that, without him. I don't want him only if Gitteridge goes down." Norris stuck out his hand. He had received more than he'd expected, more, he suspected, than Cinq-Mars had intended to relinquish. His critical need in the negotiation was impunity, for himself, but more important for his organization, which could not afford discovery by either the authorities or their mutual enemies.

Cinq-Mars judged the offered palm. "Why is time of the essence, Mr. Norris?" He, too, had a critical need. He had to rescue a police officer from a blast.

"It's happening, Émile. Her name is Julia. She does her bomb today. Shake on this deal and see about setting her free."

"Is this the cop bombing?"

Norris nodded.

"Where? Who? Tell me now."

"Shake on this deal, Émile."

"I can give you the Czar," Cinq-Mars told him.

The news surprised Selwyn Norris. "How?"

"He's had heart surgery. Given a choice, he had the job done on this side of the Atlantic. In the States—your home turf. I can give you the time and place for his next follow-up appointment. We traced him down by the star tattoo he wears on his chest. No heart surgeon could have missed that."

"I think you just gave him to me, Émile."

"Bear in mind that every call you make risks sending a signal to the wrong party. Start with the most eminent surgeons in America. That'll lead you there quickly."

"Do you know what you're doing?" Norris asked. Then his head jerked back with understanding. "Of course you do. Shit, it's a tough world we live in, Émile."

Cinq-Mars had provided information that would result in an assassination. No arrest. No trial. No conviction. No law. No order. Merely execution.

"You didn't trade for that one, Émile," Norris reminded him, and his tone conveyed skepticism and amazement in equal measure.

"Not my jurisdiction," Cinq-Mars pointed out. "If a felon should leave my jurisdiction and never return, am I saddened to be denied the arrest? Some cops would answer yes. Today, I just want him gone."

"Ah." Norris understood. "You're getting something out of this."

"Such as?"

"If he's gone, Julia has a chance to stay out alive." He had presumed from the outset that Cinq-Mars needed not only to rescue her but also to restore her life. He had not guessed how he'd get there.

"Her best shot, I'd say," Cinq-Mars confirmed. He had to keep himself distant from the likes of Selwyn Norris, who would never bring an agent out if it compromised an operation. He, on the other hand, would compromise any operation if it meant rescuing the innocent. He had to keep that line clear. The last thing he wanted was an arrest. He wanted her high and dry, to save her, believing that rescue honored the life and sorry death of Hagop Artinian. "Tell me—who, where, when."

"This is guesswork. When? A little after two when the game ends. The bomb plant will come earlier. Where? A club in an upscale neighborhood, a busy intersection nearby and valet parking where the cars get crowded in. According to my people, our first choice is the Montreal Badminton and Squash Club. It's on the edge of Westmount—Émile?" The detective seemed pale, stricken.

"Tremblay," Cinq-Mars determined, fear swift within him.

"Why him?"

"He's booting the Angels out of our computer system, taking away their big advantage."

"Go, Émile. Fifty minutes to blast off. Shake on this deal first."

Cinq-Mars hesitated. He had what he had come for. He had traded away what he was willing to give up, although he was sorry to have mentioned Beaubien. That man's life was not going to know much peace. Probably he'd suggest that the captain consider immediate retirement, take himself out of the line of everyone's fire. He was getting Julia, he had LaPierre, and the Russian would be erased, as people in another profession might put it. The lines had blurred. He was sacrificing Gitteridge to Norris, and perhaps to death. He also had to surrender his initial desire to take out Selwyn Norris. He had wanted to get at the man who had put Hagop Artinian in a position to die. He didn't have the wherewithal to make an arrest. At least he might curtail his network, or get him out of town. What he needed

the most here was Julia alive and Rémi Tremblay safe. In the overall scheme of things, this was one deal with the devil in which he
could rest easily enough. For starters, he wasn't entirely sure who
played the devil in this bargain and who was the good guy. He did
know that he wasn't squeaky clean. He breathed deeply. He had
handed over information, knowing full well that it would probably
result in an assassination. For sure, he wasn't clean at all.

"One more thing," Cinq-Mars added.

"Don't you ever quit?"

"This isn't about me. It's possible that your car has been leaked to
the other side. Undertake precautions."

"Noted," Norris said. His eyes conveyed seriousness. "Thank you."

With the door open and one foot on the icy pavement, Cinq-Mars
dutifully raised his hand. He shook. The oath between them, he knew,
was that solemn.

"Good luck!" Norris brayed, but Sergeant-Detective Émile Cinq-
Mars had already slammed the car door behind him.

The policeman scurried back to the cruiser, jumped in, and commanded Mathers, "Get me to a real phone! I don't trust these damn
toys and radios!"

Julia Murdick lugged dynamite in a computer satchel.

They parked, facing uphill, in front of a tractor-trailer, on Atwater
Avenue. Julia's destination was below her, partially within view.

Exceptionally careful getting out of the car, she moved now in slow,
prodigious motion, planted both feet on the curb and clutched the door
with her free hand to hoist herself upright. She lacked confidence in
her body, was wary of the footing, anxious not to jostle the explosive.

Under that load, the short walk downhill from the car to the club
was treacherous. Salt and sand had been layered over the ice, but
slippery patches on the slope remained, and she put her arms out to
maintain her balance. The driveway that adjoined the sidewalk just
above the property for the badminton club was level and, with relief,
Julia turned in. She noticed the valets. Somehow she had expected
very young men, these struck her as older. For one infinitesimal fraction of a second she thought that one had given her a look, a nod, a

greeting of some sort. Could that be possible? Was the place populated by Norris's people?

More confident, Julia picked out the blue car she'd been told to
look for. It was one of the largest, one of only a few that color. She
walked to the end of the snow-topped wall that separated the driveway from the parking lot and sat on it a moment as though contemplating a matter of no particular urgency. The valets were looking
elsewhere. In a trice, Julia slipped over the wall, dropped into snow,
and bent down, hidden now behind parked cars.

Suddenly she was breathing heavily. She needed to calm herself, to
quit making so much noise. She couldn't stop. Her breathing was
rampant and hectic, she feared she might faint. What if she passed
out? Then what? Then Jean-Guy would blow her up and Carl
Bantry—sweet Arthur, poor Arthur Davidson—would be dead too.
That's why he was along in the car. As life insurance. If she threw
the bomb away and bolted, they'd kill him.

Or maybe they planned to blow her up, then shoot Arthur and
dump him by the side of the road. The thought pulled a cord around
her heart. Jean-Guy held the remote detonator. All he had to do was
press the button. Norris could do nothing to stop him. *Selwyn?*

She moved between the wall and the back row of cars, finding
progress difficult along the crusty snow and frozen puddles. She
slipped once and uttered a short cry. This time she remained still,
hung herself on a breath and listened. As far as she could tell, she'd
not been detected. Julia moved down a row of cars and crawled past
the Crown Victoria on the passenger side and around by its rear. She
checked the license plate. Confirmed. The space between the bumper
of the Ford and the car behind was too narrow for her to pass. She
could not stand up and be spotted. Julia chose to get down on her
belly and shimmy between the two vehicles under their bumpers.
Carefully, she pushed the bag with the bomb ahead of her and felt
the city tremble under her belly, the traffic of trucks and buses, the
ancient volcanic quiver of the mountain explosive again at her fingertips, and she slithered through to the other side.

Returning to her crouch prematurely, she bumped her head on a
tailpipe. It hurt.

If you're going to do it, Jean-Guy baby, do it now. She thought she'd made too much noise.

The next problem was immediately apparent. Little space existed between the Ford and the car alongside it. This was not a parking lot where cars were jockeyed in and out. After the postluncheon games were played, the participants would emerge at approximately the same time and await their cars in turn. In the interim, the vehicles were tightly packed. She did not know if she could open the driver's door wide enough to stuff the bomb—about the size of a laptop computer, only a little fatter—inside.

She could hardly fit between the two automobiles. She had to get over on her side and push herself along the ground where both cars were narrower. She moved the bomb ahead of her, the case was getting mucky. She wanted out of this. She wanted to save Arthur and herself and see no more of this business. She wanted to go back in time and change everything. *Selwyn. About that giant step backwards.* At the front door she raised her arm and pressed the latch, and the door opened and a chime sounded. She could not reach in and remove the keys from the ignition. No way. That was definitely impossible. She had to rely on traffic to cover the chime with noise, and for the moment its consistent roar seemed sufficient. *Organized crime, my ass! You call this planning? Selwyn Norris never would've planned anything this badly.* Then she checked herself—his influence had precipitated her predicament.

With the door open as far as she could manage, Julia reached an arm in, and it fit, but only in one direction, toward the rear. She could never reach over the front seat with the bomb, then direct it back underneath and set the positioning device—a lever intended to snag the bottom of the seat—as she'd been taught. This was trouble now. The Czar and the Angels would not take kindly to failure. They'd be suspicious, for sure. Besides, Norris knew about the enterprise. If she had a hope of being saved, it lay with him, today, now. She had to follow through on all things and hope that he was a superior mastermind to the Angels. She had to find a way to get the damn bomb planted without killing herself in the process.

Gently, she removed it from the sack and rested it on the ground. Persuaded by the wind, the door wanted to close on her, and she used the back of her head to keep it pried open. She propped herself on an elbow and tried to guide the package onto the seat. No use. The best that she might hope for was to tuck the bomb under the seat from the side.

Julia tried to wedge it in. She forced the bomb hard, but it would not break through. The case was too large for the side space, it would have to bend in half to fit, but the shell of the case was hard. The damn chime from the open door kept sounding, driving her to a pique of fury. She removed the bomb completely and lay on the ground, panting.

She had to do this. She had to succeed. She had to find a way.

She thought, could she open the window, then reach inside and insert the bomb that way, take her chances with being spotted?

No, no, she had to do this properly. She had to find a way to do it right.

Julia came to a higher crouch, her body pinned between the two vehicles. Keeping the bomb on its side, she was able to angle it up onto the front seat. If only she could leave it there. If only the victim would return to the car and oblige her by sitting on the bomb, oblivious to its presence. Rearranging herself so that she was able to curl her right hand over the casing, she guided the bomb on its side between the seat and the door toward the rear footwell. She got it through but couldn't maintain her grip and the bomb tumbled onto the floor.

Julia gasped.

She panted, waiting, as though reaction from the fall might be delayed. As though dynamite was sleepy, and awakened would yawn before it roared. The traffic was loud, intense in her ears, she heard a commotion of horns, the chime from the open door repeating itself endlessly, but the world for her was quiet, dormant, at peace. She waited. Breathing.

A horn bellowed and she jerked in a sudden spasm.

Damn.

Reaching in again, furious, she discerned that the bomb had fallen on end, a difficult position. She wiggled a hand along the rear floor until the casing nudged her palm, and worked her other hand in as well, higher, and lowered the bomb to lie flat upon the floor. *Gently gently.* Without proper purchase, she was able to budge it by tiny increments, slowly guiding the bomb forward and under the front seat.

She kept up the action with her fingers.

The bow of the casing tilted downward into a lower section of floor. Then the rear of the bomb went over the hump and settled under the seat. She almost cheered. *You're good at this, girl!*

Julia had still to reach inside, twisting her arm backward, and fiddle with the positioning mechanism. She struggled to raise the lever. The imbecile bomb maker had not made it long enough! She had the arm straight up, but the seat was too high above the bomb for the lever to make contact.

Hearing a bus noisily ascend Atwater, Julia gave the door a shove and it shut.

She sat paralyzed a moment. She needed to summon faith. Once planted, would the bomb explode? At what juncture would Norris intervene? Did he expect her to do it, to blow up the car with a policeman in it? Was that a piece of the puzzle, a portion of her disguise? Would he, like the Angels, stop at nothing? Her dread was interrupted by a quick, unwarranted burst of tears, and she wiped them off her cheeks made cold by the wind. Now she had to move. She had to escape. She had to keep on playing the game until there was no game left to play.

Julia clutched the empty computer satchel and retreated. She went around the way that she had come, sliding under the rear bumper to get through and walking in a crouch up that side. She scampered low to the ground along the front row of cars and made it to the rear wall. No one had sounded an alarm. No one had challenged her. Slowly, she raised her head, looking through the glass of a Mercedes. She spotted one of the valets, idly pacing back and forth, eyes to the ground. The other was unseen. She jumped, leaped off her toes, and pulled herself up, dropping her rear onto the stone wall that was low on one side, high on the other. She spun on her bottom, stood again, and commenced walking away from the scene, her duty close to being accomplished.

Julia strode back up the hill to the Cadillac, opened the back door, and climbed in.

"All set?" Jean-Guy asked her. He was driving.

"All set."

"No problems?"

"I had *plenty* of problems! Are you kidding me? I couldn't get the door open, your damn lever arm is too short, I had *plenty* of problems. *Christ!* I dropped the damn thing, I thought I was dead."

Jean-Guy was chuckling to himself. "If you dropped it and it went off, you'd never know."

"Yeah yeah."

Arthur reached for, and received, Julia's hand in the back of the Caddy. They sat, eyes front, waiting, wondering. Jean-Guy turned around in the front seat and smiled at them.

"I like this part best," he said. "Waiting for the pop."

Julia was still. Frantic inside. Blood pulsed in her temples. The car was cold, its engine off, yet she perspired and tore off her wool hat. She exercised her anxiety by tousling her hair, fluffing it up, then patting it back down into shape. She waited.

"It's a nice day," Arthur surmised.

"One thing I don't talk about it's the weather," Jean-Guy said.

"Please don't talk to my father in that tone of voice. He's fragile." She had to keep up appearances.

Half-turned in his seat, Jean-Guy grinned at her. "I love the time before the pop," he repeated.

He was a psycho-killer-fanatic, Julia now knew. His cool demeanor, his sour disposition, had hid it from her. She had no illusions now. She was sitting in a car with a man passionate about his profession. His work inflicted horrible, swift death. She was his accomplice. Worse. His apprentice. He was her tutor.

"They're coming out," Jean-Guy noticed.

Below them, members were emerging from the club and hanging about the entrance. Many would have to wait until other members emerged, so that the cars on the end rows could depart first.

"God! You didn't leave me much time. I could've been caught!"

"Can you see the car?"

Julia turned in her seat, first one way and then the other, and stared down through the rear window at the club. Atwater Avenue wound up the mountainside in great curves, with the bottom portion divided by a median. Traffic came in waves, depending on the lights at the base. She saw nothing going on in the parking lot. "No," she answered. "Maybe when it backs up."

"Keep looking."

"It's a nice day," Arthur murmured.

"Heather, take this."

She turned.

He passed her the remote control.

The killing device.

Looking back out the window, Julia scanned the street for a sign of Norris. The day was dreary, gray. Drivers had begun to climb into their cars, and one or two had made it out to the street. The Crown Vic hadn't budged. More men were showing up under the canopy at the door, more cars were being backed up into their possession.

Eight cars departed.

Twelve.

The blue Ford Crown Victoria swung into view.

Jean-Guy saw it move in his side mirror. "Bingo," he said.

Julia watched.

She saw the driver tip the valet and tuck his coat in under his knees, as a woman might a dress, sliding in behind the wheel. Three other men approached the car, and each got in a separate door. "Jean-Guy!"

"Shit."

"There's four men in that car!"

"Probably cops. We'll blow them all away."

"Jean-Guy! We can't blow up four guys!"

"Maybe we can, maybe we can't," he postulated.

"You don't have orders for that!" She had to think fast, she had to think smart. His position was precarious. He had to make a decision, and either way the end result would be different than anticipated by his superiors. Kill four men instead of one, or abandon a mission with a bomb already tucked in place?

"The car's ready to pop. It hits a pothole, it could go off. A whole shitload of people could get whacked."

"Jean-Guy! You can't start a war on your own! We can't whack four guys. Your bombs don't go off by themselves."

"They could," Jean-Guy pointed out, and shrugged.

"Can we go now?" Arthur asked, making life difficult for everyone.

"Shut his yap," Jean-Guy suggested. "I got to think."

Arthur preferred that he not do that. "It's a nice day," he said. "I'm going for a walk."

"Daddy!"

"Stop him!"

"Daddy!"

"It's a nice day."

Below them, the Crown Vic pulled out into traffic and headed in their direction.

Jean-Guy started the car with his free hand. He turned out onto Atwater, wheels spinning. "Hold him!" he ordered. Julia was clutching her supposed father, but she wasn't sure what to do, to keep him with her or let him go. If he escaped, she could run after him. But surely Jean-Guy would shoot them or something. Or maybe not with those cops nearby. She was confused about what he was doing and why and how she should respond, and Jean-Guy reached back and helped her corral her father, which limited her choices.

"Jean-Guy, four guys!" Desperate now. "You can't whack four guys!"

"Watch me. Hit the button, Heather. *Now!*"

She held the remote device, and looked at Arthur Davidson, who ceased to be in character. "No," he said, and reached across to take it from her. Jean-Guy spun the car in a half circle and jammed the brakes to block their half of the road. His two passengers were thrown across the backseat, and Julia saw that Jean-Guy held a remote device of his own. He carried a backup. She tried to reach for it. He pressed the button.

She turned.

It wasn't the car that blew, the car kept coming, it was the tractor-trailer parked by the side of the road that lifted off the pavement. The explosion convulsed the street and her mind and made her heart stammer and the air go out of her lungs. As it passed by, the Crown Vic was lifted high off the road. Its back end flew up and the car crashed straight down, its front grille striking the pavement, and the car tumbled end over end over end, then settled on its four wheels, the tires blown out, the windows shattered, and bounced onto the median.

"Gimme that!" Jean-Guy snarled, and he grabbed the remote device out of Julia's hands. He was pressing the button. She looked. The car did not blow up. "You didn't plant it! You didn't plant it!" he was screaming at her.

She heard herself respond. "I did. I planted it."

He hit her across the face with the device, and she fell back and Arthur made a grab for Jean-Guy, only he punched him off and leveled his pistol at them.

"I planted it," she maintain quietly, resolutely, shocked.

Debris was falling out of the sky and some pieces smacked the roof.

Jean-Guy put his foot to the floor and peeled uphill. They saw the SWAT team, distinguished by their flak jackets and rifles, coming on the run from their roadblock high on the hill, and Jean-Guy cut left, onto a small street that he found out seconds later led nowhere. Dead end.

"Out of the car!"

She could hardly move. She couldn't sense her legs. She was tangled akimbo, and her brain felt ruptured, blown.

"Out now!"

Somehow she obeyed and sensed Arthur supporting her, and looking up Julia saw college students on the stairs to their campus above an escarpment, ascending and descending like angelic beings, and she should be one of them she knew, but she was not, she was not.

Jean-Guy aimed his pistol at her again.

"I planted the bomb," Julia maintained through her fog. "I did."

"Who's got the most to say?" Jean-Guy asked, and answered his own question. "The computer prick. Him I'll bring back alive." He aimed the pistol between Julia's eyes.

"No!" Arthur said. He jumped between the gun and Julia, and Jean-Guy fired and Arthur went down, he crumpled, and Julia was

screaming silently now and looking at her hands and the brain matter on them and the blood on them and Jean-Guy was shoving her up the stairs.

"You'll do," he snarled. "Get up! Up the stairs! Now! Go!"

The college students were ducking on the stairs, but there were too many of them for the police to risk a shot. Jean-Guy and Julia climbed, and she bumped against the students, who cried out, and she found her legs again, and she was running from all this, running, and she would run until her heart burst and the sun blew her head apart, and at the top Jean-Guy turned her and she ran that way and he held her and then turned her downward along a path through the trees and over rocks and through snow and they fought their way down through an urban woods and at the bottom of the bank came out on a row of mansions and Jean-Guy led her up the walk of one. He held her partially in front of him.

Julia wiped the fluids off her face and stared down at her hands.

Jean-Guy rang the doorbell.

A woman answered. He aimed his pistol at her, his hand just forward of Julia's face, his elbow resting on her shoulder. He had the presence of mind to speak English. "Car keys. Right now." They weren't far away, on a little hook above a shelf near the door. Julia saw the woman's face drain of color, she saw that and noticed it, and when the woman looked at her a hand went to her mouth, a gasp, as though the sight made her want to vomit.

Jean-Guy dragged her down to the driveway and stuffed her in the Jeep. He started it up and drove. "Keep your head down or I'll blow it off," he warned, and Julia did what she was told. She held on to her seat with her knees on the floor and her face shoved down into the cloth. Blood that was not her own seeped off her face. She didn't want to open her eyes again. *I'm going to die,* she promised herself. *I'm going to die soon. Arthur, Arthur, I'm so sorry, Arthur. Daddy!*

He lay on his back on snow and told himself to hang on. He didn't know how bad it was. He wiggled his toes, he could feel those. He wiggled his fingers, he could feel those. Some old cop said, "Can you hear me, sir?" and he thought that he had heard himself answer yes, which meant he could hear and he could speak, unless he had dreamed that part. The blast had turned Cinq-Mars end over end and pitched him out of the car, and all he knew for certain as he passed in and out of consciousness was that he could still wiggle his toes, he was wiggling them every chance he got.

He heard the sirens at a distance. They were coming from both directions, from down the hill and up. His view was of the sky, of a few leafless trees, of the penthouse suites of the high-rise that clung to the cliff halfway up the block, the boots and men's chins. Some cops were leaning over, talking to him, but he wanted them out of his way, he was trying to talk to his wife, to Sandra, trying to get a message through and the cops were in his way and he listened to the sirens, they were closer now, they were right up to his ears it sounded like and he was telling himself to hang on, *hang on, and wiggle your toes.*

He was telling Sandra how much he loved her and she was listening.

"Émile. Émile."

Mathers was leaning over him and his face was all bloody and smashed up and he didn't need to look at that sight, it could make a grown man weep. Mathers was already weeping himself. Somebody pulled Mathers away and made him lie down in the snow so that they lay side by side and they turned their necks, both of them—*I can turn my neck*—and looked at each other and more sirens were wailing.

Boots surrounded him. Men with guns. He closed his eyes.

He felt himself swooning, spinning. He fought that. He listened to a siren way off, among many sirens, way off, way distant, and he concentrated with his eyes closed and he dismissed the bedlam around him and felt a blanket being placed upon him and he didn't know if that was death's shroud but he listened to that siren that was coming his way, drawing near, and even as he felt himself lifted, and a voice next to him say, "On my count! One! Two! Three!" and he was lifted up, then raised, rigid, in the air and he opened his eyes and they were moving him, paramedics and cops, into an ambulance. He kept listening. He needed to follow the sound of that one wail. It wasn't coming for him but he needed that one siren to peal all the way into his heart and into this place because that siren he could count on, he didn't know why, it was real, that siren kept him alive.

"Émile. Émile!"

They'd put Mathers in beside him.

"Émile. Can you move your toes?" Mathers whispered.

It hurt to breathe. It hurt to turn his head. He looked over at Bill Mathers all bloodied up. "There's nothing wrong with my fucking toes," he said. "But I'm missing a shoe. You?"

"I walked over to you, didn't I?" Mathers whispered. "Didn't I?"

"I don't know for sure," Cinq-Mars whispered back.

He closed his eyes. He found his siren. It was close. So close that when the ambulance started up the hill with him aboard, it passed the next ambulance coming in. He heard that siren wind down and stop. He smiled. His pains felt good enough. Pain was a good thing to feel. Pain was meaningful enough. That siren wound down and he could hear Sandra say, *I love you, too, Émile, hang on.*

I will.

Then the siren on the ambulance in which he was riding began to wail.

20

Sergeant-Detective Émile Cinq-Mars entered the cellblock and walked the row from end to end surveying prisoners. His right eye was black but open, the left side of his forehead swollen. A Band-Aid covered an edge of his lower lip, and another strip of bandage had been taped under his right ear. He had missing patches of hair that exposed stitched cuts on his scalp. His left hand and wrist were taped, only the fingers poking out from gauze. What's more, he possessed a look, a countenance, a disposition that would brook no quarrel, and instinctively the prisoners feared him. They didn't know him, but he looked like a man who'd been chewed up by a dog and was now raring to chew back.

He returned to the gate. Bill Mathers was there, looking worse than he did, and Alain Déguire accompanied three guards from lockup. "Move the other prisoners out," Cinq-Mars told the guards.

"We can take your guy to a private room, shackle him down," a guard suggested.

Cinq-Mars gave him a cold look, and the guard promptly changed his mind. They jumped to his bidding then, and the prisoners were shackled and led from the cellblock in single file and a tone reflected on the faces of the authorities, a quickening, induced not one prisoner to protest.

The guards departed, and the detectives approached the lone prisoner left behind. His cell was situated two-thirds down the row, and the junior detectives walked part of that distance where they could see

402

him and then hung back. Cinq-Mars stood in front of the bars and looked down at the man, who hadn't moved, who remained immobile on his slab of steel as though his life had been drained out of him. He was smoking a cigarette.

"I should be worried," André LaPierre testified. "A cop empties out the block, the poor sap left behind doesn't usually survive."

"You've heard those stories."

"Word gets around."

"You believed them?"

LaPierre shifted his eyes, smoked. "I try to keep an open mind. What happened to you, Émile?"

"I got caught in the middle, André. Bill and I got bounced around in a blast."

"I'm sorry to hear that."

"They went after Rémi. He made it out alive. We all did."

LaPierre smoked. "People don't usually walk away from dynamite."

"We saw it coming and took the bomb out first. Didn't count on a second bomb, that's what got us into trouble. I guess they didn't trust their bomber. Just like they didn't trust Lajeunesse when he was sent to bump me off and they sent along a backup sniper. This time, a backup bomb."

"What's the world coming to, Émile?"

"I might let you walk through this one, André. Do a few paces."

He exhaled and brought his feet off his bunk onto the floor. Crushed his butt under a heel. "Time's gone by, Émile. Could be too late for that."

"It's a risk."

Cinq-Mars was quiet then, and gradually LaPierre grew more conscious of the finality of that silence. "What do you need?" he asked.

"You'll remember I gave you the gatekeeper's logbook, from down at the docks. Before I did I made a copy for myself."

"I figured. That was my case, Émile. You had no business interfering."

"Your name doesn't come up, André. I've looked all through it. Kaplonski had to go in by the main gate and come out that way so that he was implicated. That's how they do things now. But you came and went without signing in."

LaPierre reached for his smokes. He nodded while lighting up another. "Big place, the docks. More than one way in and out."

"You know a few of them."

He shrugged. "Been there. Done that. So what do you want from me?"

Cinq-Mars was staring at him coldly now. "A woman's gone missing. Last seen in the company of the Angels' bomber. He stole a car, ditched it, picked up a ride somewhere, I imagine. Nobody's shown at any of the clubhouses around town."

"There's a million holes in the wall, Émile."

"I want you to check the ship for me, go aboard the Russian freighter."

LaPierre sputtered, shook his head, ran a hand through his hair. "You don't ask for much, do you, Émile? Since when do I owe you any favors?"

"You can walk through this. Do a few paces."

"I've been cited, Émile. I'm public."

"You killed for them. They know you're not holy."

"They also know I'm in a susceptible situation." LaPierre stood, paced. Smoke flew out from between his lips. "You want me to board the ship?" he wanted clarified. "Wired?"

"Way too risky. Take a cell phone along. Find a quiet moment to report."

He kept pacing. "I could go down on this, Émile."

"Your choice. But you don't want to be an ex-cop in maximum security."

"You motherfucker," LaPierre protested. "You sweet motherfucker. You know how bad this is? You got any idea?"

"You're the one who wanted to dance with the brokenhearted."

LaPierre tried to calm himself, but he was having trouble. He was excited by the prospect of a way out, but terrified by the consequences. He might die. "Who's the woman?" he asked.

"You know her as the Banker's Daughter. Heather Bantry."

LaPierre stopped then and stared at him, his mouth open. "She's your mole? First you sent boys. Now you're sending in girls?"

"CIA sent her, André. Me and you, we're taking her out."

"And I walk?"

"You get the charges beaten down."

"Émile, *Christ!*"

"Prove yourself and we'll see."

"Sure. I don't see the prosecution participating here, Émile. I don't see my lawyer fine-tuning the deal."

"André," Cinq-Mars reminded him gently, "all the evidence is in my hands. Prove yourself on this one, and we'll see what can be done."

"You'll let me walk right through and out the other side?"

"I want Heather Bantry out alive. I think Hagop Artinian would be willing to trade a conviction on his killer in exchange for that young woman's life. Hey, André. You wanted to be the big bad cop. You're always telling me you eat shit. Here's your chance to do it your way. Here's your big opportunity to walk on the dark side, see what that gets you. At least you'll be legit for a change."

He had to think about it a minute, roam around in his cage. Any time he looked over at Cinq-Mars he saw that smashed face and the cuts on his head and those determined hawk eyes. "What's the plan?" he asked him.

"You go in. We follow. Me and the two boys. I don't want the bad guys to know we're coming. I don't want a hostage situation. I don't want a quick exit or sudden death if we storm. I don't want the SWAT cleaning up my shit. I don't want the Wolverines taking it over and pulling some high-tech glitch. We're going east of Aldgate, André. Kill or be killed. But we need someone to guide us through that ship. I can't afford to get lost in there. We need someone to clue us to the situation. We require a point man, André, and for the next five seconds I'm pointing at you."

LaPierre crushed another cigarette under his heel.

"I've got no time to spare, André. What's the word?"

"Guard on the gate," LaPierre told him, already reaching for another smoke. "Get me out of this fucking zoo."

"Guard!" Cinq-Mars hollered. "On the gate! Prisoner coming out."

They drove down a truck-lane with twenty-foot fences on either side topped with barbed wire. At the end of the road they parked.

"The gate's behind us," LaPierre said. "I'll go through first. You follow."

"How do you get in?" Déguire asked him.

LaPierre held up a key chain on his ring finger.

Déguire lowered his brooding eyebrows and sucked in his oversized lips, resisting the inclination to stuff the key chain down LaPierre's throat.

"All right," Cinq-Mars reiterated. "You've got your phone. You know my number. Board that ship, find out if she's in there, where she is, and call back to give us the coordinates and the best approach."

"I should have a gun, Émile."

"Not today. In their eyes you're suspended, so you're not carrying a weapon. You're scared, worried, looking for a way out. They know you left a trail—they made you leave it. See what you can bargain for yourself. Get in, get out, get us the information. We'll be on your tail. By the time you penetrate, we'll be onboard ourselves. If you get into trouble, let us know any way you can. Now go."

They watched him walk back the way they'd come, his shoulders hunched in the cold, collar up. The pedestrian gate bordered the truck entrance. LaPierre had keys for both, but as they were walking in he naturally used the smaller entrance.

"I wonder if she's there," Déguire pondered.

"She's there," Cinq-Mars revealed. "I was informed. André better not report otherwise."

LaPierre went through the gate, leaving the padlock unsnapped.

"How do you know? Are you telling me they brought her through the main gate?" Mathers asked, incredulous.

Cinq-Mars shook his head. "As a matter of fact, I called the gate-keeper to double-check. Nobody we care about has been through that way. But that started me thinking. Is there another way in? They brought Santa through the gate and back out again to make things look bad for Kaplonski, not because it was necessary. By keeping that in mind, I realized that they must have other ways in and out."

"Then who told you she's here?" Mathers pressed.

"Yakushev. The ship's captain. Do I have his name right?"

Mathers was feeling unsteady. This seemed murky. "Émile? How far can he be trusted? This could be a trap."

"Could be," he agreed. He looked from one young man to the other. "Both of you, be aware of that possibility at all times."

They watched LaPierre turn the corner around a shed, vanishing. Cinq-Mars passed his car keys back to Déguire. "There's a box in the trunk, bring it up front."

He came back carrying a large brown carton. He opened it in the backseat, and on top he found protective vests that were not department issue. Superior quality. It wouldn't be easy changing into them in the car in the cold.

"I didn't want LaPierre to know," Cinq-Mars said. "We can't be sure whose side he's on."

Buried under the vests were three Auto Mag .44's with reloading dies and six boxes of ammunition apiece. "Another surprise," Cinq-Mars told them.

"Where'd you get these?" Each was nearly a foot long.

"A gift. Thirty-five hundred, U.S. Used."

"We're sanctioned?" Mathers felt the weight of the pistol in his hand.

"Let's not get carried away, Bill. Let's just say that after four cops get blown to the rooftops and back down again nobody's asking too many questions." They labored to put on the vests and pull their jackets and coats back on. They jacked mags into the pistols, and it was time to leave. "A word. Six rounds per mag only. Now, ask whatever you want to ask," Cinq-Mars instructed them. "Now's the time."

Déguire had something. He had such a dark, foreboding look on his face, a life forged by worry, but Cinq-Mars was used to that now. "Why no backup? I'm not dissenting. I'm just asking."

"That's fair, Alain. Several things. To start with, we have no jurisdiction. That vessel is off limits. Which is another reason it could be a trap—they know I won't give this up to Wolverines or Mounties. I hate chaos. Which is why I put LaPierre in, to help us with our coordinates but also to fog their air. Also, and this is major, I don't want to save that woman from the Angels just to serve her back to them on a platter. She was involved in a hit on cops. She gets out of our hands, she'll be mauled by the system. But that's nothing. Putting her in jail is no different than turning her over to the Angels, no different than signing her death warrant. She won't be in jail a week before she's dead, the Angels will see to it. No. I will not let another kid die. We can't save Hagop, but I'll be damned if I let them have this young woman, too. Understand something. I want her out alive. After that I intend to set her free. Her only crime is wanting to be on the side of justice. I don't usually convict people for that. I sure as hell don't send them to their deaths."

The two younger cops indicated their consent to the terms, knowing that he was right. In prison, the woman would die in a twinkling, assuming that she had made it to trial alive.

"One more thing you should know. I'm not an idiot. We *do* have backup. It's not sanctioned. It's not official."

"What do you mean?" Déguire asked.

"Friends," Mathers guessed. "Just like that time with Lajeunesse."

"You can't not trust everybody, Alain," Cinq-Mars advised him. "You have to trust a few. Remember that when old farts like me aren't around anymore."

"So we got cops behind us?"

"A couple of Mounties, a couple of SQ, a couple of city boys from the beat. We call ourselves the Wolverettes." He was wearing a sheepish grin.

"Anything else we should know?" Mathers asked.

"East of Aldgate," Cinq-Mars mentioned as he opened his door.

"Are you going to tell me what that means, or do I have to die first?"

"Kill or be killed, Bill, that's all you need to know for now."

They clambered out of the car, big pistols in their overcoats, and headed for the gate at a clip.

They climbed the gangway, and Cinq-Mars set the pace, not so fast that he'd wear himself out. On deck he was panting. Scanning. He did not speak, and the men followed him toward the fortresslike structure of the wheelhouse over the vessel's stern. This time they did not ascend the outside but entered by a companionway at deck level, and inside they waited, breathed, listened.

"Up or down?" Mathers asked.

"Alain," Cinq-Mars instructed, "in all situations, watch our back. Bill, you guard our flanks. Keep at least seven eyes open at all times."

They went up, climbing the narrow steel steps and moving lightly. The churn of the ship's systems camouflaged any sound they made, and at the first landing Cinq-Mars knelt to peer around a corner. An empty corridor. He went along it, rejecting the stairs at hand to select another set farther up. They ascended into light, into a bright white-washed chamber, and guarded their eyes. Cinq-Mars led them in the direction of the bow this time, pistol upraised, and took to stairs again.

Halfway up they heard voices.

Bent and cautious, they continued along, coming up under the wheelhouse. Cinq-Mars waved his pistol hand to indicate to Mathers to continue on. "Go up," he whispered. "See if our captain's there. Don't be noticed if you can help it."

Mathers took the stairs two at a time. The companionway door was open and, crouching, he peered through at different angles, finally poking his head inside once, briefly. Men were talking Russian. He returned, unspotted.

"No," he reported. "Two sailors I recognize from our first time through."

"The captain's quarters ought to be close."

They searched their level. Opened doors. In one a sailor was startled in his bunk. "Captain?" Cinq-Mars asked him. *"Capitaine?"*

The man gestured with his thumb. As an afterthought he came out in his underwear to either challenge him or offer further instruction, but spotting the weapons, he retreated, shutting the cabin door.

Cinq-Mars turned full circle in the narrow passageway and leaned against the bulkhead. Gestured with his chin. He had located the captain's quarters. He and Déguire waited on either side of the door, and Mathers formally knocked.

Captain Vaclev Yakushev answered. He was wearing the same dull sweater with a larger hole now in one elbow that he'd had on when they'd first met. Cinq-Mars was again taken by how short he was, and believed that he must be tough to have endured in his profession despite his size. His gray-and-black beard had grown out more fully. The captain looked first at Mathers, at his pistol held low, then at the two men on either side of him. He invited them in by holding the door open and waving with his free hand.

He'd been expecting them. On his bunk he'd spread plans of his ship, both a side view and an overhead. "Here," he pointed, "is the girl. She's down deep." He pulled the side view across and ran his finger down the different levels, indicating the way of passage to the bowels of the ship.

Cinq-Mars stopped following the man's finger and looked into his eyes instead. "Why?" he asked him.

"I gave the girl my word. She would not be killed on my ship. I did not know they would bring her back here. I do not honor these men."

Mathers was looking across at his sergeant-detective curiously.

"Go ahead, Bill," Cinq-Mars invited.

"Captain, I was wondering what happened to your accent. Nobody learns English that fast."

They supposed that the slight softening at the corners of his mouth was his impression of a smile. "Old KGB trick," the captain explained, reverting to the accent again. "If enemy believe you speak only with accent, they not recognize you when you speak like them."

"You weren't conscripted for this fight, were you, Captain?" Cinq-Mars considered.

The captain agreed. "I was not. This is not honorable."

The cell phone rang at that moment, and Cinq-Mars answered. "Hello?"

"The Fifth of March, I presume," the voice said in impeccable English. A great roaring racket in the background made him difficult to decipher.

"Who's this?"

"We haven't had the pleasure. Some of your friends call me the Czar. Your friend LaPierre wants to have a word. I'll put him on."

First the racket grew louder, then a man screamed into Cinq-Mars's ear.

"André? André?"

The horrible screaming lapsed, then resumed again.

The English voice said, "Welcome aboard, M-Five. Feel like cutting a deal? Give me a call."

The connection was terminated.

Cinq-Mars stood with the phone at his ear.

"Émile?" Mathers prodded.

Finally he put the phone in his pocket. "Study the map," he commanded, and his tone was pure rage. "Memorize what you can."

The three men took twenty seconds to study the ship's plan, then departed the cabin, working their way down into the hold of the ship.

For Cinq-Mars the decision was simple. Whether the captain had dispatched them to the depths of the stern, where crew quarters ran off the engine and systems' rooms, in order to trap them there or whether he had given them specific directions to help save Julia, that was the place they had to be. Ambush or rescue, he could not avoid the seventeenth level belowdecks on the Russian freighter. They took an elevator down fourteen levels, then walked down stairs the rest of the way. There they entered a labyrinth of corridors and rooms, where the steady throb of the ship's works echoed off steel bulkheads. There they took a step, paused, paused again, and ventured another step forward.

Cinq-Mars carried his left elbow at the level of his chin, his hand resting on his upper right arm. On the elbow he supported his opposite fist, clutching the Auto Mag perched on its side, the barrel running across the biceps. His arms protected him from shots to the face, the bulletproof vest shielded his chest. For every stride, he moved his left foot forward, a short stride, then brought his right foot to his left heel and bent the knee, shifting his weight. Behind him, Mathers adopted the regulation police stance, both hands on his pistol, walking on the balls of his feet so that, if hit, he'd fall on his face and be able to keep firing. Déguire carried his handgun at the level of his eyes, pointed up, his arms bent, and stepped sideways, crablike, eyes moving both forward and back.

They crossed a catwalk.

The three men moved from light into shadow, the ship's pulse reverberating through their shoes. At a corridor they conferred. Mathers was the most positive of their position, insisting that he possessed a good memory of the plan, and they followed his suggestion. This deep, it was hard to know which direction was forward, which aft. They moved on.

Mathers had chosen well. The corridor that ran across the beam of the boat would lead to a network of staterooms, supply rooms, gear rooms, and repair facilities. Down one of these the young woman, supposedly, was being held.

They listened, but nothing was to be heard save the racket of generators and the hollow thrum of hot-air ducts. Cinq-Mars continued forward, Mathers behind, Déguire trailing.

They moved on, and Cinq-Mars signaled for a huddle. "I'm going up on the run. Hang back. Start creating space between us."

He jogged ahead, and the younger cops covered him. They watched him stop at a corridor, check it, then cross and wait for them. Mathers came up next, then Déguire. Each took a peek, and no one had to mention that once in the narrow corridor they would have less visual range, and less room to maneuver. No tributary corridors were available for them to flee to in case of an ambush. They'd be sitting ducks.

"Bill, take the point," Cinq-Mars ordered. "Alain—"

"—the rear," Déguire concluded, the crease in his brow tightly knit.

"Each room gets checked."

Slowly they worked their way down. Cinq-Mars swung every door open and investigated the cavity within. Halfway down, Mathers tapped his shoulder. The blank edge of a newspaper had been torn away and stuck to the door. On it was written, *"Welcome, M5."*

Cinq-Mars signaled both men to guard the corridor in opposite directions. He backed them farther away from the door in case it blew. He believed the steel door would provide him with adequate protection, but to open it, he squatted low. His two colleagues alternated between glancing at him and protecting their flank. Cinq-Mars reached for the door lever. Tugged it down. It yielded without igniting a blast. He opened the door a fraction. Felt no trigger, no line. Then he shoved it open so hard and fast that it banged against a wall inside and he held out his free hand to keep it from bouncing back. Cinq-Mars aimed his pistol and his shoulders recoiled, then he appeared to slump forward and he landed on his knees. Mathers cried, "Émile!" and turned toward him and Déguire shouted, *"Bill! Down!"* and fired and Mathers, on his belly, looked back and saw behind him a huge Hell's Angel fall with a shotgun in his hands.

"Run it down!" Cinq-Mars instructed them, bent way forward. They didn't know what had happened to him. The two young cops jogged swiftly to opposite ends of the corridor and checked their situation. Both signaled all clear. Déguire checked on his victim and found no pulse. The pistol had fired more quickly than anything he'd ever handled. He'd hit him four times, minimum. The man bled through the mouth, and through exit wounds in his back. "Walk it up!" Cinq-Mars called to them. The cops returned to him, stepping backwards all the way, pistols at the ready. Cinq-Mars had recovered to his knees, and they looked to see what had made him fall.

Sergeant-Detective André LaPierre hung in the doorway, his head no higher than a man's chest. The beanpole of a man had been cut low, his legs sheered off above the knees by the bloodied chain saw on the floor behind him.

"Get him down," Cinq-Mars ordered. "He's still alive." He guarded the corridor while the men unwrapped chain and lowered the unconscious man to the blood-soaked floor. Both men were managing, but the moment he saw the sawed-off portions of legs in a corner Mathers puked his guts. Cinq-Mars was on the phone, urgent and whispering. "Medics. Seventeenth level belowdecks, the stern. Find the captain or anybody else to guide you down. Bring them on the run, full body protection. Otherwise, stay out. I want surround sound. I want full SWAT support on the perimeter. Get it now. Out.

"Bill," Cinq-Mars said in part to chase him out of there, "get blankets. Back the way we came. There're bunks in some of the rooms."

Mathers followed orders, although in the first cabin the memory made him heave again. He wiped his mouth and face on one sheet and snatched the blankets off the other beds. He came back on the double, with Cinq-Mars and Déguire providing cover.

413

"Wrap him. Keep him warm." Cinq-Mars tore off his own belt, slung it around one bloody stump, and pulled with all his strength. He knotted the belt, then used a screwdriver off the workbench there to twist the tourniquet until the wound did not bleed so much, and he lodged the screwdriver in back of the belt. LaPierre had lost quarts. He wasn't giving him much of a chance. Déguire had his belt off by the time Cinq-Mars finished, and they did the same for the other stump. Mathers stood guard, waiting for a Hell's Angel to show, wanting one to show, longing to drop a few before the day was done. "All right," Cinq-Mars decided, "we leave him. Help's on the way. We can't do anything more."

"Come on, Émile, we can't just leave him," Mathers objected.

"That's what they want. To stall us and divide us. Bill, I don't want this happening to the woman. She's only a kid."

Mathers considered that aspect and changed his mind.

"Understand, this is a diversion. They want to slow us down and separate me out. They have one of two objectives, maybe both. One, they want to escape. Two, they want me dead. I expect them to take another shot at me before making their break. I don't intend to let them be successful."

"Where do we look first, Émile?"

"Follow me." He had his own memory of the ship's plan. This time they walked quickly, moving targets, unpredictable and quick. He led them down a flight to the level of the engine room, and they huddled there behind a bulkhead. Cinq-Mars made another phone call. "Make contact with the ship's captain. Shut the vessel down for two hundred seconds. All electricity. All air. Lights, everything. For exactly two hundred seconds I want perfect quiet. Got that? Over."

He looked into the faces of his young colleagues. "Load up, Alain, you're short."

Jacking another mag settled Déguire down, although his fingers quavered. He was scared, but he looked like the Grim Reaper, while Mathers's big brown eyes had bulged to the size of pucks. "What's up, Émile?"

"For all we know they're off the ship already. The leader's meticulous, we've seen how he's cleaned up a crime scene. He probably has a way out we don't know about, that nobody knows about, not even that captain. He's old KGB, remember, not some doofus choirboy with the Hell's Angels."

"So?"

"I think he might want another shot at me. I think he wants me down. I could be wrong. But he needed to buy time and he's bought it. All we can do now is assume he's still aboard and interfere with his plans." Cinq-Mars punched a number on his phone but didn't send the call. "He asked me to call him back. When the lights go out, I will. When the lights shut down, we enter the engine room. Why'd he bring us down this far if not to pull us down farther? We work our way through the engine room in the darkness and quiet. Keep an ear for André's cellular to ring. That'll clue us if the guy's aboard, maybe where. I'll talk to him. I'll call him back. You move on the sound. When the lights snap back, go. Keep one eye high, always. They like snipers. Remember, Julia comes out alive."

The shutdown did not occur as automatically as he had expected. First they heard the ventilation system expire, then various generators that warmed the giant holds. Finally the electricity was cut and the ship lay in darkness and utter silence.

"Hand on the shoulder of the man in front. Let's move."

He had memorized the way and made it across to the door without a fumble. Cinq-Mars opened the door. They entered the mammoth engine room, and what they hadn't counted on were the back-up emergency lamps aglow here and there. The gloomy lights cast strange and ominous shadows. He did not know if the light would help or hinder, but for now the lamps guided them through the dark and they moved across to the protection of a scaffold of pipes. Cinq-Mars pressed the Send button on his cellular.

Away in the distance a cell phone twittered.

Cinq-Mars discerned the shapes of his two young officers moving up.

"Mr. Cinq-Mars?" the phone voice answered.

"What do you want?" he asked, hushed.

"You'll die here today," the man whispered, "or you'll deal."

"What deal is that?"

"The identity of the third party LaPierre was raving about. I want the foreign agent, M-Five, his name, rank, outfit, and address. What do you want?"

"The woman."

"Yes, she insists she works for you. I fucked her mouth. You still want her?"

Cinq-Mars waited.

"Do you?"

"Yes."

"Even up. The woman for the foreign agent. Keep your phone turned on. I'll be in touch."

He terminated their connection.

In a crouch, Cinq-Mars moved swiftly through the dark. He was out of time. Above and alongside them rose the silent machines, as though this room was a mortuary for pistons and power. Someone caught his coat and he gasped. It was Bill Mathers.

Cinq-Mars punched the Redial button for LaPierre's phone again, but this time the call did not go through. His prey had not fallen for that ruse twice.

Mathers and Déguire had maintained visual contact with each other, and Déguire signaled that he was moving up. Hunched over, Mathers and Cinq-Mars chose a different slant toward the same general area. In the faint gloaming they spotted other forms, other men crouched and waiting, scanning the black universe for signs of life. The cops had so far remained invisible to them. Next to Cinq-Mars, Mathers indicated that he would cross a space to gain a third advantage on the viper's nest. Cinq-Mars agreed with a nod.

Despite the open space, the darkness here was sufficient cover, but he was only three-quarters of the way over when the lights flickered on and Bill Mathers was hit by sniper fire erupting from the steel rafters. Déguire and Cinq-Mars concentrated their fire aloft and brought down the shooter, his body wrenching backwards, then slumping forward and contorting grotesquely on a rail. The rifle fell, clanging in the brightened works and echoing like bullets ricocheting.

"Cover me!" Cinq-Mars yelled. He already saw the retreat of the tall, dark-haired man, and others, including Julia, backwards out of the room. He had foiled their ambush. Similarly, the gang had with-stood his own attack. He changed clips on the go.

A burst of gunfire caused Cinq-Mars to slump to the floor of the ship, and Déguire silenced that volley with a burst of his own. That shooter ran, passing through the same exit as his friends.

"Bill!"

Cinq-Mars turned him over.

Mathers was breathless with fright and pain, his only wounds to his vest. "Holy. That hurts."

"Can you stand? Let's get out of the open."

He needed help but managed to shuffle to a sheltered abutment.

"What happened?" Mathers begged to know. He was holding the burning points on his chest.

"She's alive, Bill. She's still alive. Her hands are tied behind her back, they've got her with them, but she's alive. Did you see her, Alain?"

Déguire had run over and was shaking as he drew a hand across his lips. "Her mouth is taped."

"Go!" Mathers urged them. "Go! I'll follow if I can."

Cinq-Mars and Déguire ran in pursuit, and Mathers hobbled behind them. They took the door with extreme caution, knowing that each delay gave advantage to the Czar. The door opened onto a stairwell. The only direction was up, but they couldn't spot anyone through the grillwork above them. The stairs exited at many levels, and each had to be checked. Cinq-Mars had the sinking feeling that he had lost them. Higher up—he'd lost track of the floors—he found the hatch used to depart the ship, riding a basket pulley, now cut, to a platform under the pier. In the darkness, in a labyrinth unknown to him, where the pursued had all the keys and the hunters would encounter only locks, Cinq-Mars knew that he'd lost them for good this time.

He breathed heavily, Déguire at his side. Stared at the abyss. Mathers came alongside eventually, panting, hurting. "What now?" he demanded. He feared that his partner had quit.

"He wants to trade Julia for the CIA guy," Cinq-Mars told him. "That should keep her alive for a while. As long as she doesn't give up Norris herself."

Mathers slumped against a wall to nurse his pain. "What do we do?"

"We wait."

Mathers was half-laughing, half-weeping, shaking his head and muttering.

"What's the matter with you?"

"I nearly got blown up today. I did somersaults in a car. I seen some things—André's cut-off legs. I got shot—vest or no vest, it hurts like *fucking* hell. Now you're telling me that all we can do is sit on our asses and wait?"

"It's called police work, Bill." Neither Mathers nor Déguire could tell if he was being serious, bitter, or wry.

Cinq-Mars put his pistol in his pocket and confirmed that his cell phone was open to receive. "Come on," he said. "Let's check out life on deck. Prepare yourselves. There'll be shit to pay for this."

Mathers was given a hand up, and the weary men mounted a gangway topside.

The survivors, and other detectives, hung around in the common area outside Cinq-Mars's cubicle, putting their feet up on chairs and desks to give their bones a rest. Tremblay had finally been released from the hospital—in the initial blast he'd suffered cracked ribs and a concussion, had been ordered held for observation, and unlike Cinq-Mars, had acquiesced. Only Déguire had not been roughed up during the day, but he was mentally whipped. He'd killed a shotgun-toting Hell's Angel and contributed, along with Cinq-Mars, to the death of another, the sniper. Déguire had never deployed his weapon in the line of duty before, and periodically he shook. He was pale, knotted up. Occasionally he'd flash on LaPierre's legs, shunted to a corner, blood soaking through the cloth of the trousers. Nobody was letting him go home alone.

The bruises that Mathers had suffered in the blast were discoloring quickly and beginning to swell. He constantly moved his hands to his face as if to make sense of his pains. He'd recovered from the shots to his bulletproof vest, but any time he wanted to move his left arm he lifted it first with his right hand.

Cinq-Mars tilted a chair back and rested both feet on a drawer jutting out from a colleague's desk. The department had opened its war room down the hall—what was really an event room intended to cover demonstrations and riots—but no sign of the young woman or her abductors had been reported, and no one really knew who they were looking for.

All the news was bad. André LaPierre had died. The Russian had called back and, expecting to be taped, had reverted to speaking with an accent. "Third party I want where to me I find him. In exchange, you to get girl. Call me between midnight and two minutes after with decision. You to use André's number. When I see you come through your end, get girl back. Not until."

A murderous choice.

The phone rang in Cinq-Mars's office, and he struggled to his feet. He slouched in the doorway to his cubicle, studying the black device on his desk. He didn't like the possibilities. He knew the Wolverines were hunting him down, anxious to be debriefed. Possibly they wanted to skin his hide. He hadn't slept in twenty-five hours and couldn't sleep now and wasn't up to being questioned by cops with a grievance. He'd already been grilled on the biker deaths aboard ship, although in that climate the interview had resembled a celebration rather than an interrogation. In time, he well knew, that would change. His caller could also be Sandra, who phoned regularly to plead him home. He picked up.

"Émile. It's been a day." Selwyn Norris.

In his weariness he was breathing into the phone. "I've lost her twice," he admitted.

"I've got more bad news."

He didn't want to hear it. Émile Cinq-Mars planted a fist on his desk and supported his weight. "Tell me."

"My doorman spotted a suspicious vehicle leaving the garage—a van that had no business inside. With all that's gone on today, he thought I should be informed."

"And?"

"I took your warning to heart, Émile. Checked my Q. Fortunately, I thought to use the passenger door to gain entry. Émile, it's wired to blow. I now require the services of the Bomb Squad."

Cinq-Mars covered the mouthpiece with his palm and stretched the phone cord to the edge of his cubicle. He whispered through to Tremblay, "Bomb Squad, at the ready." The lieutenant-detective jumped into action, and other officers began rising to their feet.

"Seal the garage off until we get there, Mr. Norris. Let nobody in. Make sure everybody's out."

"I've taken care of that. Émile, do you understand what this means?"

Cinq-Mars listened to dead air awhile. "Yes." His voice had gone hoarse.

"Émile, I'm going to disappear."

"All right. Leave your car keys with the doorman. Make sure he doesn't take the car for a spin."

"Done. I'm sorry, Émile."

"Yeah," Cinq-Mars told him, and he was not feeling particularly vindictive, "I'm sure we're all very sorry."

They hung up.

Tremblay had joined him in the cubicle. "Tell me."

"Mountain Street. Alain and Bill know the address. Inside a garage, there's an Infiniti Q Forty-five wired to blow. *Wait!*" Everyone froze. "This is a hit by the Angels. They trigger by remote, they do that a lot. That could mean we have to sneak the squad in and scan the street for a bomber."

Tremblay and Déguire left on the run. Only Mathers hung back with his partner.

"Émile, can't we turn this in our favor? Now that they know Norris by name and address, they can give us back the woman, or trade for something else."

Cinq-Mars rose to his feet. His body felt utterly fatigued, his mind bruised and blasted. "That's not what this means, Bill."

"Why not?"

"Norris might've been important enough to them that they'd be inspired to give us Julia back. That was a genuine hope, Bill, but nothing else rates. They didn't find him so fast through Lajeunesse. Look how long it took us after we had identified the car. If they fingered

Norris, it's because she gave him up. Who can blame her? She lasted a helluva lot longer than André, and André was a rough boy. She had to have witnessed what happened to him. But the second she gave up Selwyn Norris, that instant, she signed her own death warrant." He looked to one side, saw his own reflection in the window. "She's gone, Bill. We lost her. God, I hope it's swift. I pray we don't count the pieces."

As the import of the news dawned on Mathers, he arched his back and neck and let his head drop forward. He wanted to scream, he wanted to tear the walls down. Instead he slumped into the chair again and held his head in his hands. Cinq-Mars merely turned and continued to stare at the window, as though his very soul and not merely his reflection was trapped between the panes. He felt the young woman's death in his throat and heart, and he couldn't see a thing outside.

In the common area on the other side of the partitions, they heard the rush of voices and the frantic bray of commands.

"Wait," Mathers said, reviving. His head remained downcast, but he had raised a hand, letting it waver in the air. "You told me one time that we wouldn't give up on that woman until we found her in a closet with a meat hook through her heart. That hasn't happened yet."

Impatient with him, generally devastated, his anger only beginning to swell, Cinq-Mars wasn't in the mood for false optimism. "Don't be naive, Bill."

"No." He commenced a chopping motion with the hand, raising his head. "No, Émile, listen. You're right. She never could have held out against them. When the Russian called you the last time, he already had the name. He asked you for a name he already knew. They never could wire that bomb this fast. They already had Norris."

Cinq-Mars was interested. "You're starting to think like me, Bill."

"When you call back at twelve, you're free to give him Selwyn Norris, because he has him anyway. He has something else on his mind. He wants something else."

"Sure. He'll make me listen to her scream, like he did with André." He didn't want to think about André screaming.

"He's only testing you with Norris. To see if you'll come across.

421

He has something else in mind, Émile. We still have air."

He didn't know if it was fatigue or a pervading sense of despair, but Cinq-Mars didn't last long with the new wrinkle. He rejected the promise of hope. "I won't know what he has on his mind until I call back, and when I do I won't like it."

Tremblay poked his head in. "The action's under control. We'll go in by the street behind."

"It's only a car. Don't get anybody killed."

"Listen, Émile, I'm sorry, but the Wolverines are here again."

"Get off it."

"I can't hold them back forever."

Émile Cinq-Mars put one hand on his forehead, covering an eye, as though the next word he intercepted would blow his skull off. He peeked first at Mathers, then at Tremblay, and a way out occurred. "Rémi, Bill has a perspective on the bomb, thinks it might open a door for us. Tell the Wolverines I have to go on-site, top priority. I need an edge before my midnight call."

Tremblay was happy to accept any viable excuse. Cinq-Mars had saved his life that afternoon, getting the bomb out of his car. As he'd said to him when they were both in the emergency ward awaiting treatment, one out of two isn't bad. They had never figured on the truck. When that blast had gone off and they'd smashed around in the tumbling car, he had counted himself out. The last thing he remembered was reciting the names of his children. "I'll tell their captain. Radio silence, Émile. Go in by Drummond. Promise me you won't stop off—no expeditions. You look like shit cast in lead and cooked in a microwave."

The detectives didn't say much on the drive back to Selwyn Norris's apartment block. Cinq-Mars had forty-six minutes to kill before his midnight call and didn't relish spending it talking to Wolverines. They'd want his full report—Norris, Julia, his excuses for invading the ship, for making a deal with the Czar without consulting them. They might want to arrest him for overstepping his authority—to punish him for not joining them. This beat that. They located the path the Bomb Squad was using to get to the rear of the building from the next street over and ran into Déguire there. Somehow, strangely, the three were glad to be reunited, as though what they'd been through required a slower form of separation.

Cinq-Mars slouched on the back steps leading to the parking garage and listened to the news from Déguire. The bomb was unusual. Wired to the driver's door, it appeared to have no timer, yet the Bomb Squad hadn't detected an electronic detonator either. Two blow sticks would rip the car but not do significant peripheral damage. They speculated that because the bomb at the racket club had been so easily disposed of, the bikers had rigged this one not to be removed. The squad had been working meticulously to extract the driver's seat, having already taken off the door. The car was washed in bright lights. Residents in the high-rise, beginning with the bottom floor, had been taken out the back way and bused off-site.

Cinq-Mars checked his watch. Five minutes to midnight.

Mathers showed with coffee. "Where'd you get this?"

"There's no one upstairs. I found an apartment with the door open and a coffeepot left on."

"You're incorrigible, Bill. You should be arrested."

They drank.

"Will you make the call?"

"Do I have a choice?"

"What'll you say?"

"Nothing. He'll kick my teeth in. I'll beg his pardon."

Mathers left him alone after that.

Cinq-Mars wanted to punch a wall. He compulsively checked his watch, and time seemed not to move. He counted down the seconds. Every joint in his body ached. He waited. He had to dial between midnight and two after. Déguire and Mathers gathered on the stairs below him. He stabbed the number with his middle finger. He'd split the difference. One minute after midnight. He touched his ring finger to the Send button.

When the blast that afternoon had blown their car off the pavement, Cinq-Mars had lost a shoe. As the car somersaulted end over end, he'd followed the wild progress of the shoe around the vehicle until the flat sole thwacked him across the nose. He remembered yearning to leave his skin before he was actually killed, and after they'd landed, and settled, alive, he felt that he'd betrayed himself, thinking that way, that he'd given up too soon.

Cinq-Mars raised his head. "Alain, did we scan the street?"

"Yes, sir." He seemed to be breathing easier, settling down.

"No bomber?"

"No sign. We've discreetly checked all the parked cars on the street. But he could be in a building."

"Not their style. What's the squad saying about the bomb?"

"Can't be removed without being tripped."

"Clock?"

"Haven't found one."

"Remote receiver?"

"Not found. I told you before."

"Alain—go fast—check—*now!* Ask if a cell phone is attached to the device."

Déguire possessed accreditation on-site, in that the Bomb Squad had named him their liaison with detectives. This allowed him to get close to the car without being challenged. He ran on the double, and Mathers watched as Cinq-Mars hit the Power-Off button. At first the two of them seemed hardly to be breathing, then suddenly they were breathing rapidly. They burst down the stairs and together waited for the news. Déguire was at the car standing under the blazing lights. He spun around. "Yes!" he yelled back. "Yes, sir!"

Everybody out now! Cinq-Mars hollered, and he and Mathers went under the cordon ribbon and raced across the basement floor. "Bomb Squad—out now! Who's got the keys? Where're the keys?"

Mathers manhandled cops to get them moving out.

"Sir?" The man in charge of defusing the device pulled his head from the vehicle and stood. He extracted keys from his jacket, displayed them in his palm. He was a big curly-headed guy with chubby fingers, and Cinq-Mars wondered how he'd ever gotten into this line of work with those fat hands. "What's going on?"

"She's in the trunk! A woman's in the trunk! Throw me the keys and get the hell out!"

"Émile!" Mathers brayed.

Cinq-Mars hit his chest with his fist. "If I don't phone, the Czar does!" He checked his watch. Two after twelve. He held out his hands to catch the keys.

"Sir!" the big cop pointed out to him, "the trunk could be wired. We got lines all over. Some are trips, some are decoys. I haven't run them all down, and this bomb is definitely not defused."

"Toss me the keys," Cinq-Mars said calmly. "The bomber's phoning that cellular any second now, and when he does, the car blows."

The cop tossed him the keys, peeled off his flak jacket, and handed that across to him as well. Mathers helped his partner slip it on.

"Out, Bill. Think of your daughter and run."

"I'm behind the pillar in back of you."

"Bill!"

"Don't argue."

"I'm behind the other one," Déguire declared.

The rest of the cops scurried.

The instant the last one was gone, Cinq-Mars opened the trunk.

"Bill! Now! Hurry!" The young man returned on the run. Cinq-Mars pulled the half-conscious young woman partway out of the trunk and Mathers reached in, grabbing her by the legs. She was bound and gagged and sedated. They handled her like a rolled rug and ran and Déguire held open the near door. They reached him just as LaPierre's cell phone warbled. Déguire pulled the fire door shut behind them, and the Q45 sucked wind and blew.

In the stairwell, the men and the bound young woman collapsed into a pile on the floor. The blast shook the air out of their lungs, seared their minds, and their hearts felt bludgeoned. They scrambled to their knees again, and Cinq-Mars ripped the tape off Julia's mouth. He bent over her and jerked up straight again. "We need an ambulance here!" he hollered to the cops on the stairs above him. "Get the ambulance down here!"

The three detectives were all on their knees with Julia in the middle, their fists upraised, their mouths wide open, their faces rapt with wild grins.

"Get that ambulance!"

The woman, they wholly believed, was breathing.

EPILOGUE

———

THE WHISTLE

Wednesday, June 1, and Monday and Tuesday, July 11 and 12

She had gone home.

Julia returned to her family's summer farm and the comforting care of her mother, who would come up on the weekends to wonder what was wrong with her and to cook weird, delicious meals. She was grateful for the care she had received from Sergeant-Detective Émile Cinq-Mars—Julia had been portrayed by him in the media as an anonymous biker's moll, released due to a lack of evidence.

"You fell in love with a Hell's Angel?" her mother queried.

"Mummy. Don't ask."

"Was it really terrific? Did you get to ride on his Harley? You're not into rough trade sex, are you, Jul, honey?"

"Mummy!"

The detective's ploy was to lure as many of the bad guys as possible into believing that they'd made a mistake about her, that she had been one of them all along and not a mole. If he planted a doubt, they might forget about exacting revenge. It was also necessary for him to finesse his colleagues and the judiciary. He didn't want her to be arrested for any part in the whole business, for that would surely place her life in jeopardy.

The plan might not work. They could only hope.

Julia knew that the Czar understood that she had been a mole, for she had told him about Selwyn Norris when, horrified by what she'd seen and scared to death, she was no longer able to withstand his threats. In her mind, the plan could never work. The Czar knew that she had betrayed him, betrayed them all. But Émile Cinq-Mars

429

continued to insist that she be patient. So she stayed alone on the farm during the week and tried to keep busy, puttered and did her best to grow things in the wild, neglected gardens.

One day a car came up the drive, and her heart was pounding with terror. She fled to the bushes, lay down on her belly, and watched. To her relief, Okinder Boyle stepped out of the car. She was delighted to see him, anyone from that world who was a friend. She took him into the house, served him a cup of tea, and gave him a cranberry muffin she had made herself. "Émile sent me," he told her.

"What's up?"

A police officer had been intercepted displaying a picture of her around the campus of McGill University, trying to ascertain her true identity.

"A cop?"

"Not a good one."

"What does it mean?"

"The Czar is still after you, Julia. And if he's after you, he'll find out who you are, sooner or later. You're not safe here anymore."

She wept then, spontaneously and abruptly, and Boyle cradled her in his arms. After she pulled herself together, she asked him what she was supposed to do.

"Émile and me, we've come up with an idea."

Julia was to travel to the island where he had been born and raised. A place sufficiently isolated that she'd be safe, a place where she had no connection. She had to depart the family farm immediately, and leave no trace.

"My mother?"

"Call her now. Tell her you have to go. That you can't tell her where. Give her no clues. Tell her that when it's safe again you'll be in touch."

"When will it be safe?"

Boyle gritted his teeth. But when he spoke he was upbeat, positive. "Émile says that day will come. You have to hang on."

"For what? What will change? What *can* change?"

"Émile says something will happen. He's waiting for a sign. Everything will be different then."

Boyle had relations on the island willing to provide a room and ask no questions. She'd be safe there, out of harm's way. He'd drive her in his rental car, then return to the city himself.

"And where is this place?"

"The Bay of Fundy. Off the coast of northern Maine. South of Campobello Island, you know, where Roosevelt spent his summers? You're going to a special place."

On the island of Grand Manan, a road runs west from the town of North Head past woods and wildflower highland meadows to a look-out, then veers down to a rocky beach. In the evening tourists arrive to observe the sunset, the view scanning the bay across to the coast of Maine. At times during the summer Julia Murdick had spotted whales feeding offshore. The Whistle, as the lookout is known, named for the fog whistle that blew warning from this place years before a light station was erected instead, attracts island residents as well. As a local man had advised early in her visit, "This is how you tell the tourists from the locals. Tourists look across the water to watch the sun go down, locals look up the road to see who's coming down over the hill." It's a place where men and women talk and laugh and make jokes, a place that has provided her a welcome. People ask no pressing questions.

Most nights, Julia comes down for a beer or two, to partake in the banter, the stories of fishermen's lives, tales from the past. It's a happy place. As her host informed her, "People with nowhere to go are going to go somewhere."

That made sense to her. She was like that, she had nowhere to go, and so she had gone somewhere. To the Whistle. This was a gentle place, a restorative place, that, despite its isolation, was somewhere.

She walked the island trails, strolled the rocky beaches. She went lobstering with men happy to show her how.

She hated her aloneness though.

Showed her tattoo to no one.

Sergeant-Detective Émile Cinq-Mars had warned her, she mustn't have it removed until her life was safe again. Doing so might invite discovery.

"When will that be?"

"The time will come," he'd promised.

One morning, Okinder Boyle knocked upon the kitchen door of the house where she was staying. She gave him a big hug. He was beginning his vacation, and Julia was delighted for the company. Boyle was a feature writer now, no longer an underpaid junior columnist, with particular responsibility for crime. They had a lot to catch up on and the morning and the noon hour passed quickly.

He had something to show her. This was his island, his home, and he was proud of it. He launched a brother's dory and took her onto Whale's Cove, into the family weir. The weir was constructed with stout poles embedded in the bottom of the bay and bound together to form a heart shape. Nets were slung on the poles, the leading edge taken into shore. As herring followed the tide into the cove, conning the shoreline, they veered into the net. The design kept the fish moving in the same direction, following the curves of the net, always missing the opening.

"So the exit remains wide open, but the fish are trapped?"

"That's it. Their habit is to trace the shoreline. In the net, they swim along the edge, which guides them when it turns to the other side of the weir away from the opening. They repeat the same swimming pattern over and over again, a modified figure eight, until the fisherman comes along and ties up the net and calls for a seiner to empty his catch."

She could understand that. She could see how fish might be trapped even when the exit was as large and inviting as had been the opening.

"Julia," Boyle told her as they bobbed upon the water. "It's over."

"What is?" she asked.

"Look."

From the backpack that he had brought along containing their lunch, he pulled out the front page of the *New York Post*. She gazed at the dead man in the cover photo and read the story inside. "I don't understand," she said finally. "Somebody shot him, then somebody came along and cut off his shirt?" The dead man had been visiting a hospital in Baltimore.

"To expose his chest. You're not going to recognize the face, not after the bullets. But you will notice the tattoo—the Eight-Pointed Star. And his surgical scar."

Julia looked at the photograph again. The Czar was dead, his dreaded tattoo, a more elaborate example of her own, shining below his covered face.

"Why would anyone do that?" she insisted. "I don't get it. Who would kill a man, then cut off the front of his shirt?"

"It's his gift to you," Boyle told her.

"What? Whose?"

"Your CIA guy. He wanted you to know."

She was quiet.

Selwyn Norris had had the Russian assassinated. He'd instructed the assassin or assassins to cut the dead man's shirt away to expose the Eight-Pointed Star for the tabloids. Selwyn had had him killed for his own reasons. He had revealed the tattoo so she would know that she was safe now. Or safer.

The killing was described as a gangland slaying. A settling of accounts. An episode in the war between rival drug lords. Julia Murdick knew better.

"You're going to stay awhile?" she asked Boyle.

"Two weeks," he said.

"I can use two more weeks here. I was wondering, after that, maybe you can drive me back to the city?"

"Be happy to. Your risk factor has gone way down, Julia. But you know, there are no guarantees," he cautioned.

"Risk?" She smiled. "Tell me about it."

He returned her smile, and did not disguise his admiration.

Boyle rowed the dory out of the weir before starting up the outboard again.

Seals swam off the starboard quarter. A guillemot, a black bird with white wing patches, one she'd learned to identify during her stay, bobbed in their wake. She watched it for a long time, a small bird swimming alone on a great sea.

As Bill Mathers drove onto the Cinq-Mars farm, his daughter was already shouting to the horses. They were greeted by Sandra Lowndes, who promptly scooped up the child and led her guests to the nearest paddock. Cinq-Mars emerged from the barn, dusting himself off.

"Donna! Bill! How are you?"

Greetings were effusive on this sunny afternoon, although Cinq-Mars noted that his partner seemed to prolong his opening smile an indefinite time. He finally sidled up to him while they watched the little girl ride an old gray gelding, her mother walking alongside to hold her up. "Why the smirk?"

"Have you detected a smirk, Émile?"

"The look doesn't become you."

The smirk expanded into a smile, and finally into a gentle, self-satisfied chuckle.

"All right," an irritated Cinq-Mars inquired, "what canary did you swallow?"

"Surely you've heard about Baltimore."

"I know about Baltimore," Cinq-Mars told him. He'd been on vacation. "That's nothing to smirk about. It's a brutal business."

More seriously, Mathers nodded. He was right, of course.

"I had a hand in it," Cinq-Mars admitted.

"You?"

"I told them where to find him, who his doctor was."

"You were right to do it, Émile. It's better this way."

"Is it?"

"Julia Murdick gets to stay alive. Isn't that what you wanted?"

"It's what I wanted," Cinq-Mars agreed. He was watching the horses, his wife, the child. His dog, Sally, came running out from behind the barn and rolled in the dirt at his ankles.

"Last night," the junior detective began, "I was watching TV."

"Some people get to lead a life of leisure, I suppose," Cinq-Mars murmured.

"Oh? You don't watch the tube yourself?"

He shook his head, arched his eyebrows. "On occasion," he allowed.

434

"PBS. Mystery! Do you know it? Last night it was Sherlock Holmes."

"Holmes is a fine fellow. I admire him."

"Do you?"

"Sure thing. Intellect over brawn."

"But no cream puff. He'll resort to drastic measures when called upon. Last night, for instance, Watson was surprised when Holmes took a pistol out of a drawer. He asked him, We go armed? And Holmes answered—but perhaps you can tell me how Holmes answered, Cinq-Mars."

Émile Cinq-Mars put one foot up on a lower rail of the paddock fence, his eyes on their wives, the little girl, the horses. The summer had been warm, the grass beyond the fences tall in the breezes, although the land could use rain.

"It's a gruesome business, Bill. Julia Murdick's safe, we can hope. The Czar is dead, but another Russian will replace him, be sure of that. We've escalated the rules of engagement, contributed to the assassination of a criminal warlord. No charges. No trial. Merely summary death. Do you think the man's replacement will show us any quarter for that?"

"He won't think about us for the killing."

"I suppose not. We'll keep that hidden. We'll add cowardice to our list of transgressions."

"Émile, don't."

"What?"

"Beat yourself up."

"Do you think I'd give my enemies the satisfaction? Bill, let me tell you what Holmes told Watson."

"Please do."

" 'Always,' " Cinq-Mars recited sternly, " 'carry a firearm east of Aldgate, Watson.' That's what he said. He's right to say so. It's a logic I try to follow."

Bill Mathers was wearing his smirk again.

"All right," Cinq-Mars said, disgusted. "Wipe that look off your face. Nobody said you weren't a good detective. This doesn't prove it either, you just got lucky."

Mathers stayed smiling.

Ducking down, Cinq-Mars put a leg, then his head and shoulders, between rails of the paddock fence. The rest of his body went through. Mathers chose to go over the top, and they strolled slowly toward the child and horses. "Holmes was a man who relied upon his intellect, his cunning, his powers of deduction. We should all be so lucky. He recognized that sometimes he had to step east of Aldgate—the tough part of London by the docks—and carry a firearm. For us, it's more than that. We have to step east of Aldgate and make deals with criminals. Sanction murder. Run civilians undercover. If the truth be told, I started this by going after my source—Selwyn Norris—and ended up striking a bargain with the devil, leaving him unscathed. Tell me that's right, Bill. Sure, it's the best I could do under the circumstances, it saves that silly, brave young woman—I know that—but tell me it's right. When Holmes advised Watson to always carry a firearm east of Aldgate, I could accept his logic. There's no excuse for stupidity. At times you need a weapon. But this isn't fiction. Now we need more than firepower. Now we need to engage the enemy with more than our wits and our resources. There are times when we had better be ruthless, when we have to work around the law, or the enemy will win."

"Do you believe that?" Mathers asked. He was no longer smiling.

"I'd like not to," Cinq-Mars told him, "and I'm not going to work that way if I can help it. I know where that logic got André. For Holmes, east of Aldgate meant packing a weapon. For us, it means an escalation. Who knows where it'll end? Our enemies instinctively will exploit our ethics as a weakness. Do we tolerate that? Do we let the bastards win? Do we say, we're ethical, we're within the law? The country, the society, the Western world may be destroyed but at least we will choose the honorable course, now the barbarians must answer to God. Is that our plan? Or do we do what Norris and André did? Do we become our enemy? Do we meet the bad guys on the streets, or on their country estates, and treat them for what they are—enemies, warriors to be fought and brought down with firepower? Do we behave as they do?"

Mathers cast his eyes to the land beyond. He sighed heavily. "I thought we won," he argued.

Cinq-Mars raised an eyebrow to that. "Bill, you've got to get over your youthful naiveté. We caught Hagop Artinian's killer, and the Angels delivered him to justice. Good for us. The perp turned out to be one of our own, a good cop once upon a time who went east of Aldgate and came back warped and dead. Maybe we're all ruined once we cross that line. So far, we saved Julia's life, and Norris took out our mutual adversary, the man who tried to trick me into blowing her up. Gitteridge got whacked. The Wolverines have been set loose with a huge budget because that child was killed, that poor little boy. Meanwhile, the Rock Machine is looking to strike a deal with the Bandidos out of Texas to bolster their ranks. I don't know who they are, but do we need another international biker gang on the scene? Something tells me we'll be making their acquaintance sooner rather than later. So what's improved, Bill? Everything helps, we've had some success, but overall we haven't made a dent."

A mare snorted loudly and the child laughed at the sound. They played in the sun, horses and dog and young girl and women and off-duty detectives, and it seemed a fine day, an illustrious day, a beautiful, hot, lazy day of summer, the world carefree and calm. After a while, they retired to the back porch for drinks and a barbecue, and smoke drifted upward into the branches of the maple tree there, swirled around, and vanished into the bright blue of the high, wide sky. This was a day when it seemed that summer would never end, when winter was forgotten and appeared unlikely to return, when the world was wholly at peace with itself. This was a day like that, dreamlike and fleeting.

The End

ACKNOWLEDGEMENTS

The author thanks his agent, Anne McDermid, for making such a monumental difference, and all the editors who have contributed to the novel, especially Susanna Porter at Random House, New York. Particular thanks to Kate Parkin in England; Ed Carson and Iris Tupholme in Canada; and Ruth Coughlin in the U.S.